LIT RIFFS

a collection of original stories

inspired by songs

edited by matthew miele

Pocket Books
New York   London   Toronto   Sydney

POCKET BOOKS, a division of Simon & Schuster, Inc.
1230 Avenue of the Americas, New York, NY 10020

ISBN: 0-7434-7026-5

First MTV Books/Pocket Books trade paperback printing June 2004

10 9 8 7 6 5 4 3 2 1

Art Direction: Jeff Keytone and Deklah Polansky; Design: Chie Araki; Photography: Photonica

Manufactured in the United States of America

For information regarding special discounts for bulk purchases,
please contact Simon & Schuster Special Sales at 1-800-456-6798
or business@simonandschuster.com

contents

INTRODUCTION

neil strauss

There is a beautiful album from the '60s called *Odessey and Oracle*. Recorded by the Zombies, it is one of the most meticulously arranged and stunningly executed albums of the rock era. It unfolds like a paper rose, each song twisted together by themes of memory, loss, love, and the changing of the seasons.

For years, I wondered what wondrous tale held all the songs together, what feat of conceptual derring-do lay behind the music. And then, one day, my chance to unravel the mysteries of the album came: I would be interviewing the Zombies for *The New York Times*. And so I asked the question: "What ties all these songs together?" The band's answer: nothing. They are just songs, the members said, unrelated in any way.

I was stunned. I grappled with their answer for days afterward, until I came to a conclusion: They were wrong. Sure, they may have written and recorded the songs. But I had listened to them. I had the pictures in my head. They were mine now. And so, as I continued to listen to the songs, I wove them together into a fifty-page musical, a tale of murder and intrigue, heartbreak and betrayal. Zombies be damned.

There are some songwriters who don't like to discuss the meanings of their lyrics or the intention behind them. They don't want to interfere with the interpretations their fans have imposed on the music, they say. When I heard this answer in interviews, I used to think that it was a cop-out. But the beauty of music is that it is, as Marshall McLuhan would say, a hot medium. It occupies only the ears, leaving the imagination free to wander (unlike films or the Internet). The closest equivalent is literature, which occupies only the eyes. The intent may belong to the artist, but the significance is the property of the beholder.

Lit Riffs then are the synesthetic experience that occurs when the senses cross, when sound becomes text. The converse experience is far from a rarity: books have led to countless classic songs and albums. Some of the best work of David Bowie and Pink Floyd was inspired by George Orwell; Bruce Springsteen based a song on Jim Thompson's *The Killer Inside Me*; U2 brought Salman Rushdie to musical life with "The Ground Beneath Her Feet"; the Cure made Albert Camus a goth icon with "Killing a Stranger"; Metallica brought "One" into focus with Dalton Trumbo's *Johnny Got His Gun.* Cribbing from everything from the Bible to Yeats is a time-honored tradition among songwriters, as much a staple of the art as coffee and cigarettes.

Though there are exceptions (from Haruki Murakami to James Joyce), far fewer writers look to music as the jumping-off point for a story or novel. Yet the simple act of listening to most songs, even nonnarrative ones, triggers a narrative or imaginary video in the mind. For example, many can't help but imagine a fist connecting with Britney Spears when she sings "Hit Me Baby One More Time," even though that's not even what the song's about. It's simply their personal interpretation (or perhaps, for some, it's wish fulfillment).

Thus, twenty-four writers—from leading novelists to top music critics—were asked to riff on a piece of music. The authors included here were instructed only to choose a song, write a story inspired by it, and provide an explanation of their choice. They were free to choose whatever music they wanted—even if, as in the case of Darin Strauss's Black Crowes–derived be-careful-what-you-wish-for tale, it wasn't a song they necessarily loved. And they were free to interpret in any way they saw fit, even if, as in the case of Victor Lavalle's story, a droning, lyric-less song by the White Stripes reminded him of Iceland, which made him think of ice cubes, leading to a haunting fable of death and decomposition that is far from simple White Stripes homage.

Some stories here, like the Lester Bangs piece that begins (and in fact inspired) this collection, and Neal Pollack's dissection of alt-country posers, are music criticism disguised as narrative. Others, like Toure's Biblical Bob Marley parable, take the lyrics literally and tell the story of a song in prose form. Many, like Elissa Shappell's John Cale tale, riff on the metaphor, mood, and message of a song. Tom Perrotta mixes both the Tom Petty original and the Johnny Cash cover of "I Won't Back Down" into a vignette capturing the strange, mixed-up feelings that arise in grade school when social and parental pressures collide.

In her wonderful tale of Vietnam vets and the misfit obsessed with them, Lisa Tucker takes not just a song—"Why Go" by Pearl Jam—but also the album, the genre, and the period of the music, and rolls it all into one memorable story. In the process, her tale manages to capture the reason why a sad song can actually be uplifting to listen to—because it lets listeners know that they are not alone in their feelings, that there is someone else in this world who understands them.

Elsewhere, Anthony DeCurtis places the music of the Beatles squarely in his story, as a backdrop to the narrative. Julianna Baggott flips the script on Bruce Springsteen, exploring the point of view of one of the female characters, Crazy Janie, who tramps through his songs. Jennifer Belle writes a prequel to Paul Simon's "Graceland." Tanker Dane finds his "Hallelujah" not just in the version by Jeff Buckley, but in his tragic death. And Ernesto Quiñonez finds his inspiration the furthest afield, basing his elegy to the heyday of tagging on the aura of the video for "The Message" by Grandmaster Flash and the Furious Five.

While rock fans tend to be obsessed with lyrics, basing their stories on words, Hannah Tinti looked to the music—the modal interplay, the harmonic innovation, the high-flying solos—of a Miles Davis composition in order to structure a poignant moment intertwining a man falling with a man ascending.

Taken together, all these stories, interpretations, and points of view make up the greatest compilation album you can't listen to. Of course, all of the above story analysis is my own, and has nothing to do with the actual intent of the author (just as their interpretations have nothing to do with the intent of the actual songwriter or performer). Perhaps I would have been better off writing a song based on these lit riffs and completing the circle.

Of course, due to greedy music publishers, the lyrics to each song could not be printed in their entirety, which is an advantage in many ways because you should be experiencing the original inspiration as music (instead of text) anyway. In fact, just download the songs and, if so inspired, come up with your own lit riff. And if you ever happen to run into a former member of the Zombies, remember to tell him that he was wrong. Those songs do mean something.

MAGGIE MAY

lester bangs

Wake up Maggie
I think I got something to say to you.

"Maggie May"
Rod Stewart

Years later, flipping idly through his collection of ten thousand albums, he settled on an original mono copy of Sonny Boy Williamson's *Down and Out Blues* on Chess, slid it on the turntable, then lay back in his pasha's throne of a chair, contemplating the irony of it all: the wretched ragged wino on the cover of the LP, and what on earth he would do with a fourteen-year-old girl if she spread her legs before him, begging to be fucked. The wino might do better, he chuckled to himself. After all those *Vogue* manikins, the would-be Bardots, next year's Lorens and closing-time pickups;

This fictional piece was inspired by the song "Maggie May," by Rod Stewart and Martin Quittenton, but not by the lives or activities of any real person. Nothing herein is based on any actual circumstances or events, or meant to impute actual conduct, motives, or intentions to any real persons.

with some of them he'd been so drunk he'd never be able to say with absolute certainty that . . . no, there was just no way. Right now he'd rather be sipping this hundred-year-old brandy and digging Sonny Boy running down those same old lines he first heard when he was living on mashed potatoes than fuck *anything*. Sonny Boy was juicier than Brooke Shields would ever be. It had been better to sit and starve, nursing his desperation till some kinda break came his way. When it came, it wasn't the kind of break he'd had in mind. Which only figured.

It was 1966. There she was, the Perfect Slattern, propped atop that barstool ugly and coarse as only far-gone alcoholics can be, forty if she was alive but still looking all there in a leathery kind of way that surprised him, that turned him on, but here *he'd* somehow ended up, ditched by a friend who unlike him had enough money to keep on drinking, and he looked at her and she at him and a pact was thereby sealed before a single word was spoken on either side—now is that true love, or what? Mutual convenience perceived through alcoholic fog was more like it. He walked over and slid up onto the empty stool next to her, and she took one look at him—his hair, his clothes, his hangdog face—and immediately knew who was buying the drinks. She asked what he'd have, he ordered a shot of rum and a pint of Guinness. He wanted to court blackout or at least unaccountability before he had a chance to think about what he might be getting into. He drank so fast even she was a little surprised, laughing and drawling something like, "Surely I can't look *that* bad— Christ, I just came back from the powder room. Or is Art really *that* agonizing?" And she threw back her brass mane, opened those full lips, and laughed again, a true healthy hardehar this time, nothing self-effacing or ingratiating about it. She had him, and she knew it, and somehow his position as Henry Miller–style roué without a sou to his still unfamous name, living off his wits and special Way with the Ladies, did not seem to save much face or cut too far into her cynicism. He was just too pathetic, anybody could have him for a meal, but she was the one willing to take him out of sheer strumpet benevolence if nothing else—and since she now owned him dick to dorsal he might as well get an equivalent eyeful of his Owner: she looked good. Damn good. Better, in fact, at least to him at that moment, than all those damn ersatz Twiggies flitting around Carnaby Street on Dexedrine scripts and boyfriends in bands with first albums just breaking the U.S. Top 100, the kind of girl you saw everywhere then and he'd fucked enough of to know he didn't really like them, because anorexia somehow just failed to light his fuse, ninety pounds of speed-nattering Everybird, never read a book in their collective lives beyond *Shrimpton's Beauty Tips*, less soul than Malcolm Muggeridge's mother, just sitting there waiting for someone to happen but sufficiently plugged into the Scene to let them in on which name it was gonna be hip to drop next week. He always thought when he fucked them he oughta come away with purple bruises on each hip, war trophies of the 'orrid bone-bangin' he'd endured just 'cause some poof on the telly told them all that you just could *never* be *too* thin. . . .

Now, here, next to him, sat a middle-aged slut with bulging reddened alkie eyes, leering through rotten teeth, just beginning to go to fat in a serious way. He began to get a serious hard-on, and he wondered for a second if he had some kind of Mother Fixation, then decided that he couldn't care less. He got harder with the decision to stand his ground, incest be damned. Looked straight at all of her, as she at him: he estimated size 38 tits, beginning to sag a bit but that was all right, the way of nature wa'n't it?, globes that heaved up from a rather low-cut frock even for that neighborhood, and like the rest of her those breasts might reek but retained just a pinch of that pink, plump, girlishly buxom *crèmecast* of milkmaid tenderness, and gazing rapt and rigid he could not help but wonder awestruck at just what manner of pagan secrets might lie deep in the pit of cleavage. Surely there was *something* down there, one had but to dig breastplate-deep to dredge up treasures untold (the Twigs, of course, had no tits whatsoever and were all prissily proud of it), perhaps jewels and musks she'd carried all the way from the narcotized dens of the mystic East, where she'd spent her girlhood tremulously awaiting the needs of some fat sheikh who was so stoned and overstocked fuckwise he never even got *around* to her, so in revenge she stole into his inner sanctum and purloined his most prized rubies, opals, amulets, and blocks of pure hash and opium, hiding them in the handiest place, and though the master didn't catch her at theft he did find her encroaching on his hophead den and in punishment booted her ample ass clean out of his fleet of tents and into the molten Sahara sands, a white-hot sea where she'd've roasted like a squab had she not hitched a ride from missionaries, whose camel deposited her on the outskirts of Tangiers, where she sold her virgin essence to some stogie-smelly Yank robber baron who came quick anyway, but after he OD'd on absinthe she picked his pockets clean, netting not only enough money to keep her off the streets and in the bars for a while but a ticket to London via Luxury Cruise, in the course of which she enjoyed a brief affair with the son of a famous American expatriate or so he claimed, but then he apologized for his rather pallid passions explaining that Dear Old Dad had bequeathed him a palpable preference for boybutt. She didn't believe a word out of his mouth and they both had the time of their lives getting drunk like Boer War vets on the anniversary of the Big Battle, forgetting all about sex for the nonce. Landing on Blake's native soil, she made a beeline for the seediest part of London Central, renting a crummy room she decorated with a reproduction of Man Ray's famed *Box with Two Peaches in the Sky* taped up on one wall, which cheered her up no end.

Man Ray might have been a gay porno star as far as his knowledge extended. He didn't know said lithograph was worth twenty-five pounds if it was worth a shot on the house. On the other hand, she had never heard Otis Rush's original 78 rpm rendition of "Double Trouble" on the Cobra label, which he just happened to be the proud owner of. Clearly it was a match made in heaven, especially when he looked down and discovered himself delighted at the sight of one peremptory ripple of flab around her middle. That hula hoop of fat, he knew there was definitely no turning back now, so downward yet anon did slither his ogling orbs to grow themselves all wet at the sight of two more than amply supple legs in black fishnet stockings crossed under the hem o' that minidress, the whole thrilling vista tapering in most sublime tribute to Jehovah's very handiwork in two black patent leather shoes with stiletto heels could slice a porkbutt clean asunder. And amazingly enough, she wanted none other than that scrawny excuse for a failed fop HIM!

By now they'd practically consummated a week of orgiastic gymnopeds via eyes alone, so she paid up quick and out they scooted. Fairly *ran* down the block and up the stairs, through her door, where then she did after all think to stop and ask, "Like my Man Ray?"

"What's that? Some billboard for a new poofter play?"

She charitably ignored this idiocy, choosing instead to trip and shove him backward onto her scummy rumpled bed, the sheets and blankets not washed in weeks because she was too busy at the wine to remember them so they stank like sick goats but little he cared being drunk and lust-racked, too, so they commenced to make what Shakespeare, who could get at least as down 'n' dirty as say Texas Alexander when so he chose, once called "the beast with two backs." An apt description in this case, because the pair set to rutting like hogs been penned apart all winter, or dogs sprung from sexually segregated pounds (a pup-population control measure once actually tried in America, resulting in one lockup fulla

Rovers crawling around the room all day leaving bowwow jizz all over the floors, and another wherein the bitches thus imprisoned and deprived set up such a tempest-trough of yipyap yelpings and piteous yowls not unreminiscent of chalk squeaking on blackboards that the whole idea was abandoned overnight and a platoon truckload of panting Fidos imported special to the Lady Bowzers for a full-scale K-9 orgy just to shut 'em the fuck up) (happened in Keokuk, Iowa, case you wondered where the locals'd be fool enough to concoct such a scheme in the first place), they were hungry, and nosh awhile they did, groinwise that is, grinding away in to-the-hilt gimme-glee sloshed swill-sploshes of Eau de Poozwax Straight Up & Mulching Mit More Spizz-Overflow than whole popovs with some o' them Twiglets occasioned—it splashed across the grimy walls and soaked through the putrid coverlets, one rampant rivulet running down the bed cross the floor under the door down three flights of stairs and all the way out into the street where it conjugated unnoticed with TB sputum, not that the two lovers in question noticed any such minor details inasmuch as by that time they were too busy eating each other just toothpick-shy of outright cannibalism, after which they did it doggie-style and rocked so mighty they damn near broke the bedposts, the springs meanwhile playing at least five different Bartók string quartets and "From the Diary of a Fly" at once, causing an eighty-nine-year-old widowed pensioner in the next room past the wall which was about as thick as the cover off a copy of *Uncle Scrooge* ca. 1948 to seriously consider attempting to make his way down the stairs, a feat he had not accomplished in a decade and a half, so as to thereafter hit the street and see if he himself could purchase the last hit of whoopie he'd ever know except even allowing for the stairs he was still thinking WWII prices which'd mean he couldn't afford much beyond a quick whackoff into an old handkerchief while peering through a peephole at some grainy loop or two of (sign on door claimed) Mexican lezzies havin' at each other orally which mighta been still a heap better'n nothing (I tried it once on 42nd St. and it was great, but felt filthy afterward so never went back) except Pops here ain't even really had it up since the Rosenbergs were burned so what the fuck. . . .

When they were done dogfucking they sprawled back awhile to rest and pant and contemplate just exactly what they mighta forgot to try. Licking assholes? They talked about it but agreed it was finally neither's style. Mild B&D/S&M? Well, both were tired. So they tried something really daring, truly *avant*, beyond the pales of known thrash: they snuggled up for warmth, and hugged and kissed, with full passion but also gently and tenderly, sometimes just barely grazing each other's liptips (which *really* reactivated the lust-pustules in both bodies), for about twenty minutes. They kissed. Like kids, which was what he in fact was, and made her feel like all over again, which was the best feeling she'd had in years if not ever. When fully reprimed, they fucked once more, a long, slow, languorous workout in nothing but the Missionary Position, and when at last they came it seemed as if some timeless primal river was unleashed headwaters between the two as they writhed in one slow sliding tangle of YES from the core to YOU and no other . . . it was almost like some sort of, well, *religious* experience, mystical somehow, certainly elemental, the mindless melding of two principles always drawn together yet always warring everywhere, no confluently conjoined once-in-lifetime-memorable rapture among all manner of fucks high and low and every pit stop in between but this was one of the few ever that anybody's lucky enough to get which really actually on some intangible certainly beyond verbalization level *matters* . . . what you keep on looking for every time you lie down, and suspicion or nerves or reminiscence of some past lover who warn't so hot or drug-numbness or outright hatred or simple boneweariness or god knows whatall else seems to come between you and it every time damn near . . . and True Love has *nothing* to do with it, on one level it's nothing more than pure chemistry, though on a level a high degree or in-front mutual trust helps plenty, and finally maybe it's just dumb luck: THIS TIME.

When it was over, they lay in silence for upward of an hour, lost in commingled dreams, drained beyond movement, finally he sat up and said: "What's your name?"

She looked at him in silence for a full minute before answering. "Thanks a lot, SHITHEAD. That'll do for you as far as I'm concerned. As far as mine goes, just for that you'll never know. Now get dressed and get the fuck out of here."

So he did, a little sheepishly to be sure. He wanted to apologize, but felt so, well, dazed and confused right then, that he had no idea how to even begin to try. He knew he had done something stupid, ugly, and thoughtless, but he hadn't really meant anything by it, it was simply a product of his inexperience, which of course mortified him even *more*, till he felt he'd better get dressed and go or he was gonna wind up sitting there paralyzed. He'd never in his life felt more like a little boy, just as she had never felt more used, fucked, and then slapped down, put in what any cur of a male would be sure to think of as her rightful place, if for no other reason than that she was poor and single. She hated him, and all men, at that moment, and there was nothing in the world that could have changed that at the time.

When he was fully dressed, he stumbled across the bed, nearly breaking a leg and spilling across the floor, but no, he made it to his feet, though he still felt too wretched and ashamed to stand straight up all the way, so he kind of hunched across the room, hesitating by the door. He turned a bit, but was afraid even to look at her.

"Get out." It was the voice of a sidewalk as it hits a drunk in the face. Except he was no longer drunk. He felt it, every dollop of loathing, contempt, finality. Sick in the pit of his gut, moving with the spindly gait of somebody staggering away from an automobile accident, he turned the knob on the door and let himself out. She turned her face to the wall, which was oily and stained in places and where she faced it almost black with the accumulated dirt and lives of so many people, most of them down-and-outers, over so many years, and she cried hard, bitter convulsive tears that seemed to come tearing out in great chunks like the face of some cliff smashed away by . . . what? One too many assholes? Solitary middle age with no real prospects in sight? The sudden sensation that it just might be the sum total of her life, for this was all she had managed to piece together in over four decades, and what in god's name did she have to look forward to? Who wants a fifty-year-old hooker who's particular about her services (no S&M, no showers, no really kinky stuff of any sort) in the first place? Or get in on the ground floor of some new, "straight" business . . . yeah, sure. Even waitresses had to show some list of past employments. All she had to show, really, was a succession of men: two failed marriages, countless lovers, most of them as callous as this one had turned out to be or worse, various marginal forms of employment (go-go dancer, topless waitress, hooker, massage parlor, call girl . . . it all boiled down to the same thing), no family contacted in decades, no kids, not even a pet, no library or record collection amassed over the years that could now be presented to herself as some kind of evidence proving she knew not what . . . nothing. Alcoholism. A lifetime of self-con, pretending she was some schoolgirl on a spree when everybody else her age was married, employed, or both. She was so ill equipped for real life, she reflected, that she wouldn't even know how to commit suicide properly. Fuck it up no doubt. She laid her face in the black place where the two walls met, while more sobs heaved up from her very guts like boulders. In the next room, somebody turned up a radio playing some awful, maudlin song; they didn't want to have to hear her.

He staggered on down the street, still in shock, found his way home, sat down, and tried to piece it all together. On one level it was all so simple, on another it was just too abrupt a jolt from too great a height to too miserable a sink. That plus the knowledge that he'd hurt someone, and he did have some though hardly a complete idea just how badly, and it was the person that on that day of his life he wanted most in the world to avoid hurting. Again he felt himself overwhelmed by feelings of helplessness and self-hatred. He sat like this for hours, barely moving a finger joint, almost in a trance, as the darkness fell over the city and filled the room. Finally, around 10 p.m., he got up and turned on the lamp. Then he sat down again. He knew that punishing himself this way, to such masochistic extremes, he was only reconfirming, again and again, the very conviction of immaturity which had, aside from the pain he'd inflicted, made him feel that way in the first place. But he was young and male and selfish enough to be more concerned with whipping himself and turning it into a grand melodrama than with what she must be going through. *Well,* he thought ruefully a couple of hours after turning out the light, *at least here's another song for you.* Which of course made him feel even more ashamed. He fell into a fitful sleep, sitting up in his chair. He dreamed that he was a dog pawing the legs of passing women, all of them classy, fashionable, gorgeous, and looking up he saw the sneers on their faces. "Stupid mongrel mutt, go piss on somebody else's leg." One kicked him, and he went limping away. No one in the streets would even look at him, not even the beggar children: he was a mange-ridden stray.

She did not sleep. All night and all the next morning she sat on the bed, after the last tear had choked out, and stared at absolutely nothing. In the early afternoon she moved one limb. Then another. A bit at a time, she physically collected herself. For what she was about to do she hardly needed a mind. Finally she looked in her purse: £6. She snapped it shut, stood up with it in her hand, and walked out the door, which she did not bother to lock. Down the stairs, down the street, into another bar. It was a bar where lots of low-rent johns hung out, and she was going to be broke again soon. She took a stool and ordered a drink. And another. And another.

When he awoke, he felt stiff and sunbaked, sitting up like some mummy in a chair. He remembered everything, and the self-loathing had not abated, but at least now he was capable of planning and executing some course of action. For some reason he trusted himself just a hair more than last night. He left his apartment and headed straight for the bar where they'd met. When he didn't find her there, he walked out and headed down the street, looking in every bar along the way until he came to the corner. Then he walked back, checking every bar on the other side. He didn't drink.

Three hours later he walked into a dim, small bar on a side street, he saw her, hesitated, then clumsily approached. Her back was to him; she was looking down into her glass of wine. Standing behind her, he said, "I'm . . . so *very* . . . very *sorry* . . . I didn't mean it . . . I mean . . . I just didn't know . . ." The more he talked, the worse he was. With all the dignity of the longtime alcoholic who knows she's drunk and couldn't care less because unlike in the movies there are worse things in the world, namely, almost everything else in the world, she turned to face him. In the deadest voice possible she intoned: "You-have-got-some-fucking-nerve." She looked at him; he couldn't meet her gaze. She grew almost waspish: "Wasn't yesterday enough? I'm not gonna give you the rest of your kicks by beating you. Although I will say you are a miserable whelp and one of the poorest excuses for a man I've ever met. But you know what? You're not even the worst. Don't kid yourself. You're just another creep on the street. Now go wallow in somebody else's miseries. I'm sure there's a candidate just down the bar." She paid for her drink, making sure to leave a tip, picked up her purse, and walked out.

He didn't see her for two weeks. She felt better after the confrontation, but surprised herself with the realization that she also felt sorry for him, he really *didn't* know what he was doing. He really *was* just a kid. She was taking a lifetime of sons-of-bitches out on him. Not that he didn't give every indication of quite likely growing up to be one fully as practiced at true brutality as the rest. It was just that, somehow, even as she sensed his selfishness, she couldn't help being touched at least a little by his confusion, his genuinely repentant albeit masochistic manner, and her own inclination to give him the benefit of the doubt. *Why?* she kept asking herself. And finally concluding: *Maybe just because you have at this point absolutely nothing else to do with your life.* Which, once she'd articulated it, was obviously as pathetic a reason for doing absolutely anything as any of his. *Fuck it,* she thought, tricked her landlord and a couple of others she forced out of memory as soon as the episodes were done, and started drinking again, moving slowly from bar to bar at her own unset pace.

He hadn't been able to look a woman, any woman, in the eye since she'd told him off in the bar when he'd gone to find her. For several days he sat in his room; finally he called a friend and told him the whole story. "C'mon," laughed the friend, "she's just a whore. Don't be a sucker." "Fuck you," he said.

Crass as his friend had been, he'd come away knowing one thing: she was no more perfect than he, and he'd been putting her on a pedestal purely in the interests of his masochism. Whether or not she might actually be a prostitute was a matter of no moral judgment to him one way or the other. If he had suspected she was one, it had been a secret excuse to romanticize her. Slowly, somehow, without further contact, he began to perceive her as a human being. As all that fell into place, his anger at himself assumed a more fitting perspective. Finally, he saw that even his groveling apologies—perhaps in a way *especially* them—were at bottom selfish. She'd been right. For some time now, he'd been in the habit of treating women with casual unconcern—like shit. It was an act that worked more often than not, but it also ensured that he'd always end up with the same kind of woman, and ultimately alone. Now that he had encountered somebody he was capable of caring about, he'd exploited her in a way that was probably even worse—to expunge his guilt over all the others he'd mistreated, to put himself in their place, to know how it felt to be treated just that shabbily. He also felt that, if they could ever clear all this up, there might be some possibility for . . . what? Something more than what he'd been accustomed to. On the other hand, it might just be that all it had amounted to was an incidence of random lust, proof of which lay in the very fact that the instant they'd tried to verbally communicate, all hell had broken loose. He wondered at times if he shouldn't just forget the whole thing, or take it as a lesson learned and go on with his life. But gradually he came to realize that one way or another she was almost all he ever thought about. Which might mean that this was just a particularly twisted teenage crush, but he had to find, see, and at least try to talk to her again. For better or worse.

She'd been on the bottle long enough to have long since lost track of the days. In one bar she ran into a guy she'd once lived with, a comparatively decent sort, who'd given her some money. "Take better care of yourself," he said evenly but with real concern. "You're too good a person to go out this way." She asked him what the fuck he cared. "I guess I probably don't," he admitted, "except insofar as we were once lovers; if I cared for you enough to live and sleep with you then, part of that must still exist now. You see what I mean? I don't know if I loved you. But I did care. And I still care, and maybe I always will. I don't know what's happened to you and I don't think I want to, but do me a favor and try to pull yourself out of this downslide. You know that's a coward's way out, and I never would have been attracted to a coward in the first place. You're the same person and so am I. I don't want anything out of you now except that you maybe show some of the spunk that drew me to you in the first place. I mean, what the fuck? Why kill yourself over some asshole? Why give him the satisfaction? Just *start* is all I'm saying—put one foot in front of the other, and keep doing it. Things'll get better, not today or tomorrow, but by and by. You'll see. I've been down there, too." He laughed. "Otherwise, terminate the soap opera with some style: go get a pistol out of the nearest fuckin' pawnshop and BLOW YOUR FUCKIN' BRAINS OUT!"

They stared at each other for a long moment. Then both laughed at the same time, not loud and hearty by any means, but for real. It was her first real laugh, since . . . well, yeah, since all that. "I'll even loan you the money," he said. They laughed again. Between his sense of humor, the pep talk, his shaming her for being maudlin and giving yet another creep any satisfaction whatsoever, plus the basic knowledge that at least one other person in the world actually cared with no strings attached, she came out of it.

"Let's go fuck," she said.

"No," he said. "Not today. Nothing personal."

"Okay," she said, and stopped drinking.

They embraced and kissed lightly, without tenderness or passion. They walked off in opposite directions. She had absolutely no idea what she was going to do with herself. It was enough merely to feel good, to nourish some resolve, however vague. She went back to her apartment and thought about her options for the rest of the afternoon. There certainty weren't all that many of them, but how many did most people have? Fuck it. The first thing was to make some firm decisions, second thing to stick to them. Set her life in order. She picked up pad and pen and made a list:

(1) Sober up. Stay that way.
(2) Don't fuck anybody else for money.
(3) Don't fuck anybody you don't really want to.
(4) Find some sort of straight job.
(5) No more self-pity, no matter what happens.

That was enough. It took her three days to sober up. She faked an application form and got a shit job filing papers in an office building. Temp work termed permanent. It was hell. But she just did what she'd always done when she was fucking for money: shut off her mind and let Bach or Mozart play instead. Bit by bit, day by day, she regained her self-esteem. Even made friends, of sorts, on the job. Of course none of them were the kind of people you could really *talk* to—they were all women, and they all actually thought being a secretary was going to lead somewhere, or they just wanted to get married, and generally spoke in banalities of their lives and the things they had just bought or were planning/hoping to buy. She made one male friend who lasted exactly a week and a half, until he made a crude and clumsy pass at her over lunch, and when she politely refused, he began to sulk. After that he wouldn't talk to her. Fuck him. One day she realized she had been celibate for over two months. At night she read or listened to the radio, what she could stand of it, which was very little, or watched TV, what she could stand of it, which was very little, mostly old movies and news. She thought about her life. It hadn't been so good, in fact much of it had been an outright nightmare. But then she thought about the women she worked with, and their lives, with or without men, what they had amounted to so far or possibly ever could: they were so timid they might as well never have been born. She was better off with the nightmares. She'd learned a few things. When that thought hit her, she couldn't help laughing out loud.

Meanwhile he sat in his apartment, thinking about her when he wasn't dwelling on his own problems or mentally combining the two. He was still determined to find her, but she seemed to have disappeared from the bars. Nobody seemed to have a clue as to her whereabouts. One day he thought, *I wonder if she is dead,* and a chill ran through him. He was still writing songs, but none of them were about her. He wasn't ready yet—or he was afraid. The songs weren't about anything in particular. He knew he was stagnant, knew he had to do something with his life and his music, but had no idea what.

Months passed. One day he turned a corner in the middle of London and almost bumped smack into her. They were both startled, then both laughed in spite of themselves. It had been too long for high dramatics of any sort. "Well, well," she said calmly, a bit too calmly she thought. "Of all the ghosts in this town. And just how are you? Still fucking women just so you can shove them face-first in the dirt five minutes after?"

She was surprised at the lack of malice in the way she said the words. Somehow they felt almost obligatory; somehow, she knew, she wanted to talk to him. About what, she had no idea.

He blushed. That was when she knew why she wanted to talk to him, and why she felt just the slightest bit foolish for making the little speech she'd just concluded. "I . . . ," he began, and stopped. Still an adolescent. They looked at each other. "Let's go get a cup of tea," she said.

They sat down in a restaurant around the corner and stared at each other a while longer. To her, it felt downright comical. Still, she knew just how much she was enjoying the power she was now holding, the feeling of totally controlling the situation with a man for once in her life. She didn't like the idea of letting that go. At least she knew she didn't want to right this minute. *But what the hell did that mean?* She had no desire to hurt him; if anything, she felt playful. But that, too, seemed a kind of unnecessary mockery, in spite of her memories. She wanted to talk to him, she repeated to herself. If only she knew where to begin.

He began. "I was a terrible fool. Please forgive me."

"Stop." She was beginning to get irritated already.

"No, no, you've got to listen. Please. I was wrong and I hurt you. And then I compounded it later."

"That you did."

"Well, at least I can tell you that I know all that now."

"Congratulations." She was being too cool, too terse, it was some form of overcompensation, she knew it. What she didn't know was why. Which meant that suddenly she was no longer in control. And given *this* state, that left a real mess: two cartoon characters, trying on balloons. No, that was forced cynicism. She didn't know what she felt. One thing she did know: she had been on automatic pilot for what seemed like an eternity. This was like two babies stumbling across a playpen toward each other more than anything else, but even *that* was more than anything she'd felt with anyone else in so long that . . . she was fascinated, pulled in, and she didn't know why. She kept telling herself the whole thing was stupid—she should just get up and leave.

"I've thought about you a lot."

She didn't say anything. She had thought of him as little as possible.

"I've also been trying to find you for months. Not to ask any kind of absolution, but . . . you made me understand certain things about myself. When you weren't even around. I guess that sounds selfish, but . . ."

"Yeah, especially considering humiliating me was your ticket to Total Enlightenment." She grew impatient again. "Look, I know you're young. But I've just been through too many assholes in my time. Maybe to someone else, especially a girl your own age, it would have meant less. Maybe to some it would have meant nothing. People have that attitude a lot these days. I—"

"I don't either. Maybe what you're really saying is that I

have nothing to offer you. Aside from whatever you might have to offer me."

"Well, I could give you pointers on the etiquette of how not to treat women like shit, for starters. The next person you fuck might appreciate that."

"What can I say? You've got me over a barrel. I blew it. I can't even apologize anymore. All I can say is one thing: Will you go to dinner and the movies with me this Friday night?"

"Why on earth should I do that?"

"I honestly don't know. I might not if I was you. I'm just asking. You can say no."

"Dinner and the movies—how charmingly *teenage*." She knew her sarcasm was flat, stalling for time.

So did he, finally. "So stop playing around: What's your answer?"

She looked at him. "Yes."

Now neither held the cards. "What is this?" he asked simply and sincerely.

"I swear," she sighed, "I haven't got the *slightest* idea. If I did, I'd be glad to tell you."

"Maybe it's good. This way."

"What's good?"

"I don't know."

"This conversation is absurd. The tea's gotten cold. I have to go, I'm late getting back from my coffee break." She gathered her things and stood up. "See you Friday night. You know where I live. I'm generally home after six o'clock; other than that, I'm not particular about time. Just don't come barging in, in the middle of the night, ever. I've been through that one once too often. And *especially* don't come barging in drunk, ever. Which reminds me, I'm trying not to drink now. Just thought I'd let you know I don't mind going to bars, but don't expect me to get wasted on anything with you."

"Okay."

She walked out. He tasted his tea. It *was* cold. She'd left him the check. He paid, left a tip, and walked out.

She had trouble concentrating on her work. It was just that it was so *boring*. So, ultimately, were Bach and Mozart, at least when you had to hear them inside your head. Here she was, a woman in her forties, with a Friday night date with some rock 'n' roll teenager. She didn't even like rock 'n' roll.

Friday night he showed up at exactly 6:10 p.m. "What kept you?" she joked.

"Huh?"

"Nothing. So, what's on the agenda? What's the movie? What kind of exotic meal you got planned for us? A foreign restaurant, I hope? And will I be expected to fuck you in return at the end of the evening?"

He didn't say anything; he looked hurt. Instantly she regretted the last sentence that had come out of her mouth. "Look, all I meant is that *I'm bored out of my skull. I work in a morgue.* You're a teenager, they're supposed to be up on all the latest kicks. Well," she tried to joke, "*Show me some kicks. I'm a desperate woman.*"

He didn't know she was joking. "You work in a morgue? Really?"

"No. I wish I did. It's a morgue for dead papers—writs, subpoenas, wills, old lawsuits, on and on and on. Dead bodies would be a definite improvement."

"Oh."

He was nervous. So was she, but in a different way. Clearly, each wanted something different out of the other. Somehow they just kept missing. She decided to try a more direct approach. The most direct.

"What do you want from me?"

He didn't answer for a couple of minutes. "I'm not really sure, except I think somehow it has something to do with— don't laugh now—*soul*."

"Who's laughing? I'm flattered. But then, I'll take just about anything I can get these days. Soul. Why me?"

"That's a lot harder to answer. Maybe because . . . you're the sort of person who would joke about your job by describing it as a morgue, or wish it was instead, or maybe it's just that . . . I think you want something from all of this—meaning all this around us, life, work, whatever—that you're not getting. And you're not gonna stop struggling. Or"—he laughed—"at least *complaining* until you get it. Or at least find out what it is."

"What if I'm not missing anything? What if there's nothing there to miss?"

"You aren't the type to settle for a good answer when I finally managed one, are you? You gotta push it to the next level of impossibility. In fact"—he laughed again—"I wouldn't be surprised if you turned out to be impossible all the way around. Maybe"—he stared at her for a long moment, not kidding at all and both of them knew it—"that's the last word with you. Maybe that's how you get your kicks after all. You get your kicks by seeing to it that everything remains impossible. And I don't even mean anything so banal as you and I. I mean a serious effort, conscious or not, in futility as a way of life."

She hadn't been ready for that. It was too close to the exact center of her most basic fears. All she could do was own up. "You're right. I'm into absolutely nothing. Waiting around to die. So what's a bright, talented young lad like you doing with the likes of me?"

"I don't exactly know, just yet. Why should I? Maybe I agree with you. Maybe I think you don't want to believe your own arguments. But I don't want to turn this into a philosophy seminar. I'll tell you this: I'm not in love with you—"

"That's good—"

"—I just like being around you. And I think by now I've earned the right to ask you at least one question: Just why in hell do you wanna be around the likes of me? Some dumb kid who doesn't know whether he's coming or going, loves and even writes and sings music you hate—like you said the other day, we have absolutely nothing in common. So why did you say yes? And why do I get the feeling that this whole conversation amounts to more of the same? JUST WHAT DO YOU SEE IN ME, HUH?"

"I . . . can't honestly say. When you're as old as I am, you'll understand better, and I don't mean this to sound condescending, what I mean when I say that ninety-nine percent of men, that I ever encountered at least, are one hundred percent shits. The odds don't look too good, given my age, my work, my financial situation, my marital status, how many children I've contributed to our ever-expanding social future, my history as regards booze and the like—any way you look at it, I'm a bad bet. I hope you appreciate I'm telling you the truth."

"You're also deliberately leaving out all the emotion."

"That's because I don't feel any yet."

"That's a lie."

"No, it's not. I haven't felt any in a long, long time. I shut all of it off. You kids can afford to throw that emotion stuff all over the place—us older folks, especially women, are rather more spent. And I don't fit in anywhere. Never have. I never will. You, on the other hand, have a whole 'generation' to back up any horseshit you get yourself into. You're lucky, but I'm not jealous. You'll end up one of two ways: just like me, or just like the rest of the people on my job. Either way you'll be unhappy. This 'generation' stuff is just a con to try and sell you something I know, I've seen it before, the same catchphrases. But the last word is I'm desperate. And THAT'S"—here she bore down almost with a vengeance—"WHY I'M SPENDING FRIDAY NIGHT WITH YOU INSTEAD OF ALONE WITH A BOOK, OR THE RADIO OR TV I NEVER PLAY."

"So you're desperate. So are millions of other people, but they're not with me. You are. How come?"

She felt cornered. "Because . . . I'm just narcissistic

enough that when I look at you, I see some of me looking back, and I like that. I want a yes-man—"

"Ah, come on—"

"Okay, then, I want a mirror. Or somebody who shares some of these feelings you call futile. I want to talk like this, even if we're both just digging one big hole that leads nowhere, as I strongly suspect, I've been starved for talk like this for longer than you can imagine. Most people never do it, and when I start to—"

"I know—"

"They get weird."

He looked her in the eye. "That's 'cause they're afraid of you. Because the very fact of you raising the questions threatens the very foundations of their lives, what they live for and why."

"Don't you *dare* deny how scared you are of me—"

"Yeah, but that's different. . . ."

"So what? Maybe we're wrong and they're right. Maybe we should just shut up and go buy something."

"Okay—whaddaya want?"

"Absolutely nothing anybody's selling, at least not at any price I can afford. Two months on the coast of Spain might be nice. How about *you? Surely* there's some new rock album you're just *dying* to own."

"I already bought it, the day it came out."

"Well then, a new stereo."

"Old stereos are better, at least for the kind of music I usually listen to, and I already got one."

"A new guitar."

"Already own two."

"Strings."

"Thirty-four pence apiece."

"Amp."

"When I have more money."

"Clothes."

"Why? Soon as you get caught up, they change all the fashions so you just have to start all over again."

"That sounds exactly like something I would say."

He grinned. "Maybe that answers your question of why we should be together."

"Or why we should stay away from each other at all times."

"Face it: we're both snobs."

"We don't like anybody or anything—"

"That's 'cause nobody and nothing is good enough for us—"

"Or so we *think*—"

"So here we are, pretending we're right and they're wrong—"

"When really we both know better—"

"If we don't they'll be letting us know real soon."

"Would you rather spend the rest of your life in prison or the nuthouse?"

"That's a rough one. Gimme some time. Neither."

"My answer exactly."

"But what's gonna happen when we get to the point—"

"Wait, I already know what you're about to say—"

"When we both think the same thing—"

"Always—"

"So we no longer need to talk at all?"

"I guess we'll just have to wait and see."

"Either that or find out what we can't stand about each other and go our separate ways."

"All right. So we've agreed about all the things we *hate*— so much so we don't even need to discuss them. . . ."

"Yeah . . ."

"Yeah, well, what about the things we actually *like?*"

"What about 'em?"

"Well, JUST WHAT ARE THEY? I mean, *I wanna see an itemized list.*"

"Can't be done."

"Why not?"

"Guess."

"We don't like enough things to fill out the fingers of one hand much less a whole sheet of paper."

"Right again."

"Though there is one thing . . ."

"Yeah . . . ?

"Well . . . I'm kinda hesitant to bring it up . . ."

"For God's sake, WHY?"

"Because . . . well . . ."

"Are you talking about what I think you're talking about?"

"Uhh . . ."

"You are. After all we've been through."

"Yeah, but look at it this way: when the rest of human experience is totally worthless, and we see eye to eye to such an extent we can barely talk, that leaves just ONE THING."

"Hmmm . . . and what if that runs out, too?"

"It won't."

"Why?"

"Trust me."

"Why?"

"You've got nothing better to do."

"True enough."

"Hey."

"What?"

"Let's fuck."

"I thought you'd never ask."

From that night it began to seem as if they measured their time more in terms of when and for how long they had to be apart than when they saw each other. They became so attuned to each other's thought patterns that conversation did indeed sometimes become all but superfluous. Yet, curiously, that was all they lived for. Or so they thought. So he thought. There was never the slightest doubt in his mind.

After a few months, she began to have second thoughts. They were *too much* alike. Lovers brought something unexpected, some tension to the relationship that made it click, cook, and change. This was more like brother and sister. Which she never told him, but she increasingly found less than dizzyingly erotic. It was simply too pat. Yet there he was, as happy as she had ever seen anyone be in her life. Her reservations made her feel guilty, and the fact that she didn't voice them compounded the guilt. She was hiding plenty from him, more all the time in fact. She couldn't stand the thought of him being unhappy. If things continued on their present course, she was going to end up bored out of her fucking mind. She was beginning to feel like his mother: precisely because she understood all this and he didn't. Whereas he felt like a 100 percent fulfilled LOVER, if not a flat-out husband.

One thing was clear: they were not communicating. He just thought they were. He was living in a dream that she had the power to break in a moment, with a word. She had never heard of anything more unfair in her life. And what was most unfair about it was that it was nobody's fault. There were no villains, no excuses, no nothing, and she was going crazy. Something had to give. There was no solution, short of death. And she was not prepared to die. He was healthier than anyone else she knew. Why shouldn't he be: she, as he'd put it so often, repeating the phrase till she could scream, "completed" him. Completed him. Was that even fair to him, assuming it was true? What sort of life could he possibly have, when both of them were so alienated, and the crucial difference was that she had had over forty years to acclimate herself to it, even view it with a certain wry detachment, whereas he, being a child of the sixties with all that that entailed, thought there was no reason on earth why he should acclimate himself to anything? Why shouldn't they just be happy? Wasn't that what it was all about? Hadn't they found it in each other? *But we aren't* supposed *to be happy,* she wanted to scream.

She thought about it all the time. How could he not notice? Had he gone senile? Maybe his whole generation was senile, with their Beatles and drugs and notions of happiness as some inalienable birthright instead of an occasional holiday that sneaks up on you while you figure out a way to fuck it up. She was just too set in her ways. Whereas he could bend to anything, and did, regularly. Which was one of the main reasons why she was beginning to feel like a mother. Who the hell was she to remake and define his whole life? Yet that was seemingly exactly what he wanted. What else was there for him? It was sickening. Once they were alike; now they were both her. One was more than enough.

One day she sat down and made a list of possible solutions:

(1) *Commit suicide. Then he would be free.* Unacceptable. As pointless as life was, she had no intention of checking out until absolutely necessary. Besides, who was to say that he might not kill himself in grief immediately thereafter, becoming her shadow even in death?

(2) *Confront him. Tell him she couldn't stand it anymore. Then ask for his advice.* Trouble was, she suspected he wouldn't have any. He had externalized his own emptiness to the point he thought she was perfect. Perfect. Some joke that was. A forty-six-year-old divorcée and intermittent alcoholic subject to chronic depression and conviction that life is meaningless and empty, an individual with zero interests, no

skills, shit job, ex-hooker, no children, now carrying on an obviously deeply sick relationship with a boy almost twenty years her junior, half her age. Maybe she had let the whole mess get started in the first place simply as a hedge against the fact she'd never had children. Now she had a son. Whom she fucked. Who imitated her in every way he knew how. Lord help us. If this was perfection, give me a country of miscreants, mutants, psychos, and cripples.

(3) *Demand they break up.* Break his heart. Deprive him of his sole reason for staying alive. *HURT HIM.* And herself as well, no doubt about it. Back to the office and the papers and slimy men making hideous propositions over chili dogs? The coffee klatch? Bach and Mozart, even? She'd rather kill herself. *She* would have nothing to live for in that case. Yet somehow she got by before him. How? She could not remember.

(4) *Force herself to develop some new outside interest which was sure to alienate him.* A cult? Antirock crusade? Rightwing politics? Jesus freaks? The Chamber of Commerce? Fascinating Womanhood? She would rather learn bass (as he had in fact even on occasion urged her, for Christ's sake) and join his damn rock band. And she hated his singing as well as his songs. She would rather be dead.

(5) *Kill him.* At least if she did it right, he'd never know what hit him, never know unhappiness for the rest of his life. But she had no right to do this. Besides, it would break her heart; she would kill herself first. Besides, she couldn't stand the thought of either prison *or* the mental ward.

(6) *Simply disappear.* Pull a Judge Crater. Somehow that

seemed the most cowardly way out of all. And more than likely, they'd end up back together.

It was a single word which made up her mind for her. One morning she awoke, turned her head on the pillow, looked at him sleeping so blissfully beside her with one arm wrapped around her naked body and even a sleeping hand cupping her breast, and she thought: *I am his guru.* GURU. That was the end. To be anyone's "guru" was more than she could bear, whatever the consequences. It was funny how life worked. Nothing had changed. Just one word. But that word made all the difference in the world. For her it was like "Hitler" or "nigger" or any of those other buzzwords that set alarms raging in the human heart. She would murder a busload of schoolchildren in cold blood before she would be even one single human's "guru." Just looking at him there on the pillow, she wanted to vomit.

But what to do? Stealthily she crept out of bed, padded into the kitchen, and over a cup of coffee plotted. Out of six possible escape hatches, no single one of which was satisfactory, perhaps she could contrive a combination kiss-off that might work. Yes. She dressed, making sure to keep as quiet as before so he'd sleep on while she plotted, then drove the car to the liquor store, where she bought a half gallon of Johnnie Walker Black. Arriving back home, she began to mix it with the coffee, fifty-fifty. Drank it down pretty fast. By the third cup she had hatched fifteen more schemes, each more outlandishly unworkable than its predecessor. By the time he awoke, she was drunker than she'd been in years, plotzed, zonked, a mess. She checked the bathroom mirror: yep, it'd done the trick. She looked *fifty* years old if she looked a day. Keep this up for a week and she'd be a hundred. How could he possibly want to fuck that, much less idolize it?

He walked into the kitchen and blinked, still half asleep but palpably shocked: "What are you *doing?*"

"Whaddaya mean, waddami doin'? I'm having a li'l *fun*, thaz wad I'm doin'. Wat the fugh's it to ya, anyway?"

She knew this wouldn't be enough. He commenced to grill her: "Is anything *wrong?*"

"YA DAMN RIGHT SUMTHINZ WRONG. LIFE STINKS, TAZ WAT. I TRIED TO ENJOY IT, BUT IT WUZZA LIE I'M GONNA DRINK UNTIL I CROAK."

Jeez, was this corny. But he was buying it. Was there no depth to which her respect for him could not sink?

"But . . . but . . . everything was going so well . . ."

"YEAH—SO *YOU* THOUGHT. I *HATED* EVERY SECOND OF IT." Well, there was certainly enough truth in this. "I'M JUST TOO SET IN MY WAYS. NOT YOUNG LIKE YOU. GWAN AN' LIVE. I WAN' DIE."

"But WHY? You've got ME, we've got EACH OTHER."

"BIG *DEAL*." Better soften the payload a bit. "All we are is MIRRORS of each other. We used to be two IN . . . INN . . . N-DIVVIJAWLS . . . NOW WE'RE JUST ONE . . . *LUMP* . . . not even hardly HUMAN. . . ."

He began to cry. Well, tough shit. "But we've shared so *much*—so many *ideas*, made so much *good love*, enriched each other in SO MANY WAYS . . .

"YEAH, THAT'S WHY I WANNA DIE, JERKOFF . . . ain't no YOU or I anymore . . . just WE . . . face it: WE ARE BORING AS SHIT. Wanna drink?"

"NO. I want . . . God, all of a sudden I don't know. . . ."

Time to up the ante with a little gross-out: "I DO. YER RIGHT ABOUT THE LAV MAKING AT LEAST"—yanking her dress up and panties down, ripping the latter in the process, spreading her legs as crudely as she could—"HOW 'BOUT A LI'L POO-ZEE? C'MON, BUSTER BROWN— LESSEE YA *LAP THAT CUNNY UP* . . . or"—in the world's absolute worst Mae West impression—"PIPE ME YER WAGSTAFF, BIG BOY, I WANNA FRESH LOADA A.M. JIZM RIGHT *HERE*. . . ."

He was getting physically ill. On the other hand, so was she. This project obviously called for more extreme measures. She ran out and jumped into the car, drove it 90 mph to a shabby house well-known as headquarters of the local Hell's Angels chapter, and invited them all back to the house for a gangfuck. This was asking for serious trouble, but anything was better than being Baba Ram Dass. Fourteen of them came roaring after her. When they arrived back at the homestead, she lay down in the middle of the living room floor, hiked her dress again, and hollered, *"C'mon, boys . . . firs' come, firs' serve . . ."*

They didn't look any too eager—but then he like a damn fool had to go and try to protect her Maidenly Honor. He picked a fistfight with them. They beat him to a pulp, one of them demanded a blow job from her, she refused, sirens began to be heard in the distance, they all did the quickest disappearing act she'd ever seen outside the movies. She drove him to the hospital. While he was laid up in there three straight weeks, she hired one whore after another to go into the ward disguised as nurses and seduce him. It didn't work until she spiked his orange juice with a triple dose of street acid: she sent three different girls up that day, and he fucked, sucked, and orifically jimjammed his little brains loose. With the third one of the day she pretended to innocently wander in on them—"*What is this? I thought you LOVED me?*"

"I *do*, I *do*," and damn if his hard-on don't wilt outa guilt. The hooker stalks out in disgust while he grovels, begging forgiveness till it reminds her so much of the first time he ever pulled that act, way back in the beginning, she wants to puke. Instead she whips out a copy of Garner Ted Armstong's *The Plain Truth* and begins to hector him at the top of her lungs, liberally peppering this gibberish spew with extensive quotes from said publication, the whole rant to effect that if *only* he would *see the light* of *Jesus Christ our lord* he'd forget about them wicked wimmin forever. By now he's practically catatonic. Meanwhile she's taking more swigs of Johnnie Walker Black, holy rolling and mouthing scatological rants all mixed up together at the top of her lungs, till it brings half the hospital staff down on them, who toss her off the premises immediately.

In fact, she is denied entrance to the hospital for the remainder of his stay. So every day by messenger she makes sure he's sent copies of *The Plain Truth*, Gerald L. K. Smith's *The Cross and the Flag*, *Communism, Hypnotism and the Beatles*, *The Watchtower*, and *The Journal of Krishna Consciousness*, as well as more hookers in nurses' uniforms, drug dealers disguised as staff doctors, forcing every sort of street dope on him from acid to speed to Placidyls to methadone, slimy strangers who regale him with long, involved tales of all the sexual high jinks she's supposedly been pulling with 'em while barred from his hospital ward.

By the time his broken bones are healed he's ready for the nut ward, but she carts him home, and all he'll say is "We gotta have a talk." At last.

So they sit down in the kitchen. He leans forward over the table, looks her square in the eye, and says, "I realized one thing in the hospital: you're right. I don't know what you're up to, but whatever it is, I haven't felt this good in years, broken ribs and all. As Crowley said, 'Nothing is true; everything is permitted.' So, from here on out, we are libertines."

This is more than she can take. The whole thing has backfired. There's only one way out: find some way to make him a rock star, get him a hit record and out on tour, then maybe she'll be free. . . . So she pulls out her ace in the hole: "Well, look, I've been reading *NME* a lot while you were laid up, especially the classifieds, and it says here the lead singer of this band is splitting, the band needs a new, dynamic-individual-type lead singer to break them in America. I think that might be you. . . ."

"Might. Trouble is, one of those Angels stepped on my Adam's apple—my voice sounds like shit."

"Well, hell, look—do yourself a favor, go on down and try out for it anyway. What've you got to lose?"

Answer, of course: nothing. What she's got to lose is one king-size albatross, as he gets hired and the rest is history or what passes for it. He ends up one of the biggest superstars in the world, while she goes back to the bars and stays alive on the occasional check for not all that many bucks he sends along. . . .

Now, you'd think after she went to all that trouble for him, practically made him what he is today, that he'd be more grateful, but he's not. One day he shows up with an acetate, looking kinda sheepish, and says, "I thought it only fair you be one of the first persons to hear this. . . ."

She takes the *St. Matthew Passion* off the box and slaps on this circle of black plastic without even a label. What is it? Whadda *you* think?

When it's over, she very calmly takes it off, hands it back to him, pours another tumbler full of Johnnie Walker, and says, cool as you please, "Well, I certainly gotta hand it to you: you've come full circle: from SOB by minded nature to reeducated rather sweet fella, which I guess never really suited you inasmuch as your entire personality disappeared into mine and you became merely an adjunct of my apathy, clear through to your present status as SOB who knows just exactly how big a slime he is and is gonna clean up off it I have no doubt."

"Yes, and I owe it all to you."

"Well, not exactly. Though the thought is certainly touching. I'm not sure exactly who you owe it to, but please leave my name out of it. Just send a check every now and then. . . ."

"Good as done . . ." He slides the acetate back in its sleeve and splits pronto, a little nervously methinks. But so what? You'd be nervous, too, if you had to go through life worrying that somebody might spill the beans on you at any moment. She's not about to do so, of course, because she couldn't care less as long as she never has to listen to it, and he keeps sending what after all is only her fair share of the royalties for, uh, "inspiring" his biggest hit. As long as he does and she keeps her mouth shut in public, he's happy, she's happy, the record industry's happy, and all's well with the world.

Of course, she still laughs about it: "Yeah, poor old guy . . . only man I ever knew with real potential. Trouble is, if he'd've told the truth in that stupid song, not only would nobody've bought it, but instead of World's Foremost Casanova Tinseltown Division he would today be a mere drugstore clerk in South Kensington. His sex life would be more satisfying, as I'm sure he recalls it was for a while there. I guess in the end it all boils down to a matter of priorities: Would you rather be the ship or the cargo? He made his choice, I made mine, and I hope you've all made yours. Cheers." And she raises her glass again.

From *Psychotic Reactions and Carburetor Dung* by Lester Bangs, edited by Greil Marcus, copyright © 1987 by the Estate of Lester Bangs. Used by permission of Alfred A. Knopf, a division of Random House, Inc.

THE NATIONAL ANTHEM

jonathan lethem

Dear M.,

Our long letters are pleasing to me, but they do come slowly. Lulled by the intrinsic properties of email, I've been willing to let most of my other correspondences slide down that slippery slope, into hectic witty ping-pong. But our deep connection, for twenty years or more now unrefreshed or diluted or whatever it *would* be by regular communications in person or on the phone, is precious to me, and demands more traditional letters. I suppose three-month breaks are not so much in a friendship once treated so casually that we let nearly a decade go by, eh?

You asked about A. We've finally broken it off, the end of a nearly three-year chapter in my life, and a secret chapter as well. For, apart from you, safely remote in Japan, I've confided in no one. Her horrible marriage survived us, a fact that would have seemed absurd to me at the beginning, if some time traveler had come back to whisper it in my ear. The break was mutual—mutual enough to give it that name—and I'd be helpless to guess who is the more scarred. We won't be friends, but we were never going to be. Dissolving a secret affair is eerily simple: A. and I only had to quit lying that we didn't exist.

Did I tell you about "The National Anthem"? I don't think so. This was the first night we stole together from her husband, the first intentional rendezvous, at a bed-and-breakfast outside Portland, Maine. A. always traveled with a Walkman and a wallet of CDs, and that night, as we lay entwined in a twee canopy bed, she insisted on playing me a song, though there was no way for us to listen to it together. Instead she cued it up and watched me while it played, her ungroggy eyes inspecting me from below the horizon of my chest, mine a posture of submission: James Carr singing "The Dark End of the Street." I recognized it, but I'd never listened closely before. It's a song of infidelity and hopeless love, full of doomed certainty that the lovers, the love, will fail.

"I've got a friend who calls that 'The National Anthem,' " she said.

I gave her what was surely a weak-sickly smile, though likely I thought it was a cool and dispassionate one. She didn't elaborate, just let it sink in. I didn't ask who the friend might be—the unspecificity seemed as essential to the mood between us as the dual rental cars, the welcoming basket of cookies and fruit we'd ignored downstairs, or the silent fucking we'd enjoyed, our orgasms discrete, in turn. To press one another back into the world of names, of our real individual lives, would have seemed a rent in the shroud of worldly arbitrariness that enclosed our passion. Of course this was morbid, I see it now.

"There's a Bob Dylan song," I said then. " 'Ninety Miles an Hour Down a Dead End Street.' I think it's a cover, actually. Same thing: 'We're on a bad motorcycle with a devil in the seat, going ninety miles an hour down a dead end street . . .' "

"Yes, but this is 'The National Anthem.' "

By refusing the comparison, A. put me on notice that this wasn't a dialogue, but a preemptive declaration. She'd be the one to manage our yearnings, by her foreknowledge of despair. Fair enough: her jadedness was what I'd been drawn to in the first place.

Of course you know, M., because I've told you stories, how we rode her jadedness—our bad motorcycle—down our own dead end street. It wasn't kept anonymously cute, with baskets of cookies, for long. The perversity of the affair, it seems to me now, is that under cover of delivering her from the marriage she claimed to be so tired of, A. and I climbed inside the armature of that marriage instead. By skulking at its foundations, its skirts, we only proved its superiority. However aggrieved she and R. might be, however dubious their prospect, it wasn't a secret affair, wasn't nearly as contemptible as *us*. Certainly that can be the only explanation for why, in a world of motels and with my own apartment free, we so often met at her place—at theirs. And I think now that though I mimed indifference whenever she predicted immanent destruction, I'd *lusted* to destroy a marriage, that I was far more interested in R. than I allowed myself to know.

But I don't want to make this letter about A. You've written at length about your uncertainties in your own marriage—written poignantly, then switched to a tone of flippancy, as though to reassure me not to be too concerned. Yet the flippancy is the most poignant of all—your joshing about your vagrant daily lusts in such an unguarded voice makes them real to me. Having never been to Japan, nor met your wife and child, I've been guilty of picturing it as some rosy, implacable surface, as though by moving from New York to Tokyo and entering a "traditional" Japanese marriage you'd migrated from the complicated world into an elegantly calm piece of eighteenth-century screen art. I'm probably not the first person guilty of finding it convenient to imagine my friends' lives are simpler than my own. It's also possible I began this letter by speaking of A. in order to discredit myself as any sort of reasonable counsel, to put you in mind of my abhorrent track record (or maybe I'm just obsessed).

Let me be more honest. I don't spend all that much time imagining Japan. However much you and I speak of our contemporary lives, I picture you as I left you: eighteen years old. You and I were inseparable for the first three years at Music and Art, then distant in our senior year, then you vanished. Now you're a digital wraith. When I try to think of your marriage, I instead tangle, helplessly, in the unexamined questions surrounding our first, lost friendship. I don't mean to suggest *anyone* doesn't find a muddle when they recall that year, launching from twelfth grade to the unknown. But it is usual to have you lucidly before me, daring me, by your good faith in these recent letters, to understand.

Do you remember my obsession with Bess Hersh? Do you remember how you played the go-between? That was junior year, just before the breach between us. Bess was a freshman, an eighth-grader. You and I were giddy dorks in rapidly enlarging bodies, hoping that being a year older could stand in, with the younger girls, for the cool we'd never attained. I'll never forget the look on your face when you found me where I waited, at the little park beside the school, and said that Bess's appointed friend, her "second," had confirmed that she *liked me, too.*

Shortly after that, Bess Hersh saw through me. I hadn't known what to do with this coup except bungle it when she and I had a moment alone, bungle it with my self-conscious tittering, my staring, my grin. I tried boy jokes on her, Steve Martin routines, and those don't work on girls in high school. What's required then is some stammering James Dean, with shy eyes cast to pavement. Those shy eyes are what gives a girl as young as that breathing room, I think. You, you mastered those poses in short order—I'd wait until college.

Soon, agonizingly soon, Bess was on Adam Reisner's arm, and I felt that I'd only alerted the hipper Adam to her radiant presence among the new freshmen. But I still cling to that moment when I knew she'd mistaken me for cool, before I opened my mouth, while you were still ferrying messages between us so that she could project what she wished into the outline of me. I still picture her, too, as some sort of teenage sexual ideal, lost forever: her leggy, slouching stride, the cinch of worn jeans over that impossible curve from her narrow waist to the scallop of her hips, her slightly too big nose and fawny eyes. I wonder what kind of woman she grew into, whether I'd glance at her now. Once she gave me boners that nearly caused me to faint. Just typing her name is erotic to me still.

Funny, though, I don't remember speaking *to* her more than once or twice. I remember speaking with you about her, *chortling* about her, I should say, and scheming, and pining, and once, when we were safely alone in the Sheep Meadow in Central Park, bellowing her name to the big, empty sky. I recall talking this way with you, too, about Liz Kessel, Margaret Anodyne, and others. I recall the dopey, sexed-up love lyrics we'd write together, never to show to the girls. You and I were just clever enough, and schooled enough in *Mad* magazine, Woody Allen, Talking Heads, Frank Zappa, and Devo, to ironize our sprung lusts, to find the chaos of our new-yearning hearts bitterly funny.

When, six months on, you first began combing your hair differently, and when you began listening to New Romantic bands, and when you began dating Tu-Lin, I was disenchanted with you, M. Violently disenchanted, it seems to me now. I felt all the music you listened to was wrong, a betrayal—you'd quit liking the inane, clever stuff and moved on to music that felt postured and sexy instead. I felt you'd forgotten yourself, and I tried to show you what you'd forgotten. When I'd third around with you and your new Vietnamese girlfriend, I'd seek to remind you of our secret languages, our jokes—if they hadn't worked on Bess they should at least still mean something to you—but those japes now fell flat, and you'd rebuff me, embarrassed.

Of course the worse I fared, the harder I tried. For a while. Then that became our falling-out. I must have appeared so angry—this is painful speculation, now. Of course, what seemed so elaborately *cultural* or *aesthetic* to me at the time—I faulted you for hairstyle, music, Tu-Lin's Asianness—all appears simply emotional in retrospect. I was threatened by the fact that you'd gone from pining for girls to *having* them, sure. But I'd also invested in you all my intimations of what I was about to surrender in myself, by growing up. By investing them in you I could make them something to loathe, rather than fear. Loathing was safer.

Oh, the simple pain of growing up at different speeds!

A page or two ago I supposed I was going to build back from this reminiscence, to some musings on your current quandary, your adult ambivalence about the commitments you entered when you married (I nearly wrote *entered precociously*, but that's only the case by my retarded standard). But I find I'm reeling even deeper into the past. When I was seven or eight, years before you and I had met, my parents befriended a young couple, weirdly named August and Sincerely. I guess those were their hippie names—at least Sincerely's must have been. August was a war resister. My parents had sort of adopted him during his trial, for he'd made the gesture of throwing himself an eighteenth birthday party in the office of his local draft board, a dippy bit of agitprop that got him singled out, two years later, for prosecution. Sincerely was a potter, with a muddy wheel and a redbrick kiln in the backyard of her apartment. She was blond and stolid and unpretentious, the kind of woman who'd impress me now as mannish, a lesbian perhaps, at least as a more plausible candidate for chumming around than for an attraction (I felt she was a woman, then, but she must have been barely twenty, if that).

We'd visit Sincerely often during the six or eight months while August served out his sentence, sit in the backyard sipping ice tea she'd poured with clay-stained hands, and in that time I very simply—and articulately, to myself—fell in love. I was still presexual enough to isolate my feelings for Sincerely as romantic and pure. In stories like this one, children are supposed to get mixed up, and to imagine that adults will stop and wait for them to grow up, but I wasn't confused for a moment. I understood that my love for Sincerely pertained to the idea of what kind of woman I meant to love in my future life as a man. I promised myself she would be exactly like Sincerely, and that when I met her, I would love her perfectly and resolutely, that I would be better to her than I have in fact ever been to anyone—than *anyone's* ever been to anyone else.

So my love wasn't damaged by August's return from jail

(he'd never gone upstate, instead served his whole time in the Brooklyn House of Detention, on Atlantic Avenue). I didn't even bother to resent his possession of Sincercly, which I saw as intrinsically flawed by grown-up sex and diffidence. August wasn't a worthy rival, and so I just went on secretly loving Sincerely with my childish idealism. The moron-genius of my young self felt it knew better than any adult how to love, felt certain it wouldn't blow the chance if it were given one. Not one day I've lived since has satisfied that standard. Of course, it is strange and sad for me now to see a shade of future triangulation in that emotional arrangement—I'd cast August as an early stand-in for R., a man I would pretend was irrelevant even as I fitted myself into his place in life.

What I'd promised to hold on to then, M., is the same thing I'd raged against losing when you began to grow away from me, when I failed the test presented by your sultry new self that senior year. How ashamed that promiser would be to learn—had some malicious time traveler drifted back to whisper it in his ear—about the pointless ruin of my years with A. Those promises we make to ourselves when we are younger, about how we mean to conduct our adult lives, can it be true we break every last one of them? All except for one, I suppose: the promise to judge ourselves by those standards, the promise to remember the child who would be so appalled by compromise, the child who would find jadedness wicked.

Yes, my childish self would read this letter and think me poisoned with knowledge, but the truth is that what I flung against A. so recklessly *was* my innocence, preserved in a useless form. The revving heart of my hopefulness, kicked into gear anew, is the most precious thing about me, I refuse to vilify it. I hope I fall in love again. But it's a crude innocence that fails to make the distinctions that might have protected me from A., and A. from me. For by imagining I could save her from her marriage, by that blustery optimism by which I concealed from myself my own despair at the cul-de-sac lust had led us into, I forced her to compensate by playing the jaded one on both our behalfs. What I mean to say is that I forced her to play me that song, M., by grinning at her like a loon. Like the way I grinned at Bess Hersh. I gave A. no choice but to be the *dark lady*, by being the moron-child who thought love could repair what love had wrecked. A motorcycle that's gone off a cliff isn't repaired by another motorcycle.

Well, I've failed. This whole letter is about A., I see that now. You wonder whether you can stand never to know the touch of a fresh hand, the trembling flavor of a new kiss, and I'm desperately trying to keep from telling you the little I know: it's sweeter than anything, for a moment. For just a moment, there's nothing else. As to all you're weighing it against, your wife and child, I know less than nothing. The wisdom of your ambivalence, the whimsical, faux-jaded wit you share in your letter, as you contemplate the beauties around you, all that poise will be shattered if you act—I can promise you that much. You're more innocent than you know. I speak to you from the dark end of the street, but it's a less informed place than you'd think. All I can do for you is frame the question I've framed for myself: Where to steer the speeding motorcycle of one's own innocence? How to make it a gift instead of a curse?

I think we need a new national anthem.

I'm ending this letter without saying anything about your incredible tale of the salaryman masturbating on the subway. Well, there, I've mentioned it. I'm also grateful to know that Godzilla's not what he's cracked up to be, that he's just another mediocre slugger with a good agent and a memorable nickname. What a joy it would be to see the Yankees take a pratfall on that move. Bad enough when they pillage the other American teams, but that the world is their oyster, too, has become unbearable. Of course, the Mets go on signing haggard veterans and I think there's no hope at all, but you can be certain Giuseppe and I will be out at Shea having our hearts broken this May, as always. In our hearts it's always spring, or 1969, or something like that. I only wish we had some outfielders who could catch the ball.

Yours,

E.

author inspiration

Yo La Tengo has been one of my favorite groups for ten years, not least because in their curiosity and generosity they remained fans and critics even as they became artists themselves. Their covers of other musicians—in this case, the prodigal songwriter Daniel Johnston—convey a quality of curatorial pleasure not so different from the premise of this anthology. Aside from that, anyone whose heart isn't broken by that song hasn't ever been in love.

BLUE GUITAR

amanda davis

I wish I had a blue guitar,
a blue guitar to play all night long

"Blue Guitar"
Cowboy Junkies

Meg dreams that someone is coming for her. It is a clear and urgent dream and she wakes full of hope, but twisted in the sheets, as though a struggle has ensued. She dresses slowly, pulling on her cleanest pair of worn blue pants, a tight white T-shirt that she believes hints at her figure under the blue-and-white smocks Raylene makes all the Clover waitresses wear. She rouses her little brothers and pours them bowls of cereal, makes herself coffee, and herds the boys to catch their bus, all the while consumed by an unshakable feeling that the day ahead contains an electric promise: something is going to change.

Meg checks on her mother, still asleep in her darkened bedroom, then goes down the hall to the bathroom and appraises herself. She pulls her dark hair back in a clip, and then, studying herself in the mirror, takes the clip out and shakes her hair loose, so that it hangs in waves that frame her pointy face. Her pale cheeks are flushed and her eyes shine. She applies mascara, eye shadow, lipstick. She looks pretty, doesn't she? Pretty enough for whatever is coming?

When Meg arrives, the restaurant is already busy. Her shift proceeds normally enough. People come in, she takes their order, smiles, brings them food, all the while waiting.

You are so jumpy, Raylene says. Why the bee in your bonnet? Settle down.

Meg only smiles. Raylene is not the type to be confided in. But she is bursting with it, with expectation for the future in every pore. At lunch she needs to say something. I had a dream, she tells Leah, the other waitress, who widens her eyes appropriately. I think something's going to happen today.

I'll tell you what's going to happen, Raylene calls from halfway across the restaurant. You're going to get your butt in the back room and bring out more napkins, before I throw something at you, that's what.

Leah gives Meg a sympathetic smile, but then it gets busy and that is the last Meg speaks of it. The day ticks by with frustrating predictability and the feeling fades, the dream fades, and all that is left is the Clover Restaurant.

It rains and then stops. People complain about the weather and then talk about the forecast for tomorrow, the next day, next week. The dinner rush is in full swing, and the end of the shift creeps toward her. Meg is mopping the counter when, coming from the entrance, she feels a dry heat that causes her to look up, to see him there in jeans and boots and a worn canvas jacket. He is pleasant looking, but nothing special—brown hair and the beginning of a dark beard. He is shorter than Meg had hoped, and when he hangs his jacket on the rack by the door, she sees he is a little heavy, too. Still, she feels that heat coming off him and her pulse quickens. That has to count for something.

There is nowhere free but the counter. He strolls there slowly, not looking straight at her, but Meg can feel him watching just the same.

Later Meg imagines ways it might have turned out differently. She could have put her notepad down, untied her apron, and taken a break, though the restaurant was too crowded for Raylene to let her off without a scene. Still, she could have slipped out to go to the bathroom at least—who could argue with that? Meg could have excused herself to Mr. Wilson and Tom, her regulars, and wiped the counter clean with one sweep like she always did before walking into the back, because a clean counter made her feel calm, returning to it was okay, while the dirty ones made her feet ache with the hours to come. She could have walked back through the swinging door and continued out to the Dumpster. Could have leaned against the brick wall and smoked a cigarette, slowly, until her hands stopped shaking.

But she doesn't. Instead, she watches this man saunter forward and holds her breath until he sits down. She tries to smile, but Leah brushes by, and for a moment it seems as though he will order from Leah, but he doesn't. Meg watches Leah open a box of straws, and the man clears his throat. He waits until he has Meg's attention before he speaks.

You got good coffee? he says. I need a good cup of coffee.

Meg licks her lips. She tries to swallow. For no sound reason there is something about him that makes her feel the future rush at her with enormous speed. It's okay, she says. Not the best in the world, but it'll probably do.

She clenches her fingers to keep from rocking and he turns his attention to the menu, greasy and pie-stained. I'll take some, he says. And some of that there.

Meg follows his finger to the peach pie under glass. Right, she says. Okay. And it is like having a fever: she fades in and out of consciousness, all the time aware of becoming a planet orbiting around a sun.

Her shift disappears in a blur of motion. Sometimes time behaves strangely in the restaurant—days lurch forward or hang still, minutes taking hours to tick by. But this is different. This is like being on fire.

He is leaning against a battered blue pickup when Meg gets off. He flashes a wide smile and she swallows again, but doesn't let herself smile back this time. She doesn't have to. It was decided, it had all been decided before by her bones and her blood, by some other being, some other Meg back in that room full of dishes. It was already settled when he paid the check and put his hand over hers: she hoped it would feel like this.

You want one? he says and thrusts a pack of reds at her.

I got my own. Meg holds her purse close and feels them in her pocket, the pack smooth and loose. She can't quite look at him, not directly. He hands her a lit cigarette, as though she hadn't answered. She didn't seen him with two in his mouth, lighting one for her, but it is damp, and Meg knows she is touching a place his lips have been.

You're not from around here, she blurts, so loudly that they both laugh in surprise.

No, he says, but now she can look at that dangerous grin, at his big teeth, his small, dark eyes. I'm from Texas. Small town. You wouldn't have heard of it.

Try me.

He runs a hand through his hair so it pokes up on top and looks at something over her head. It's called Shuville, he said. *S-H-U*, not like footwear. It's about four hours from any-where you'd want to be.

You still live there?

No.

A car passes, and then another. Each leaving the restau-rant for the highway that twists out toward the horizon. She watches them go, waits for them to disappear from sight, one after the other. Any other night she might be out here alone, staring at that line that divides land from sky, wondering when she'll ever get a chance to head there herself. She drags deep so he won't see her hand tremble.

It's nice out, he says. She turns to him. It is about to rain again. He leans back on the hood of his truck, one arm propping him up, the other holding his cigarette. His blue jeans end in cowboy boots, and that makes her smile.

You want to go for a ride? he says, and pats the side of his truck.

Where to?

Don't know. Maybe we'll just find someplace.

Meg takes another drag and looks over her shoulder, back into the restaurant where she can see Leah watching, Raylene shaking her head. There is no good reason to go, she knows, but there is no way she won't.

You got something better to do? he says.

No, Meg says. I guess not.

They drive fast with the windows rolled up and don't speak. His truck is old and dented, the seats patched with duct tape. It rattles and runs loudly and it smells like tobacco and sweat. And something else. She sees an orange pierced with a thousand cloves wedged in the slant where his dashboard and windshield meet.

You do that? Meg says, and points, but he seems not to hear her. He stares ahead looking calm, sure of where he is taking her.

At some point he turns on the radio and for a while they listen to a guitar and a lonesome voice sing to each other. Meg thinks of her twin brothers. She hasn't until this moment, but she thinks of them now, fixing their own dinners and eating in front of the television with the sound turned low. They will have the lights off, she knows. And they will sit too close with no one to tell them not to. Maybe one of them will be called on to bring Mama something. Maybe they will spend the night in silence.

Meg shakes her head to empty it and tells herself to focus on now, on this very moment, not what she is missing. She watches the headlights spear the dusk, then turns a little to watch him, too.

What do they call you? she says. What's your name?

Jackson, he says, and she isn't sure if it's his first or his last, but she doesn't ask.

Aren't you going to ask me mine?

It's Meg, he says. I can read.

Meg reaches over, unpins the nametag, and tucks it in her pocket. She had forgotten it was there.

It begins to rain lightly at first, then heavier. They drive into the night, and Meg sleeps and wakes, forgetting where she is or why she is there, forgetting how it seemed right to climb in the truck in the first place. But she isn't afraid. She is thankful for the motion, happy to think of her life growing small behind her.

Where are we? Meg says, raising her head from the glass when she sees a white church loom in the glare of their lights. Are we still in South Carolina?

Jackson doesn't look at her, but she sees him smile. You ever had catfish? he says.

She sits up now and peers into the dark. Sure I have.

Well, I thought of this place to take you to a while back and that's where we're going.

And they make catfish?

Like nothing you ever had before.

You know I have to work tomorrow? Meg says. You know that?

I figured as much.

Well, how far is this place?

Let's just go, he says. We're having an adventure, sweetheart, let's just have it.

Meg nestles back down, the road underneath them singing her back to the dream: She is at home, sitting on the front porch of their once-white house. Only it is white again, peeling paint grown smooth, and she understands somehow that it is Before. That her father is still alive, that her mother is well. That the boys are healthy and round-faced and that they all wait for her through that screen door, if only she will stand up off the steps and turn around and walk inside.

But Meg cannot do it. Her limbs are heavy and she cannot make herself rise to meet them. The sun fades from the clear sky until it is purple and then dark, and it grows cold. Then light spills beside her from the windows of the house, but still she cannot stand, because even in the midst of it, she can tell it is a dream and can't bear to take it one step further.

Something lurches her out of that place. She wakes with wet cheeks and wipes them hard, hiding her face from Jackson.

They have stopped. She raises her head and looks around. It is dark and she doesn't know where they are. He leans his chin on the palm of his hand, elbow propped on the truck window, still as granite.

What is it? she says.

Scrapyard.

It emerges from the darkness then, the elements of metal piled in high towers as far back as she can see. There is a crane, too, empty and orange, with a bucket that looks like it could swing out as far as where they sit.

Where are we?

Nowhere, he says, and throws the truck into gear.

My granddaddy owned that yard, he says a while later. It's other people's now, but that was where my daddy was born.

I thought you were from Texas?

Yeah. He turns the radio back on and spins the dial, looking for something he doesn't find. He turns it off and the silence feels sudden to her, large.

You born in Texas?

Yeah.

When did your people leave South Carolina?

We're in Georgia, he says. He looks over at her then and seems to be adding something up, something that she can't see. My daddy wrote songs, he says finally. He wrote these songs and he got known for them and that would have never happened if he'd a stayed here.

His words are fierce, his voice low. She isn't sure what he expects of her. The windshield wipers slap back and forth. You out here visiting some folks?

He cracks the window and lights a cigarette, flicking it with his thumb. My daddy left here when he was seventeen. Hitched his way to Nashville. Knew he'd never go back. His real name was Jackson, too. He never did come back here after that, but he talked about it. He told my mom and he told me. Didn't tell me directly, I guess, but I know he meant to.

There are things hiding in the darkness all around them. Probably was hard for him, leaving everyone behind like that, Meg says.

He was a good person. Jackson hits the steering wheel with an open palm. He tried all along to be a good person.

My daddy died, Meg says, startling herself enough to sit up straighter.

He didn't mean for what happened to happen, Jackson continues as though she hadn't spoken. He was a good man, everybody says so.

I'm sure he was.

You have to make choices, Jackson says. You have to look at your life and what it holds and then you have to ask yourself what's missing. That's what he always said, and he was right. So sometimes you have to give up what matters most in the world to you because it gets in the way of something else.

He is focused on the road, not looking at Meg, but she feels as though the things he says are being delivered in a random order for her to reassemble, everything a clue to something she can't know.

They hit a pothole. Jackson passes a white van. There is no one ahead of them.

Did you know him? Your father?

Of course I did, Jackson says, turning to her with a sharp look. Of course I did.

They are quiet for a while and then Jackson pulls the truck into an all-night gas station and Meg stays in the car while he fills up.

In Meg's house, the absence is everything. One car turning the wrong way on a one-way street and the world stopped moving forward. Sometimes Meg lets herself think about the other family, the mother and daughter belonging to the drunk man driving the other car. She wonders what they have become, whether that night ruined them, too. The newspaper said the other driver was *survived*, just as her father was *survived*, but it was the wrong word, she knows. They don't survive him, exactly. It is more fragile than that, more precarious. She and her brothers were crushed into tiptoeing shadows, moving soundlessly through the house so as not to disturb their mother, who rarely left her room before and now refuses to leave it at all. Meg doesn't think of that as surviving him. They survive despite him.

The rain has let up, but the darkness is inky, the center of night. Meg grinds the heels of her hands into her eye sockets until she sees bright spots of white, and opens them to find Jackson staring at her through the window. She rolls it down.

You want a Coke? he says. I was asking if you wanted something to drink.

I'm OK, she says.

Well if you want to use the facilities, this would be a good time. We still got a ways to go.

Meg nods. He opens the door and she climbs out of the truck. Her legs nearly buckle from hours of driving. In the sharp fluorescence of the ladies' room she splashes water on her face and tries to neaten her hair. In the mirror, her eyes are wide, wider than she remembered, and she has the strange sensation of staring at an older vision of herself, as though the evening has aged her. I've been up all night, she mouths, but it feels different from that. It feels as though she's been looking at a teenage version of herself for years and her reflection has suddenly caught up with her.

Neither speaks when they began driving again. She holds the Coke that Jackson bought her but doesn't open it, and eventually it grows warm in her hands.

The night is bleeding into a predawn haze by the time Jackson turns onto an unmarked dirt road. They bump along and drive up clouds of dust, until they find another road, even more rough, that leads them to a weather-beaten shack, which leans impossibly. There is loud music playing, they hear it through the closed windows as they drive up, and the light from the shack gives it the orange glow of an invitation.

We're here, Jackson says, and climbs down from the truck.

Meg sits there for a minute, wondering at what she has done, at where they are, but then he opens her door and offers his hand, and his touch is all it takes to push away her questions again.

She straightens her smock and follows him up the dirt path. As they approach, laughter rings out over rowdy music, a loud thumping beat, yowling voices. Jackson holds the wooden door for Meg and she plunges into a room of dancing people. The place is thick with sweat and smoke and the heavy odor of fried food. The noise rushes through her.

Jackson takes Meg's elbow and steers her toward a raw pine bar. While he shouts for beers, she watches the whirling couples, each one moving faster than the next.

They mind us in here?

What? He leans in close, but still she has to yell.

They mind us coming in here like this? She sweeps the room with her hand, trying to show him how her color doesn't match, how they are different from everyone else there.

I don't think so, he says, but he presses his lips together and she is sorry for having asked.

We'll only be a minute, he yells. If you mind it, I mean.

No, she says. No, I just—she circles with the hand again, then forces herself to clutch a wet beer with it instead. I just was wondering is all.

He nods, his jaw set. Come on. He steers her back beyond the ever-spreading dance floor, until they come to a rough doorway that opens into a larger room crowded with rough-hewn picnic tables. You wait here, he says, and points.

She sinks onto a wooden bench and he disappears again. The dark floor has worn smooth with age, but it is clean. A few people sit at nearby tables. Two coffee-skinned men in matching baseball caps and a huge woman with dark curls tumbling down her wide back are hunched over eating with great concentration, as though the place were quiet.

Panic takes Meg by surprise. Where are they and how is she ever going to make it back in time for her shift? The thought propels her to her feet and she lurches toward the door, then takes a step back when she sees Jackson weaving toward her, a plastic tray piled high with food and more beer gripped tight in his large hands.

This is worth it, hon, he says. Worth the whole night's drive. Don't know what it was, but I had to take you here. Haven't been here in years. Too long. But it's the same. Catfish to make you cry. Here, taste—

He shoves a paper plate at her. Though her stomach rumbles at the sight, she lifts the sandwich gingerly and sniffs it.

Go on. His eyes are bright and focused on her. She flushes, but takes a bite, and the bread is warm and soft, the fish crispy outside and flaky inside, warm and tasty. She closes her eyes and takes another bite. Wow, she says.

My mom took me here first, when she and my dad split, Jackson says. She lit out of Texas and we drove for days. Took me here and it was the best place I'd ever been. They played more country then, more old-timey stuff. First time I remember hearing the banjo. And I always meant to come back. Even when I was touring around.

Touring? Meg wipes her mouth with a paper napkin.

Yeah. I'm on the radio all over, he says. You didn't recognize me?

She stares for a moment, then shakes her head slowly and notices the light in his face dim a little.

Well, I'm known, he says. Get recognized lots of places these days. Half the people in that restaurant of yours were whispering the minute I walked in. That's some of why I figured you wanted to come with me. A little touch of fame. That's why I picked you—seemed like you needed something special to happen.

Meg stops chewing and puts the sandwich down. The magic of the evening rushes away from her. What do you mean? she says, but thinks she knows—she just wants to hear him say it.

It's nothing against you, sweetheart, he says. Never mind. Eat your sandwich and then we'll dance.

I have to work tonight, Meg says. I have to get back.

He scowls. I said eat up. For chrissake. He takes a toothpick from the tray and leans back to clean his teeth. Most girls would kill to be in your place. It's the least you could do, considering.

She takes another bite, but the flavor has gone. He had not recognized her as the stranger he was waiting for. He had not fallen prey to a dream, as she had. He took pity on her. He brought her along to flatter himself.

She pushes the fish away. I don't want any more, she says. I'm not hungry.

They do not dance.

When he has finished his sandwich, and what is left of hers, he gets himself another beer and sits there, not looking at her. Finally he rises and she follows him to the truck.

For the first few miles they are silent. The sky has started to pink, tendrils of color leap up and across the horizon. The land is stark and lush at the same time. Empty and full of life.

Meg presses her cheek against the cool glass and watches the fields pass. She is not sorry she got in the truck or drove all night, but she does not like this silence or the emptiness that accompanies it. It is different from the bouts of silence they shared on the way down. Those belonged to both of them. Now they each have their own.

She thinks of her brothers asleep on the floor in front of the television, no one to put them to bed. Their limbs will be tangled, their cheeks flushed, the dark circles under their eyes softened by their dreams. She can almost smell them, feel their weight as she carries first one, then the other up to bed. But she will not be there to do that tonight. Tonight they are on their own.

She rubs her temples with the tips of her fingers. You didn't need to do me a favor, she says softly. You don't know me. My life isn't something you needed to rescue me from.

He stares straight ahead, but his mouth twitches.

What makes you think you have that kind of power, anyway?

He doesn't answer. Meg loosens her seat belt and pulls her legs up under her and for a while they watch the sun come up.

Sorry, he says a while later in the full light of day.

What?

Sorry. About before.

Oh.

Aren't you going to say thank you?

You sure do have a lot of ideas about what I should do, Meg says, and that hushes him for a while.

Well, anyway, he says a little later. I am. Sorry, I mean. I just thought you looked different in there. Like you might want to have an adventure.

So you thought you'd do me a favor. Drive me all the hell across the state for some fish?

You sure are prickly all of a sudden. I didn't see you complaining before.

She bites her lip, but doesn't feel like explaining what she thought would happen: that he *had* come to rescue her, to hand over his heart, cracked open. She had no reason to believe this beyond the shaking and the way she couldn't catch her breath when he'd sat down, when he'd touched her. Surely that wasn't his fault.

The trees have moved closer, but still there are places where they can see the red clay hills. She tucks her hair behind her ears and catches a whiff of the catfish. It was real good though, she says. The fish. Thank you.

He glances over and squints. You making fun?

No. She exhales. No, I mean it.

You do?

Yes.

It is the best I've ever had, he says. But I don't know why I brought you there. I've never brought anyone before, least of all a stranger. That place means a lot to me. He looks over at her and smiles, and she sees it again, the whole reason she came with him in the first place.

What's your music like? she says.

He hesitates and licks his lips. It's like what we were listening to before, he says finally. Kind of like that. Old-time country and a little blues. Just me and my guitar, mostly. I write my own stuff.

Oh.

You like that music?

She looks at her hands and they seem to belong to someone else entirely. I guess, she says. You'll think it's strange, but I don't listen to music much.

Oh, he says. He sets his jaw again and she feels the wrongness of what she said, but it is too late, and anyway, it is the truth.

I don't know if I believe you, she says a little later. About your career? I mean, if you're so well known, how come your truck is so beat-up?

His hands grind at the steering wheel. Don't talk about my truck.

Why? It's a mess.

The back of his hand connects with her chin before she can move out of its way. She tastes blood and promises herself that she will not cry, even as tears leak out.

Bastard, she whispers. You didn't need to do that.

They pull off the side of the road. I thought you were someone else, he says. That's the truth of it. I thought you'd be someone I could tell things to but you're not like that.

You don't know what I'm like. You don't know anything about me.

Sure I do, he says, his eyes narrow and mean. You grew up in that town and so did your folks. You dropped out of high school and probably wouldn't have been able to finish, but you're pretty, so people treat you nice anyway. You hope maybe someday you can get a decent house. You hope maybe someday you can marry some dumb ex-jock with a steady job and pump out a few little monsters, and by the time you're thirty you'll look like an old lady. That's who you are.

Her face is hot. She tries to open the door, but he reaches over and swats at her hands. Won't open from the inside, he says. You can't throw yourself out on the highway.

She crosses her arms and looks for a familiar sign, a landmark, something to tell her where she is.

He started to laugh. Aw, he says, sticking his bottom lip out. Did I hurt your feelings?

She pulls her knees to her chest, refusing to look at him.

You going to cry?

You don't know anything.

Oh, I don't?

No, she says softly. Asshole. You don't.

Tell me one thing I got wrong, he says, and uses his finger to count. One thing.

Okay. She turns to him. I graduated from high school second in my class. I had a scholarship to college and I even went. Did a whole year before my dad died. I bet that's a year more than you. My mom is sick, she has been for a long time, and I have two little brothers, so I had to come home and care for them. I had to come home and work for them. And no, none of us are from this town, we moved there when I was seven and my dad got a job at the plant. You don't know who I am or what matters to me and you got no right to judge my choices when you just met me. You never walked two steps in my shoes.

He doesn't answer, but after a minute he throws the truck into gear and they pull out on the highway again. Ten miles later he says he's sorry he hit her.

Too late now, she says. You did it. I can't pretend this is fun anymore. I just want to go home.

When she finally begins to recognize things, it is well into morning. The twins will have woken without her and fixed themselves cereal. They will have turned on cartoons and probably missed their bus. And with no one to notice, no one to drive them, what is the harm in that?

Raylene will have opened the restaurant, grown impatient when Meg didn't show up at ten and called the house. No one ever answers that phone. It is a wonder they even remember it is there.

You going to get in trouble? he says. For being late? You going to be late?

She sighs. I'm already late.

Oh. He reaches over and turns the radio on, then spins the dial until he comes to a song he likes. It is one she recognizes, a sweet, catchy love song. She smiles.

You like that?

I do.

He smiles, too. I wrote that—it's not me singing it, but it's my song.

She looks over and sees how bright his face has grown, how young he looks, and stifles the urge to rumple his hair. He hit you, she reminds herself, but it doesn't fade the impulse.

Guess this didn't turn out like either of us thought, she says.

He gives a short laugh. They pull into town. She diverts him from the Clover and gives him directions to her house. When they get there, he pulls the brake and comes around to let her out.

Thanks, she says.

Yeah, well—

Well.

He leans over and kisses her on the cheek. She feels herself pull back but waits until the truck has disappeared around the bend before scrubbing at her face with the edge of her smock.

The boys must have made the bus and gone to school after all. The house is quiet. Instead of calling the restaurant, or showering and making her way back, Meg crawls into bed and tumbles into a dense, dreamless sleep.

She wakes in the early afternoon and takes a quick shower. She dresses and walks down the hall. The bedroom is dark and smells strongly of her mother. Vials of pills stand at attention beside the bed. Meg watches the blankets rise and fall and is comforted.

Later Meg busies herself in the kitchen with baking a cake—the twins' birthday is tomorrow—but humming behind everything, she feels a dark, slow coldness that she can't push away. She pours the batter into pans, careful to shake each one so it will settle. There is no other way to go but forward. Night is coming and her cakes will go in and be baked. She is tumbling toward something old and worn, ugly but unavoidable.

She didn't graduated second in her class.

She didn't graduate at all.

She opens the oven and places the pans gently, one by one, careful not to spill or burn herself. Then she closes the door.

Is that you, Meg? Her mother's voice is thin and distant. Meg?

She does not answer. Instead she sits at the kitchen table and lights a cigarette, stares out the window at the familiar yard and trees. It is her house, the house her grandfather built. For a few moments out there in the world she forgot this: what it smells like here, what it feels like. Sitting at this table is like breathing, baking in this kitchen is like wearing her own skin: she knows where everything is, where it belongs. She can tell the time by the shadows on the cabinets, by the timbre of her mother's voice.

Meg?

She spins the saucer she's chosen as an ashtray. Outside the light is golden. She takes one last long drag and then scrapes the ember of her cigarette along the edge of the saucer until its tip falls off and lies there, still smoking. She watches it for a moment, then she licks her thumb to press it out.

UNTITLED

jt leroy

They're in the trenches and shells are skimming the tops of their heads, bodies blown up right next to them, and these eighteen-year-old men who aren't really men but boys like me are shaking like a dog squeezing out a peach pit, cryin' and callin' for their mommas. It's in almost every war film I've ever seen. And it would always piss me off, too, illustrating just in case you missed it, how the horror of war could reduce a grown eighteen-year-old soldier to the state of a three-year-old howling to her. But it always would hit me, too, in that sore place: Would I ever become man enough that mama ain't a person or place I call out to, war or not? I thought when I hit eighteen, that delineating line of manhood, I would be done with callin' out to Momma, no matter what was flying over my head.

I was at that crag of maturity, eighteen, as I sat in the waiting room of a dentist who gears his practice to "young adults with drug and alcohol issues." So the chairs are bright red and the music that same rockness designed to somehow appeal to "young adults with drug and alcohol issues." And it's as easy to tune out as elevator music.

I'm just a newly-off-the-street eighteen-year-old. I can't even go to a fucking normal dentist. I gotta go to one that my NA sponsor insists I go to. One that won't let me, the constant low-down dirty-dog drug abuser (as he somewhat nonaffectionately calls me), con the dentist into giving me drugs, like say, Novocain. And it's not announced or introduced, it's just thrust on me, like a mortar launch, as I sit there waiting to get my tooth filled. My hands are sweaty with the thought of getting drilled with only acupuncture. And I am supposed to avoid situations that might make me wanna pick up, to use. Anything stressful, besides getting my tooth filled with no painkiller.

I am supposed to be doing this crap. Taking care of myself, cleaning up the wreckage of the past-type shit. But, fuck me, this comes outta nowheres! There is the way certain songs can fly out at ya like a liberated cargo load from a passing truck, smashing through yer strat of well-fermented armor. And I am thrown into a battlefield as the Foo Fighters launch into "Everlong" through the dentist's sound system.

"Hello, I've waited here for you. Everlong . . ." And I know Dave Grohl probably wrote this about some chick . . . and at first that's what my wits ping to. All the fucked-up relationships . . . torturous, can't get enough of, can't get out of . . . with lines like he is almost groaning out. "Ya gotta promise not to stop when I say when . . . " It's gotta be a very

SM'y relationship he's goin' on about, and, man, do I know that. . . . I've said those words myself to many a lover . . . "Don't stop, even if I beg you to . . ." The lover that holds all of you, all the control and your helpless as a . . . baby . . .

And the drill skids in deeper, closer to that nerve. . . . And my hands grip at the red cloth of the couch. And I know Grohl pro'ly did not write this song thinking about his dang mama . . . but for me his words describe what I've never been able to quite say myself, about every relationship I've been in and how they are all her . . . my momma, and me trying to escape what I somehow know is crazy, but then needing more, the intense craving of her, calling out even though you know she won't come. Or can't anymore . . . and *bang*, I am there watching my mother slip a needle in her arm, sloppily telling me I can have what's left, the drug mixed in with her darkened blood, in the syringe. . . . And how it would feel when I would take her inside me. Wrap her arm, too lost to protest, around me like a lead apron.

And Grohl is singing her for me and it's worse that he's not even screaming. It's his voice sounding almost subdued, pleading over the panicked music: "Breathe out so I can breathe you in."

And the throb is excruciating as he goes on and on. And the most exciting point I ever got to was never saying "when." Just seeing how far someone can go, will go . . . before they come back. And he's giving voice to it all. I never said "when" to her, to my momma. I'd go as far as she could— fuck, I went way further.

And if she came back, I'd do it again. I'd never say stop. Cuz now somehow I have to say good-bye every fuckin' day I don't take her in me.

Every day I have to remember the bodies around me, her body. . . . And that I do actually know how to say "when" and mean it. And how still as old as I will ever get . . . way past outgrowing the dentist for low-down, dirty drug abusers . . . as grown-up as U ever think I am . . . all it takes is to hear "Everlong" and I know, I'm still calling out to her, still hoping she will somehow come and it will all be . . . fixed.

"Hello I've waited here for you. Everlong . . ."

DIRTY MOUTH

tom perrotta

You can stand me up at the gates of hell,
But I won't back down.

"I Won't Back Down"
Tom Petty

I was walking home from school with Mark Hofstetter, listening to him defend the highly dubious proposition that a pound of feathers weighs just as much as a pound of pennies, when Larry Salvati grabbed me from behind and slammed me up against the rusty chain-link fence that bordered the lumberyard along Grand Avenue. Larry and I had once been best friends, so I was more baffled than frightened by his surprise attack.

"Whadooinarry?" It was close to Halloween and I was wearing a set of wax vampire fangs I'd just bought at Frenchie's, so the question didn't come out right.

"You think you're so high-and-mighty, don'tcha?" Larry asked.

Craig Murtha and Bobby Staples, two seventh-grade hard guys who were flanking Larry, nodded and muttered their wholehearted agreement with this unfair assessment of my character.

"Goody Two-shoes."

"Little altar boy."

"Don'tcha?" Larry repeated, slamming me back against the fence once more for good measure.

"Narree," I replied.

In an attempt to facilitate our discussion, Larry plucked the wax teeth out of my mouth and tossed them over his shoulder into the busy street, where they were promptly run over by a passing Boar's Head delivery truck.

"Darn it," I said. "Why'd you have to go and do that?"

"Listen to him," said Craig. He crossed his eyes, screwed his face into this doofusy-looking grimace, and spoke in a dumb Mortimer Snerd voice that was apparently supposed to be an imitation of me. "Oh gee, whiz golly, gosh darn it to heck. Why'd you have to go and do that?"

Craig was mean, but he was also short and scrawny and hadn't yet taken to carrying concealed weapons, so I glared at him with the contempt he deserved, a course of action that had the added benefit of keeping me from having to look at Bobby Staples, who was taller and way more intimidating. I don't care what anyone says: it's just not right for a twelve-year-old to have muttonchop sideburns.

"Oh, shoot," said Bobby in a voice as deep as Richard Nixon's. He looked like he should have been overhauling a transmission somewhere, or breaking up asphalt with a jackhammer. "You broke my freaking fangs, you son of a bad person!"

Craig and Bobby slapped five and burst into a storm of hysterical laughter. Just to be on the safe side, I started laughing, too. It seemed like a good idea to operate under the assumption that this episode was just a big joke, rather than a mysterious confrontation that might take a nasty turn at any moment. The only two people who didn't seem to be enjoying themselves were Larry, who had tightened his grip on the front of my windbreaker, and Mark, who was looking on with wide, terrified eyes, his hands folded against his chest as though in prayer.

"Hey, Larry," I said. "You wanna let go of me?"

Larry looked like he was considering my request, but then he made the mistake of checking with his goons.

"No fucking way!" said Craig. "Not until he says *shit*."

An odd feeling of relief came over me. Up until that moment, I honestly hadn't understood what was going on, what I'd done to run afoul of people whom I'd normally make every effort not to offend.

"Yeah," chuckled Bobby. "Make the little angel say *shit*."

The previous week, in the locker room after gym class, I'd told a bunch of my classmates a funny story about my uncle Frank, who'd been walking his basset hound near the Little League baseball field when a resident of one of the nearby houses—a town councilman—came outside and started yelling at him for not cleaning up after his dog. Uncle Frank got mad—he'd never liked the councilman—and denied that Lorenzo had made a mess.

I saw it! the councilman insisted. *I saw it out my window!*

The hell you did, Uncle Frank told him. *I've been watching him the whole time.*

They got into a heated argument, which ended with my uncle saying that if his dog had actually done what the guy claimed, he, Uncle Frank, would pick up the poop with his bare hand and carry it home, that's how certain he was that he was right.

Is that a promise? said the councilman.

Damn right it is! said Uncle Frank.

At this point, the councilman took my uncle by the arm and led him straight to a steaming heap of turds that had just been deposited in the tall grass behind the left field fence, presumably by Lorenzo.

There, smart guy! the councilman gloated. *What do you say to that?*

My uncle actually seemed to be enjoying himself as he told the story to me and my parents after we'd finished our dessert.

But what happened? I asked. *What did you do?*

What could I do? my uncle replied. *I picked it up. I walked all the way home with a pound of fresh dog shit in the palm of my hand.*

In the locker room, I told the story exactly the way my uncle had, except for one small detail. Instead of saying the word *shit*, I'd spelled it out, which led someone in the audience — it was Larry, I suddenly realized — to ask if I was really afraid to say it.

"I'm not afraid," I explained. "I just don't like to curse."

• • •

Mark Hofstetter surprised me. He was a science nerd, a smart but notoriously wimpy kid who spent most of his time fooling around with his telescope and chemistry set, and building scale models of cities like Reykjavik and Helsinki out of LEGOs. I wasn't expecting much from him in the way of backup, but he actually grabbed Larry by the arm and tried to separate his hand from my jacket.

"Come on," he said in a reedy, trembling voice. "This isn't funny. Leave him alone."

Craig Murtha stepped up and jabbed his index finger, hard, into Mark's chest.

"Who's gonna make us, Poindexter?"

"Yeah," said Bobby. "Whaddaya gonna do? Build a bomb and blow us up?"*

Mark hesitated, searching his database for some kind of snappy comeback, but then thought better of it. He let go of Larry's wrist and retreated a respectful distance from the fray.

So now we were back at square one. Larry shook me impatiently.

"Come on," he said. "Say *shit*. It's not that hard."

There was an odd pleading note in his voice, as if he didn't understand why I was putting him to all this trouble.

---

*Ironically, about fifteen years after this incident, Mark was hired as an engineer by the Raytheon Corporation and has devoted his professional life to developing high-tech ordnance for the U.S. military.

"No," I said stoutly. "You're not gonna make me say that word."

"What word?" Craig asked quickly, hoping to trip me up.

"S-h-i-t," I replied.

Larry looked back at his buddies, obviously stumped about what he was supposed to do next.

"He says he won't say it."

"Make him," Craig commanded. "Make him say it or else."

"Or else what?" I inquired.

"Or else . . . punch him in the fucking mouth!" Bobby said.

With a gasp of alarm, Mark took off running down the sidewalk, his arms flapping wildly around his head as if he were being attacked by a swarm of bees.

"I'm getting Mr. Lorber!" he shouted over his shoulder.

"Who's Mr. Lorber?" Craig wanted to know.

"The crossing guard," I explained. "The one who sits on the folding chair."

"Big Fat Joe?" said Bobby, using the man's more familiar name. "Is he Sharon Lorber's father?"

"Grandfather," I explained.

"Man," said Craig. "Does she have big tits or what?"

"They are pretty big," I agreed.

"No kidding," said Bobby. "I'd like to get my hands on those watermelons."

"Guys," Larry reminded them, "he's gonna tell on us. We gotta get outta here."

Craig let out an irritated sigh and slapped me lightly on the forehead.

"Just say *shit*," he told me. "That's all we're asking."

"Yeah," said Bobby. "It's just one stupid word."

"I don't care," I said. "You can knock my teeth out if you want, but you're not gonna make me say it."

"Come on," said Larry. He was staring at me with what looked like panic in his eyes, and I could see what sort of a box I'd put him in. He didn't want to hit me, but he also didn't want to back down, not in front of his buddies.

"Say *shit!*" Craig repeated.

"Or else," added Bobby.

"I'm sorry," I said. "I refuse."

Craig threw up his hands in defeat.

"All right," he said. "Fine. Be that way."

"Yeah," said Bobby. "Be a little pussy."

"I don't care if anyone else says it," I explained. "I just don't want to say it myself."

Craig knitted his brow, as if he needed to think this over. Then he touched Larry's arm.

"Go ahead," he said. "Sock him in the mouth."

Larry looked upset. "Really? You really want me to hit him?"

Craig squinted uneasily down the block. "Just slug him and let's get the hell outta here."

"You sure?" said Larry.

"Whaddaya, chickening out?" asked Craig.

With obvious reluctance, Larry raised his fist, which suddenly seemed very large and grown-up looking, and drew it back behind his ear. I closed my eyes, steeling myself for the blow, which I knew was gonna hurt like anything. Larry's dad had been a Golden Gloves boxer in his youth, and he'd once given my Webelos troop a demonstration on the proper way of throwing a punch. A couple of seconds went by.

"Go on," said Bobby. "What are you waiting for?"

I was curious about the delay, so I opened my eyes, just in time to see a shiny maroon-colored Lincoln Continental pull up right in front of us. Larry must have known whose car it was, because he let go of my windbreaker even before Monsignor Mulligan stepped out of the car and spread his arms wide in a plea for peace.

"Boys, boys," he said with just a hint of a brogue. "What would be the trouble?"

To my amazement, Craig Murtha made the sign of the cross.

"Nothing, Father," he said. "We're just fooling around."

"That's not how it looks to me," said the monsignor. He pushed between Bobby and Craig and headed straight for me, shouldering Larry aside as he approached.

"Are you all right, son?" he asked.

"Yeah," I said. "I'm fine."

"Why are they picking on you, lad?"

Larry and I shared a moment of eye contact before I replied. It lasted just long enough for me to see how relieved he was that he hadn't had to hit me.

"They wanted me to say a dirty word," I told the priest. "But I wouldn't do it."

Monsignor Mulligan stared at me for a few seconds. He was a short, rotund man with a bald head and shrewd blue eyes. There was a look on his face that I'll never forget—not of an adult approving of a child, but of one man respecting another.

"Good for you, son," he told me, laying a soft hand on my shoulder. "Good for you."

The priest turned and frowned at my tormentors, all three of whom hung their heads in shame. He had just ordered them to go home and ask God for forgiveness when Mark came trotting up, with the very unhappy-looking crossing guard lumbering and wheezing along behind him, sweating profusely and clutching at his chest like Fred Sanford.

"Everything . . . okay . . . here?" he huffed.

"Fine," said Monsignor Mulligan. "Score one for the good guys."

Big Fat Joe hitched up his belt and took a moment to catch his breath. He shook his head in disgust as he watched Larry, Bobby, and Craig heading down the street toward McDonald's, walking so fast they might as well have been running.

"Little bastards," he said. "Someone should give 'em all a good swift kick in the ass."

"Amen," said the monsignor.

You'd think I would've been feeling pretty good about myself when I got home that afternoon. I'd stood up to some bullies, stuck to my principles, and been praised for my courage by the priest and the crossing guard. Mark said I reminded him of the Hardy Boys, who never backed down, not even when the bad guys had them tied to their chairs in some abandoned mansion by the river and were rubbing their hands together with sinister glee, gloating about how Fenton Hardy, the boys' famous detective father, would never be able to find them, *at least not until it's too late, ha ha ha!*

Flattered though I was—I'd been a huge Hardy Boys fan a couple of years back and still secretly believed they were pretty cool—I didn't feel much like a hero. All I could think about was Larry Salvati, and how miserable he seemed the whole time he was gripping my windbreaker, threatening to bust me in the mouth. He kept staring at me with this sick-puppy-dog look on his face, like somehow the whole stupid situation was my fault, like it never would have happened if I hadn't abandoned him midway through fifth grade and forced him to team up with jerks like Craig and Bobby.

Larry and I had been best friends for almost two years. He had a lot more freedom than me, and a wild streak that I really admired. He was always pushing me to go one step further than I wanted to, like that day we climbed into empty trash barrels and rolled down the sledding hill at Indian Park over and over again, making ourselves so dizzy we could barely stand up, or that day we let ourselves into his next-door neighbors' house with a key they kept under the welcome mat and made ourselves turkey sandwiches.

Larry's mother had died when he was in second grade, and his father worked a lot of overtime at the sheet-metal factory. His father also happened to have a pretty large collection of porno magazines—not just *Playboy*, either, all different kinds, including the really disgusting ones you could only buy in New York—and he didn't seem to mind if Larry and I looked at them from time to time. At Larry's insistence, I borrowed a copy of *Swank* and kept it stashed in my bedroom closet, cleverly buried—or so I thought—in a stack of Richie Rich and Sad Sack comic books. I don't know how my mother sniffed it out, but one day I came home from school and found the magazine—it had a picture of a blond woman sucking her own enormous breast on the cover—sitting right out on our kitchen table, along with my usual snack of cookies and milk. I lied and said I'd found it in the woods behind the Little League, but my mother didn't believe me.

"Tell me the truth," she said. "You got it from Larry, didn't you?"

"It's his dad's," I said. "Larry let me borrow it."

My mother shook her head.

"I feel sorry for Mr. Salvati," she said. "It's terrible what happened to him. But I never liked him, not even when his wife was alive. That man has such a dirty mouth."

I couldn't argue with that. Mr. Salvati was one of those guys who said *fuck* in normal conversation, as if it were a perfectly ordinary word, and seemed to think *shithead* was a term of endearment.

"He's always nice to me," I told her.

"I'll tell you what," my mother said. "I feel sorry for his son. He's not getting the kind of adult guidance he needs."

My parents didn't exactly force me to stop being friends with Larry. But they did bar me from going to his house after school and weren't as nice as they used to be when he came over to ours. They encouraged me to spend more time with my other friends, nice kids like Mark Hofstetter. Slowly but inevitably, Larry and I drifted apart, a separation that became more and more pronounced as he started running with a pack of tough older kids, troublemakers like Craig and Bobby.

I must've been unusually quiet over supper that night, because my mother reached across the table to feel my forehead.

"Are you okay?" she asked.

"Fine."

"You've barely touched your food."

"Something bothering you?" my father wondered.

"Actually," I said, "I've got a little stomachache. Can I be excused?"

I went up to the bathroom, locked the door, and sat down on the closed lid of the toilet. My legs felt weak and my heart was beating fast, but I knew what I had to do.

I took a deep breath and clenched my muscles. I strained with all my might, but nothing happened. I scrunched my face and tried again. For a second, the word got trapped in my throat, but I managed to force it out in a harsh, barely audible whisper.

"Shit."

I laughed at the sound of it, then felt myself relax a little. It was easier than I thought.

"Shit," I said again, this time a little louder.

I opened the bathroom window and poked my head out. The sky was blue-black, speckled with nameless stars. I must have said my word a dozen times to the crisp October night, and each time I felt a little lighter, a little less burdened by my conscience. I only wished Larry had been standing there with me, so he could hear my apology.

When I was finished, I shut the window, flushed the toilet, and washed my hands. Then I headed back down to the kitchen and rejoined my parents, both of whom were watching me with worried expressions. I smiled and picked up my fork.

"Mission accomplished," I told them.

author inspiration

I've always loved the Tom Petty song "I Won't Back Down." It's an anthem full of exuberance and defiance, which are two of the great rock 'n' roll emotions. I also love how vague it is — you have no idea who wants the narrator to back down, or what particular principle might be at stake — as if it were somehow the human condition to be under pressure to compromise yourself and your beliefs. It was certainly easy for me as a teenager to hear the song and believe that it was somehow about the pride and pleasure that are the emotional payoffs of resisting authority—parental, governmental, whatever. A few years ago, though, Johnny Cash did an amazing cover of the song that made me think about it in a whole new way. Cash's version has none of the brash energy of the original—it's weary and mournful, as if Cash understands the cost of not backing down, the isolation and weariness that come with a lifetime of trying to be true to yourself. I was hoping to capture both aspects of the song in "Dirty Mouth," to celebrate a moment of youthful defiance and inner strength, while also acknowledging the mysterious sadness that the narrator feels afterward.

"HALLELUJAH"

tanker dane

Well, I've heard there was a secret chord
That David played and it pleased the Lord . . .

"Hallelujah"
Jeff Buckley
(Lyrics by Leonard Cohen)

t is no longer, this instrument they played. Though not in
its final resting place, for it will be found again, just not
by the well-intentioned or inspired, nor by the suitable,
even the capable. But it matters not. Anyone is invited to find
it this time, provided they can: corroded and covered in
algae, the neck warped, frets rusted and the double truss rod
buried in sediment. The ivory bindings around the sound-
board split from the time spent submerged, the acoustic body
once hollow, now flooded and the adopted dwelling of a flat-
head catfish.

A guitar having wept, bled, screamed, and soared lies on
its side. All at once splashed down, adrift, sunken, and silent
since the incident. Infamous and extraordinary, never anything less than sublime. To be strummed once more near im-

possible due to its wretched condition, yet this guitar, having been responsible for one musical miracle after another, just may and must be the subject of its own divine rescue. The age unknown. Its intial purpose unclear, but assuredly simple as compared to its eventual calling and final catastrophe.

This unassuming lute first handed down, then inherited, bartered, bought and sold, gifted, won and lost, then finally found. The most innocent way its most glorious. Nicked and scratched, smashed and cracked, the instrument wrecked and repaired as often as it changed hands. And changed shape. The lute was the shape of a pear, then a circle, then a square, before it got in the hands of the man who split it in half and played it in two. Went unrecognized for an extended time as a table, then a toy. Picked out of the trash and given away by a man to a boy, who gave it a name. Then stolen twice: first by a thief, then by the boy who stole it back from the thief, who renamed it the same.

The name never stuck, as no name would after several hundred years. A gitarer, a quintern, a guitarra . . . with each owner it became anew, in name, in shape, in sound, in song, but never in string.

The strings never changed, never snapped nor allowed the instrument out of tune. The string gut wrapped tight on the original lute remained, even now, underwater. Each string shimmering in the stabs of sunlight cutting through the kelp layered above, tempting and taunting the schools of sunnies and the stubborn rainbow trout who pass every half moon. The strings are neither prey, nor predictably attached to a rod and reel, but bare prints. Fingerprints. Multiple fingerprints, tens of thousands on each of the five strings, perhaps more. The G almost double the D, the E less than a quarter more than the A, all of them unable to compete with the the C. Whether solo or strummed in a chord, all of them intact, unable to be wiped or swept away with the changing times or tides. Equally apparent, but hardly in importance. In fact, only a minute fraction stand above the rest. The most recent fingerprints, played just minutes before the instrument was befallen, would remain the most recent. Played by the hand stripped of flesh and flopped on its side in bone beside the instrument. The hand, along with the other in bone behind the instrument, responsible for the fingerprints. Once bound in flesh making the most important fingerprints. Prints producing the finest notes. The most natural notes, notable notes, notorious notes. The notes responsible for the refrain.

"The final refrain!" and the accompaniment. "The accompaniment at last!" and the tempo. "The exact tempo!" and the melody. "The perfect melody!" This guitar, crafted by the hand of a carpenter, crafted for the composition, the perfect composition, the only composition. The possibility the right notes would be played, the proper chords struck? A near impossibility, no doubt. But not for one, the destined one, the defiant one . . .

Never a note or notes ever played to compare to these. For all of its time, all of its music, all of its solos, improvs, freestyles, riffs . . . this guitar never sounded so grand yet ghostly, so harrowing and haunting; so hallelujah. The hand of the man to play the part, to fulfill its intent of truth, is to be saved as soon as it ceases, sacrificed as soon as his gift is given, with one final breath—his song to the world . . . to save the world.

Playing on the streets and down in the pipes of New York is both a dangerous and daunting way to make a living. At least that's how I felt in the beginning. Song after song yielded no tips. My guitar case was changeless for four days and four more hours before three quarters finally splashed down. "Hallelujah" was the song I remember playing at the time, or it could have been the one before . . . I'm still not sure which tune struck the right chord, but I like to think it was "Hallelujah." It has been part of my street list ever since.

WHY GO

lisa tucker

maybe someday another child
won't feel as alone as she does

"Why Go"
Pearl Jam

'm a Vietnam vet wannabe. That's what I told my parents last Friday night, when they started in on how sad it was that I was watching *The Deer Hunter* for the twelfth time instead of going out with friends. I told them they were right, but *Platoon* was checked out again. My mother bit her lip; my father laughed nervously. The next morning, when I came downstairs in my thrift-shop army jacket, my mother got up and left the kitchen table. Dad acted like he had to go do something in the garage, after he mumbled yes when I asked if I could borrow volume seven of his Time-Life series *The Vietnam Experience*.

It's Wednesday afternoon, and I'm on my way to the community center downtown to attend a support group for Vietnam vets. Luckily, my parents know nothing about this.

I called the guy who runs the group and said that my

uncle died in Vietnam. I told him that I'd never known Uncle Johnny, but I wanted to understand more about his life. The guy was cool; he said I could come to the meeting for the first half hour or so and ask questions. He said I should be prepared because, on occasion, these support group sessions can get intense.

I smiled then in what my mom calls my "sardonic way." She says I could kill someone with that smile, "metaphorically speaking of course," she always adds, too quickly, like she's trying to convince herself that her daughter's not *that* kind of crazy.

I didn't think this support group could be any more intense than the ones at the hospital where I was. The guy on the phone said the point of the meetings was to make the vets feel better. To give them some sympathy, let them know they're not alone. Not alone, rather than completely alone, with everyone forced to watch while they break you down, make you admit you're nothing but a messed-up kid.

I should make one thing perfectly clear: I don't really want to be a veteran. And I'm pretty sure I'm not crazy either.

There are only three guys at the meeting, plus the moderator, Ken. I'm not surprised; I read some stupid article that claimed Vietnam is "over" now that it's the nineties. Ken tells them why I'm there and asks if they are okay with it. They all say sure, and then Ken says I can start whenever I want. First, I ask if they knew a guy named Johnny Thomas. None of them did, no surprise, since Johnny doesn't exist. Then I ask them to tell me what it was like during the war.

A bald man in a wheelchair introduces himself. His name is Andy; he's big, fat, with a long red beard and pale blue eyes. "I want to get this straight," he says, smiling at me, tapping the arm of his wheelchair. "This contraption has nothing to do with Nam." I assume he's saying something deep and I make my face look serious so he'll tell me the rest. But he goes on to say that he was in a skiing accident twelve years ago and severed his spine. He says the worst he got in Vietnam was just rashes and diarrhea. "I lived through three years over there just to come home and fall down a hill. Not even a mountain for Christ sakes. Is that shit-ass luck or what?"

Ken looks a little uncomfortable; I figure he's thinking I'm a little young to hear words like *shit-ass*. I want to tell him that *fuck* is like a mantra for me; sometimes I say it ten times in a row, sometimes more, just to get myself back to my center. Whatever that is.

Another guy, Jeff, speaks up. He's tall and keeps crossing and uncrossing his legs. "It's all luck, that's true. Some dudes would get so short they could smell home, only to have their guts torn out. And I used to think there was some kind of reason, but there wasn't. Just bad luck."

I don't say anything but I nod my head. There was no rhyme or reason to who got to go home at the hospital either. Jessica had been there more than two years, and yet I got out instead of her.

Ken asks the third man, William, if he wants to tell me

anything about his experience as a prisoner of war. William is thin and pale, with short, very dark hair. He seems out of place in the navy blue suit he's wearing. He doesn't look up, just shakes his head. I stare at William, and I get the feeling he could tell me something I need to know. How long it takes to get over it. If you get over it.

Ken tells William that he doesn't have to speak if he doesn't want to. Andy says that's right and uses his hands to move his wheelchair farther back against the wall. Farther away from William.

Jeff uncrosses his leg again. "Where was your uncle Johnny? What company in Nam?"

I shrug. "My mom won't talk about it. It's almost like she wants to forget about Johnny." Which would be true, I'm sure, if Johnny were real. My mom is good at forgetting. She hasn't mentioned the hospital once in the two months I've been home.

Ken leans back and says, "We don't believe in that. One of the goals of our group is to remember and tell other people what happened." He folds his hands. "It's not a political thing. We're about personal recovery. And finding peace."

It hits me that Ken is a vet, too. I wish my parents would find me a shrink who was a vet. Someone cool like William maybe, instead of old and boring like Dr. Simpson, my current shrink, who told me last week how encouraged he is by my performance in school, but who sounded almost as nervous as my father when he asked what was going on with this "Vietnam business."

I lick my lips and ask if they've found peace. I look at William when I say this, but Andy answers me.

"I guess if we had, we wouldn't be wasting our time here," he says, laughing. "But I know I'm a hell of a lot better off now than five years ago, when I started coming. I don't have the dreams anymore and that alone is worth the price of admission."

The group is free; Ken told me that on the phone. I decide I like Andy.

"What kind of dreams?" I ask him.

He smirks, but not at me, at the wall. "The usual, I guess. Blood-and-guts type of things. No glory, that's for sure. Always enough guilt to feed an army."

William is looking down at his shoes. Wing tips, just like my dad's, but scuffed up, with one of the laces unraveling at the top.

Jeff rolls his head on his shoulders until his neck cracks, loudly. Then he looks at Ken, as though he is waiting for him to say something. Ken looks back and asks Jeff if he wants to talk about his current nightmare.

"I don't think the kid needs to hear about that," he says. "You have to protect them. It's the one thing I did right with mine. Kim and Jeff junior have never had to deal with any of this."

I wonder if his kids are really as out of it as he thinks. I ask him how old they are and he tells me Kim is nineteen and Jeff junior, seventeen. I want to ask if they've ever been in trouble, but I don't.

William looks uncomfortable; he's leaning forward and pulling the back of his jacket down with both hands; his forehead is oily with sweat. It's at least eighty-five degrees in here; the community center air conditioner is broken. I wish I could think of a way to get him to take off that jacket.

I look at my watch; my half hour is almost over. I wish I could get one of them to tell me about those dreams, especially the guilt part.

I dream about Jessica almost every night. I see her the way she was that last day, sitting in the activity room slumped on the floor, banging her hand quietly against the green wall.

Ken looks at his watch, too, then at me. I know he wants me to go now; he probably wants to give Jeff a chance to talk about his nightmare and William a chance to talk, period. But I still don't move. I have to ask them one thing.

I lower my voice and pick at the skin on top of my hand—a nervous habit they couldn't break me of in eight months at the hospital. "Did it ever get so bad you felt like killing yourself?"

Jeff flinches, Andy shakes his head, and William just stares at me. It's up to Ken to say what they're probably all thinking, especially Jeff, whose face has turned blotchy, angry red. "The point was to stay alive," Ken says softly. "That was the whole point."

I pull up more skin on my hand until I can clearly see the outline of the bones underneath. I've been misunderstood; I have to explain; I have to tell them I know, while you're there, you just want to make it through and out. But what about afterward? What about when you're home?

I'm not a vet though. I get up and leave. Only after Ken shuts the door behind me do I realize I've forgotten to thank them.

My parents are pleased because they think I've given up my Vietnam "phase." They're glad I don't watch all those depressing movies anymore. Instead, I lie on the couch and think about the dreams I'm having about William. He's right there, next to Jessica, sitting in the activity room, and he's telling me something I can do to help her.

I call Ken two weeks after the group and tell him I have a question for William. I say my uncle Johnny was a prisoner of war, too, and I have to know what it was like. Ken is less friendly this time; he says he can't give out any information about group members. He says William's privacy has to be respected. He says I should probably ask some relatives for more information about my uncle.

I do my fuck mantra when I hang up the phone but it doesn't help. I can't stop thinking about William. A guy who might be older than my father. A guy who I know almost nothing about. A guy who I saw once, sitting in a grade-school chair, saying nothing, sweating in a too tight businessman blue suit with torn-up shoes.

I wonder if I am going crazy.

●　　●　　●

I kept hoping I would run into him somewhere. Where I live is pretty small (Grandville, Illinois, only 36,814 people, according to the highway sign); things like that happen. But not this time. Not at the bank or the mall or the post office. Not even outside the liquor store, which I thought was a damn good place to try.

So I have to lurk outside the community center on Wednesday afternoon and wait until he comes out of the session. I didn't want to do this because I'm afraid Ken might see me. Ken could even call my house, since he knows my last name. Then he'd find out there's no Uncle Johnny, for one thing. Also, my parents would find out what I've done and think I've lost it again.

They're very conscientious parents, according to Dr. Simpson, my shrink. They just want what's best for me. When they checked me into the hospital last year, they felt like they didn't have a choice. The doctors told them I was depressed, possibly suicidal; my mother, and later my father, agreed. I felt a little sorry for them when they wanted to visit me and Dr. Michaels, the head shrink, told them they couldn't. When they did get to visit, they always cried about how messed up I was, especially when I would do my fuck mantra and refuse to talk to them the whole time.

It became so easy to cut myself off from everyone. I'm thinking maybe William will understand that.

I see Andy roll his wheelchair down the handicapped ramp and then get lifted into a special white van that's waiting for him. I see Jeff walk slowly, head down, across the parking lot, and then get into a blue station wagon with a bumper sticker that says, "Proud Parent of an Honor Student at Grandville High." My parents have that sticker; they put it on the back of our Volvo at the end of my sophomore year, two months before I went to the hospital.

Finally Ken and William come out together, talking quietly. I hunch down behind the steering wheel of my car: a brand-new red Toyota; it was waiting for me in the driveway the day I got home.

"Isn't it beautiful, honey?" my mom said. Her smile was so forced it looked painful. "Now you can just zip over and pick up Karen and go out for pizza or head to the mall whenever you want."

Karen was my best friend before. I haven't seen her except in the halls at school since I got out. She seems nervous around me, even though she, like everyone else, was told by my mother that I was away at a boarding school. Karen invited me to a party a few weeks ago; I told her I was too tired to make it. I know my mom must have found out—Karen's mother is a receptionist at my mom's medical office—but she never mentioned it.

Ken stays with William until they get to a blue Chevy parked only five spots down from me. William gets in the driver's seat. Ken leans his head down and says something to William through the window; then, as Ken walks away, William turns on the engine and starts to back up.

I wait until Ken is about ten cars away, and then I turn on

the Toyota and quickly catch up to William's car, which is just leaving the parking lot. He heads right on Stenton Avenue; I follow about one car length behind.

I lose track of him twice during the drive, but both times I'm able to speed up and find him. I have my radio on full blast, one of my favorite bands, loud guitar, drum taking over the beat of my heart, guy screaming why we have a right to be angry. I love music again. Sometimes I'm almost grateful to the hospital for giving me that.

William pulls into a big apartment complex, the Strafford Arms, a run-down place on the north edge of town. I've never been here before. My family lives on the west side in what Realtors, and my mother, call an upscale neighborhood. Instead of a rich neighborhood, which is what it is, comparatively speaking. We're a very rich family, at least for this town. My mother says that's because she works and always has, but I know several other kids whose parents both work that don't have the money we do. My mother is a doctor, my father, an electrical engineer.

"This place is one of the most expensive in the country. Our insurance doesn't come close to paying the bills." My dad told me that, in tears, one time when he was visiting me at the hospital, without my mother, and I wouldn't look at him or say anything but *fuck*.

William gets out of his blue Chevy and starts to walk toward the big door at the front of building D. I get out and follow him a few steps behind; I walk all the way up the stairs and see him unlock the door of apartment 217. After he shuts the door, I stand outside, trying to decide what to do next. I suddenly realize how strange it might seem if I just show up at his front door.

I sit down on the green rug in the hall to think. I wish I had a cigarette, even though I don't smoke. Everybody at the hospital talked about wanting a cigarette all the time, and after a few weeks, I did, too. I even smoked one outside, with a guy named Benjamin, because when he found that half-empty pack of Winstons in the trash, we both knew it was as if he'd stumbled onto gold.

I'm afraid to go to the door, but I'm not afraid of William. I know that some people think a lot of the Vietnam vets are crazy, but I've read enough to know they're wrong about that. Plus, I'm not afraid of crazy either.

It's almost dark out and I'm still sitting on the green rug, staring at William's door. I can't stay much longer. My parents eat dinner at exactly seven o'clock—except when my mother's on call—and if I don't show up, they might call the police. (They've done it before. Once when I spent the night with my friend Brian in the hills outside of town, having sex in his car. The other time when I went into those hills by myself, after Brian moved to California, and I camped in the woods for three days before the police finally found me.)

My watch says six thirty; I've got to do something. And of course I will do something because I can do anything now. I'm invincible; I can do whatever it takes. I can sit in the little windowless room, padded in rubber, with the hundred-watt light-bulb hanging from the ceiling, surrounded by a wire cage, and not even want to cry, no matter how long they keep me there. And I can knock on a total stranger's door, if I feel like it.

I do, so softly I'm not sure he could hear me, but after a minute or so, he comes to the door. Still in the blue suit from the meeting. He doesn't recognize me at first, so I explain that I'm the girl with the uncle who died. He stares at me for a minute; then he asks if I want to come in.

His voice is just like I knew it would be. Low, melodic, real. He doesn't sit down but he tells me I can have a seat on his couch. Two of the brown cushions are covered with magazines and papers, so I sit down on the third one, near the window. He stands by the TV, across the room, silently looking at me. Then he reaches into his jacket pocket and takes out a pack of cigarettes. He lights one, but before he can put the pack away, I ask him if I can have one, too. He hands me one and his Zippo lighter; I light my cigarette and start coughing.

"You don't smoke, do you?"

"No, not really," I say, stifling another cough. "But I want to learn how."

"Why would you want to do that?" He looks out the window. "I'm sure you've heard it's bad for you."

"It's bad for you, too," I say, dropping my ashes in a yellow plastic bowl filled with butts on the end table next to me. "I don't buy all that research anyway. I think it's part of some government plot to trick people into forgetting about the real problems in the country by making them so busy hating smokers."

I think about what my mom would say if she could hear me. She's fanatical about the damage people do to themselves when they smoke. She always complains about her patients who won't quit; she told my father that she'd like to refuse to take any patients who smoke, but her HMO won't let her.

William's mouth moves a little. Almost a smile.

He brings out a white plastic chair from his kitchen and sits across from me. He smokes the cigarette until it's almost down to the filter; then he tells me he has to go to work in about five minutes.

"Where do you work?"

"At the mall," he says. "Sears. In the furniture department."

So that's why he has to wear a suit. But I'm not disappointed; I didn't want him to work behind some desk at a bank or an insurance company. The mall is as good as anywhere to make a living. I remember my dad saying how sad it is when older people have to work in retail or fast food, but I don't feel sorry for William.

"I've got to go, too. My parents have dinner at seven."

He pauses for a minute, and then he says, barely moving his lips, "You haven't told me why you're here."

I stand up and move toward the door. "It's a long story. I'll have to save it for some time when you don't have to work."

He picks up his wallet and keys from the top of the television. We walk out of the apartment and down the stairs: him in front, me trailing behind. When we get to the parking lot, I ask if I can come again tomorrow morning.

"Don't you have school?"

"Yeah, but I can skip whenever I want. I already have enough credits to graduate. It doesn't matter what I do now."

He shakes his head, but he says I can come if I want. Then he gets in his blue Chevy and leaves.

I resist the temptation to follow him to Sears instead of going home.

That night, I dream about William and Jessica and me, but we're not in the hospital anymore. We're in a silver boat and William is holding Jessica in his arms—she's so small, the size of a baby—and he's rocking her and singing. The song sounds like a hymn, but it's sweeter than any I ever heard at the All Saints' Episcopal Church. When I wake up, I don't remember most of the words, but I still hear one line, repeating: "Go across the water, to the other side; Find the peace you've longed for, always been denied."

As I get dressed to go to William's house, I decide I'll bring him a present.

The present is ready at ten, but I wait until eleven to knock on his door, in case he's a night person. But he doesn't answer. He isn't home. It occurs to me he's done this on purpose to avoid me, but I don't want to believe that. I sit back down on the green rug and wait, with the present behind me, so he won't see it right when he walks up. I want to explain it first; I don't want him to feel strange about getting a gift from someone he hardly knows.

I don't have to wait too long. He nods when he sees me; he says he had a feeling I might show up during the ten minutes he was gone, but he had to get a few things from the mini-market. Cigarettes and coffee, he mutters, can't live without them.

I follow him through the apartment door, still holding my present behind me. When he motions me over to my spot on the coach, I sit down and tuck the present under the coffee table, out of sight.

This time he gets the white plastic chair right away and sits down. He's not wearing the suit; he's wearing blue jeans and a black, short-sleeved shirt, but he still has the wing tips on. Maybe the only shoes he has, I figure, and that's okay with me.

He leans back in his chair. "I called Ken last night after I realized I didn't remember your name. Stacey Janzen."

"Pretty boring name, huh?" I'm nervous about Ken knowing I came over here, but I try to sound casual. "Did Ken tell you I called him earlier for your address?"

William exhales a puff of smoke and it swirls and disappears in the sunlight streaming in the window. "He did. He also said he wouldn't give it to you."

I cross my legs and smile. "But, hey, I'm pretty resourceful, huh?"

He doesn't smile back. "Why are you here, Stacey Janzen?"

"Well, like I told Ken, my uncle Johnny was a POW, too, for a while, and I thought that maybe you could tell me what it was like."

He puts out his cigarette and stares at the glass ashtray next to him. "Ken used to work for the VA. He mentioned something about calling a friend of his to find out exactly what happened to your uncle." He pauses. "Do you want him to do that?"

He knows, I'm sure of it. And in a way, I'm glad. It's hard to lie to William after hearing him sing last night in my dream.

"No." I sit up straighter. "No, I guess he shouldn't call them."

William gets up and takes a styrofoam cup out of his grocery bag. While he sits and sips his coffee, I walk over to his window. It looks down on the corner of the parking lot where the green trash Dumpsters are. I see a white bird feeder hanging from the window ledge and ask if he hung it there.

"Yeah," he says. "I like to listen to them in the morning."

I feel my breath coming quicker. "Sing to me, Stacey," Jessica would say. She was my roommate, the youngest kid at the hospital. There were rumors that her dad or an uncle had done something to her—like half the girls in the place. "My sister used to sing to me in the morning."

"Dammit, Jessica, I can't do that. Okay, okay, just stop crying."

"Do you want a drink?" William asks, pulling out a can of Pepsi from the grocery bag. I say sure, and he hands me the can. While I'm sitting on the couch, drinking, he asks me again what I'm doing here.

"I want to give you something." I reach under the coffee table and pull out the present.

He stands up and puts his hands in his pockets. "You feel sorry for me, is that it? Some kind of charity work at school? Or maybe for your church?"

He doesn't sound annoyed, but his voice has lost the melody. I want to explain that I don't feel sorry for him at all, but I can't find the words.

Finally I say, "I've been dreaming about you."

He sits back down and looks at me. "And what am I doing in the dream?"

"Open the present first," I tell him, with a note of pleading I can't keep out of my voice. "Then I'll tell you."

He reaches across the coffee table and I hand it to him. He takes off the purple wrapping paper carefully, without tearing it. It's a T-shirt, men's size medium. I got it at this store where they'll put anything you want on a T-shirt. On William's T-shirt, I put in bold black letters:

Do Not Lose Hope
Our Hearts Will Always Be Free

"Thanks," he says, and pauses. "You wanted me to have this because I was in prison in Nam?"

"Yeah, sort of. But it's from a poster I made a few months ago. For another friend of mine."

I taped it to the wall of our room the night before I left, over Jessica's bed. But she was on so many meds, I wasn't even sure she read it before the counselor took it down.

William smiles then for the first time, and I realize I've said, indirectly, that I think of him as my friend. I blush, something I never do, something I pride myself on being above. I hope he doesn't notice.

"Who was this other friend?" he asks, putting the T-shirt down, carefully, on the floor next to him. "A vet?"

I shake my head. "A kid. A little kid, only thirteen. Her name was Jessica." I realize I've used the past tense. Her name is Jessica. *Is.* Even if she doesn't know it half the time now.

He stares out the window for a minute; then he tells me he has a kid. A boy named Matthew, fifteen years old now, who lives in Seattle with his mother.

"That's far. . . . Do you ever get to see him?"

"No. Not since my ex-wife remarried when Matthew was five."

I lean forward. "But you're still his dad."

"Not legally," he says, lighting another cigarette. "I signed some papers so he could be adopted by his stepfather."

The pack of cigarettes is lying on the TV; I ask William if I can have one and he says sure. When I walk across the room, I notice William's hands are trembling.

"Give me a light, okay?"

He picks up the lighter; I put my hand under his wrist to stop the shaking. He lights my cigarette, but I don't let go of his wrist.

He looks up at me. "I really don't understand what you're doing here."

I drop his hand and walk to the window. There's a red bird perched on the feeder. "I told you already; I keep dreaming about you."

"You're a kid, Stacey," he says quietly. "You shouldn't be dreaming about me."

I take a puff of my cigarette, without coughing this time. I turn around and stare at him. "It's not a sexual thing. I'm not here for a fuck."

He doesn't seem shocked or embarrassed; I knew he wouldn't. "You don't have an uncle though?"

"No." I sit back down on the couch. "But I do have a friend named Jessica. And I can't see her anymore because she's locked up."

"Your friend's in prison?"

My throat is burning from the cigarette; I can't answer his question. I pull the skin on top of my hand until it hurts, until the surrounding skin loses all its color. Then I take a deep breath and tell him that Jessica is in a mental hospital.

He sits there for a few minutes without saying anything; then he picks up the T-shirt I gave him and goes through a door on the other side of the room. When he comes back out, he's wearing the shirt, and he asks me if I want to go to McDonald's for lunch. I tell him I'd rather go to Wendy's because it's farther from school.

He whistles a song as we drive to Wendy's in his blue

Chevy. It might be the hymn in my dream, but I'm not sure. I can't hear that song anymore now that William is whistling.

I was a big grunge fan in the early nineties, and one of my favorite albums was Pearl Jam's *Ten*. I loved the band and the lyrics suited me: angry rants about poverty, violence, alienation—and especially, the treatment of children. I was in grad school at the time and the topic of my dissertation was youth politics. Songs like "Jeremy" and "Why Go" seemed especially meaningful.

I started the story inspired by "Why Go" back in 1995, when I was on my third copy of *Ten* and still pissed off about all the kids who were "diagnosed" and sometimes even institutionalized because they couldn't or wouldn't fit in. As the story evolved, though, it became less about child politics and more about the human condition. The world is full of people rejected by mainstream culture; Stacey isn't as alone as she thought. This is a possible answer to the question of the song "Why go home?"—to make a connection with the other strangers, to maybe even achieve a limited form of transcendence, with anger still intact.

ALL THE SECURITY GUARDS BY NAME

aimee bender

So I go down to the lobby, and everybody's there,
and they say: "Take off that foolish hat.
Put down the chair."

"The Lobby"
Jane Siberry

I moved in ten years ago, with one suitcase and a broken-ness, like the bird that has hit the window by accident. If you're that bird, you are surprised for the rest of your life, because air, which you know better than anything else, is not supposed to turn hard and painful. The air should be soft enough to soar inside. That's the worst of it for the stunned bird, whose body heals fast enough; for me, too.

I had my suitcase and a small hat on, a proper hat with a brown band, and the building rose up next to me on the corner and the front door was open, and there was a For Rent sign up in one of the high windows, enough to invite anyone inside, except no one else on the busy street was stopping but me. The security guard at the front smiled and asked if I was interested in looking, and I nodded, yes please. My one suitcase, getting hard to hold. The handle slippery with my anticipatory sweat. I hardly even noticed the lobby then, what with its silvery walls and the tinkling sound of glass mobiles above.

The room they were offering was everything in its right place, and the spectacular view of the far-reaching corners of the city made me finally put the suitcase on the floor and stretch out my clenched hand, and take off my proper hat and sit down in a chair. I'll take it, I told the security guard, who apparently felt safe enough to leave his post for longer and show me the excellent bathroom and spacious closet. We signed papers together, and someone came rolling by with a sandwich cart, and I ate a turkey on sourdough and lemonade with cherries floating redly beside the ice cubes. When the security guard left, I rolled around on the towels, white as salt, still warm from the dryer.

It took me honestly a year to notice that I had not gone outside once. Who ever needs to do such a thing? When there is a fine restaurant and bar, and so many different rooms galore from floors 1 to 42. And the security guard team there twenty four hours keeping it safe for all of us, and a basement in case of war. A bomb shelter. A greenhouse terrarium. Iron balustrade fire escapes and ballrooms if you want to throw a ball. On the seventh floor, you'll find rooms of mothers, and they will hold you on their laps and stroke down your hair. I try to see when they leave to go home, but whenever I knock, they are always there. Beautiful mothers, with tired, warm eyes. I bring them armfuls of flowers from the nursery on the third floor, and I take hours to make the decision: who gets the lily, who the rose, who fits with dahlia, who is all orchid. And then there's his room, down the row from mine. Our meeting in the hall, oops, was that your foot? Sorry, sorry, hello. Hello. That first lunch together, in the squares of reflected sunshine. Who would notice the absence of fresh air in the presence of all this? The thought did not cross my mind for a year and then it crossed it so fast I missed it and it took three more years for it to cross again for long enough to consider, and then three more after that to gain the strength to form some questions and then three more still to decide on an answer. After all, did I really miss the rest of the world that much, which I could see so clearly outside my window? I could hear the nasty traffic outside, and sometimes the yelling. And him in his room, and me, lying in bed together on Sunday mornings with someone bringing us coffee, and the liquid look of his eyes, and the way he says he loves me and knows me. I love to let him know me for me. He hates it when I return to my room to shower.

But all that is other information. Don't get sentimental on me now. All that is past history, and the ten years is up. You, all of you, standing around here in the lobby, don't you have other places to go? Aren't you late for work already? Everyone is in perfect gray suits, both men and women, but the heels for the women are all different heights so that each woman becomes the same height, or that appears to be the grand plan. The very short woman is wearing heels that are almost a foot and a half high. She is wobbling like crazy but she understands the power and purpose of unity. The tallest woman is in flats. There are men here, too, but their heights are different: it's the women who want to be alike. They want to perform their oneness, against me. They turn in profile and become a series of portraits over the tall glass windows. Over the growing whiteness of the snow outside.

They all speak at once. There is no reason, they tell me, to leave here except for the reason of leaving, and there are seminar sessions they hold in the conference halls to remind me that leaving makes no sense, that it is a foolish idea. And that that new hat is foolish and that the idea, once again, is foolish, in case I did not hear the first time. Put down the chair. All I need. And he is here. And love is here. And the building is enough, isn't the building enough? A building, with everything you need in it, should be enough. The warmth of a welcome lap. Look, outside, at the tumbling, cold snow. There are starving people, and not only in China.

On this day, the day I decide it is not enough, he is reading the paper. No, he is broken in pieces on the floor. He is about to die; no, he is reading the paper. He is unconscious. He is bleeding on the floor from pain, the pain in his heart starting to flow out his mouth in red rivers. No, no, he is reading the paper: the funnies section. He likes to read me the comics out loud even though they don't make sense without the pictures. I don't ever understand the joke.

He is dying, they say, in tinny voices, through the intercom into my room. Look at his pallor. Soon he'll be dead on the floor from your callous departure. He is choking. He is suffering a wound inside his gut that is eating him, wormlike, from the inside out. I have to look again. Listen, I say out loud, it's true that he is sad, but he is also reading the paper. I say it as firmly as I can but the intercom only works one way. I make the finishing touches on my new hat, made from discarded towels, and dead flowers from the room of mothers, and seashells I tore from the mirror border. I tie it under my chin in the now unbordered mirror while he reads the paper aloud.

Let me tell you a comic, he says. Let me tell you about this one, see there's this apocalyptic landscape and a dog is in it with only two legs left and he's about to tumble into a priest and instead he—

You were once, then, the whole sum and total of the up and down and north and south, in my body a quiet peacefulness. The warm lap I find when I look in your eyes. Please. The rescue of your gentle hands. Thank you. But then the warm lap that lasted about ten minutes until I had to sit on my hands in order to withstand the peacefulness and then no hands but no legs either, crossed, in order to hold on to the quiet, and then the gag over my mouth, too, and no words, and your love is a blanket I could fall asleep under forever.

The women in the lobby with their equilateral heels wait as I descend. Tap tap tapping. They know I'm coming. I take the stairs, winding down and down, the chair bumping against the rail, and there they are, everyone, all their faces in rows against the snow outside. And I smell the ocean off my brim and maybe it's only that that keeps me walking, the smell of fish and sea salt and roses, with the chair so firmly raised in my hands. He's reading the paper, I declare, but my voice is small. They shake their heads together. Nope, they tell me. Foolish girl you are. He is shivering cold. He is small and weak. He is useless and cannot move. You selfish, unfair girl.

He is reading the *paper*, I say. There's this comic of a dog in the apocalypse.

No suitcase this time, and a new hat. I bring the chair higher, so that it rakes the underside of the glass mobiles and pokes them into clinkings and ringings. Hold on. The door. I have to elbow my way through the suits to get there. I don't even recognize the security guard this time, and usually I know them all by name: Safety Smith. Shelter Perry. Comfort Jackson. Solace Sherwood. Sanctuary Wu. Custody Koffman. Asylum Jones.

When you have only seen the world through glass for the last ten years it is daunting to imagine it unglassed. The bare world, unclothed by windows. I remember danger. I am not stupid. Someone clicks on the lobby speakers and there's his voice, loud, everywhere: Oh *no*, he says; You can't leave him like that, they say; Excuse me, miss, says the security guard; Ring! trill the mobiles, and Suck Suck goes the glass door, and then in a wash there's that same air from long, long ago, flooding in. New air. Large air. They all shout at me through the closing door. Please! Stop! Never! Crisis!

Outside, enter the blurrier world. It smells blastingly full out here, like popcorn and cars and trees and shit and bright sun—not quite sweet, and a little bit gross, but my nose is about to fall off my face from the change. And the noise! Honk honk. Fuck you. The boom of a bass line.

I won't turn even though I can feel their faces, mouths open in O's, pressed up against the glass, all the same height. I know the way he's sitting in the room that was mine, his foot on his knee, the slow closing of the paper. The pulse of sadness living in the arch of his eyebrow. I loved him, truly. I loved the mothers with their wide-open laps who have been telling me gently to go for months now. Last I saw, they were ankle-deep in petals, and their hair had grown white. We are all dying. I still have the chair in my hands, fingers brittle from holding it so hard, and I put it down and sit. Snow crunches underfoot, and car exhaust smokes out everywhere. The chair is sturdy. I'll take it a few more blocks soon, away from the faces behind me, and sit down there, too. If I have to, I will sit my way across the entire city.

My brain has a lobby. It has a lobby at its front tip, where the thoughts wait after they have come out of hiding, from deep down inside the murkiest corridors of the mind. They fly down the fire escape and pause in the silvery room, deciding if they will launch themselves into the world. Some never do. Some slink right back down into the bomb shelter forever. But others make it out. Today. I take a breath and let the bird go, her song and my story, where it exits the door of my mouth. This is the action I will take. This is all I can ever give, the most I can give always, and my darling, my love, it will have to be enough.

And I still can't get over how Siberry can have a line so absurd—"Take off that foolish hat. Put down the chair"—and wrap it in such beautiful three-part harmony and reverberating keyboards that it becomes almost holy. Suddenly, the foolish hat is really, really important and holding up a chair seems like the right thing to do. I've often puzzled over how to replicate that tone clash in prose—how to make the ridiculous luminous. The song also got me thinking about the idea of lobbies, of waiting rooms, of places of pause and limbo. An interim space. How much time we spend in our internal lobbies, waiting. Deciding to go out or go in. Waiting for someone to come out with a clipboard and call us. Wearing our foolish hats and holding our chairs with both powerful hope and defiance.

SHE ONCE HAD ME

anthony decurtis

I once had a girl, or, should I say, she once had me

"Norwegian Wood (This Bird Has Flown)"
The Beatles

It was a gray Tuesday morning in early December, and as Julian Marks stood at the window staring at the Hudson River and the soft sky above New Jersey, he found himself longing for a cigarette. He felt the yearning in his chest. It was so voluptuous, lighting the match, smelling the sulfur and putting the filter to his lips, feeling the smoke hit the back of his throat and then sucking it into his lungs and then luxuriantly exhaling. Voluptuous, but now just a memory. Like drinking, haunting the clubs, chasing girls, and getting high—cocaine, which he loved, and pot, primarily—smoking had become too debilitating an indulgence once he'd begun to slog his way through his forties. Somehow, getting older seemed almost exclusively to consist of passages like that, a continual judicious editing of potentially dangerous pleasures from his life. It was a process that sometimes seemed designed to eventually render you entirely safe, just in time for your death. Outside his window, a beautiful blue bird flew by, floating on the wind, heading north along the river.

Marks was fifty-two now, and he never felt better, physically at least. He worked out for an hour every day, which bored him to stupefaction, but, once again, seemed necessary. While he was not as thin as he was in the whip-thin splendor of his pop-star glory days two decades or more ago, his weight was well within the acceptable range for his height, which was five feet ten inches. His cholesterol was normal; ditto his blood pressure, though salt, too, had, alas, gone the way of smokes, whiskey, fast girls, and blow.

He walked away from the row of windows overlooking Riverside Drive, crossed the loft-size room, and seated himself on a stool at the kitchen counter, his urge to smoke forgotten. His dog, Gracie, a 160-pound Saint Bernard, sauntered into the room and dropped herself clumsily at his feet. After six years together, longer than all but one of his girlfriends and wives, neither of them required a greeting. Their intimacy was deep and assumed. It was 7:20 a.m., and he knew that within twenty minutes or so, she would need to eat and go out. And she knew that he knew. He popped *Rubber Soul* into his CD player, poured himself a decaffeinated coffee, added some skim milk, and began to think about his day. The sound of "Drive My Car" flooded the apartment.

After mentally rifling through his possible responsibilities, he realized, happily, that the day essentially required nothing of him. Deal with the dog. Call his manager to discuss the developing logistics for his annual six-week club tour in the summer. Check in with his girlfriend, Angela, who lived in Boston, where he would be going this weekend. Make arrangements for the session he was set to do in Philadelphia in a couple of weeks. That would be good. Catherine Williams, a singer-songwriter whose debut album (*Unavailable*) had been one of the previous year's most dramatic breakthroughs, planned to record one of his songs ("The Darkest Night") for a B-side, and she had asked if he would play acoustic guitar and sing backup on it. He was looking forward to that.

As he drank the last of his coffee and began to dress to take Gracie out, however, he felt that dreadful inward tug of looming, unfinished business, something vaguely discomforting that required his attention but that he had conveniently put out of his mind. At first, drifting in the sweet fog of the just-awakened, he wasn't able to recover it. He teased himself with the possibility that he had made some kind of internal mistake, that despite the unsettled feeling in the pit of his stomach, no emotional loose ends remained to be tied.

But instincts never lie. As the strains of George Harrison's sitar on "Norwegian Wood (This Bird Has Flown)" faded, it came to him. When he had arrived home the day before from seeing Angela in Boston, he had found a letter from Hannah. He and his former lover hadn't communicated at all in nearly ten years—she would be close to forty now—but in her characteristic way she wrote as if they had just spoken moments before. She was like a ghost who could pass through barriers and boundaries of all kinds. Time never seemed to pass in her hothouse inner life; it was always, eternally, right now. Hence no need for chitchat, small talk, catching up, filling in the gaps. The heat was always on.

"I heard 'Disappearance' on the radio the other day, and thought of you, of course," she wrote. "That was always my favorite song of yours. It made me think of how we used to meet every morning at my apartment on Cottage Grove, how you would come to me, light a fire in the fireplace, play me the songs you were working on and we would spend the entire morning in bed. Wasn't it good? How have you been, my love? What is your life like?"

Those mornings she referred to were among the most erotic experiences of his life. He could still remember lying next to her, the smell of their sweat and their sex filling the room, and looking out at the trees and sky beyond her window. He had been married and living in Boston, not far from where Angela lived now, actually, when he met Hannah after one of his gigs at the Thermometer, a local club. As he was playing, he had seen her walking across the room to join some friends at a table. She was tall and slender, and she moved with exquisite grace. He liked that she had not dressed as if she were going to a club. It was summertime, and she wore a light blue silk blouse, a long, dark blue skirt, and sandals. Her straight blond hair fell nearly to the small of her back. He looked over at her occasionally as he performed, and she always was looking directly at him. Her sloe eyes were both serious and playful.

Their affair began that night. When he left the club with

her, he had hoped that by sleeping with her he would get her—and all the girls like her, whom he had a hard time resisting—"out of his system." His marriage was fading at the time, he now realized, but then he wanted to be able to return to the monogamy he had been struggling, with intermittent success, to accept. Somewhere inside himself he knew, though, that if Hannah had gotten into his system so quickly, she would not leave so easily.

Their conversation was easy and flirty as they walked the early-morning streets to her apartment. He set his guitar case down, and she removed her sandals as soon as they entered her studio. It was 2 a.m. "There's not much to see, but let me show you my room," she said. "Sit anywhere." He looked around and noticed there was no convenient place to sit but her large, low bed. He sat on her rug, watched her, and waited.

She was a literature student, and wooden bookshelves lined the walls. She put on *Blonde on Blonde* and poured them each a glass of red wine, looking quietly pleased with herself as she moved deliberately about the room. She sat on the edge of the bed, then lifted her bare legs onto it and lay back on the pillows. She looked over at him and smiled playfully. "Does this seem just unspeakably bold?" she asked. "It's time for bed."

He got up, carried his glass to the nightstand, and lay down next to her. When they kissed, which they did immediately, her lips felt like soft, liquid flames. Her eyes, impossibly blue and never closed, glazed over, defenseless. They were light pools, glinting in the darkness, that provided another way to enter her. As they kissed and touched, he could feel her emptying herself into him, letting the outlines of her personality dissolve so that he could reconstruct her according to whatever shape his desires might take. "Do you like your version?" she asked, aware of how she had already signaled her compliance to whatever he wanted. "Another fine edition of you," he said. Her molten hollowness inspired a violence in him; the willing sum of his fantasies, she seemed perfect and, therefore, perfectly violable. She felt those feelings in him, and they thrilled her.

When he entered her, she moaned and slowly turned her head to her left. He wanted to look into her eyes, so he pulled her hair to the right until she faced him. She lay there, her eyes were wide, her mouth open. He pulled her hair harder until her neck, long, white, pulsing, was fully extended. "You're hurting me," she whispered, but there was no judgment, demand, or even plea in the statement. It was a mere declaration of fact, and it was entirely up to him how to proceed. He pulled harder and she shuddered. Everywhere his mouth could reach he sucked and bit on her, leaving her marked.

They finished with her on her back, her legs extended along his stomach and chest, her long, elegant feet resting on his shoulders, her high arches and smooth soles pressed against his face and lips, his cock thrusting rapidly and forcefully into her. Her eyes were closed now, and she was whimpering. She seemed to have no spine or will. When they were done, he collapsed on his back next to her, gasping for breath. Stretching out her long body, she reached over and took his cock, slick and drenched with their juices, into her hand and stroked it. The ridge of its large, thick head was so sensitive he could barely stand her touch. She then rested her head on his stomach and licked him clean. "I feel like a virgin," she said. "I've never been fucked like that in my life."

Marks was roused from this reverie by the thud of Gracie planting herself by the door. When he looked over at her, she was sitting like a sphinx, her back erect, her face bright with expectation. It was hardly the first time she had pulled him back from a funk or a descent into the quicksand of his past. Her openheartedness and readiness for experience, her grounding in the present and eagerness for the future, had led him to adapt that annoying fundamentalist acronym—WWJD—to his own purposes.

"What would Jesus do?" became WWGD: What would Gracie do? He'd ask himself that question whenever he felt emotionally paralyzed, perplexed, or overwhelmed by feelings he couldn't comprehend, turn into action, or use in some effective way. As clearly as he could tell from Gracie's behavior, that question typically had one of four answers: get something to eat, find something or somebody to play with, take a nap, or go for a walk. He found that those four options usually did the trick for him as well, snapping him out of pointless obsession. This morning, obviously, he would take a walk.

It was cold and damp outside, but he and Gracie headed toward Riverside Park and the Hudson anyway. It was easy for him to think there, and there was something cleansing about the cold. They entered the park near 120th Street and walked down the long stone stairway that ended near the vacant tennis courts, Gracie pulling all the way. Then they headed south. Marks had loathed the cold until he got the dog, who loved it. Now he experienced it through her and actually got excited for her as fall yielded to winter.

He still had to decide what to do about the letter. Its arrival made him feel like the French poet Paul Verlaine, unwillingly shocked out of bourgeois comfort by the appearance on his doorstep of the young madman Arthur Rimbaud. For years he had been unable to resist Hannah whenever she turned up. A friend had wryly termed his relationship with her, which had gone around about four times since the initial fire of that first affair, "the crying game." It was an apt description. Hannah's passion for intrigue was inexhaustible; she seemed incapable of settling into a relationship that wasn't an unending tumult.

For his part, he was addicted to her, there was no other way to put it. When he would be on top of her staring into her face, he felt like Narcissus, gazing into his own reflection in the pond and, beyond that, into the bottomless depths of himself, in which it would be all too easy to drown. The feeling was both exalting and frightening, as if he could sink in there and lose any grip he might have had on the external world.

Gracie dragged him toward the dog run, but, much as he loved watching her raise havoc there, they didn't enter and join the canine fray. He wanted to continue walking along the nearly empty promenade, under the canopy of bare trees. The spare chill around him provided an ideal complement to his introspective mood. Who could tell what Hannah's reemergence at this point meant? A divorce? A dead husband? She had written from Wilmington, North Carolina; maybe she was living there now. Marks thought of those stalker profiles security experts compiled for celebrities and politicians. Mobility is a key characteristic of someone whose threats must be taken seriously. He and Gracie turned to walk back toward the apartment.

His CD player must have been set on REPEAT because *Rubber Soul* was still playing when he opened the door—the reflective strains of John Lennon's "In My Life." He fed Gracie and then picked up his phone to make some calls. He had a message. It was Angela. "Hi, sweetie," she said, her voice warm and clear. "I'm sorry to call so early, but I wanted to see if I could catch you before I went off to my day. It was wonderful seeing you over the weekend, and I can't wait for Friday. I really miss you. Let's talk tonight, okay? Love you—bye!" He put down the phone and lay on his couch.

Angela was just completing her first semester of teaching English at Harvard. She was a Byron specialist. In terms of sheer brainpower, she was the smartest woman Marks had ever been involved with—and, amazingly, the least pretentious. What he loved about her conversation was that she as-

Their sexual conflagrations were just one thing. He also regarded her as his best, most discerning, and most sympathetic audience. Her (admittedly disturbing) desire to erase herself and become him made discussing ideas with her or playing songs for her like collaborating with a second self. She had been the muse for his richest and most mysterious album, *The Secret World*. Where he was concerned, nothing was too subtle for her. There was no nuance she didn't get.

Finally, though, it was hard to tell if he had her, or if she had him. He had left his wife for her, and then, predictably enough, everything fell apart soon after. This bird has flown, indeed. Not long after that, he moved to New York, his favorite city, and tried to build a new life. Still, Hannah never escaped his mind. A couple of years later his album *Wilderland* won a Grammy, and she wrote him a letter after seeing him perform on the awards show. This time, in the endlessly witty ways of reality, she was married and he was single.

"I never took much," she wrote, "and I know that everybody must give something back for something they get. But I feel like I have lost everything. I think of you all the time. Every day I imagine coming to see you." Inevitably, they started up again, though she was living in Vancouver. When he would fly to see her, it was like the buildings in New York evaporated as he made his way west, finally deliquescing into the watery outdoors of the Northwest, a haze of gray and green shadings. He begged her to leave her husband. She couldn't. That was it for that time around. And even that had not been the end of it.

sumed the intelligence and interest of anyone she spoke to, and assumed nothing else. She carried her beauty with equal ease, though not without pride. Her considerable vanity amused him because she was so nice a person that she couldn't allow herself to acknowledge or accept it. She somehow thought that if she kept her vanity a secret from herself, no one else would notice it. But the pleasure she took in compliments was palpable, which made it fun to compliment her.

When they met three years ago, she had just turned thirty and she had no idea who he was. He was surprised that didn't bother him and wondered if it meant he had achieved some previously unanticipated level of maturity. Later, when she described him to one of her friends after their first date, that girl had enthusiastically given her the rundown: the 1974 debut album, *Waiting for You*, that had drawn comparisons to Dylan; the Grammy; the string of songs that had become part of the singer-songwriter canon: "You Loved Me Then," "Biding My Time," "More Wood for the Flame," and a handful of others.

As with Hannah, he and Angela had had blinding sex on their first night together. But what he most remembered was the long, leisurely bath they took the next morning, because she had the day off and didn't have to leave for work. In the steam of his large, stone bathroom they had talked for what seemed like hours. Her vulnerability touched him. Uncharacteristically, he spent more time listening than speaking.

"I was diagnosed with cancer when I was twenty," she told

him. "I can't tell you how frightening it was." She was from Kansas, and in a flat Midwestern accent that sounded exotic to his East Coast ears, she plainly described the radiation and chemotherapy. He looked at the gorgeous body that had withstood all that, and, strangely, he began to stir. He wondered about the source of his arousal, and then stopped wondering about it. He couldn't imagine having to be so strong at such a young age.

"After a period of remission," she continued, as calmly as if she were talking about someone else, but with no detachment, "it came back when I was twenty-four. I was devastated. I had to leave graduate school for a semester and go home to Lawrence for treatment. To top things off, I had been having an affair with a professor in my department who was separated from his wife. While I was away in the hospital, he went back to her. I found out through a friend of mine who had called to cheer me up and share the gossip from back at school. She didn't know I had been seeing him."

He sat there soaking, watching as she leaned against the white tiles behind her, her platinum hair wet and sticking to the sides of her face. As she spoke, he had been thinking about the failure of his marriage and the romantic agony of his run-ins with Hannah. He had often wondered how he would ever be able to tell someone about them without feeling pathetic. The depth of Angela's story made him feel that he could safely tell his own.

Just before her thirtieth birthday, Angela had just passed the five-year mark since her cancer recurrence, and her doctor had given her a clean bill of health. "I'm ready for a new beginning," she told him excitedly. "I want to be part of that," he thought, but said nothing.

He had fallen asleep on the couch, and when he woke up, the room felt chilly. He got up, nearly stepping on the dog, who was sleeping on the floor next to him, and went to the woodstove to build a fire. He gathered up the many newspapers that were scattered around the room, and he removed four logs from the pile against the brick wall opposite the windows. He also took the letter that lay on his kitchen counter and placed the logs and the paper in the stove. He got a wooden match from a kitchen cabinet and lit the paper. The flames quickly filled the belly of the stove, and he could already feel the heat coming from vents on the side.

He walked over to the window and stared at the river, as still as a pane of glass this morning, reflecting the clouds. "Isn't it good?" he thought, and as "If I Needed Someone" played, he began, quietly, to sing along.

author inspiration

I first heard "Norwegian Wood (This Bird Has Flown)" in 1965, the year The Beatles' *Rubber Soul* was released. I was fourteen years old. I remember noticing the strange, dreamlike sound of George Harrison's sitar, and the sense that the song told an actual adult story in a way that most of the pop music I had heard to that point didn't. Those impressions weren't conscious; I probably just felt that the song was "different" in some way. As I grew more sophisticated as a listener over the years, I discovered how the song's narrative was broken by surreal details and information that John Lennon had left out. In later interviews, Lennon would say that the song was his way of writing about having an affair without revealing it to his wife, Cynthia. Those facts—and the song's reflective tone—inspired me to imagine a songwriter who, unlike Lennon, had lived into his fifties and had occasion to evaluate the impact on his life of a past affair.

MILESTONES

hannah tinti

Since there are no lyrics, I've listed the performers instead, to give readers some idea of whom they're listening to. I've used all of the musicians' names in the story.

Trumpet: Miles Davis
Alto Saxophone: Julian "Cannonball" Adderley
Tenor Saxophone: John Coltrane
Piano: Red Garland
Bass: Paul Chambers
Drums: "Philly" Joe Jones

"Milestones"
Miles Davis

D own on the street they are all trying to cross at once. It's a hard, crisp fall day and the people are crowded on the corner, eyeing the light, and when the yellow cab runs the red and angles itself in the crosswalk, they rush forward and split and divide around it like water. These are city people and they all know where they are going, taking fast steps—one, two, three, four—and dodging around things in their way, like newspaper stands and lunch carts grilling rows of chicken legs and tourists with matching purple windbreakers looking up and unshaven men on the steps of the church, crouched beneath statues, blankets over their heads and cardboard signs at their feet—*Help me I need help PLEASE ANYTHING*. There's a double stroller coming in on the right. There is someone shouting Spanish into a pay phone. There are watches for sale. And bags. And hats. And small plastic frogs swimming in water.

Above all of this, the rope slips. And there he goes. One moment Red has his hand out, steadying as he pulls the squeegee down the side of the twenty-seventh-floor window, grinning as the secretary wearing the green blouse inside picks her nose, and the next he feels the roof braces shift and one side of the scaffolding drops and he is putting his heel down into nothing, into empty air, and the rest of him follows behind, like a string of beads falling off a table.

Red has fallen before, off his own two-story home. Tripped over the edge while reshingling and landed on a small fir tree he had planted three weeks earlier to symbolize the birth of a new baby, a girl, who'd come so early that her ears hadn't developed yet—there were just small openings with tiny flaps of skin above. She'd immediately been placed in an incubator, and that was where she was when Red fell off the roof—in that tiny plastic bubble, her ears just beginning to bend and fold. The tree collapsed underneath Red's weight, and he heard those branches snapping more than his leg, which came apart in three places.

Now the floors whiz past him—twenty-six, twenty-five, twenty-four—and Red is waiting for his safety line to catch. There is a harness across his shoulders and underneath his arms with a large metal ring in the back for a rope to go through, and that rope should be stopping him now. Meanwhile he is remembering how to fall, with his shirt flapping and his stomach sinking and his body turning and his hard hat gone.

On the sidewalk, no one looks up. Not even the tourists. They are busy moving around a truck that has taken a corner too quickly and knocked over the lunch cart that sells kebabs. Raw meat hits the gutter and the owner is holding on to the side of his face, singed by his portable stove.

A man breaks away out of the crowd and enters the lobby of the building. There is something special about him, the way he carries himself, as if he is determined to make good. He nods at the security guards, and they smile back. He turns into the narrow hallway and there is an elevator waiting, already full of people. He steps in right before the door closes. There is a woman standing next to him, wearing a blue overcoat and smelling like lavender. The scent is coming from her hair.

This man is going to quit his job today, a job he has worked at for fifteen years, and soon he will never have to ride this elevator again. Last night he ordered a gin and tonic at a bar, and when he tasted the lime, he suddenly remembered being in love when he was twenty-two, with a girl he'd met working at a fish fry—tall, slender, and knock-kneed, her skin so pale it would change color when you touched it. On Mondays the fish fry was closed and he would pack food and a small thermos of gin and tonic and they would go to the beach, stretch out on a blanket in the sun, and take turns reading short stories out loud and swimming in the icy water.

It was, John remembered, a time when he was happy, and he was not happy now, living alone and reading Kierkegaard and masturbating every night into a sock. Leaning against the bar, he caught a reflection of himself in the mirror above. There was no denying it—he was middle-aged. He lifted his fingers to his mouth as he swallowed the gin, as if he needed to push the alcohol farther down his throat. He remembered licking the girl's neck on the blanket, how salty it tasted, and he ran his tongue over his own wrist. All he felt was hair.

He would change what he could—he would leave his job. In the morning this made everything seem different. The sky was brighter, the colors people wore passed in a blur, and even when he stepped onto the elevator, he could sense it—a certain snappiness to things, to their possibility.

John can't help himself—he starts to hum. *Fascinating rhythm, you've got me on the go.* The other people in the elevator exchange glances and try to move away from him, but there is no place to go. John does not care—in fact, so determined is he to change his life that he hums louder. Still they are going up and up and John's ears begin to pop. He taps his foot back and forth, keeping time to the jingle in his throat.

The lavender-smelling woman touches her elbow to the side of John's coat as she reaches into her bag for a tissue. There is something in her eye and she is looking at the ceiling of the elevator, at the tiny little escape hatch, holding the skin below her lashes so that the pink shows. John watches her. He hums.

When John was twelve years old, he bought a plastic model of an eye for a science project. The model was the size of a bowling ball and came apart into soft pieces, pink and blue and red, with a sliding see-through lid over the iris. John made lists of diseases that blinded, chemicals and birth defects. He learned to read the alphabet in braille. He set books out on the table and drew charts with Magic Markers and came in second place at the science fair, just behind the kinetic energy roller designed by Philly Joe.

Later, John told the girl he fell in love with about it on the beach. He talked about her pupils, her cornea, her sclera and iris, her vitreous body and aqueous humor. She told him that when she was a child and something was caught in her eye, her mother, a nurse, would use her tongue to remove it.

The elevator stops at the fourteenth floor. The doors open and three people step out before the doors close again. The remaining passengers move away from John into the corners, and the lavender woman rearranges herself so that she is no longer touching anyone. She lowers her head, dabbing at her lashes with the tissue in her hand. John wonders if he should offer to lick it out.

•   •   •

Red has been washing windows for five years. Before that he was a housepainter and before that he shingled roofs and before that he was a truck driver and before that he was a mover. He carried pianos on his back. The hammers hit the strings on each step down the stairs, and with the crushing weight of wood on top of him, Red felt it was not an instrument anymore but all of his disappointments in life, groaning. His parents were killed in a car on the highway while Red was at a moving job, and that did it for him—he couldn't carry anything anymore.

He met his wife at a truck stop. She was driving a refriger-ated case full of turkey parts; he was pulling a load of Nabisco. They made love in the parking lot, his cab beneath a row of trees. She held on to the back of the driver's seat and he braced against the wheel, the smell of cigarettes on his fin-gertips. Her hair covered her face in the dark. He parted it and pulled it aside and looked at her nose. It was round with a slight turn at the end, and he could see straight up inside.

Before long she was pregnant and Red was climbing roofs. It was good to be working on homes, to be in one place, with a woman who made him sandwiches. He opened his lunch bag each day and reached inside with the expecta-tion of hard-boiled eggs, of tuna fish, of salami and cheese and grapes and cookies and small containers of applesauce. He pressed his back against the chimney, spread these items out on his napkin, and felt loved.

After the baby came they needed money and he began washing skyscrapers. On his first trip over the edge, his knees had wobbled. Don't look down, he'd been told—it'll seem like miles. He didn't, but he could still see the reflection of what was behind him in the glass as he ran his squeegee across, and he could feel the wind shifting the scaffolding beneath his feet, and the metal of the railings seemed cold, no matter how long the sun had been shining on it. Bugs ran into the windows. Occasionally, a bird.

Red's daughter's ears never did grow in. She had a hearing aid to make up for a twisted canal, and there was no outer cartilage, just those tiny flaps—the beginnings of ears, a ridge of semicircles—that her mother helped to hide with her hair.

At the breakfast table that morning his daughter had told him that she loved someone. Me, I hope, Red said. And she said yes, but she meant a different kind of love. She meant movie love. There was a boy in her first-grade class who wore glasses and she was making him a valentine. She had already picked out the paper and was working on cutting a triangle for the front, because he liked triangles.

It made Red think of the fir tree. Too much damage had been done when he crushed it, and so while his daughter was still in the incubator and maybe going to die, he'd torn the plant out by the roots. It hurt him to do it, because he felt it might have saved him. When he fed it into the wood chipper, the machine choked. He pulled the pieces out, his hands sticky with sap, and he'd thought, I love this so much. I love this more than anything.

John steps out of the elevator with the lavender-smelling woman. They are standing on the same floor. He asks her, does she need any help? Can he do something for her? The speck—he can almost see it—seems to be caught in the corner of her eye. She is nearly crying, but says no and reaches out for the wall, then begins to guide herself, sliding her hand toward the door to the ladies' room.

John's assistant has her hair piled on top of her head like an ice cream cone. He says hello to her and wiggles his eyebrows in a way that means *coffee*. She can tell that something is different. He notices that she notices and he feels glad. He wants to shout, I am different today! But instead he grips the handle of his office door and turns it. This office is a corner office, with windows from ceiling to floor, and as he puts down his briefcase on his desk, he sees Red go flying past in one vertical movement.

The man is more of a blur, really, a flash of something large that makes John jump and then think—*Did I see that?*—and rush over to the window and press his forehead against it, looking down at the body twisting and turning. A piece of rope is trailing behind, attached to the man's back like the tail of a kite. John bangs his hands against the glass, thinking for a moment that he will be able to grab hold of it.

There is nothing he can do, so he watches. John's legs ache as if he has been running. He sees the body flail along the side of the building and his stomach drops—the same queasy sensation of an elevator slipping before it catches itself—the suspension for a moment in the air it leaves behind. John leans into the frame of the window and realizes he is biting his lip. There is blood; he can taste it with his tongue.

His secretary comes in behind him and places a cup of coffee on his desk. Here you are, she says, and John decides, right as he hears the sound of the cup and saucer clink together on the table, that he going to wait outside the ladies' room until the lavender woman comes out. He is going to ask her to lunch and ride the elevator down with her, and if he is lucky—very, very lucky—she will marry him and his life will change and he will never have to come back to this.

The owner of the kebab stand is sitting on a milk crate and pressing a package of frozen meat to his face. He is looking up at a police officer and giving a description of the truck that destroyed his lunch cart when he sees Red's hard hat and pauses, thinking it is a falling bird—just as one of the purple-windbreaker tourists lifts the lens of her camera and focuses on a gargoyle and presses the shutter and captures it.

The hard hat is white. On the side, it has the letters *CABM* stamped in blue by the company Red works for, Chambers American Building & Maintenance. The hard hat is given to each man his first day on the job. It lands a full fifteen seconds before Red does, in a fountain in front of the building.

There is a woman on her way to an interview. She has three children at home and a husband who has disappeared, and now, suddenly, here is a shimmering explosion of water over her pink silk suit that leaves dark stains across her shoulders, blurs the ink on the copies of her résumé, and flattens her hair.

There is a boy delivering a plain cheese pizza. This pizza is on its way to a good-bye party for a receptionist who has worked at her company for forty years, but now the thin cardboard box is drenched, and the pizza boy turns his head in surprise as lucky pennies wash onto the pavement.

There is a dog walker with seven dogs—two dachshunds, a beagle, a golden retriever, a pit bull, a Burmese mountain dog, and a mutt. Bits of plastic fly through the air as the hard hat hits the bottom of the fountain and the dog walker can't help himself—he lets go of every leash and brings his arms across his face and the dogs run for it, shaking the water off their bodies as they go, breaking out in all directions.

Red is still waiting for the safety catch. He wonders at the length of the rope. The wind is tearing at his legs, blowing so strongly against him that he thinks for a moment it is holding him up. Red stretches then, reaches his hand out, and it knocks against the side of the building and he hears his fingers snap. The world is moving toward him like someone opening their arms, wider and wider until he can't see anything else.

The second splash booms.

Police sent to investigate the lunch cart pull out their yellow plastic tape and quickly circle the fountain. For good measure, they also place two sawhorses on the sidewalk. They radio for an ambulance and fire trucks. They spread out to find the dogs.

The tourists finish taking pictures and climb onto their bus. The street vendors hide around the corner, their stolen goods wrapped up in blankets. The homeless men of the church slide their cardboard signs out of sight. The woman in the pink suit has removed her jacket. She holds it now in the breeze, waving it back and forth like a flag. She has fifteen minutes to dry out.

The owner of the kebab stand drops his frozen meat and stares at the scaffolding, still dangling at the top of the building. It is a tooth hanging on by a thread. The fire trucks arrive. They park on top of an abandoned case of plastic frogs and the toys splinter across the street, all broken eyes and webbed toes. The firemen pile out, hook up hoses, roll their ladders. They ask what happened and are told: cannonball. The dogs are collected. The pizza boy moves on. There are more pedestrians coming down the block. More taxis and buses and limousines and motorcycles. The police swing their arms and keep it all moving. Some people crane their necks at what is floating in the fountain. Others simply dodge around this new thing standing still.

author inspiration

"Milestones" is one of my all-time favorite pieces of music. The energy is like a busy street in New York City, all that motion and franticness, where your eye pauses and begins to follow one person, one story, before it gets caught up in the bustle again. One section in "Milestones" made me think of a man falling, and another section made me think of a man rising, which is why Red is falling and John is going up in the elevator at the same time. I was interested in personal vertical movement, in comparison to the horizontal movement of the street. I also tried to follow Miles Davis's structure, using the solos as moments to go into the lives of the characters before they get caught up in the music again and are lost.

DEATH IN THE ALT-COUNTRY

neal pollack

No one could set me right
But mama tried, mama tried.

"Mama Tried"
Merle Haggard

I was underneath my 1967 Chevy pickup when I found
out that Blake had died. It was a slow resto job, but it
didn't matter because I loved that car. I'd already pulled
the original 283 and put in an '86 350 four-bolt, block-bored
.030 with high-compression TRW pistons. I couldn't decide
what impressed me more: the custom Corvette cam that I'd
transplanted from an L82 or the Edelbrock performer mani-
fold with a 650 CFM carb that I'd so carefully restored. Well,
now I was installing a high-volume oil pump, and nothing
was going to stop me.

"Isn't that right, Lyman?" I said to my basset hound.

Lyman looked up. I put out a grease-stained hand for him
to lick. He obliged. Then he went back to chomping on his
pig's ear.

I rolled myself out. It was time for a cold Tecate, and a new album on the boom. It'd been a while since I'd listened to that Townes Van Zandt tribute for cancer survivors. I'd also been eyeing volume two from the Gram Parsons compilation reissue boxed set.

My cell phone rang. It was Randy.

"Rick, where are you?" he said.

"In the garage."

"Oh, man."

"What?"

"Blake's dead."

I was silent.

It'd been a while since the death of a friend of mine.

"Fuck," I said. "How?"

"He was on the Kennedy. Tires blew out on his Ford Explorer. They found his head on the median."

I sobbed a little into the phone. But I adjusted myself quickly. Blake didn't like it when we cried. Blake had been a man. He'd partied like a man. He'd played his vintage Hank Martin Stratocaster like a man. And we were going to send him out like a man.

"Let's start planning the funeral," I said. "Come by tomorrow."

"Totally," Randy said.

I went inside and had a stiff shot of bourbon, Gentleman Jack, superpremium. Sad times meant breaking out the good stuff. It was hard for me to think about anything, so I turned on the computer. So many digital photos to look at. There we were, me, Randy, and Blake, at South By Southwest, with our cowboy hats on. That'd been some party in the park. The Drive-By Truckers played before anyone had heard of them. We stayed up all night doing Stooges covers with Alejandro. Blake was so happy. He'd always said that the best festival parties were the ones that the A&R people didn't know about.

I scrolled to a photo of Blake singing "I Will Always Love You" at Big Lula's Ukranian Village Cowboy Karaoke Night, and I got a little choked. Did you know that Dolly Parton wrote that song originally? Well, she did. "It was a real good tune," Blake used to say, "before the wrong people got hold of it."

I was starting to get some good ideas for the funeral.

The doorbell rang. It was the UPS guy. I'd ordered a bunch of corrugated tin. A lucky break had landed me this installation gig for a sculpture garden in Lawrence, Kansas, but now my friend was dead, and my project could wait. The tin would have other uses.

I wanted to do a sculpture for Blake, starkly beautiful and really cool, completely representative of his tastes and interests. Blake always said he loved my work, particularly the Wilco album cover I'd designed and they'd rejected. Blake said mine was better than the one the band had finally chosen.

"Don't do business with Tweedy," Blake said. "You'll always end up getting hurt."

Blake was an honest man and I wish he wasn't dead.

Randy and I planned one other funeral. Back in 1992, a guy named Gary got shot in the stomach. He was riding his bike on Irving Park, coming back from a rehearsal of a Brecht play he was directing. The shot came from nowhere, and they never found the shooter. There was a lot of blood. Gary died in the ambulance.

We'd known Gary at Northwestern. He was the biggest Nine Inch Nails fan in the world. One time he came back from spring break and said he'd partied with Trent Reznor in Jamaica. None of us believed him, but he had the photos to prove it, and from then on, it was nothing but "bow down before the one you serve" in our dorm.

Naturally, Randy decided to throw Gary a Nine Inch Nails funeral. There'd never been a dead guy in our life before, and we wanted to mourn properly. Gary's girlfriend thought it was a good idea, so we sent out invitations telling people to wear leather and chains. "Prepare to Be Dominated," the invitations read, "As We Celebrate Gary's Life."

It was a crazy S&M party. We invited the rat lady, and she brought all her animals, including a mongoose and some kind of miniature lynx, and I had Cynthia Plastercaster bring her mold of Reznor's dick. The dancers in cages were a nice touch. A guy we knew from the Fireside Bowl scored us a smoke machine. Sergio from Weeds donated a case of tequila. Best of all, we hired a DJ who knew the Nails, and he had Reznor make a tape saying, "Fuck you, Gary. Meet you in hell in about twenty-five years."

I got a couple of girlfriends out of that night. Not like I meant to, of course, and neither relationship turned serious. But sometimes grief makes people close.

This all came to mind while I was thinking about how to send off Blake. Randy came over. I broke open some Knob Creek. We played my Xbox and shot around some ideas for the Blake gig.

"Maybe we should do it at The Roundup," I said.

"Nah," said Randy. "They had two memorial services there last month, plus the diabetes benefit."

"Right," I said.

"What about Bill and Sarah's Record Barn?" he said.

"Too small."

We sat around for a while, listening to Whiskeytown. Randy poured himself a double, and I had a beer to go along with my shot. He scratched himself through his cowboy shirt.

"Pig roast," he said.

I said, "Yes."

The building I live in now used to be a Mexican-owned auto-parts store before I bought it. That was back in 1996, so I got a really good deal. My realtor scored me a big lot behind the house. I fenced it in so the neighbors wouldn't steal my outdoor art, built a patio, bought a couple of used picnic tables, started growing tomato and weed, put up some trellises.

Blake said, "Man, you need yourself a barbecue pit."

Everybody back in Kentucky had them, he said. There was nothing like slow-roasted meat and good-old country banjo picking. They used to roast pigs at his prep school all the time. So he came over one afternoon with a shovel and a bundle of hickory, and we dug.

It was a beautiful pit.

"We've gotta have a pig roast," he said.

That first roast was all Blake's idea. We started calling some bands we knew. They'd get free beer if they played, we told them. Word got out on our email lists that we'd have a prize for the best-looking pair of overalls.

Blake carved the tops out of some leftover beams I had in the garage. He said the centerpiece of the party would be table-saw races; people could trick up their saws however they wanted and cut them loose on the track. We provided the electricity; the ones that went the farthest without breaking won. Blake made the call on my PA: "Oh, yeah. It looks like The Virginia General is gonna win the first ever Pig Roast Table-Saw Race, right here in the heart of Pilsen! We've made some crazy table saws, that's for sure!"

On the day of the party, we went to a slaughterhouse in Back Of The Yards and came home with a prize hog. We tossed it in the pit with the wood and coals and slammed shut the cast-iron doors. The article in the *Reader* about our party said, "The highlight came when they opened up the pit and the hog appeared in all its apple-mouthed glory." There were nearly a hundred of us. We slapped that hog up on a table and picked away; I've never had meat so tender or satisfying. In later years, people started coming to the roast because they'd heard it was cool, not because they really belonged there. But the first-year people knew we'd been part of something great, and every one of us wore our First Annual Pig Roast T-shirts proudly.

So of course we had to have a pig roast to remember Blake. He deserved the party of all time. His death had made us very sad.

The bands from the scene all agreed to play, even Washboard Billy. The musicians donated money so we could rent a stage. We got a beer sponsor. Randy made some calls and the radio station from UofC agreed to carry the music live. A lot of people I knew were having kids now. I even set up a play area for the kids, with a magic show, and piped-in kids' music.

We knew Blake's funeral would be a success, but we weren't prepared for just how successful. The roast was supposed to start at three. People started showing up around noon. I was glad that twenty or so of us—his really close friends—had stayed up drinking the night before, because it was obvious that we weren't going to have much of a chance to talk.

We had to make a keg run early. By 5 p.m., my backyard was just brimming. I couldn't believe that Steve Albini showed up, and the guys from Tortoise. Blake had some Mexican friends, too, so we had a norteña band playing *cumbias* on the sidewalk as everyone came in.

Randy got onstage with his band, Hellhound Hayseed. He played the guitar, and there was a drummer and a stand-up bassist. Washboard Billy, to everyone's surprise, was there with them. Randy leaned into the microphone.

"This one's for Blake," he said. "He was the goddamn best guy, and he'd want you to eat some pig."

The crowd went nuts.

The bassist played a few notes. The drummer started in. Randy sang Blake's favorite song, like he did every Monday night at the Roundup:

Jug of wine
Jug of wine
I'm gonna drink another
Jug of wine.
When I'm with you,
I feel fine,
Without you I'm just fixin'
To drink another
Jug of wine.

Oh, jug of wine
Jug of wine
I'm gonna drink another
Jug of wine.
Our love is dying
On the vine
And so I think I'll go home
To drink another
Jug of wine.

I grabbed the nearest girl and started to dance, even though this wasn't much of a dancing song. It was just hard without Blake. I needed to feel close to someone. Randy sang, and the crowd sang along:

Oh, jug of wine
Jug of wine
I'm gonna drink another
Jug of wine.
My baby drank
Some turpentine
And so I think I'll go home
To drink another
Jug of wine.

"The pig is ready!" I heard someone shout. "The pig is ready!"

And there it was, in the pit, a really beautiful forty-pound hog. The people were starving, I guess, because they didn't even let us get it onto the table. I turned the crank and it rose above ground level, still on the spit. Hands started flying, tearing at the skin. Even the table-saw races stopped. Everybody was gathered around the pig, grasping, groping, and shoving little globules of fat into their mouths. There wasn't nearly enough food for everyone. Blake would have probably thought it was funny.

Over by the back door, I saw an old couple. The woman was small and kind of stooped. She wore a nice pair of dark slacks and a black, frilly blouse. The man had on a navy blue pin-striped suit. His hair was slicked and austere. They were the only people at the party not in jeans. But they were my guests, so I had to greet them.

"Howdy!" I said.

"We're the Rosens," said the woman.

"Who?"

"Blake's parents," the man said. "You invited us. We came from Lexington."

"Sure!" I said. "Sure! Blake's parents! Wow! Come in. We're almost out of pig!"

"We don't eat pig," he said.

"Oh," I said. "We've got coleslaw."

"I'm not so hungry," said Blake's mom.

"Of course," I said.

Randy and Washboard Billy launched into their cover of "Mind Your Own Business."

"I love this song!" I said.

Mrs. Rosen started to cry. Her husband put an arm around her. She seemed to get swallowed into his suit.

"If it makes you feel any better," I said, "we used to have parties like this pretty often. Blake was real happy and fun and had all kinds of friends. This was his favorite kind of music."

The mother just kept crying. Blake's father stroked her hair. He looked at me with pity.

"Blake was our son," he said. "We don't care what kind of music he liked."

"Oh," I said.

God! I was so dumb. I hadn't even thought about it before. These were real people, Blake's parents. It wasn't about a scene or a pose or what kind of a turnout you could get at a funeral. Regular people work all day. They don't have time to

plan parties or think about the most appropriate song for any occasion. I looked at Blake's parents and thought, now that's how to mourn. That's ordinary folk and how they feel. That's what they sing about in country music, at least the old country music, not the synthetic stuff that comes out of Nashville now. And that's what was missing from my own day-to-day life. Blake was a real person. They don't come around that often.

It's been a few days now. I've cleaned up from the party and cut out the newspaper clippings. I'm putting them into a scrapbook that I'll send to Blake's mom.

Goddamn Blake, man.

I've been sitting here listening to his Roy Acuff records. They remind me of him.

I SHOT THE SHERIFF

touré

Every day the bucket a-go a-well
One day the bottom have a drop out

"I Shot the Sheriff"
Bob Marley

Bob knew they'd catch him when dawn came. Now, after midnight in the forest, he could hide. But there were footsteps all around, passing right by him, the bodies stinking of rum. And there was a sinewy line of smoke leaking from his pocket, floating out from the gun buried inside it, the rickety gun that just hours ago had spent a single bullet with the same miraculous precision that David had used to fell Goliath long ago. In a few hours a floodlight called the sun would ease on and the rummy bodies would surely find him and rush him off to a sham trial and a public hanging. But in the forest, in these last moments of earthly freedom, he had the stoic, chin-high courage of a man marching to the gallows for an act he believed in, for this murderer knew that heaven awaited him. Bob shot the sheriff. But he didn't shoot no deputy. Bob was a simple man who grew the sweetest sugarcane in all the county. But each dawn he awoke looking forward to nothing but the hour the sun closed up shop and he could be alone in his candlelit shanty with a good book. Reading a book, he felt, was like planting a seed in the mind. After many years he'd read every book he could find and felt his head brimming with sweet cane. He decided everyone in his hometown had to know this joy, and soon all his profits from sugarcane went to buying books for his neighbors. After each harvest he walked through town giving books to adults and children, dazzling them with stories of the wondrous places the books would transport them to. As sweet cane began growing in minds all over town, everyone came to love Bob. Everyone but Sheriff John Brown. No one could recall how John Brown had become sheriff. No one had ever even seen anyone in the government from which he claimed to derive his authority. But they knew he never went anywhere without his gun, a solid hunk of gleaming black steel so large it looked like a mini-missile launcher. He came round to collect taxes quite often, even though many suspected his badge was homemade. It was a flat slab of gold fashioned, he said, into a five-point star. Most saw five little daggers pointing away from his icy heart. And in the center of that so-called badge someone had stamped the words *Sheriff John Brown*. When he wasn't collecting taxes, he was making overproof white rum that he drank straight from a label-less bottle. Whether he was collecting taxes, making rum, or doing anything at all, Sheriff John Brown was drunk. He'd been drunk for years on end, so long no one could recall what he was like sober. Even he couldn't remember what he was like sober. He had a little moonshine business but he never made money because he drank all the potential profits, and what's more, his overproof rum was so strong even the numbest livers in town refused to process that liquid fire and sent it right back up to the throat. Men said drinking Sheriff's home brew felt like sucking on Death's own nipple. The old ladies wondered how anyone but the devil's spawn could drink rum that toxic all day, every day, and not die. Sheriff thought if he could just take one or two harvests from Bob, with all that free cane he could finally turn a profit, or at least be assured of having plenty of rum for the winter ahead and the one following. But only Bob knew just when to harvest the cane, and each season, before Sheriff could begin moving in to snatch Bob's crops, he was at the market imagining all the books he'd buy for his people. Oh yes, Sheriff John Brown hated him. One day Sheriff waddled into town to collect taxes and saw everyone reading. He didn't know what was inside those books for he couldn't read, but he could see in their eyes that seeds were taking root in all those minds. "Kill them before they grow," he told his men. "Kill them before they grow." His men snatched every book they saw and promptly burned them all. Bob was crushed. He wanted to fight, but no one had ever challenged Sheriff and lived to tell the tale. So Bob went back to raising his cane, and after the next harvest he returned with a stack of books double the size of the last one. But on tax day Sheriff came and took their wages and their books. Men carted off books with children still attached to them, children dragged through the streets while clinging to their books as if to life rafts. Bob saw all this and returned to his land in a fury, planting his biggest crop ever. After the next harvest he'd buy so many books there wouldn't be enough men to find them all, wouldn't be enough fire to burn them all. But one dawn months later Bob awoke to find his crops gone. Sheriff had come in the night and stolen his world. He went inside and stuffed a bag with some clothes, a candle, and a book he could read over and again because his journey would be long. He was going to walk as far away from Sheriff as his feet could stand, because if he stayed he knew one of them would end up dead. On his way out he stopped to say good-bye to his friend Gabriel. Gabriel tried to talk Bob into staying, but they both knew leaving now was prudent. So Gabriel gave Bob a gift he could use on his long, possibly dangerous journey. Bob tried to refuse but Gabriel wouldn't hear it. He gave Bob a gun, but it was the lamest little gun in the world. It was so small you could close your fist around it. It was so rickety it looked as though it had Scotch tape holding its insides together. It was so old it was basically a high-tech slingshot. Gabriel had only one bullet to give Bob, but a bullet from that old thing was likely to slide out of the barrel with less force than you could muster throwing it. Gabriel told Bob if he had to fire it, he should first pray God was on his side, because without His help that bullet just might peek out of the barrel and fall right at Bob's feet. Bob took Gabriel's supposed gift just to avoid being rude, but he knew the little contraption couldn't possibly hurt anyone. Bob hugged him good-bye and turned to go. Then, all of a sudden, he saw Sheriff John Brown, twenty paces away, aiming to shoot him down. There was no time to think, no time to pray. Bob aimed his little gun at the man with a half-spent bottle of rum in one hand and a gleaming missile launcher in the other, and pulled the rusty trigger with no idea what would happen next. But the hammer kicked Bob's one bullet in its ass with all the force it had and that bullet took wings, for that day God was with Bob as He'd been with David long ago, and that blessed bullet flew straight and fast and ripped right through Sheriff John Brown's toy badge, through his sagging tit, and plunged right into his heart, dragging one of the badge's daggers into that Grinchly organ, leaving him on his back, spouting blood like a geyser, soon to be dead. Bob shot the sheriff, and soon he would die for it, but one day he would be pardoned, for the ultimate deputy is God.

author inspiration

1. Bob Marley is the most important recording artist in the world. Chris Martin, the lead singer of Coldplay, a Brit and thus a Beatles fan, told me once, "Everyone goes on about the Beatles being the most important artists of all time, but they're not, Marley is. If you go to any country in the world, you'll be fine if you know how to play some Bob Marley songs. No one in Angola is gonna be impressed if you play

'Paperback Writer,' but if you play 'No Woman, No Cry' . . ."

2. "I Shot the Sheriff" is a story song, and one with a good, dramatic climax that allowed room for some backstory. Many story songs have good characters but no climax or the action takes place offstage.

3. Nearly everyone knows "I Shot the Sheriff," and unless you lack a brain, you love it.

A SIMPLE EXPLANATION
OF THE AFTERLIFE

victor lavalle

Aaaaaaaaaaahhhhhhhhhhh!
Aaaaaaaaaaahhhhhhhhhhh!

"Aluminum"
The White Stripes

She was half in the water, on her back, stained with beer and drowning. A man had grabbed her, dragged her, brought her out to this lake. She coughed a lot. It wasn't even voluntary. He pulled her head up and forced it down. The back of her skull cut on rocks each time. She vomited underwater, but as he pulled her out again, she gasped, sucking the bile into her throat once more. Her sweater was wet, but her pants were dry. While her face was in the green water, little black fish swam past her eyes.

Some kind of stunt fish maybe. They'd come in a school of a hundred, right up to her face, then jolt away. Oodles of these tadpolelike, dust-mote-sized fish. Inconvenient as it seems, she struggled with the fish even as she fought against dying. She blinked defensively. She kicked her legs so hard. The man was kneeling on them. Her body gasped even after she was unconscious. The man held her under for three minutes more.

This happened between green mountains. Not that far from a popular roadway. Right near a modest town of about two thousand. In the shadow of a large device that was built in 1992.

Five enormous vats had been constructed on a hill overlooking the town. They held and heated water. They were different colors: two orange, two yellow, and one red. They were even beautiful, incongruous with the wooded hills. Travelers, on their way to ski, often saw them from the road and stopped to take some pictures.

The five tanks were arranged in a circle on the hill. Rising from the earth in between them was an enormous metal stem with a translucent dome on top; this looked like a toadstool and it made a spectral snapping noise. At night it cackled, too.

When the day was sunny, the dome shone silver. Under a bright moon it turned white. But it was actually clear, the rest just messy false perception. The dome was a device for stealing water from the air.

It was built because the groundwater was terrible. Underground wells had been good to the people here for more than fifty years, and then suddenly all the water that came up smelled like tiger breath. Water with a rancid aftertaste and often burning. They tried decontamination through various chemical means, but it stayed gamy. The townspeople couldn't even trust drinkable Tardash Lake anymore. Every trickle from the earth had curdled.

To condense water out of the atmosphere, the inside of the dome was filled with nearly frozen water. Just above zero degrees. One of the five tanks, the red one, was a refrigerated unit that supplied the inside of the dome with a chilled stream. The cold water sat around inside, filling the apparatus, and this caused the outside of the dome to bead, sweat, collect whenever wind rushed across it. As the moisture turned to drops, they slipped down the outside into gutters at the base of the raised dome. That newfound water went into the five tanks. Four were stored for winter while the fifth was refrigerated and pumped back inside the dome.

The shape of the surrounding mountains had turned this valley into a wind tunnel. On the hill the air came constantly, and all the machine had to do was squat there and accept.

In the coldest months, January through March, the machine slumbered. Otherwise the water chamber inside the dome would freeze and crack. And for those twelve weeks the people of the town would bathe with some frugality.

Now he stops touching her. She lies faceup in the water. The man who killed her stands by a tree in privacy.

The town is steps away. Boys often come through here to play among mice, worms. The town was doing bad before the mayor proposed the moisture condenser. Every summer they thank him on the street, at restaurants. It dies down only when the cooler days make everybody moody.

Faceup in the water. The way her head is tilted she was looking back, seeing the dome upside down. A bright day, and because of the shining glass she mistook it for a piston valve, like on the trumpet she played for six months in grade school. What enormous music, if played correctly! She regretted that she'd never hear the note.

The man plans to weigh her down in the muck by putting stones in her jacket, but there are boys in woods. Loud kids jumping on twigs, or is that snapping the water condenser? Either way, it makes the murderer panic; he's a worthless coward who runs away.

But the kids are actually far off. They're moving in the other direction. Wouldn't have found these two for hours. It's just that in these woods sounds shimmy directly up a tree from the other side of the valley. A fox can seem to be on your lap when it's howling in the next county.

The noise of boys provides time alone. If there were any wiggle left in her, this would be her chance to run. Flies tickle her fingers, but she can't itch anymore.

The rocks right by the water smell of turpentine because two days ago a local artist wanted to put stones around his doorstep. He came here and chose fifteen. His clothes stank of the turpentine he'd been using to thin his oils. That smell will camouflage her decomposition. It'll take even longer to discover her in this position. It'll take all winter, because soon there will be snow.

In a few weeks

Today there's a dead woman, faceup, half in the dirty

water, with sunlight warming her exposed skin. The sun is also changing the water. Turning the surface to mist. Into an invisible gas that supplies the device just yards away.

Why do you think we get buried?

Or burned, or otherwise hidden away. No one wants to see the corpse, that's true; your loved one's yellowing eye. But also, we evaporate. She evaporates. Right now, it's begun. She dissipates through her pores. From there a breeze catches on to her newly released ether, then traps it flat against the dome. Otherwise the day is uneventful.

The three prominent mountains around the town are called Redrush, Ici, and Cloak.

The woods ran yellow and orange just months ago. Mothers received bright leaves pasted on poster board from their children. But now the most appealing thing about the woods is made of metal moving parts because the condenser sure looks prettier than naked maple trees.

The town is used to the device, it's been there for years, so the technicians, the schoolteachers, dairy farmers, and shop foremen don't look at it. Even the kids aren't spooked by the condenser's sounds, they find other ways to get scared in the woods.

So the woman is slapped flat against the outside of the dome, but goes unnoticed. Though what would anyone have done? It's not as though there's the outline of her body in full view. It's her soul up there, which, relative to a person's figure, is rather small.

The outer surface of the dome shows these millions of smattered water drops, in no discernible pattern, simply dripping down the sides, but she has condensed into a perfect oval of gray liquid amid them. She slides down as one flat, gray, soggy disk.

She weighs forty-four grams. Water that drops into the gutter to be drawn down into the second yellow vat. In there she's no longer a disk, more of a gray bubble. Floating in the town's drinking water.

She floats for such a long time.

The water in the first orange tank drains, and then the next orange tank is tapped, and so forth around the circuit. When the land begins its thaw in April, seven months from now, the machine will be reinvigorated and condensation begins again.

She doesn't know where she is in the yellow vat because she isn't thinking anymore. There isn't any point where she imagines, I'm in a tub, I'm floating in water, I was killed, I had nice toes.

Eventually she won't hold. That little sphere of soul is going to dissolve by and by. Definitely by the time her yellow tank is tapped. Once it is, her ether will be pulled in all directions. Fifty houses flush toilets simultaneously. Two hundred people brush their teeth. A woman washes dishes and grunts that the work is tougher than usual today as she tries to get these new gray streaks off her plates. Where did they come from? she asks her husband.

A young boy refills the ice tray in his home. For nights

and nights the dead woman will cool his pop. He never much notices the little gray center of each ice cube. Have you? That foggy imprint is like a signature. It's more accurate than any given name. The young boy takes a cube to bed. He chews it. He would like to drive a truck when he gets older. She's the last taste in his mouth before he sleeps.

I chose "Aluminum" by the White Stripes because it sounded a lot like Black Sabbath to me. Since I was raised on heavy metal—Metallica, Iron Maiden, and Anthrax were my top three—it made me feel nostalgic. There are no lyrics, just Jack White's voice (highly distorted) crying out again and again. As the music shifts, the single line, "Aaaaaaaaaahhhh-hhhhhhh," takes on different meanings. At first it sounds ominous, then pained, then sad, but finally, triumphant. At least that's how it sounded to me.

I'd been to Iceland recently, camping in the countryside for a month. While there, I'd seen an emormous water tower in which water is kept and heated to help the people of Reykjavik get through the harsh winters. The look of it stayed with me. For a long time I'd wanted to write a little fable that explained why ice cubes have that little gray ball in the middle, because when I was a kid, I never understood how it happened. The look of that gray blob always seemed eerie to me.

So when I heard "Aluminum," a few stray pieces clicked together: the water tower, the gray blobs in ice, a song about transcendence, and another image that had been on my mind, a dead young girl facedown in dirty water. So then I wrote this.

THE ETERNAL HELEN

heidi julavits

You're all what you perceive
What comes is better than what came before

"I Found a Reason"
Cat Power
(Lyrics by the Velvet Underground)

lgar and I met in first class, on a Viking Air flight from New York to Helsinki. I was en route to an Emotional Rigidity Retreat at a Lapland ice hotel, a birthday present from my best friend, Pam. At first glance, Elgar appeared to be a businessman, a very, very tired one, or maybe *jaded* is a better word. He had clearly seen too much of something. He wore a navy flannel eye pillow, the elasticized leather straps winding around his cranium and pushing his hair upward into a pouf that shuddered under the direct blasts from his air vent.

I ordered red wine from a bald steward; I leafed through the literature Pam had given me about the retreat and half-watched the Scandinavian in-flight movie about a woman and a man with a pack of sled dogs. In the opening scene, the man and woman are waving good-bye to a village of indigenous Sami, who seem to find the man and woman very stupid. The man and the woman slalom through a graveyard where all the tombstones are covered in fur, or maybe it was a Scandinavian form of lichen, but it looked to me like fur. It is night. It is day. It is night again. Morning dawns, the sky is overcast with dismal fish-scale clouds. The woman cuts her finger on a sharp piece of jerky. The man has a cough. The dogs fight. That afternoon, as they're crossing a lake, the ice cracks open. The dogs and the man drown. The woman cries inside her sealskin hood, and her tears freeze on her cheeks as she builds a pathetic snow crucifix beside the hole. The woman retraces her steps and returns to the Sami village. The women point at her and laugh as the fat chief leads her into his fornication hut. Without words, without the music, the scene was hardly more upsetting than a car commercial.

The bald steward paused the movie for the duty-free service, and my seatmate fumbled with his wallet. A business card dropped onto my tray table. I picked it up. It read, Elgar's Disposables.

Elgar, I said. That's a strange name.

Elgar pushed up his eye pillow, revealing a solitary, dumbstruck eye. He looked at me. He looked at me. He returned the pillow to its previous position.

Elgar was the name of a Swedish warrior, he said, who raped his way across the arctic tundra. Or so my mother told me.

You mother is Swedish? I asked.

No, but she was fondled once at a skating party.

I'm sorry to hear that, I said. My name is Helen.

Very pleased to meet you, Helen, Elgar said, and offered me a flask.

We got very drunk together and made fun of the woman in the movie, who was violated by every Sami male this side of the Gudvangen fjord. When Elgar stood to use the rest room, he left a doglegged sliver of white paper in his seat. It looked like a Chinese fortune. It read: *The woman who lies prone on the bed must have a reason, otherwise she is pathetic.*

I phoned Pam in New York from the baggage carousel, propellering Elgar's business card between my first two fingers. Pam was back at home again after serving a ten-day sentence in a white-collar prison for hacking into her son's school database and enhancing his Dante grade. Her computer skills made her an unparalleled friend and travel agent.

Sounds like your usual loser, Helen, Pam said. She was invested in my hating men as much as she did. She was forever sending me to retreats where the man-as-monster message was the subtext to every chanting session and massage.

He's actually a bit of an unusual loser, I said.

What does he look like? Pam asked.

I described his eye pillow. I described his beard. There wasn't really much else to describe.

I imagine having sex with him will feel lonely and anonymous but hurt a great deal, Pam said. I imagine he'll have hairs on his penis like a cat, and that the hairs will reverse inside of you when he pulls out and draw blood. Where did he go to college?

I admitted I did not know.

Sounds like a Haverford man, she said with some wistfulness. Did you know Haverford is harder to get into than Brown?

Really? I said.

Really, Pam said.

She agreed, grudgingly, to book me on each of Elgar's Viking Air flights.

I went to the Emotional Rigidity Retreat at the ice hotel. The retreaters, all nine of them, were rich American woman like myself with diamond rings on the wrong fingers and faces twitching full of that greedy hope you encounter at spas and PTA meetings and sample sales. We wore parkas with the hotel's insignia on the hood, we practiced chanting in an igloo, and drank white wine that looked green against the igloo walls. We took turns confessing the story of our most recent failed romance. When a woman finished her confession, usually in tears, the retreat leader would point a finger at her and laugh uproariously. It seemed cruel initially, but by the end of the weekend we were all laughing and pointing fingers inside our mittens, and the woman we were laughing at would blush and bend her head, as though she were an unfunny person who'd inadvertently told a first-rate joke. I left the retreat with a drawstring chamois gift bag full of lip balm, antacid tablets, and a white pleather journal with the word *Resolve* embossed across the cover. Inside was an epigraph: *Nothing increases a woman's resolve like repeated exposure to depravity.*

We first made love in Helsinki, after three gin drinks at a hotel bar where we were lorded over by three disconsolate elk heads and a team of straw-haired sales representatives from Swedish National Plastic. Elgar told me he was a businessman who dealt in disposable woods, the sort that is used for chopsticks, toothpicks, tongue depressors, shish-kebab spears, cut-rate coffins. Primarily, he sold wood to undertakers. He bragged about his extremely low IQ, the fact that he didn't learn to read until he was nine, and long division remained beyond him at the age of thirty-five. He traveled with a single briefcase and a nylon backpack full of pills. He always wore the same suit, of charcoal gray wool. His grandfather had invented the massaging eye pillows that Elgar wore during the greater part of every day, that are available in every duty-free store across the Western world.

Our suite had a cold mink headboard that smelled of the eucalyptus toilet water the maids splashed around the room with impunity. Contrary to Pam's predictions, Elgar was hairless below the chin, white and ill-defined. Making love to him was not unlike involving my whole body with an underdone breakfast pastry, yeasty and chilly and a tiny bit sour. We finished up and all I could see was a cooler full of mink headboards, stacked against each other like furry tombstones. I told him this as we lay against it, eating herring with our fingers from the zinc guest fridge.

You try to be appear morbid, he said, an eye pillow pushed up around his forehead goggle-style and lending the moment an après-ski feel. But I can see you're just an aimless romantic.

Aimless romance can be morbid, I said.

In an ideal world, he said. Pass the herring, please.

In fact, I've never been in love before, I said. I've decided it is senseless to look.

Glad to hear it, Helen, he said. Love is a dull and predictable business. Perhaps you were molested as a child?

Not that I recall, I said.

Elgar shook his head. So you've always lacked ambition.

We made love again against the mink headboard, which felt colder than before, even though the room was full of tepid steam heat and the smell of pickled fish and my strange compulsion to adore him, for very little reason.

We established a routine. Elgar introduced me to his Chinese tailors, and they made me matching charcoal suits with derisive fortunes in the pockets (You are no catch, madame). I dyed my blond hair white and parted it over my face so that one dark eye peered out. I'd read magazines in the hotel suite while Elgar went to lunch with undertakers and insisted on charging ludicrous prices for his cheap wood. When they refused to pay his price, he'd slam a bread roll onto the table, he'd toss wine in the face of the undertaker, or sometimes he'd simply break down weeping, his beard dragging through his coq au vin.

It was his idea to have me accompany him as his associate.

He presented me to the undertakers as Miss Winterbottom. Elgar and the undertaker would ignore me through the aperitifs, the *amuse bouches*.

Miss Winterbottom, Elgar would say after the waiter had served our first course, I see you've gained some weight.

I would squint a scornful teal eye at him between my white hair.

Honest to God, Miss Winterbottom, it could just be the light in here, but you're looking a touch too portly for my tastes. Maybe I ought to start chasing you around the office a bit more vigorously.

The undertaker would cough into his linen napkin or busy himself with his turtle consommé.

This is what I hire her for, Elgar would say to the undertaker, patting him confidentially on the elbow and sending his half-lifted spoonful of consommé spattering over his thin shirt. She is my sexual associate. I pay to fondle her freely with no emotional attachments. If it's part of the job description, there's no chance of a harassment suit. Is there, Miss Winterbottom?

I would apply a coat of gray lipstick and remove a fountain pen from my charcoal suit. I'd unscrew the top and lick the quill. My tongue would turn black.

The undertaker would attempt to excuse himself, but Elgar would order a very, very expensive bottle of Lynch-Bages, and the undertaker would agree to stay for one more course. I'd put a hand on his knee and squeeze gently. By dessert, the undertaker would be drunk and leering at me with my white hair and my one eye. His eyes would soften and a sigh would escape between his lips, on which a dab of French butter lingered.

Don't let her fool you, Elgar would admonish the undertaker. She's a wicked little cur, aren't you, Miss Winterbottom? The sad thing is, she cannot fall in love. That's what happens when you sell yourself the way she has, your heart becomes encased in scar tissue with a trampoline-like consistency. You could stamp on her heart and you'd be launched into the sky or hit your head on the ceiling, depending on where you were at the time. She could help you see the stars or crush your silly skull. And did you bring the contracts, you senseless hussy?

I would produce a thick contract, stinking of eucalyptus, from my suit coat. I did not wear a blouse and allowed the undertaker to catch a glimpse of my white breast, my mauve nipple like a tiny bird giblet, beneath which my trampoline heart beat away. I left my lapel gaping open for the rest of the meal, not caring if the waiter saw, or the busboy, or the wine steward. Elgar would unfold the contract on the table before the undertaker, pinning the papers down with the salt well and a dirty salad fork. He'd run over the terms of the contract, lightning fast, contradicting himself numerous times and referring to various subsections and Roman numerals. The undertaker would nod and nod as I moved my hand north of his knee, crawling my fingers, spider-style, up his thigh while enacting an air of erotically charged ennui.

And so as you see here, Elgar would say, directing the undertaker's wandering attention to the last page of the contract, I am quite up-front about the fact that my product is unreliable, of the poorest imaginable quality, and rarely ships when scheduled, that I do not accept returns, nor do I entertain complaints, written or tape-recorded, if the wood for which you've paid an exorbitant fee in full before seeing a single dry-rotted board fails to arrive at all. You'll see here, the signature line, where I'd like you to draw a little picture of yourself.

Elgar would snap his fingers and I would surrender my fountain pen to the undertaker, who would, invariably, draw a pathetic little stick figure, often tipping over to one side, with a very long torso, stubby legs, a tiny blank head. Elgar would fold the contract into thirds and shove it into his coat pocket, making an excuse about a golf game or a sailing appointment, even though it was November and Scandinavia was entombed in ice. He would hustle me into my coat and the two of us would scuttle importantly through the dining room, pausing at the potted spruce flanking the host stand in order to thrust the contract deep into the green needles. Elgar would put his arm under my charcoal coat and wrap it tightly around my waist, grabbing me near to him so that we weren't exactly hugging as we walked, we were more like one gangly creature that couldn't quite get its balance, but which strode confidently through the coatroom and out the revolving door as though it had a purpose in the world, no matter how contrived and awkward.

•   •   •

In early December, Elgar began to grow bored of our Winterbottom ruse, even though I wore less and less clothing to our lunches, even though I let the undertakers pinch my exposed nipple as they drew their little stick figures.

Don't you have somewhere you need to be? Elgar inquired over breakfast. We were eating in bed, and he pounded the cranium of his soft-boiled egg brutishly with a butter knife. The yoke spattered over the headboard, the brilliant yellow congealing on the fur.

No, I said.

Don't you have a job? he asked.

No, I said. I've never had a job in my life until you hired me. Yolk hung from his beard.

Everyone must have a job, he said. Look at me, for example. I don't need to work, but I do, I have a job, I have lunches with undertakers.

That's not a job, I said. That's a hobby.

Elgar raised a dirty spoon. My grandfather used to say, if a man's hobby is his job, then he is some measure of a genius.

But you're not a genius, I said. You have a very low IQ.

Nonsense, Elgar said. I only told you that so you'd pity me. I like to be pitied by strange women on planes. It reminds me of my youth.

I nodded dumbly.

Ask me what 2,345 divided by 453 is, he said.

I didn't respond.

It's 5.18. How about 33,334 divided by 334? It's 99.8. Do you believe me now?

Elgar hopped out of bed and began unwrapping his new suit.

Where are you going? I asked.

Elgar used a razor to cut open his suit coat pockets.

He held the fortune in his palm. It shuddered under the weak wind tossed off by the ceiling fan.

Engaged apathy is not an ironic form of adoration, he read.

Is that really what it says? I asked.

He pulled a second fortune from the breast pocket. *The woman who lies prone on the bed must have a reason,* he read. *But occasionally she does not. This woman is called, in some medical circles, The Eternal Helen.*

Elgar put the fortunes in the waste can.

You don't mind settling the bill, do you? he asked. I've got a plane to catch.

I pretended to read the paper while Elgar packed his pills. When I heard the door close, I phoned Pam in New York. The connection was terrible, punctuated by a lot of terrible hissing noises.

Pam? I said. Are you in prison again?

I'm at my son's jai alai match. Can't really talk now, Helen. How's Edwin?

He left me, I said.

He can't leave you. You're booked on his flight today at ten forty-five.

I wonder if I'm forcing things, I said.

He won't even know you're there, per usual, Pam said. He always wears that stupid eye bag, doesn't he? Just—

Pam dropped her cell phone. I heard the sound of boys screaming and punching each other's padded bodies.

Pam? I said.

I heard Pam cursing, *Get your hands off me, you ultra-suede phony, your kid doesn't have a hope at Swarthmore.* The ultra-suede phony said something indecipherable in a high-pitched voice, the boys screamed louder, and the line went dead.

I cut open the pocket of my new suit and extracted the fortune from inside. It read, *My condolences, Miss Winterbottom. You're in love.*

I decided not to follow Elgar that day. I went to a disreputable bathhouse and allowed a woman with a mustache to whip my naked back and thighs with a ribbon of maroon kelp. I sat in a stone sauna beneath the city streets and listened to the trolleys roll overhead. I took myself out for bad Japanese food. The fish was cold, the tea cold, the rice cold, my bone chopsticks wrapped with somebody's gray hair, and the waiter a sneering, tobacco-toothed Finn with soy sauce on his lapel. I returned to my hotel room, shivering my way along the Katajanokka in the shadow of the cruise ships, dodging tipsy Swedes with vomit on their chins. The room was green with eucalyptus mist. My sinuses yawned open and I started to weep, for no reason I was able to discern.

I woke up the next morning to a white sun. I called Pam as I drank my coffee. She was at the police station filing assault charges against the ultra-suede phony.

I don't know what you're whining about.

I could hear the click-click-click as she typed her testimony into the station computer.

You should consider yourself lucky to be rid of the pervert, Pam continued.

He's not a pervert, I said.

He's one step away from a necrophiliac, she said. That's the only reason I agreed to participate in this charade, Helen. You know what they say: Nothing increases a woman's resolve like repeated exposure to depravity.

I promised Pam I would keep away from Elgar through the holidays. I hooked up with a divorced undertaker named Silor, who was still in love with his wife, and the two of us took a cruise ship around Scandinavia. The ship's pool was turned into an ice-skating rink and the two of us slid around under the salty night skies, holding hands and feeling nothing. I called Pam from the dead middle of the North Sea, where the reception was unfathomably good.

Do you still miss him? Pam asked. What's his name again—Elwood?

I suppose, I said.

Helen, Helen, Helen, she said. Did I tell you my son "scored" in the ninety-ninth percentile?

Hooray, I said.

And that bitch who hit me at the jai alai match—I arranged it so her boy is sucking state school bilgewater somewhere in the low sixties.

Pam, I said. Sometimes I worry about you. You're becoming brittle.

I am winning, Helen. Triumphant is not the same as brittle, unless you're you.

You're becoming brittle, I repeated.

Is the sex good with the undertaker? Pam asked.

It is what it is, I replied.

I imagine it's like being fucked by a tall, white candle. That's how I imagine it. All waxy and cold. So when do you dock? And if you had to choose between Carlton and Oberlin, which would you choose? Oberlin is a lot more hospitable to homosexuals.

Is your son gay? I asked. Above me, in the dark, I heard the hum of an airplane engine.

No! Pam said. I just think homosexuals are smarter, but care less about grades. My son could have very smart, very chic friends who wouldn't compete over GPAs.

I dock tomorrow, I said.

I'll book you a flight, Pam said.

Where has he been? I asked. The airplane hum grew louder. It messed up our reception.

I don't know where he's been, but I know where he is, Pam said.

Where is he? I asked. I could barely hear her.

Look up, Pam said, and her phone cut out.

Silor and I parted amiably at the dock in Helsinki. I checked into the room with the mink headboard. I pretended Elgar was in the shower, I pretended he was wearing his eye pillow and lost in the closet. He was here, though. He was here, and

I lay on the bed, I rubbed against the mink headboard and waited. I thought, if a woman is prone on a bed, she must have a reason. I missed my flight, I missed another flight. I ate everything in the zinc guest fridge.

After three days, I showered and put on a new gray suit, fresh from its brown paper wrapping. The fortune said, *Who has more emotions? A squirrel frozen in a waterfall or Miss Winterbottom? Ha ha ha!* The suit hung off me and let the cold air from the sidewalk up inside it. I walked into a boutique and bought a white coat, a white fur hat, a pair of elk-skin gloves the color of the teeth of the waiter in the Japanese restaurant.

I wandered through town until town was gone. Soon I came to a country club. There were tire tracks pressed into the snowy road, so I walked in them. The road curved to the left and I saw the clubhouse and a frozen lake and the white golf course beyond. I saw a pair of men out on the first tee, or maybe it was the second tee. They were practicing their swings in the knee-high snow. Each clumsy swipe lofted a sparkling wing of snow into the air.

I recognized the winter sporting-eye pillow. I had worn it to bed, once, when the hotel's heating system failed.

You're not following through, I heard Elgar say. The eye pillow was pushed up into his hair.

Silor gripped his club and sliced meanly at the snow.

No, no, Elgar said. Are you thinking of your wife when you swipe at the snow?

Silor nodded, grim-faced. Elgar handed him his flask.

Well, don't, Elgar said. First rule of golf is to shelve your rage at the clubhouse. Look at me, he said. Look at how I have shelved my rage so that this driver—he shook the driver—this driver is not a barometer of my myriad disappointments. Do you understand?

Silor returned the flask. Elgar threw it into the snow. The flask sank from view.

Now then, Elgar said. Watch.

He fumbled in his hair, pushing the eye pillow over his eyes. He wiggled his bottom back and forth, he made a few slow-motion strokes through the air, he gripped and re-gripped the club.

Maybe I made a noise, or maybe I was simply breathing louder than the wind.

Elgar froze. He unslumped himself and directed his eye-pillowed gaze at me.

Miss Winterbottom, he said.

Silor turned. Saw me. Raised a halfhearted palm.

You should be ashamed of yourself, Miss Winterbottom. According to rumor, you've been a very bad employee, sleeping with the clients. How does that make us look at Elgar's Disposables? How does it make us look?

I didn't respond.

It makes us look unprofessional, Miss Winterbottom. It makes it look like we're running a class-act brothel instead of an unreliable wood supply company. I need not tell you that this creates confusion with our brand identity.

I'm actually not so confused, Silor said.

Shut up, Elgar said. You wouldn't know an orifice from a wormhole.

Silor kicked around in the snow with a black-booted foot, searching for the flask.

I think, if you want your job back, which is what I'm guessing you want, then you should take off your clothes, Miss Winterbottom, and lie down here on the snow.

He tapped at an untouched snowy spot with his driver. The driver made a whispery blue divot that the wind quickly erased.

I stared at Elgar and pretended that, beneath it all, he was a good man with some queer ideas. It was easier than admitting we were two eternally cold souls incapable of thawing, for no especially good reason. But next to him, I would never appear emotionally lacking, and isn't that the definition of a soul mate? A person who allows you to appear gloriously as something you are not and can never, will never be?

I lay in the snow and took off my clothes. Elgar picked up his antique driver and placed the wooden club on my forehead. He ran the club along the ridge of my profile, he slid it down my throat, between my breasts. This sounds so humiliating, I know, but I cannot explain that this was a moment of tenderness between two Eternal Helens, this was a moment of gorgeous depravity for the invulnerables of this world. Elgar lifted a snowy boot and pressed the treads into my chest.

And where will you send me, Miss Winterbottom? he asked. I want to see the stars.

I was about to answer when my phone rang. Silor wrestled with my coat, and the phone fell into the snow, leaving a little heart-shaped hole.

Silor handed the phone to Elgar.

Hello? he said.

I looked at Silor. Silor shrugged.

Miss Winterbottom, how wonderful to hear from you. And how's your son? Got into Harvard I hear? Yes, yes, I believe there's an excellent amount of homosexuals there. Would you like to speak to your predecessor?

Elgar dropped the phone on my belly. I put it to my ear.

Pam? I said.

I don't know what the hell he's talking about, Pam said. Who's Miss Winterbottom?

Pam, I—

Don't listen to a thing he says, Helen. The man's a necrophiliac, I swear he is. You'll be dead before he gets another hard-on. I'm thinking maybe this method of mine isn't working for you. Have you thought about getting a job, Helen?

I have a job, I said.

You've never had a job in your life. You don't know what work is. Did you hear my son got into Harvard? That little bastard owes me everything. I told him if he doesn't call me twice a week, I'll make sure he flunks out.

I dropped the phone into the snow and propped myself up on my elbow. I was alone on the golf course. Two pairs of footprints led into the woods. I heard laughter between the trees, I heard Pam's voice distantly saying *a squirrel in a wa-*

terfall or maybe it was *you're too spineless Helen* or *look up*. I looked up but the sky was the same color as the snow, and the whole world felt like the inside of something, like a furred, soundless interior, safe and empty. I started to giggle, or cry, I wasn't sure which, but the snot on my face made me colder than an avalanche worth of snow. I reached for my coat pocket to get a tissue. Instead I discovered a tiny filigree of paper, airmail thin and crumby to the touch, as though it had just been cracked free of its cookie prison.

It said, *If a woman is not built for laughter at her expense, she is not built for love.*

author inspiration

Cat Power's mournful cover of the Velvet Underground's "I Found a Reason" is all the more haunting a rendition when you listen to the original—a jaded, jangling, tongue-in-cheek love song that bears no resemblance to Cat Power's quasi-dirge. I liked the idea of doing a "third-generation" cover, one that would blend Reed's jaded with Marshall's haunted and collapse the two versions into one that spoke to both approaches. The main characters, thus, are loosely based on what I know of Reed and Marshall. Helen hides behind her hair, as Marshall is famed for doing at performances, and Elgar is a picky eater who dines at fancy restaurants. I used to waitress at an aggressively romantic French restaurant in Manhattan that was, inexplicably, a favorite of Reed's. But there was a lot of velvet, and since, in the name of romance, the restaurant was dark (and abutted the Holland Tunnel), you did feel you were underground. Regardless, Reed was a refreshingly grumpy presence in the midst of the near-nightly wedding engagements and the banquette snuggling and the vaguely desperate quality to everyone's supposed happiness. That incongruity—a curmudgeon in the house of desperate love—is what, I hope, my version captures.

SWAMPTHROAT

arthur bradford

> *I'm on my way to the promised land . . .*
> *I'm on the Highway to Hell . . .*
>
> **"Highway to Hell"**
> **AC/DC**

William "Swampthroat" Simpson was my idol. He was a heavyset, lumbering oaf of a guy who wandered around our town with his head down and long, stringy hair covering his eyes. When he was seventeen, years before I met him, a chain saw slipped from his hands and bounced up into his neck. He lost four pints of blood that day, but they saved him at the hospital. To cover up the damage, the doctors placed a series of skin graphs on his neck, leaving his throat scarred and covered in patches of different colors. It was difficult for him to shave properly after that and there were often stray whiskers, long and curly, sprouting from his neck. This was why we all called him Swampthroat. He wasn't fond of the name and always introduced himself as William, but he allowed us to call him Swampthroat all the same.

I first met Swampthroat when he started dating my older sister, Robin. He was twenty-four years old then and I was sixteen. Robin had sort of a wild streak and it was considered an unusual thing to do, to go out with a guy like Swampthroat. I was sitting on the couch when Robin first brought him home. He clomped inside wearing big leather boots, tracking dirt onto the floor.

"Next time take your boots off," Robin said to him.

"Sorry," said Swampthroat. He had a deep, scratchy voice. It was sort of timid and quieter than what you'd expect. Maybe his vocal chords were damaged, too. He saw me sitting there and walked toward me, still tracking dirt behind him.

"My name's William," he said, extending his hand.

"Hi," I said. His hand was fat and meaty. It was dirty, too.

"You can call him Swampthroat," said Robin. "Everyone else does."

Swampthroat nodded in agreement and we shook hands.

Robin led him upstairs and they went into her bedroom. Robin liked to listen to loud rock music. Swampthroat enjoyed this kind of music as well, and together they would listen to it for hours. Robin wasn't bad looking or unpopular and I wondered at first why she would want to be associated with a guy like Swampthroat. But, as I came to see later, it was his reckless side that made him attractive.

Later on that day, after he and Robin had left the house, our mother came home and said, "What's that smell?"

I said, "Swampthroat was here."

That winter Swampthroat drove his van off a bridge. He'd been going fast, hit some ice, and went into a skid. He and his van landed in the shallow river below the bridge and he nearly drowned because the impact knocked him out. They found him lying facedown in the cold water. No one was sure how long he'd been lying like that, but it was determined that because the water was so cold, it had slowed his heart down and allowed him to survive without oxygen for an unusually long time.

"You're a lucky man, William," the doctor said.

Without his van Swampthroat had no way to get to work, so Robin let him use her car, a little hatchback, which had once belonged to our father. Swampthroat crashed that car, too. He hit a deer one night and then plowed into a pile of rocks. The car could still drive though and Swampthroat chased down the deer, which had been limping by the side of the road. He then killed it with one of the large rocks from the pile he'd run into.

"It was suffering," he explained.

Swampthroat stood at our doorway with blood on his hands, telling us the story. Outside, in front of our house, sat Robin's beat-up hatchback. Tied to its roof was the dead deer.

"You idiot," said Robin.

"I didn't want it to go to waste," he said.

Robin broke up with him then. She'd had enough. Before he left, Swampthroat took me out behind the house and showed me how to clean and dress the deer for eating. He did it all with a small hunting knife and some rope. It was sort of like cleaning a fish, except messier, and with more fur. He presented the venison to Robin and my mother as a gift, to help offset the damage he'd done to the car. It was a lot of meat and my mother looked at it perplexed.

"What am I supposed to do with this?" she said, once he had left.

I inherited Robin's hatchback after that because I was just then learning to drive. The car worked all right even though its front end was wrinkled up and the windshield was cracked. I had to wash the deer blood off it, too. I didn't have an official license, just a learner's permit, which allowed me to drive with another, older person in the car. But I often took the car out anyway, by myself, just to have the feeling of being away on my own.

One time I was driving along the State Road and I saw Swampthroat standing by a billboard with his thumb out, hitchhiking. I was surprised to see him there and passed him by. I went a mile or so down the road and then realized he had probably recognized the car. I figured I had better turn around and pick him up. It was doubtful that anyone else would stop for him.

When I pulled up next to him, Swampthroat seemed relieved to see that it wasn't Robin at the wheel. He got inside and immediately the car filled with his damp, grungy smell, the odor of Swampthroat.

"So, you got yourself some wheels," he said to me.

"That's right, thanks to you."

"Did you eat that deer?"

"Not yet. I don't think so."

"Tell your mom to cook it up," he said. "Make a stew. That's good meat."

"Okay."

We drove for a while down the State Road before Swampthroat asked me where I was going.

"I'm just driving," I told him.

"Oh, right." He thought for a minute, peering ahead at the open road. "Maybe you could take me to see a friend?"

"How far is it?"

"About an hour."

"You have money for gas?" I asked him.

"Sure."

This was a concern because although the hatchback was small, it didn't get good mileage. I was going broke driving it around. We stopped at a gas station and Swampthroat used his last six dollars to put gas in the tank. It turned out he'd lost his job on account of not having a car. I noticed, too, once we got going again, that his knuckles were scabbed up and swollen.

"I got in a tussle," he explained.

We drove forty miles down the State Road and then he told me to slow down. He leaned forward and scanned the side of the road.

"Up there," he said. "See that sign?"

There was a hand-painted wooden sign a little ways ahead of us. It marked the entrance to a small dirt road.

"Turn there," he said to me.

When we got up close, I was able to read the words on the sign. Painted in drippy black letters, it said, "Highway to Hell."

We drove down this road, hardly a highway, for several miles. I'd never been this way before. Grass was growing up between the tire tracks, and several times the underside of the hatchback scraped loudly against the earth below, especially on Swampthroat's side where the car rode lower.

Finally we reached a sad-looking shack tucked into a nook in the woods. A small yard had been cleared away out front, and rows of blue plastic barrels were scattered about within a maze of chicken-wire fencing. Swampthroat explained that chickens of various rare breeds were living inside those barrels. The proprietor of the shack, a woman named Tilly, raised them and sold them to collectors.

"She's famous for her hens," he said, "known around the world."

A wobbly old hound shimmied it's way out from under the shack and began barking at us.

"I better go inside," said Swampthroat.

He made no mention of me going with him and I was just as happy to wait there in the car. Swampthroat walked past the growling hound and knocked on the door. It opened up and he went inside.

The hound lay down on the grass and ignored me. I watched the blue barrels for signs of the famous hens inside. I figured they must have been sleeping because I saw nothing, though I did hear an occasional cluck. Eventually Swampthroat emerged from the house carrying a small paper sack and walking more quickly than usual. He opened up the car door and threw his big body inside.

"Let's go," he said.

I started up the car, began to turn it around. An older woman wrapped up in a camouflage army coat stepped out of the house and stood there glaring at us. Her long gray hair was done up in an untidy bun with the loose strands flying about her head.

"Is that Tilly?" I asked.

"Yes," said Swampthroat. "Let's go."

A younger, potbellied man came walking out from behind the house. He was holding some kind of wooden device with a short rope attached to it.

"Let's go," said Swampthroat again.

The potbellied man stopped walking toward us and raised the wooden device up to his shoulder. It was a crossbow, a homemade job constructed of two-by-fours and regular household rope. I pressed down on the gas and we lurched forward down the bumpy dirt road, not moving very fast. A loud metallic thud rang out as something smacked hard into the back of the car. In the rearview mirror I saw the potbellied man stooped over, reloading his crossbow. We plowed ahead, barreling down that "Highway to Hell" as fast as I dared to drive, and that man didn't get a chance to fire his weapon at us again.

Once we got out to the State Road, I pulled over and we took a look at the back of the car. A metal arrow, about a foot long, was stuck firmly in the back door. It had pierced right through the car's body.

"Motherfucker," said Swampthroat.

"Who was that?" I asked.

"That's Lionel. He's Tilly's son."

We got back in the car and sped toward home with the engine roaring so loudly we couldn't hear each other speak. I was pushing it, fearing further attacks from Lionel, though Swampthroat assured me that was doubtful.

"He never leaves that house," he said.

The paper sack that Swampthroat had brought out of Tilly's shack contained several handfuls of dried-up mushrooms. They were of the hallucinatory variety. Apparently Lionel cultivated them in boxes that he stored under the house. Swampthroat planned to sell the mushrooms and return to the shack with payment at a later date, but I guess he hadn't worked out the terms to Lionel's satisfaction before he left.

After about twenty miles of high-speed progress we ran out of gas on the State Road. Swampthroat pointed out correctly that he was less likely to elicit sympathy from strangers, so I had to hitchhike to the gas station and hassle people for spare change to buy more fuel. Each time I approached a car for money, I was scared I would find Tilly and Lionel inside ready for retribution. But that didn't happen and eventually we made it back to town, where I dropped off Swampthroat and he wandered away into the night.

I didn't see Swampthroat for a few weeks after that. I asked Robin if she knew what he was up to, but she said no and added that I shouldn't be interested in his antics anyway.

"That man is trouble," she said.

"When are we going to eat that deer meat?" I asked my mother.

"Never," she said.

When I finally did see Swampthroat again, he was passed out, lying on someone's front lawn. At first I thought he was napping there, but then I examined him more closely, and I saw that he was passed out from drinking. I touched him with the tip of my foot to wake him up.

He opened his eyes and I asked, "What's up?"

Swampthroat sat up and looked around him.

"Did you pay Lionel back yet?" I asked.

"Lionel?"

"For the mushrooms?"

"No," he said. "No, I didn't."

"You should do that."

"I don't have the money."

"Oh." I didn't have much money myself. If I did, I probably wouldn't have given it to him though. I wasn't sure how much a bag of mushrooms was worth anyway.

Swampthroat got up and dusted himself off. He stumbled around, squinting in the daylight and straightening out his clothing. He wiped his eyes and surveyed the surroundings, confused, it seemed, as to how he'd ended up there. I admired him at that moment, the way he took things in stride and carelessly allowed himself to wander so far off course.

"How's Robin?" he asked.

"She's good."

"What about the venison? Did your mom make a stew?"

"No. She doesn't want it."

"Oh."

We walked together into town, where Swampthroat bought himself a large can of beer, a "tallboy." He drank it out in the open and said he would have offered me a sip, but I was underaged.

"You still have that car," he asked, "the hatchback?"

"Yes."

"I need another ride, back to Tilly's place."

"I don't know." There was a small, rusted hole in the back of the hatchback where Lionel's arrow had once been. People had asked me if it was a bullet hole, and I had told them truthfully that it was not.

"We'll stop by your house first," he said. "I've got an idea."

Swampthroat's plan was to load my car up with the unused deer meat from our freezer. We'd take it out to Tilly's place and Swampthroat would present it to them as payment for Lionel's mushrooms. He seemed to think this would more than satisfy them.

"That's a whole deer," he said. "It's worth more than a bag full of mushrooms."

I agreed to drive out there with Swampthroat but only if I didn't have to get out of the car. I told him if Lionel and his crossbow showed up, I would drive away quickly, with or without him.

"That's fine," said Swampthroat.

Robin wasn't happy to see Swampthroat back at our

house, but she softened up a little when she saw that we had come to take away the venison.

"That stuff was disgusting," she said.

"You never even tried it," said Swampthroat. The meat had been divided into several large parcels, wrapped up in newspaper, and stored in a freezer in our basement. Swampthroat grabbed the last of it and hoisted it over his shoulder. He motioned for me to leave with him.

"Where are you going?" Robin asked me.

"To see a friend," I said.

"Swampthroat doesn't have any friends," said Robin.

"I'm his friend," I said.

"Yeah, right," said Robin.

"Let's go," said Swampthroat.

We drove out to the State Road and filled up with gas for the trip. The meat was piled in the backseat and I was worried that it would begin to thaw and make things smell. I kept the windows open as we drove along.

A police car pulled up behind us and began flashing its lights. I pulled over. It was dark outside now and those lights made everything inside the car turn red and blue and red and blue. Swampthroat slumped down in his seat.

The cop was a young guy who, I think, had been in Robin's class in high school. He knew who we both were, especially Swampthroat. Everybody in town knew Swampthroat.

"One of your headlights is out," the cop said to me.

"I'm sorry," I said, "I didn't know that."

"Well, now you do." The cop scanned the back of the car, illuminating his view with the beam from a large flashlight. He seemed puzzled by the pile of meat in the backseat.

"What have you got back there?" he asked me.

"It's deer meat," I said. "We're taking it to a friend."

"Are you a hunter?"

"No." I said. There was a short pause and I then added, "Swampthroat killed it."

Swampthroat nodded. "That's true."

The cop tucked his flashlight under his arm. "I'm gonna have to take a look at that meat."

It occurred to me then that the officer might think we were transporting a human body, a person we'd killed and were now trying to dispose of. I said to him, "It's not a person back there."

The cop narrowed his eyes. "Can I take a look, please?" he said.

"Sure," I told him.

I got out and opened the hatchback for him. He examined the newspaper packages and seemed a little surprised to find that there was meat inside them at all. He was not concerned, as I had thought, that they might contain human remains. Swampthroat explained to me that the cop was looking for drugs, which we did not have. The cop finished his search, wrote out a warning for the headlight, and then let us go on our way.

It was harder to see the sign for the Highway to Hell in the dark and I nearly passed right by it. Swampthroat pointed it out and I slowed down with a screech. My single headlight shone meekly down the bumpy road.

"I hope they like deer meat," I said.

"Everybody likes deer meat," said Swampthroat.

"Except my mom and sister."

"They would've like it if they'd tried it."

The old hound began to bark as soon as my headlight hit the shack. There was a dim, flickering light on inside. Swampthroat got out and grabbed two of the larger bundles of meat. Then he ventured toward the front door. I sat low in the car, wary of stray arrows, and kept the engine running.

The door of the shack opened when Swampthroat knocked, and to my surprise, they let him in. I sat in the car for a long time, nearly an hour, listening to the radio and watching the shack for signs of movement. Swampthroat hadn't returned for the rest of the meat and I wondered if they had him tied up in there. Perhaps Lionel was holding the crossbow to his head. I would have liked to have left at that point. I had taken Swampthroat as far as I said I would and it wouldn't have been unreasonable to leave. But instead I decided to check on him. I couldn't leave if Swampthroat was in trouble. If he was, I decided, I would drive back out to the road and find that cop. I wasn't going to take on Tilly and Lionel by myself.

I crept up slowly toward the shack, trying to see what was going on inside. Once I got away from the car, I could hear their voices. I was glad when I heard Swampthroat's deep grumble. He was still alive. I got up close to the window and peered in. The three of them, Swampthroat, Tilly, and Lionel, were sitting around a table with a kerosene lamp burning between them. They were drinking beer and smoking cigarettes. Lionel had a hunting knife and he was sticking the tip of it into the wooden table so that it would stand up straight.

I heard a low growling from below and suddenly the old hound dove out from the house and grabbed hold of my foot with its teeth.

"Hey!" I yelled.

I tried to shake it off, but it growled louder and held tight. Swampthroat and Lionel came out the front door to see what was happening. Lionel yelled, "Drop it, Nancy!" and the hound let go.

I was shaken up, breathing quickly, and Swampthroat laughed at me.

"Come inside," he said. "Tilly's making stew."

I followed them into the shack where Tilly was sitting at the table wearing her camouflage jacket and shuffling a deck of worn-out playing cards. She had seemed older when I saw her before. Up closer, she was kind of pretty. Her hair was a little gray and a smudge of charcoal was across her cheek.

"Have a seat," she said to me.

The little shack was cluttered with empty cans, cardboard egg crates, and stacks of magazines. There was an old-time record player, the kind where the needle extends into a big horn, sitting on a table in the corner. Tilly's stew bubbled on top of a wood-burning stove and the whole place smelled like meat and cigarettes. The conflict over the bag of mushrooms had apparently been forgotten. Lionel pulled out a rusted metal fold-up chair and I sat down on that.

Lionel sat on a stool next to me. He seemed too old to be Tilly's son. He had a big, round face and a stubbly beard. He kept his head down, preferring not to look at me.

Swampthroat opened a can of beer and placed it in front of me. I took a sip and said, "I was wondering what had happened to you."

"Tilly saw the meat and decided to cook it up," he said.

A chicken darted out from somewhere and pecked at my foot. Tilly said, "Shoo," and waved it away. Lionel picked up his knife and began pushing it into the tabletop again. On the walls hung various types of slingshots and his trusty homemade crossbow. Swampthroat seemed at ease here so I tried to relax as well. Tilly got up and stirred the stew. It smelled good.

We played a few hands of that card game crazy eights. I wasn't very good at it and Tilly laughed at me.

"I think this boy's retarded," she said.

From then on she began referring to me as "the retard." She said it in a somewhat affectionate way, but still I didn't care for the moniker, especially since it seemed to me that her own son, Lionel, might be touched with a bit of a mental disability himself. He didn't speak much and he kept getting up to examine his weapons. He'd take a slingshot down from the wall and reset the rubber cord or whittle the handle down with his knife.

"Lionel hunts squirrels with those things," explained Tilly. "He's a real accurate shooter."

I wondered when she said this if she was trying to explain the arrow that had struck my car. Perhaps she was suggesting he'd missed our heads on purpose.

We all drank quite a few beers, and eventually, after some time had passed, Tilly announced the stew was ready.

"It would taste better if I had whole day to let it cook," she said. "But this will have to do."

We spooned out the stew into a variety of tin cups and bowls. Lionel wouldn't eat it until Swampthroat tasted it first. He was worried that it had been poisoned.

"I wouldn't do that," said Swampthroat.

"Let the retard eat it first," said Tilly.

Everyone watched as I put a spoonful in my mouth. It did occur to me that Swampthroat might have poisoned the meat, but it seemed improbable. The stew was delicious, as a matter of fact. It was seasoned just right and the venison had a nice flavor. I'd never had anything like it.

"It tastes good," I told them.

Tilly said, "Of course it does," and she began eating it herself. Swampthroat dug in, too, but Lionel waited a while, watching us for signs of distress, before he finally began to eat.

After dinner we all sat around with our bellies full and Swampthroat did a few unimpressive card tricks. Lionel got up and put a record on the old phonograph. Instead of cranking it up to make it turn, Lionel had hooked the record player up to a car battery. The record he put on wasn't an old-time record either, like what you might expect. It was rock 'n' roll from the 1970s. Blue Oyster Cult, I believe. The music sounded funny coming through that big brass horn, but it was plenty loud.

"Lionel's pretty clever with machinery," explained Tilly.

Lionel was feeling a little more social now and he offered to take me outside to shoot his crossbow. I declined, but it would've been a good idea to go out there. About an hour later Swampthroat went out to the car to get the rest of the meat and saw that I had left the engine running. Now it was out of gas.

Tilly said the nearest gas station was closed at this time of night. "You'll have to wait until the morning," she said. "You two can stay here. That's okay with me."

I wasn't too happy with this prospect, but I was tired, and there seemed to be no choice. Tilly gave me a blanket and I cleared the magazines off the couch and lay down. Lionel and Swampthroat weren't ready to sleep yet so they went outside to sit and drink. Lionel put on another record for me to go to sleep by. It was that album by AC/DC, *Highway to Hell.*

I woke up early to the sound of Tilly's roosters crowing away at the first light. Tilly was already awake. She went out and gathered eggs from her rare hens and then she cooked them up for breakfast. They were very tasty. She made me try some more of the stew, too, since it had now had a chance to sit and gather flavor.

"That's very good stew, Tilly," I told her.

Swampthroat and Lionel had slept out on the front lawn.

Swampthroat had a black eye. Apparently Lionel had hit him for something but they couldn't remember what and both seemed unconcerned about it now. After breakfast Lionel gave us a ride to the gas station in his run-down truck. I rode in the back with the old hound, Nancy. We filled a can with gas and Lionel bought some more beer. Both he and Swampthroat had some of that for breakfast.

Back at Tilly's we got my car running and then said good-bye. Tilly said I could come back there anytime. I said that I would, and as we drove away on the bumpy dirt road, I believed Swampthroat and I would return often. I imagined the four of us playing cards and listening to those strange records for many nights to come. But as we hit the State Road and got farther away, I realized this was unlikely. By the time I dropped Swampthroat off at the convenience store in town, I wondered if I would ever see him again. He was smelling bad and was newly drunk at eight thirty in the morning. I watched him lumber away from me, weaving a little, brushing the long hair from his eyes, and I wished I could be like him. I knew that I couldn't though. For me it would have all just been some kind of act, a dumb charade. That was the last time I saw him.

I got a postcard from Swampthroat several years later. He had hitchhiked to Missouri and become a father. He wasn't sure where the child was now.

"If you see a kid walking around who looks like me," he wrote, "please let me know."

"I'm glad I get to write this explanation because this story wasn't that easy for me to write. I liked the idea of writing something inspired by a song, but I didn't want to get all deep and indie rock about it. So long before I wrote the story, I chose this song by one of my all-time favorite bands, the great AC/DC. Then, when the time came to write the story, I realized that my personal experience with the actual Highway to Hell was somewhat limited. I like to party and all that, but I don't think of myself as the type who will go down in flames. When I tried to write from such a character's point of view, it came off pretty phony, so then I had to rethink the whole idea. I decided that really, like a lot of us, I'm just sort of facinated with the kinds of people who live their lives knowing they are going down fast. So then I started writing about Swampthroat, which was actually the nickname of one of my childhood friends. He may not have been aware of this nickname, but my friend Roger gave it to him and it fit pretty well. The real Swampthroat is, I'm sure, not going to hell, but what a fine name for someone who is. But now that I think about it, the Swampthroat in this story isn't such a bad guy either. I think that's also the point of the song. Even someone like Bon Scott, the late lead singer for AC/DC, who died choking on his own vomit in 1980, was not really a bad person. In fact, he was probably quite good at heart. I've heard that about Bon Scott, that he was a very nice guy.

BOUNCING

jennifer belle

Poorboys and Pilgrims with families
And we are going to Graceland

"Graceland"
Paul Simon

The only reason I agreed to go was it said on the invitation that there was going to be a real kangaroo. I couldn't believe that my friend Leslie's child was going to be nine. It had been nine years since I had visited her in the hospital when he was born. I had watched them check out of the hospital, her then husband Paul nervously carrying the baby in the car seat and loading the family into the back of the car. We had all stood in the semicircle driveway at St. Luke's. "This is my son," Leslie had said, "this is my son."

As indifferent as you may feel toward a friend (I hadn't been invited to Paul and Leslie's very large wedding for instance), there is nothing more exhilarating than holding a newborn in the hospital. And there is nothing more miserably boring than going to its birthday party one, two, three, nine years later. My appearances at these birthday parties were a heavy price to pay for those one or two moments of bliss in the hospital, when I was allowed to hold the baby after pushing my way through the large double doors, infringing on the family, and soaping my hands with disinfectant.

The invitation had a picture of a kangaroo jumping on a trampoline. For some reason I couldn't take my eyes off it.

I took the train to Croton-on-Hudson, eating a croissant in a waxy bag. The croissant was as stiff and starched as a collar. It was as far away from Paris as a croissant could get.

I looked out the small gray window as we slowed at the various desolate icy platforms. Croton, Croton, Croton, I'm going to Croton, I thought in my head over and over again involuntarily, like a Poe character. Every other seat on the train was empty. I noticed the neat rows of electrical sockets. I should have brought my computer. Actually I should have been home working.

At the stop called Tarrytown I thought I saw Blake running, trying to catch the train. But it was nobody. There was no one at all on the platform. I wondered if there was such a thing as the ghost of a relationship. Maybe the reason there were no other passengers was because every seat was taken by a ghost from my past. Those were my traveling companions: my ghosts, the velour seats (all facing in the opposite direction from where we were heading), empty electrical sockets, the strange out-of-season ad for an allergy medication called Claritin (a woman running in a field of flowers), the wrapped gift for the birthday boy, my own dim reflection in the window next to me, and of course the red emergency-brake pull handle, dangling from the ceiling like grapes in *Aesop's Fables* or a tempting sausage. I pulled the handle in my mind, and in my mind it grew from my nose like the woman in the fairy tale who wasted the first of three wishes on a sausage.

All I asked from life was the potential for something good to happen. And I couldn't help but feel guilty if I was the cause of the lack of potential. On an empty train, on my way to a child's birthday party, what were my chances of finding love for instance? And whose fault was that? The day was cold, gray, and windy. The wind blew through me, it seemed, literally. Since he left, I had felt cold. I felt like I had a window fan lodged in my chest, like the kind we had used in the country house, congratulating ourselves every minute at how well they worked.

When I got off the train and started down the stairs, Paul, the father of the birthday boy, waved to me. He was standing near his car. I was surprised to see him. He and Leslie had been through a terrible divorce and custody battle, and Leslie despised his second wife, Karen. Despised. With the exception of myself, the father always suffers the most at a child's birthday party. Hanging decorations, picking up the cake, picking up the guests at the train. Right before he waved, I had decided to turn around and go back home, but now it was too late. He had seen me. "How are you?" I asked him.

I said, "Blake and I are breaking up," just as he said, "Karen and I are breaking up." We both smiled. It was like that commercial on TV for cereal, where this fat guy is so proud and excited that he can't help but tell everyone that he has just lowered his cholesterol, and then he turns to a woman in an elevator and is just about to blurt out to her that he has lowered his cholesterol, when she turns to him and says excitedly, "I lowered my cholesterol."

I didn't know what to say about his second marriage ending. "It's nice of you to be at Harper's birthday party."

I wondered what it meant that he had come back to Leslie for the birthday party. I looked out the window. I had never seen as ugly a place as Croton. Paul had NPR playing. An author I had never heard of was being interviewed. Apparently a famous rock star had slightly based his song on a short story she had written and she was suing him. She was going on and on about what would happen, and how was she supposed to feel, if his song was, say, *optioned* to be made into a film? After all, she possessed the *rights*. "But it hasn't been optioned to be made into a film, has it?" the interviewer asked, genuinely confused. "No, I'm speaking hypothetically. I mean, say they make a Broadway show out of it like Twyla Tharp did with Billy Joel." "I'm not sure I follow," the host said. "What I'm saying is people should not be allowed to feed off other people's work. He should be obliged to explain why the ending of the song is exactly like the ending of my story," the author said.

"Karen came home after spending three months at Yaddo and said she was leaving. She met a cinematographer," Paul said.

"Cinematographer. That sounds like a fancy word for

NYU film student." I had actually met a cinematographer once, the cinematographer of the movie *Great Expectations*, but I didn't think I should mention that now. "Cinematographer. That sounds like a fancy word for unemployed," I said. If there was one thing in this world I hated, it was meeting an NYU film student and having to hear all about his "short."

"She accused me of being afraid to leave the city," he said.

"That sounds like a compliment," I said.

He laughed. "After escaping from this place I swore I would never leave the city again. So what happened with you and Blake?"

The wind churned in my chest.

"Sorry, stupid question," he said.

"No, it's not," I said. "Blake said I was a like a Pilgrim and he was like an Indian."

"What does that mean?"

Again, I said, "At the time it sounded to me like a compliment."

"But what about the *ending* of his song?" the author on the radio ranted.

"I don't know why we feel obliged to defend ourselves," Paul said.

We got out of the car before I could hear who the rock star was.

At the party I handed the kid his present, a small trampoline. I had lugged it on the train and Paul had slid it easily into the trunk and brought it into the house for me. I was proud of the gift. It was perfect. The invitation had a trampoline on it, and the trampoline perfectly symbolized my role in my relationship with Leslie, and with most people for that matter. I was proud of it, although my shrink said I was a slave to symbolism.

I had a friend who was a cartoonist and liked to draw caricatures of me. I could, I decided, ask him to do a caricature of me for the invitation to my fortieth birthday party—a cartoon of me lying down with an anthropomorphic trampoline jumping up and down on me.

We went downstairs to the carpeted rec room and sat on the floor in a circle. I sat Indian-style, not Pilgrim-style, I noticed. It was a moment before I realized that only the kids were sitting on the floor in a circle. The grown-ups were standing in the back. I was the only grown-up sitting.

Blake said that he couldn't stand it when I acted like a child. I also know he was embarrassed when his sister-in-law said they were bringing her kids to an arboretum and I didn't know what an arboretum was and she explained very condescendingly that it was some kind of a place with trees. "I grew up in New York," I apologized. "Still," she said. Fuck her.

A fat woman in a giant T-shirt with an owl on it took a porcupine out of a bag and held it in her cupped hands. Harper, the birthday boy, announced that it was a blowfish. Everyone touched it. A few other animals followed, a rabbit, an enormous snake, a turtle that was the same age as me, almost forty.

"Where's the tiger?" the birthday boy demanded.

I thought back to my ninth birthday, on which I got my ears pierced, was given a gray wool coat, and went with my mother to visit the famous artist she was having an affair with in his art studio. I never had a party with a tiger.

"Here he is," the animal handler announced, pulling a striped cat out of a crate. "This member of the cat family is a descendant of the Indian tiger."

"That's just a cat," the birthday boy said.

"Rip-off, rip-off, rip-off," one of the parents said in a harsh New York accent that suited the surroundings perfectly. The party wouldn't have been complete without that voice.

"He's one-eighth tiger," the animal handler said.

Leslie looked annoyed. I couldn't believe she lived in this terrible place, Croton, in this terrible house with framed family photos everywhere and gray carpeting and something she actually called a rec room. She said the word *rec room* completely naturally without even thinking about it. "Everyone, there's still the kangaroo," she announced desperately, like the woman in the fairy tale, clutching at the emergency brake, wasting yet another wish.

"Does anyone know what a baby kangaroo is called?" the animal woman said.

I leaned forward in anticipation. I didn't know. No one knew.

"A joey," the woman said. "And that's why we named him Joey."

The kangaroo hopped out of a large dog crate. He had

coarse gray fur the exact color of the carpet and a stiff, starched tail that hit the floor like a ship's anchor. He had big, expressive human eyes. He looked very angry.

Paul started taking pictures of each child alone with Joey.

"Make sure you get your picture taken," Leslie said to me.

"Oh, no, that's okay," I said, even though I really wanted one. But I didn't know why she would single me out for a photo. None of the other adults wanted one.

I posed next to Joey and touched his long, low tail. With the small, square window of the camera pointing at us, the orphan-thought that I would never have a child shot through me. I felt self-conscious and grabbed the hand of a little boy and pulled him next to me. Paul took the picture. I thought it would be exotic to have a picture of myself with a real kangaroo. I thought I would look like I was on safari. I thought I would look like I was a model in a magazine ad, wearing a tight dress and walking a tiger on a rhinestone leash down Fifth Avenue. I thought I'd look courageous, adventurous, athletic, and sexy. But it is just me holding the hand of a strange, ugly little boy and the tail of a miserable kangaroo on gray carpet in someone's suburban rec room. It is a picture of one of the most pathetic moments of my life.

When I got my coat to leave, I caught a glimpse of Joey standing at the rec room window looking out on the gray suburban landscape. He looked straight out toward the horizon. Seeing it through his eyes, I considered for the first time that it might be beautiful. Beautiful, compared to in here, at least.

For the first time I understood longing. I stood next to

him and we looked out the window together. It was all I could do not to burst into tears.

The children and their parents were upstairs eating pizza and cake. The animal handler was upstairs watching Leslie look frantically for her checkbook. Leslie was pretty much ignoring Paul, but Harper wouldn't leave Paul's side. He wasn't playing with his friends or opening his presents, he just followed his dad around from room to room like I used to follow Blake around when I was trying to figure out where we were going to go for brunch or something. Now I just felt like standing with Joey. My eye went to the basement door. If I opened the door, he could hop down the gray, icy hill and keep going, following the Hudson.

I walked to the door and put my hand on the doorknob.

"What are you doing?" Paul asked, coming down the stairs, startling us.

"Oh, nothing," I said, not taking my hand away, "just getting some air."

"Harper liked the trampoline, that's a pretty sexy gift," he said.

I wondered what he meant by *sexy*.

"It reminded me of something you once said to me about yourself," he said.

"And what was that?" I asked.

"You don't remember?"

"No, I honestly have no idea what you're talking about." I honestly didn't, and I was incredibly curious what it was he remembered me saying about myself, but I felt extremely uncomfortable all of a sudden, and I wanted to change the subject. "What did you get him?" I asked.

"I got him a guitar and I'm taking him to Graceland. You know, in Memphis. We're driving, leaving in the morning."

"Why Graceland?" I asked. It sounded awful. But a crazy thought occurred to me that he might ask me to go with them. I suddenly longed for an invitation.

"I don't know. Harper's a huge Elvis fan." He laughed. "When I was nine, I liked explorers, Christopher Columbus, Sir Francis Drake, I liked the Civil War, I liked a red-haired girl in my class named Jessica Hershey, but what Harper likes is Elvis. And I have to admit, some part of me wants to see it. What about you? You could come with us. I could tell you what it was you said about yourself in the car."

He smiled at me. I laughed. "I can't."

"Why not?" he asked.

I thought for a moment. "I think I have obligations."

"Maybe you don't," he said.

I thought about the greasy redhead in my building whom I hated. She tried to steal a cab from me once, and even though she hadn't succeeded, I hated her. I saw her in the nail salon on Eighth Street and in the elevator and we never acknowledged each other. I hated her wrinkled forties skin and her workout pants and whorish miniskirts and black satin shoes. She was everything I didn't want to be at her age: single, and trying so hard with her chemically straightened pumpkin-dyed hair and *Mademoiselle*-magazine tote bag. She lived across the courtyard from me, two floors below, and from my apartment I could watch her through my window, sitting alone night after night, opening her mail topless.

Then she got a boyfriend just when I lost mine. They ate candlelight dinners at the table by the window every night, at least three or four candles burning on the table every night, while I stood at my kitchen window watching them, eating cereal and milk. It was as if God had said, *Remember that cab she wanted but you got? Well, it's only fair. You got the cab, so she'll get the life.*

"You should come," Paul said. "Maybe we will be personally received by Elvis. A poor boy like me and a pilgrim like yourself."

There were no shortcuts out of this loneliness.

There was no reality TV show I could audition for.

No vacation, time-share, road trip, spa, or hospital.

No national treasure, tourist attraction, or water ride to distract me.

No prescription pill or breakfast cereal to make me feel better.

I had to bounce on the loneliness like a trampoline and let the loneliness bounce on me.

Then there was a sound, like a tiny cry, from Joey.

"That's one sad kangaroo," Paul said.

"This is the last place on earth he wants to be," I said.

I thought about the redhead's new boyfriend smoking cig-arettes out the window in his underpants after their candlelight dinners while I stood trapped in the kitchen unable to tear myself away.

I thought about how I had overheard Blake tell one of his stupid meditation friends that he was very grateful to me for allowing him to break up with me.

I opened the basement door.

Joey took a few slow hops toward the open door.

"Just slip out the back, Jack," Paul said.

Then Paul and I watched from inside as he bounced off into the gray, cold air, until he was practically flying.

author inspiration

I chose "Graceland" by Paul Simon because I wanted to try to literally adapt a song and I knew that Paul Simon, one of the greatest writers of our time, would make it easy for me. "Graceland" is a novel written in fifty-seven lines. It could have inspired me to write fifty-seven stories. I have heard Paul Simon say that "Graceland" ended a long creative dry spell. He had been feeling trapped and it released him. My story is about being trapped and released. I like to think of it as the backstory, what happens right before the song begins. The character of Paul is the man traveling to Graceland with his nine-year-old son, the product of his first marriage. I am the girl who calls herself a human trampoline. While writing it, I felt like I was trespassing in Paul Simon's song like a stalker. After my first novel came out, two different songwriters sent me CDs of songs they had based on my novel. Although the songs were both good, the experience was extremely unnerving. I have used Paul Simon as inspiration for my writing many times, and I wouldn't blame him if he really hated this.

GRAFFITI MONK

ernesto quiñonez

Got a bum education, double-digit inflation
can't take the train to the job, there's a strike at the station.

"The Message"
Grandmaster Flash and the Furious Five

"**F**orget it, Hector." Inelda Flores split open my dream like a machete hitting a watermelon. "Indio's gone crazy. Claims he's nonviolent now."

"Nonviolent?"

"Yeah, he doesn't wanna fight or tag."

I had heard this rumor that my best friend, Indio, had come back from juvie a changed guy. I didn't go straight to his house because his mother hated me, so I went to see his girlfriend, hoping she'd tell me about Indio's sudden change.

"But he's all-city," I said, "and what about TSC?"

"I don't know, Hector." Inelda shrugged. "Indio's crazy now."

My crew, TSC (The Spanish Connection), was famous because Indio was the best graffiti writer in Spanish Harlem.

He was known throughout all five boroughs, he was "all-city." Our tag TSC had been visible everywhere. You couldn't escape it. It was on every rooftop, every subway tunnel, bridge, parking sign, mailbox, wall. Indio owned the 6 train. His "pieces" were brilliant bursts of color and magic. The tag Indio 110 (the number representing the block he was from) was sacred. Only when you had achieved his fame might you be allowed to tag your tag next to his or TSC's without fear of retaliation. But since Indio had been sent away, TSC had been inactive for more than a year. During the power vacuum, another graffiti crew, the CIA, had settled in. It was now their tags that ruled Spanish Harlem.

"Hector, you got to talk to him." Inelda's head was wrapped in a yellow towel. Her mother was a fourth-grade teacher and a student had infected her with lice.

"I'll try." I was out by the hallway because Inelda didn't want me to come inside, due to the apartment's smelling of ammonia because they had just fumigated.

"I mean, he's gone crazy, Hector." Her voice was almost a whisper, like she didn't want the neighbors to hear her. "He broke up with me you know."

"He broke up with you? With *you?*" I couldn't believe Indio would dump Inelda, because Inelda was gorgeous. Her mother, Doña Flores, was one of those middle-aged women who could wear tight dresses and not look ridiculous, and all her four daughters had been blessed with the same beauty. Three of the daughters had gotten married and left the neighborhood, and every day you could hear the older guys in Spanish Harlem mourn them. They spoke about the departed Flores girls as if they had been that ice cream cone that falls to the ground before you even got a single lick. The last of the Flores girls was Inelda, and like her mother and sisters, Inelda's breasts had springs like a mattress. Her whole body gave off this flowery heat, and the neighborhood perverts had been eyeing Inelda since she was eight, waiting for her to blossom. But it was Indio who had caught her eye.

"Get out? No way." I still couldn't believe it. "Why he broke up with you?"

"Well, when he was doing his time in camp, you know I visited him a lot at first, but then he started to get weird. Instead of telling me he loved me or things like that, he'd tell me about these books to read and these movies to see, or read actually, because those movies were in some other language."

"Yeah, my boy Edwin told me, Indio gave him a book."

"Yeah, that's his thing now, giving books. He mailed me a couple of books from camp."

"I never got any books," I said, "and I sent him letters and he'd write back, short, normal letters." I had visited Indio only once because he was detained way upstate. Unless you had a car, you had to take a train and then a bus to get there. When I last saw him, I hadn't noticed anything different about him.

"He got home yesterday, Hector."

"I know that."

"Well, the first thing he did was to quiz me on those books he mailed me. Asking me all these stupid questions."

"Like ha?"

"Shit about the soul—"

"The soul?"

"Something about a soul creating worlds and leaving worlds behind. That souls only know other souls, weird shit—"

"Wow, you're right," I whispered to myself, "he's gone nuts."

"Yeah, I think so," Inelda heard me. "When I told him that I tried reading some of those books but I couldn't get into them, he said—" Inelda's face tightened. "He said that he 'couldn't see me in the same light anymore.' Couldn't see me in the same light? What kind of shit is that?"

"Do you still got the books?"

"But the fucking worst part of it, Hector"—Inelda didn't stop—"was that bitch from the CIA, Yvette, calls me. I've no idea how she got my number, and she fucking makes fun of me. Can you believe that bitch?"

Yvette Sanabria was this girl with big tits who had fallen in love with this giant retard, Lucky G. He had no artistic skills whatsoever, like his hands were made of stone. Yet his crew, the CIA (Criminals in Action), was well-known because Yvette's tags were beautiful and she had vision. Yvette was an innovator. She once did this piece on the 4 train of Blondie and established her reputation. Every graffiti writer that looked at it deemed it a "masterpiece," the highest compliment any work could receive. Yvette's Blondie was "all-platinum." There were no drips running down the piece and it took up the entire car, from top to bottom, even the windows had been painted. Yvette's Deborah Harry sang in a black miniskirt and a red leather jacket, the band played behind her as CBGB's exploded in lightning bolts of all colors in the background. Even people from the Upper East Side who hated graffiti would stare at it when the train pulled in. It was Warhol, it was American Expression, it was what real action painting was supposed to be. Soon every writer began "biting," copying Yvette's lightning bolts. Her Blondie piece lasted only three days before the city washed it, but her fame was established. Her tag, Lady Y 109, was associated with the CIA. And if you sucked, if you were a scrub but dared write your tag next to hers, you had Lucky G and the CIA to deal with. None of us in TSC could write on trains like Yvette, except for Indio. And after hearing how Indio had gone soft, I had no idea about the future of my crew.

"So, that bitch Yvette tells me," Inelda continued, "she tells me, 'You don't know men. Now I know men. See, Inelda, there are dumb men and smart men. Smart men are always unhappy. They always want more and more and think they can always do better. Now you should get yourself a dumb, ugly guy, like I got with G. Dumb, ugly men are always happy, are always spending money on you and praising you all the time. Smart men don't.' " Inelda pressed her lips and exhaled. "She fucking tells me how G always calls her sweet names and he buys her anything she wants and shit like that. How G is always telling Yvette how he feels so lucky that she loves him, and that's why he never looks at other girls. And then she tells me, 'You get yourself a gorilla like I did with G. Ugly men will treat you mo' better.' And you know what, Hector, you know what?"

"What?" I sighed.

"After that bitch stopped rambling, I wondered why I hadn't hung up on her. And you know why, Hector? It's because some of her shit makes sense. Then I got really mad."

"What you tell her?"

"Oh, I wasn't mad at Yvette, I was mad at Indio, stupid. I waited all this time for him to come back from camp and do some beautiful pieces on the 6 train declaring his love for me, and what do I get? What do I get? I get weird shit about the fucking soul. I don't want to see him ever again," Inelda said, but I knew that wasn't true. She tightened the yellow towel on her head, which had loosened a bit.

"Do you have any of those books?" I said again.

"Nah, I threw them away."

"All of them?"

"I think I found a little one under the sofa. I think I was trying to read it and fell asleep and forgot about it."

"Can I look at it?"

"It's got lice, Hector."

"I don't care," I said, "I want to see the book."

"God, all right, let me go look for it." She closed the door.

Alone in the hallway I wondered, what was Indio's problem? All this shit about nonviolence, not tagging? What was wrong with him? This was 1981. New York City had almost been bankrupt. It was a time when if things broke, they stayed broken. Poor neighborhoods were deserts full of vacant lots. It was a bleak time and I was a teenager stuck in a helpless ghetto. Then graffiti entered my life. To me, graffiti was the ultimate. The beat-up subway lines became an opportunity for me to create something to believe in. A "piece", a "masterpiece," a "burner," even a lousy "throw-up," I did on a subway car. The Stillwell stop in Brooklyn was my train yard, as it was for other writers. And I did my pieces there, better on Sunday night, less transit workers. I always carried a loaded Polaroid to shoot my work before others tagged over it or before the city could wash the train and my piece along with it. Sometimes I ran out of a color and had to improvise. Sometimes the cops chased me. Sometimes I had to stand on top of the wooden plank that covers the third rail so I could reach the top of the car and continue my piece; one slip and I might come in contact with the third rail and get fried. This was part of the fun, part of the danger, why people looked at me differently. As graffiti writers we risked our lives for art. Your life was part of the work itself and you became more famous if got caught and did time. A famous writer like Indio who got pinched was eulogized by a lesser writer like me, who kept a vigil for his return. Anticipating the new styles this pinched writer picked up in juvie or in prison from tattoo artists. New styles that now would break out to the street where lesser writers could bite off. That's what I wanted from Indio, his newly acquired styles. I worshiped Indio because to me graffiti was a calling, and it didn't matter that I was not one of its prophets, that I was a scrub and would remain a scrub. I was happy enough to be a part of an underground movement invented by a bunch of talented teenage outlaws who were responsible for the ever-changing traveling show of the subway system.

"If you get lice," Inelda said when she returned, opening the door a bit wider and handing the book to me, "don't blame me."

I noticed Inelda was wearing a light blue bathrobe. She was naked underneath from shampooing and bathing. The top of the robe was a bit loose and she had to hold it shut with her hand.

"This is it, this little book?"

"Yeah, that's it," she said, "and I'd go home and change that sweatshirt. The CIA see you wearing that, you might get jumped." She shot me an air kiss and closed the door.

I just kept looking at the little book in my hand. No more than three inches and skinny, *The Tibetan Book of the Dead*. Going down the elevator, I started reading some of it. It spoke about preparing yourself on how to die and all this stuff. I was mad just thinking Indio would be into this shit, but what really got me angry was the tag CIA on the elevator's door. In Indio's own girlfriend's project! I took out a thick, black permanent marker I always carried with me in my back pocket and tagged TSC over it. I walked out of the project and in a burst of anger started to bomb everything in sight. Nothing big and stylish. One color, one hand motion. If I saw it, I bombed it. I was tagging cars, windows, sidewalks, street signs, abandoned buildings, garbage cans, everything TSC. Then I was stopped dead cold. High above a supermarket billboard, lit by a lamppost, I saw a glorious piece: five colors, true Manhattan style, geometric lettering with serifs, loops, and arches like mosques. The background was highlighted, giving the piece a 3-D effect. There were so many little, tiny things happening in that piece, every detail worked, and I could tell the piece was fresh. I stared at it as if it didn't belong high on that empty billboard but in some place protected by sensors and guards. The masterpiece was Yvette's tag, *Lady Y of 109 loves Lucky G of CIA,* and the letters and numbers were so intertwined, so together, anyone who didn't know would think it was an abstract painting.

"You gonna fuck with that, Hector?" I heard a laugh behind me. I turned around. Yvette with an arm around Lucky G.

"I ain't going to fuck with that," I said, looking at Yvette as I flung my marker to a nearby garbage pile. Then I looked at G. "But if you want my sweatshirt, G"—it was all I could do—"you gonna have to fuck me up, cuz I ain't fucking giving it to you." Graffiti writers never give up their colors without a fight. If your sweatshirt gets taken and you land in the hospital, your dignity is intact. You are in good standing, a part of the crew. You only lost a sweatshirt that costs five dollars. But if your sweatshirt gets taken and your face is clean, you bought years of humiliation from those who were once your friends, and your tag became worthless.

"Fuck you up, Hector?" G let go of Yvette and grabbed

me by the sweatshirt and raised a fist at me. "Let me ask my honey if I should take your colors. Should I fuck him up, baby?" G's eyes were glassy and he kept laughing. It didn't really matter. High or not, I could never take Lucky G.

"Nah, baby, he ain't worth sore knuckles," Yvette said, "who gives a shit about his colors." She was chewing gum and her face was speckled with colorful dots. They must have been celebrating the finishing of the piece by doing some serious pot or something, because Yvette's eyes were insect slits.

"Hector, Hector the Garbage Collector. You just a scrub, man." She dug into her tool bag and brought out a burgundy sweatshirt with the white iron-on letters TSC. She held it up for me to see.

"Look familiar to you, huh?"

"Who you take it from, Edwin? Victor?" I said, and they both laughed. It seemed that everything I said was funny to them. I stayed quiet from then on.

"Take it?" Lucky G clutched my sweatshirt tighter, wrinkling my iron-on letters. I was sure he was about to punch me, or spit at me. Either one is humiliating enough when you know if you hit back, you'll just get more shit kicked out of you. "We didn't take shit. Your homo friend Indio gave it to us." Yvette laughed and G let go of my shirt and joined her in the laughter.

"Then . . . then,"—Yvette was laughing so hard she was having a hard time getting the words out—"then Indio says we are . . . all . . . God! . . . Ha . . . ha . . . God!" All hell broke loose. It was like watching two hyenas slapping each other five after the kill. I always hated the way Yvette laughed, like a seal barking. She breathed in and out hard. If she'd clapped the back of her hands together, I bet someone would throw her a fish. Yvette got away with that laugh only because she was a good writer and she had Lucky G protecting her.

"Look, man," Lucky G said as Yvette threw Indio's sweatshirt at my face. I caught it in midair before it hit me. The sweatshirt was clean, as if Indio had sent it to the laundry before they took it from him. I don't know how they got it, but it was definitely Indio's. "Tell your homo friend we don't need his colors. You guys are done, TSC is Memorex." They walked away and left me there, didn't beat me up, didn't take my TSC sweatshirt . They just left me there holding Indio's shirt. That's when I knew that what I had heard had to be true. There was no glory in beating me up, no glory in beating up anyone from a dead graffiti crew whose best writer had gone soft.

But now I needed to hear it from Indio. I wanted to hear it from him. I hated going to his house because his mother was aware of what we did and didn't approve. She knew we were always "getting up" to go "bomb" trains at crazy hours of the night. She thought graffiti would lead to more violence, and she had told on me since my mother and her were friends. They went to the same church, Our Lady of Carmel on 112th and Lex. It's where me and Indio met as little kids, bored out of our skulls. So I didn't understand Indio's sudden change.

I walked toward Indio's project, it was getting late. The orangey sky was a reddish yellow glow that bounced off the project's walls like a tennis ball. Above the rooftops, red-tailed hawks hovered over Mount Sinai Hospital, looking to snare pigeons. The New York skyline had already lit up and there was a middle-of-September breeze. With evening on the way the streets came alive. People were returning from work, while others gathered their friends to come out and play or drink out by the benches. When I reached Indio's project, I took the elevator up to his floor. I stood at the door and wondered if I should even waste my time knocking. But I did. His mother opened the door. She was not happy to see me. I didn't blame her. Her son was back and she didn't want anyone rekindling old habits. She only smiled a half smile and told me Indio was in his room and pointed.

I knocked and there he was lying on his bed reading a book. When he saw me walk in, he put the book aside and stood up.

"Hey, man, good to see you, bro," he said warmly. Besides his room being really clean, there was nothing different. The posters of baseball players and swimsuit models were still taped to the wall, his trophies were still by the window, his comic books were neatly stacked. His Polaroid camera was on top of the desk. I didn't see any aerosol cans, but you always kept those in a nice and dry place, like the closet.

"I got this TSC sweatshirt. Lucky G says it belongs to you. Know anything about that?" I gave it to Indio. He took his sweatshirt, neatly folded it, and didn't say anything for a little while.

"You haven't seen me in about a year and you want to talk about a sweatshirt? Come on, bro." Indio smiled.

"I just saw Inelda and she said stuff about you. Then Lucky G and Yvette said you said some shit about God? Now, bro, all I'm asking is, what the fuck is wrong with you?" I closed the door behind me. "What the fuck's going on here, Indio? What's all this stuff I'm hearing about you going soft, no tagging, or fighting."

"I don't know."

"What don't you know?"

"Just that," he said.

"So won't you just tell me, just what the fuck you don't know." I knew I wasn't making any sense either, but I had to ask him. "Tell me what you don't know, bro."

Indio sat on his bed. I sat on the floor across from him, leaning my back against the door. Indio was calm like he was sleeping.

"Things, bro, just things." He stared at the wall and not at me. "When I first entered that place, you know"—Indio shrugged—"I thought, all right, I'll just have to carve a new rep here till I get out. I'm still the baddest dog here. But then after doing dishes, a lot of dishes . . ." He trailed off. "You had to be there, Hector."

"At camp?"

"No, not at juvie, at the time when it all didn't make sense, or may be it did?"

"Yo, bro, listen," I said, and dug into my pocket, "I have some weed. We can open the window like old times and your mom will never know." Indio smiled, as if he had wanted a joint for the longest. He stared at the joint I began rolling. "So maybe after smoking some of this," I said, "maybe things would make more sense, dig? I mean, if you don't want to be with Inelda anymore, though I don't see why because she's fine, but, hey, that's your thing. And if you also don't want to be part of TSC anymore, then that's cool. Even though you're the best and want to quit, hey, that's your thing. Just don't talk stupid shit, Indio. Like some fucking crazy person." I sneaked a look at Indio, to see his expression. To see if he minded my cursing. He was nodding his head, smiling a bit.

"Got nothing to say about that, man?"

"No, I think you're right," Indio said.

"So you're retired, then?" I asked, even though I knew he had to be. If it was me in his place, as soon as I was free, I would have wasted no time in reclaiming my fame.

"Is that done?" he said, looking straight at the joint. I lit it and offered the first toke to him. He took it.

"So you don't believe in a lot of things anymore, yet you still smoke up, huh?"

"It's the earth man, the planet can't harm you," he said.

That set me off. "So, bro, are you going to tell me what happened to you or are you going to continue to talk like one of them Jesus-freak Moonies or something!" Indio looked calm, I was angry. "Cuz, bro, I got some thinking of my own to do, and I want to know if the old Indio is back or is this a Xerox. Cuz you look like my friend, you smoke like my friend, you even live where he lived, but you ain't him!"

Indio just blew out smoke and smiled and nodded his head like he had been doing all along.

"Yeah, I guess you're right, Hector."

"Nigga, talk to me."

"I don't understand it myself. If I did, I'd tell you."

"Well then, tell me, man, just tell me anything."

He finally stopped nodding and his smile went away. He looked at me and wrinkled his face. There was a long silence.

"You ever wonder why some people do certain things, and then those things make you see other things?"

"Don't know what you mean, but keep talking."

"See, there was this old man who worked at that camp. He washed dishes with me. He was real old like you see in movies, white hair, baby teeth. He was like weightless, Hector, hollow cheeks, the skin on his arms was wasted to his bone, man. That old man, he'd never talk to nobody. All he ever do was read, read, read. At the beginning I thought he was just crazy. My job was the kitchen with three others. We were that old man's responsibility. The guards were always around, but we were his helpers. I would try to talk to him, ask him what he was reading, but he'd never talk to me."

"So."

"So, one day he finally talked. He said his name was Paul and that he was madly in love and getting married."

"Get out." I took a toke and laughed. "That's beautiful, bro, I bet that old man could still get it up, too."

Indio laughed and reached for the joint.

"Yeah, I bet he could Hector, even though by looking at

him you thought he was dead. Until he really died. Just like that, the old man died."

"Well, yeah, you said he was old, right?"

"Yeah, but then I heard the guards make fun of him."

"So what? Was he something of yours, no, right?" I reached for the joint. "So why should you care?"

"Yeah, I guess not. But see, Hector . . ." Indio paused, and when I passed the joint, he didn't take it, he fixed himself in front of me as if he was going to say something that even he was embarrassed about.

"That same day, I was doing dishes—" And he paused again and looked at the wall as if he was checking if someone else was going to hear this. "I was doing dishes, all these dishes, and see, all this soap foam started building and I saw the suds, and I saw how they just went poof! But it was beautiful when you really looked at it. A rainbow was in every one of those little bubbles. Then I thought of that old man, Paul. I thought, this old geezer must have known he was going to die, but he was going to get married, what's that about? So, Hector, man, I looked back at the foam, Hector. The suds and all those dishes that I had the power to clean, and then I picked up some suds with my hands, Hector, and placed them close to my ear. I heard them pop like Rice Krispies as if they were coming alive and dying at the same time. All those suds with rainbows in them. And I could never tag like the soap could tag a bubble. It was beautiful, Hector, the colors, Hector, the style, and something happened to me, bro, I don't know what it was, but something did."

I didn't know what to say. So I reminded him of who he was.

"What are you talking about? You're the best. No one can do pieces like you, Indio." But I had to laugh a little. "Bubbles, you want to quit because of bubbles?"

"I knew you'd laugh, Hector. It's all right. I laughed, too. But I saw that old man in those bubbles, Hector, I swear I did. I saw the old man worked into all those bubbles. But in each bubble, he was in a slightly altered pattern. As if someone could somehow work a piece but change a bit of it from car to car, and when the train rushes by, you could see the piece move. Like film. The bubbles were like that, Hector, like film." I pictured it in my head. A magical train with a piece that moves. Could that be possible? Could it be done? It would take days. A throw-up on one car was risky enough; a piece meant you were somebody and took hours; but an entire train? No way, the city would clean up the train before you could get halfway.

"But that wasn't all, Hector. Later I heard the guards say that his girlfriend was also old and that she died a couple of hours after Paul had. And the guards laughed some more. That instant I looked around at all these dishes that I had to clean, man. They were piled up in all corners of the kitchen. So many dirty dishes. And the foam was building, all that white, sparkling foam, Hector. At that minute I couldn't write, couldn't paint, but I could clean all those dishes. The dishes could be saved, washed you know."

"Look, bro, I think you're crazy, but that's all right. You'll be all right. Listen, just give it a few weeks, you'll be back with us in no time. We got to get reclaim the 6 train, right? Right? The green line, that's ours, right?"

"It's like when you're thirsty, you know, Hector, you don't need the ocean, just a cup of water."

He was on some other plane. I saw his pupils grow large even though his room had a lot of light. He looked down at the floor. "Maybe the old man just wanted to feel young for a second, you know, he didn't need years. I think he was trying to tell me this, I don't know. But something happened to me." Then Indio returned from wherever it was he had been in his head. "Sorry," he said, defeated. "Sorry, Hector."

"Fuck that, man." I got up from the floor. Put out the joint. "Do what you want, Indio. Always do what you want." I was a little angry at him and just wanted to get out. Indio smiled and nodded like he had been doing all along. I left his house knowing that Indio felt embarrassed. As if he had told me something that only he thought was important.

I once heard a *santero* say, "Sometimes you play the right number and that number never comes up. Sometimes you play the wrong number and it is that number that hits." You can't really explain it. I think something like that is what happened to Indio.

I saw Indio after that, but he never tagged again. He took to going to Central Park and feeding squirrels and watching birds. One day I asked him why and he said, "It's like hunting without killing anything." Later, he got a big yellow dog, which I thought he called Sinatra, which was bad enough, but the dog's real name was Siddhartha. I went home and looked up the name and found out it meant Buddha. I wondered why would Indio name his dog after that fat statue that everyone in Spanish Harlem rubbed its belly for good luck? I tried talking to Indio again, but he never really talked much to me anymore. He would always remain in his own little whatever. At times I spot him on some grassy field in Central Park, sitting cross-legged like the Indio that he was, never looking up when others would pass by and give him odd looks. I heard some kids egged him while he was sitting like that and that he didn't even blink. I never believed it. Though I do know that the old Indio would have kicked those kids' ass.

A few weeks after graduation I saw Inelda walking alone by the Harlem Meer in the north end of Central Park. The trees were beautiful and the pond was clean. We wound up talking about high school and all that junk, crews, graffiti, trains, styles, Lucky G, Yvette. When I mentioned Indio, her faced saddened. She said he was crazy, and I agreed with her. I asked her if Indio talks to her and she said no. After that walk in the park Inelda and me started seeing each other. At first it was just fuck, fuck, fuck, and later we had a kid. This was around the time when Mexicans were taking over Spanish Harlem. The green, red, white, and eagle of their flag fluttered all over East Harlem. Indio was gone by then. No one knows where he went, his mother said he was in the army, but we knew that was a lie because the dog was gone, too. The last time I saw him was at the library. Me and Inelda were checking out books about babies, and Indio was returning a lot of books. He was scrawny, like he didn't eat much. We went over to talk to him and all he said was "Oh, hi. I don't understand these books but they fill me up." We said, yeah, nice seeing Indio, whatever, and went back to our lives.

When the eighties started to die, the city bought new trains with an alloy surface that not even flypaper would stick to. Many writers started to scratch their tags on train windows. I understood their need to tag, but I gave it up. Where were the colors, the smell of turpentine, the sound of the aerosol can? Many crews split up. Some took up Web design, graphics, some even hip-hop. I started working at the factory where my father is the foreman. Without knowing it, I've become Fred Flintstone. Now I work all day waiting for the five-o'clock whistle, and then it's yababadabadoo! The factory is hard, backbreaking shit, mixing paint and hauling steel drums. I use to look down on my father. I used to think that if you're not sitting behind a desk and don't leave El Barrio, you're a failure. I used to think that way. But not anymore. I work hard and my union has good benefits, it even paid for the birth of my daughter. And I get free paint, though for what, I don't know. At times Inelda makes fun of me: "Now you have all the spray cans in the world, Hector, and no one writes on the trains anymore."

Subway graffiti had a short but glorious history. I still say the city blew it. Subway art could have been a tourist attraction. If done right, people would have come from all over the world to see our trains. Another artistic ghetto invention America could've exported like rap music. More beauty from the gutters of NYC. Now, when I wake up in the morning to go to work and see trains rushing by me with that sterile steel shell that attracts more grime than anything, I miss the pictures, the colors, the words. And I remember Indio. Whatever happened to that graffiti monk? Man, there was a time when me and Indio would wait for hours in the cold subway stations watching trains rush by, checking out the competition or just hoping to catch a glimpse of a piece that Indio had done. Sometimes we'd never see it, the city had washed it before the train pulled out of the yard. But we knew it had existed and we had those stupid Polaroids. I never understood why Indio turned away from graffiti; whatever it was that he saw in those bubbles, God, death, or whatever, it must have been something big. Because there was nothing that brought me more pleasure than to know that strangers were reading my words, seeing my pieces whether they liked it or not. Back in those days, fame was the name of the game. "I saw your tag in Far Rockaway, nice." And I felt as if I had traveled all the five boroughs. I was getting around, I was somebody.

author inspiration

Watching MTV's late-night show *Old School Hip-Hop*, I came upon Grandmaster Flash and the Furious Five's video for their song "The Message."

It wasn't so much the words that caught my attention but rather the images of a filthy and broken New York City. For some reason, the next day I found myself waiting for the train on 149th Street and Grand Concourse. I looked for the "writers' bench," where graffiti writers would gather in the eighties. As a teen, I had admired so many, and to my surprise the bench was still there. I decided to write a short story about that period. It was really my late-seventies, early-eighties New York City I longed for. In today's age of gentrification, that period in NYC history is lost. But there was a time when we took all that neglect, crime, and poverty and turned it into art. "Graffiti Monk" is my attempt to capture some of that lost history.

SMOKING INSIDE

darin strauss

Can I have some remedy? Remedy for me, please.

"Remedy"
The Black Crowes

ragic example of me being a stupid mother came when Morrison, he's my oldest, packed an onion ring up his nose while his brother peed the carpet on purpose. Little Dylan does that: he pees. I'll open the door, burned up after eight hours helping morons at the library, and there's my bony, pale guy standing pants down with his mini-sized Oscar Mayer between his pinkies. Like he's been waiting to show me for hours. The jukebox in my head starts in on the Beatles' "She's Leaving Home," but you actually think I'd split? A parent may get notions that are no more than daydreams for herself; she's better than those.

Now, I don't scream; I shake my head and go, "Put your little noodle *away*, Dylan." Kid's only seven, you think he'd feel embarrassed. But my shirtless boy, long black hair bopping across his shoulders, does a five-second hula shake. His measly dick flaps like one of those gummi worms my ex-husband, Dave the Rave, used to let our boys eat for dinner. (Dave the Rave left us for Sheri-with-an-*i*, and if Dylan and Morrison had been this hellacious before that bastard split, no one's convinced me of it.)

"Put your goddamn penis away"—I'm trying for calm-toned, even in my rush of anger. Dylan's eyebrows go flat above his squinting eyes that steal my heart every time; his cheeks look delicate like white tissue paper. When he runs crying to the kitchen—his butt too scrawny to have much bounce—he trips on the cloudy-blue corduroys tangled at his shins.

Watching him tumble, I think (or I want myself to think), *Kid, go on and cry yourself hoarse.* But why isn't he wearing his underwear? Motherhood's got loads more carpet-pissing and vanished underwear than advertised.

Then, just like that, Dylan's up, off to hide within the majesty of my twelve-hundred-square-foot "amenity ranch home." I turn to Morrison, the older one. He's been watching Emeril Lagasse on the idiot box. (At thirteen, my Morrison's the man of the ranch.)

"Hey, there, li'l *gourmet*," I say, imitating my own mother's idea of a talking-to, like I'm pulling taffy inside the words. "Isn't your job in this life not letting your kid brother piss where he shouldn't?" That's angry-sounding, but what I feel is I'm just about used up. "Isn't it—your one job?"

"Wait, Nanette," Morrison says; he's sunk into his father's

green TV chair, which is indented and frayed black around the buttons. "Emeril's about to do it."

And right on cue, Emeril Lagasse yells, *"Bam!"* and my son's face bursts like one of those jiffy popcorn containers. I really can't help my soft spot for the zip of that boy's smile.

"Can you get that onion ring out of your nose?" I say, but not before something pulls at my attention like a magnet: Dylan's whiz has made a perfect tan frown on my off-white pile rug. Since The Rave left, I'm the oldest single mother in Pritchardville, South Carolina, by eight years.

"Mo, what did I tell you kids about stopping for junky food on the way home?" I say. In the mirror my eye shadow's runny. I haven't taken off my coat yet. "Besides," I say, my sigh showing too much of the unfun woman The Rave says I am, "it's *Mom* to you."

The thing is, I'm *not* that unfun woman, not when I don't have to be.

"Men," I'm saying now, "are allowed to call me Nanette only when they reach eighteen and take me to see The Black Crowes."

"Nanette," he says, "I didn't get it on the way home—the onion ring, I mean." He's all nasally, as the food's still in his nose. "This is from lunch."

"Take it out!"

Later, I scrubbed the carpet until I woke the old knee cramps; after that I gave the little villains my "punishment dinner," which is bread and bologna. (No matter how angry she gets, a mother has to provide.) I cleaned a half hour more before putting them to bed. And cursed the ex. But not before I logged on. I'd learned how at the library—I like books okay, but it's only a job my cousin Francis got me. I hate having to talk politely, proper, and all quiet, pretending I give a tit about Tom Clancy or Hemingway; the one perk is it gives free internet at home. Nothing beats that eBay auction site. I once got a salesman's sample "Hearth-Style" stove I didn't need—thirty bucks, give or take.

On this night, eBay had 1½ Ct. Genuine Ruby Earrings in gold-plated silver for sale, pretty nice, and a Black Crowes Signed Concert Tee (I'm a fan. Though it stings to call anyone younger than me a real rock star).

I was surfing through it all when I got this idea. I love my kids and would be lost without them, etc., but wouldn't it be quote unquote *funny* if I put them up for auction online?

Two kids for public sale. 13 and 7—Morrison and the other one. Fmr. bed-wetter and current carpet-wetter. **Would make a god-awful gift or to keep for yourself.** Buyer pays shipping and insurance. I 100% guarantee these kids to be a handful and offer a three-day return policy if not found as stated.

Right away, emails. MissThang@usfolk.net: "Can I add my 4 snot-nosed guttersnipes to auction with your 2?" KARIN@earthfair.web: "Hoping you'll take one obese, 'prime-of-life' husband for barter. I'll throw in one pair skid-marked tighty-whities and some Mitchum X-tra strength deodorant." Best thing about it, I went to bed not really in a mood anymore.

Next day, from eBay: "To whom it may . . . You are hereby prohibited from auctioning . . . *privileges invalidated.*" No big deal. If they can't dig a joke, I can join another auction site. Easy peasy.

Couple weeks later, I was cooking with Morrison—just store-bought sauce and pasta, he stirred the tomato paste while I did the noodles. Dylan was napping upstairs. The mail was an unopened pile on the table.

Out of left field, Mo asks, "If we get a dog"—his arm disappearing into the sauce pot—"would I have to still babysit?" That thirteen-year-old troublemaker smiles the way that only a kid who hasn't seen the real world can. "Billy Doric said Irish setters are like smart enough to do it for you."

This is probably because my husband was such a cock that I had to turn to something that wasn't him, but when I first became a mom, the thrill I felt for Morrison was under my skin and stayed that way—until Dylan was born. It was like a poison oak rash for six years.

And now I'm sighing at Morrison: "Who said anything about a goddamn dog?" Because the thought of a puppy heartburns me—who does Mo think would end up walking the fucking thing?

"That's shitting bullcrap, Nanette."

He's picked up language from school; he'll curse even when it doesn't make sense to. More than the words themselves, I hate that he doesn't use them right.

Anyway, he's chewing his lips, creasing his forehead—his best hard-guy face. But thanks to that squeaky clean skin of his, I always imagine Mo a sheep on a cultivator feedlot, blinking, a cream puff with no defense from the ax.

I slap his hand with all I can muster—*whap!* "What'd I tell you about language in this house?"

"*Ow,* Mom."

Like the point of a boat, his nose splits the steam that rides around his head. He's got Dave the Rave's baby blues, bluer now that they're getting all teary. "Jesus H. Crap, Nanette," he mutters.

I can't even remember my life without him; it's always a shock seeing he's not in any of my picture albums from, say, high school. Meanwhile, here I am, imitating his whine: "*Ow, a woman hit my hand.*"

He's pouting about his wrist, which is blotched red where I slapped it.

"Mom?" he says, his voice tiny and tight.

"Dylan'll probably go against the idea of a puppy," I say, nice as I'm able now. I hadn't planned on hitting him so hard. "You know how your brother can be a stubborn little shit." We laugh on that.

(The truth of the thing is, motherhood came down-to-earth when little Dylan got born. Even Morrison started to get on my nerves. Overnight he turned from this cute superkid to a clumsy thing I had to protect the baby from. And I never really got that poison oak feeling with my youngest.)

Now little Dylan himself walks in, rubbing the sleep from his eyes, his hair a wild black heave—a seven-year-old bundle of pee wearing nothing but a Black Crowes T-shirt that's not long enough to hide his goods. I should yell about this, but me and Morrison just laugh some more. The point is, I forget to look at the mail and don't notice the letter from the Department of Social Services.

Next day I went to work, it was hell as always. Every time she saw me, Mrs. Crailt, chief librarian, puckered her face as if she'd heard an insult. Too tall even in flats, that woman showed more chins than I should mention here.

"You *sure* you've cataloged *every*thing, and stacked the *what's lefts*, Nanette?"

Why are women so hard on other women? Her hair was the stringy that pasta in a can often is.

After work I open my front door expecting the usual zoo, but here's Morrison and Dylan, both close to tears in front of the TV, their heads down. Mo's clenching his free fist while some gangly man in a cardigan holds them by their hands.

"Who the hell are you?"—I'm trying to sound like more than the five foot three I am. My hands are trembling. "Get *the fuck* out of my house."

"You don't need to be alarmed, please. I'm looking for Mrs. McQuaid—their mother?" Cardigan has a breathy good-fairy voice and a wide smile. "Ma'am, is Mrs. McQuaid your daughter?" The guy's got a tight grip on my boys; his fingernails are like Sno-Kones: red, followed by a white that's bloodless.

"*I'm* the mother, thank you," I say.

"Jim Plates," the guy singsongs. "Department of Social Services."

He doesn't let go of my boys.

I'd been thirty-seven and two years married when The Rave and I did "blotter" acid in 1986. I sat alone in the kitchen and it hit. I got so cut off, Bono from U2 appeared. Bono wrapped me tight in freakishly huge hands, and he swept me from my housework, from my thinking about myself. He spun me, his massive thumbs flicking my apron off, and before I knew it Bono had me close, his chest solid against the mess of who I was. Bono held me in a way that *he* never could—*he* was miles from me, in the green TV chair, waiting on a beer—and I was snug in Irish arms in the kitchen. Together we sang the "name" songs: "In the Name of Love" and "Where the Streets Have No Name."

Later, I squinted under emergency room lights at a beaver-toothed med student. If he'd asked me, Do you think you'd end up a good mother one day?—or a mother at all?—I would've said, Shut up and play yer guitar some more. But I cleaned up. Had the boys. And got rid of Dave the Rave (though not by choice).

•   •   •

After all that, here I found myself in 2004 with gray-eyed Jim Plates, Department of Social Services, a stranger across from me at my unset dinner table. His breath was a beesting in my nostrils. I'd sent the kids outside.

This Plates guy says to me, "Mrs. McQuaid." He grins while he talks, which is a feat. "Your son, uh, Dylan, tells me—"

"Mr. Plates, how'd you get into my house?" The breath smell's not as bad if I breathe in through my mouth. I can take control of the situation. "Not to be rude, but—"

"—Dylan told me that you'd fed them 'Orange Crush and peanut butter and jelly' for dinner one night this week." He has a voice that rises at the end of every sentence—apologetic-sounding even when you're the one on the ropes.

"Mr. Plates, that's not unusual for a mom." I'm going with my cheerful voice. "Usually, I just get whatever seems best to me when I'm at the store. It ain't a stretch to say the boys love that meal." I don't want to reach for a cig in front of Plates, but I need one. "*Isn't* a stretch."

Now the guy, looking up from his file, peers at the chest I haven't got much of. And he keeps peering. His eyes are cement.

"I'm not like the type to auction my kids, really, if that's what this is about," I say brilliantly. My ceiling seems really low to me. "I mean, who is—right? Ha ha ha." I bend toward him a little, now that we're such pals. "So is *that* what this is about?"

He stoops to write again. The part in his hair makes a scalp trail, white and straight as a string. "Yes," he says.

I check my watch: 6:15. I cough—even that doesn't make him look up at me. My own house, now municipal-feeling as a DMV. Even the air seems what Mrs. Crailt calls "poor-ventilated." And what are the kids up to outside that it's so quiet?

Plates raises his head all of a sudden, as if I'm the one who's disturbed him. "Don't worry, Mrs. McQuaid." He works his easy-on-the-ear half-whisper. "I'll never let them take"—checking his notes—"Dylan and Morrison from you."

That does the opposite of soothe me. I hadn't even considered that possibility. I manage to use my librarian voice: "May I ask you to leave?"

More than anything in my life I want to be happy, I think. Could be that's the difference between me and the really good mothers of the world.

"Uh, sure, you can ask me to leave," Plates says, squinting. "No problemo." He's extrabreathy now, speaking almost to himself, his face aimed at his notepad. "We're just talking. It was my understanding that we were just talking, Mrs. McQuaid."

After that the only sound is the musical-shakerish cha-cha-cha of Plates writing. His hands are fat, pink hands.

Pritchardville, where I live, was said to be birthplace to the hokeypokey, not a rock-and-roll town. That's probably one reason that I'm not into music as much. Just sometimes The Black Crowes, to help me when I get stressed. "Hard to Handle" *has* to be about my boys. (It was just one more disappointment to learn that the Crowes didn't even write that one.) Anyway, I thought people here in Pritchardville didn't butt into other lives.

Plates called to set up a few more "talks."

It wouldn't be on any schedule, he said—maybe two next week, the week after, then more. We'd see. They'd operate around my calendar. I wondered who the hell "they" were. "More people like me," Plates laughed—*glug, glug, glug,* like Coke going too quick from a bottle.

The first meeting was set for a Wednesday, 9 a.m., at the Human Services building in Palmetto Bluff.

"Sure, come in late Wednesday, I don't mind," Mrs. Crailt yawned toward the massive bookstacks that are going to come crashing through the third floor one day. "Assuming, that is, Nanette, that you have periodicals *E* through *H* retagged."

The night before the meeting, the kids watched *Rugrats.* At the commercial, Dyl's voice cracked as he asked what the FBI was. He sat chewing on the sleeve of his Jimi Hendrix footie pajamas.

"A bunch of squares, that's the FBI," I say.

Dylan whines, "I *told* you, Mo"—as insecure as unexpectedly victorious little brothers always are. When the kids had been younger, it was adorable the way they'd acted together, Mo cheering while Dylan walked with a magazine balanced on his head. Now Morrison's shooting Dyl a look that says, "Shut up, asshole."

Dylan tells me that the elementary school principal, along with some other men, had questions—about me. And the way Morrison's staring into his hands, I know someone'd grilled him, too.

"So, what'd they ask you guys?" I try for casualness: *Hey, look, your mom doesn't give a shit about the stupid principal's office*. On the tube, the Rugrat with Charlie Brown–ish head and hair is laughing like a full-grown individual.

Mo's eyes are doing this slow side-to-side—just like The Rave does when *he's* nervous.

"Well," he says, "this guy was going, 'How does your mommy treat you,' and I was like, '*Mommy?* We just say *Mom* or *Nanette*. I was like, 'Our place's not the same as other kids' places, but it's awesome sometimes, too.' "

Little Dylan arches his back and interrupts, "Like, um, when you let us pick CDs to listen to at dinner, and how you don't yell so much when I pee on the floor—and I know I gotta stop doing that, Mom—and he said, 'She sounds nice,' the guy. I didn't tell him about you and Dad, or when you punished me for when Mo broke the glass, but you thought maybe I did it, too, even though I didn't."

"Oh," I say. Either Mo or Dyl seems to have put the TV on mute. "Oh, good."

In South Carolina, wherever a building rises three stories or more, worn-out shops or houses squat around it, jealous as groupies. That's how it is with the Human Services building—a tall, yellow-trimmed ex-mansion with high cheekbones. At five to nine, the lights are bright in its eye-windows. It's almost welcoming—nothing like what I'd imagined. Inside, there's gleaming wood. Still, I'm a little pissed as soon I walk in; no one's told me which room to visit.

A tubby in a cheap orange blouse gives me a dirty look as she marches down the carpeted stairs that I'm marching up. But then a fat, pink hand settles on my shoulder.

"Mrs. McQuaid." Plates's voice is deep in my ear. He stands at my back. "Come on, come on, we've been expecting you." It's nine on the dot.

"Oh, but—"

"Did you bring your boys?" Fat hand on my tailbone, Plates is walking me up the stairs.

"Did I—no, nobody told me—"

Plates sidles next to me at the start of the second-floor hallway, his breath minted by mouthwash that'll burn away by noon the latest.

"Oh, well, I guess that's fine, then. But Mrs. McQuaid"—he's looking at his watch—"who takes care of the kids when you're out?"

"Well, they're in school." Like that, my underarms go sweaty. Should kids be somewhere besides school?

"Of course they are." Plates, moving his lips as if he had a mouth sore, looks anything but mannish. "Sorry—I have to ask these questions, you understand."

"Yes." I'm nodding a lot. "Of course."

"This way, please." Plates has teeth that lean into one another and jostle for a better view of the world outside his mouth. He takes me by the elbow down the stairs again. My own teeth are no great shakes, I know that.

If the Human Services building once was an old mansion, what is now the empty waiting room must've been the broom closet. The receptionist has blond hair only a laboratory could invent. She keeps having to finger up her bifocals as she wheeze-laughs through a personal call. Plates and I stand waiting in place until my back starts to ache. The *Far Side* taped to her monitor features a moose with a bull's-eye for a birthmark.

When Receptionist hangs up, she and Plates start to gab—she calls him Hot Plates. The whole time, someone's piping in Muzak of Frampton's "Show Me the Way," a version with strings and keyboards like thick gloves that dull its punch—where's the Fender Rhodes, voice box guitar, the fuzz-toned lick that lifted a thousand skirts? Whitewashing like this is what separates good from evil, ask anyone. In the meantime I'm standing here like a jackass, breathing in the dead air, trying to shut my ears to this dead music.

Finally Plates asks Blondie, "Stampp's in, huh—3B?"

Back on the second floor, Plates—now a three-year-old shy to wake his parents on Christmas morning—taps on the open door of a conference room. Inside, this old, fat guy's sitting on the lip of a metal desk that could be from the Eisenhower administration.

"Mrs. McQuaid?" says the guy that I don't know yet. "You're quite tardy."

All Plates does is frown and shake his head. I take a breath. "I'm here now, though, sir." My biggest smile. "I was with Mr. Plates for a bit." Again, Plates says nothing to back me up. Trying not to lose it, I turn to the window, where the top of an elm is shivering like a humiliated thing getting yelled at.

The fat guy on the desk sighs — "Twenty minutes is twenty minutes" — he jumps to his feet and offers me his hand. It gives like a bag of flour. "Do you know what I mean?"

"Well, Mrs. McQuaid." The guy rattles the phlegm in his throat. "John Stampp. FSACWCCA."

And Plates stage-whispers, "Federal Sub-Agency of Child Welfare, Child Care, and Abuse." You'd guess something's tugging inside his cheek, the way half his face hollows up when he shrugs.

Meanwhile, this guy Stampp is saying, "This won't be too *prickly*, I hope." He hesitates before *prickly*, worming his eyebrows as if he's being naughty.

It's anger or nervousness that has me scratching my palms.

Mr. Stampp: Stick a pair of hairy ears on an egg, glue it on top of a potato, don't worry about a neck, and there you have him — plump in the way friendly neighbors are, imagine a David Crosby shaved clean. I try to look for something human in the guy's face, but what can you expect from the eyes of a man who has not an ounce of life in him?

"Sirs, can I just say something?" — sounding, I hope, not overconfident but not insecure, either. I have a flash of how they see me: middle-aged and lonely, a package of things you can't hide no matter how you talk. "I'd like to say something in my defense."

Stampp smiles and it almost seems a real smile; his cheeks gentle into ballish little circles. "Of course you may, Mrs. McQuaid." But his eyes look no more humane than smudged marbles.

"Sirs, I love my kids." I want this to sit for a while. The black-and-white George Bush tacked to the wall is the older one, the father. And suddenly, out the window, what looks like a flock of envelopes glides by with a floaty whoosh, hundreds of them swimming in the air, for some reason twirling, apart and together, papers gone bright with the sun. I want to make a big deal out of this—there's a pack of glowy little ghosts boogying just outside—but it's only Plates and Stampp with me in this wood-paneled room, and the sight would be gone before I could explain it.

"I just wanted to let you know that, sirs." I stop myself from chewing my lip. "I mean, my children are happy." What I'm saying is true, but the quake in my voice marks me as a liar.

"Ma'am, how often do the children see their father?" Smiling Stampp's voice is as bouncy as his jowls.

"Every three weeks—two and a half weeks," I say. "Every two, two and a half weeks."

I want to cut my own throat immediately. Either I should have told the truth ("almost never") or said once a week.

"Mr. Stampp is going to ask you some questions now," Plates says.

"Shoot," I say.

And he gives me a third degree, a blur of words, all my answers on the heels of new questions like cats chasing dogs: So, I see you are a musician, No, Mr. Stampp, I'm the associate librarian at the Pritchardville Library. It says here you're an entertainer, Well, sir, I'm a librarian. May I ask how much an associate librarian job receives a year by way of salaried compensation, Do I have to get into that, sir? I can check the IRS records if I have to, It pays twenty-four-six a year, sir. And I have no doubt you've a good reason for not bringing your kids here this morning, Yes, sir, I thought, I didn't know—And, Mrs. McQuaid, you are not yet divorced, Close to it, sir. I see your husband's name is David McQuaid and is it true that he makes his living as the percussionist in a rock-and-roll outfit and as a hand model, Well, sir, my ex wasn't a beauty, but he was all right, I say.

"Springfield," Stampp mutters, bending over his desk to jot something.

"*Steen*," I say. "There's Rick Spring*field*, who's no Bruce Spring*steen*."

Plates gives me this openmouthed stare as if I just dropped a china plate. By now my heart's a grimy balled-up sock. "So, can you tell me why I'm here?" I ask.

"I guess you're the comedienne, why don't you tell us?" Stampp turns back to me, his eyes showing their first spark of life. "Tell us a joke about selling kids on-line."

"No, no, *no*," I say—screw this sick-to-my-stomach feeling—"I'll tell you what is a joke. Getting a working mother out of the library to come here for nothing. Scaring kids at school for no reason."

Stampp blinks as if I'd shook him from a long sleep.

Which gives me more backbone. "I can't believe this! Mr. Plates here dawdles around with the secretary downstairs and makes me look tardy, plus, for Christ's sakes it was a *joke*, the auction thing. And coming to my boys' school? Is that allowed? Do you intimidate little boys to get your jollies? Do you have like a quota of honest people you have to mess with every month?"

"Mrs. McQuaid—"

"I'm a taxpayer!" I even stomp my foot, a little. This isn't me: more often than not I'm by the card catalogs forcing a sweet grin when comb-over perverts breathe garlicly in my face. But now anger's lifting a sob halfway up my throat. "I am a *taxpayer!*"

"Mrs. McQuaid—"

"Mr. Stampp, I have a really good girlfriend at the *Palmetto Standard*." Which is a lie. But it seems to work; Stampp's started to rub his forehead. I take a step toward the door. "You know I did nothing wrong, Mr. Stampp. I have rights. I also have my congresswoman's phone number."

"All right, Mrs. McQuaid." He chuckles sadly—I take that as a good sign. "All right now."

Plates gazes at me with this heavy-lidded, almost-smiling look that—I could swear—seems halfway dirty. It reminds me of some smirks that got me into trouble in the old days.

But I'm out the door so fast, it's like Plates's own fat hands are pushing me from behind.

When I get home, Dylan's standing to greet me, his teeny Oscar Mayer out, the floor a puddle behind him. I want to yell, but I'm afraid to, as if they'd bugged my house or something.

That Saturday, someone rang our bell. I answered in my robe, and there stood my ex, Dave the Rave.

"Hey, kitten," he says, this close to pornographic with those jeans two sizes closer to my measure than his. His mindless blue eyes still look right inside me. Of course he's doing his normal, droopy-necked lean-in, and his face—which has gotten a little puffy—moves too close to mine. Dave the Rave deals in the discomfort of women.

It's noon, I haven't brushed my teeth, so I aim my talk away from his nose. "What *now*, Rave?"

"That's it?" His voice comes as a raspy warning about how far desire could throw you if you let it. He's wearing a giant, silvery belt buckle. Had he always been so damn pale? He says, "That's all you got for me, Nan, in my old bathrobe?" His belt buckle reads, *rhythm rave*.

"Come the fuck inside, already."

By the time the Rave's pigeon-toed his new cowboy boots over the stained part of the rug, the kids have barreled in. Dylan can't stop screaming, "Dad, Dad, Dad," in his Hendrix footies. "Dave the Rave! Dave the Rave!"

Mo just ticks his head back: "Dads, what up?"

Before long, little Dyl is standing one foot in front of the other, toes circling into the floor. "There's this program, it's in school"—the kid's talking faster than normal—"and 'contemplation' is when you go into your head and you stay there and decide what's wrong and right, and if you're smart, you choose what's right."

"Your father and I have to talk now," I say.

Dylan stares at his circling foot. "When I'm bored, I watch TV in my mind."

Mo interrupts his brother with a nasty little laugh. "Dad, how'd you have such a faggot for a son, yo?"

The Rave's been inside the house less than a minute, already he's massaging his eyes and groaning. After a second he thinks of how to answer Mo. "Hey," he says, "that's what I asked Dr. Himmelfarb when you popped out, Morrison." This gets big laughs from Dyl. After that, The Rave turns serious: "Now, you guys just let me talk to the old lady, okay?"

This hushes the kids, but it doesn't get them to leave. Before I know it, the boys are running around the kitchen, quietly, and Dave the Rave and I sit face-to-face at the table. His curly (dyed) black hair looks like a poodle stretched out from his scalp down his back.

"So, Nan," he says, "what's this about the F-reaking BI?"

I turn to the boys. "Okay, get away now. Get away, kids." And, surprise of the week, they leave without a stink.

"First, Dave," I say, "it's not the FBI, it's the FSACWCCA."

He snorts and shakes his head—his take on an adult-type stare. He's given me that look twice before, once when I told him I was pregnant with Dylan, and it'd take too long to go into the other time.

"Oh, *Dave*," I say. His Drakkar aftershave is all cinnamony in my nostrils. I try not to look into his baby blues or hear this motherness in my voice; I want to punch him in his perfect turned-up nose. "Don't pretend that I am what *you* are, okay?"

"Nan"—he's sighing—"how am *I* the fuckup this time?"

I sigh right back. Arguments that could take ten hours or years often come down to one short sigh or two.

"Look, baby." He actually tries on the stupid smile I won't fall for anymore—pouty and built on what he'd like you to believe is kindness. "I just don't need the F-reaking BI calling. Not for my little guys. What father wouldn't be upset . . ."

"Don't start with *that*." His sister Rae told me that he's having problems with Sheri—a hussy, by the way, that Dave first met when she cleaned his teeth. "I think you should go now, Rave. Get out."

For the longest time, he squints like a cowboy trying to see an Indian across the prairie. I start to drum my fingers on the table. This isn't much of a game of chicken; we're both pretty sure I'm not really kicking him out. A wind hisses its way inside through the goddamn kitchen window he never caulked.

Then the Rave turns his huge, smooth hands palms-up. We both look at his long, beautiful fingers for a time.

"How's the music going?" I ask finally. "Still doing grunge ten years too late?"

He squints at me again. The wind's stopped, and I bite my fingernails a little.

"Don't do that. It augments the roughness of the cuticle," he says.

"Listen," I say, "I don't think they'll call again." When I close my eyes, I get a picture of the openmouthed, zombieish look on the Rave's face every single time I've seen him at the drums. Or having sex with me. "The FBI, I mean."

"I don't think so, either, Nan." He runs a hand through his hair, it takes him nearly five minutes. "Not that I'd know what those type of guys would do, though." His face looks baggy and colorless. "Okay, the important thing is, I want to do right by the boys, and I know I haven't, so don't bring it to the fore. Because, hearing about the internet thing, I was just—"

"Don't, Rave." My ex is the only guy who I always know exactly what he's going to say. "Dave, don't say 'concerned.' Not you."

Next afternoon, tired after pickups at the supermarket, the drugstore, the Blockbuster, and cold after getting caught in the rain, and grateful to get out of my bra, I sat on my throne, eyeing the thin black stripe that pointed across my bathroom ceiling. Brown curlicues raked out from its sides. Not to mention the sink was discolored, the varnish chipped. I was depressed, I admit that.

Soon I hear the kids sneak into my bedroom, which is officially off-limits for them; guess they don't know I'm on the toilet. I can hear them enough to make out the words "Mr. Plates"—but I have to work to catch the rest.

It's Morrison who says, "Don't you agree it would be cool?"

"Um, do you really think?" says Dylan. That boy can be so sincere.

"*Um,* do you really listen?" Morrison cries. "What'd I just say, bullcrap bag? Yes, I think. The Rave thinks so, too, right?"

My stomach squeezes into a fist. I can't be sure what they're talking about; of course I imagine the worst. Not a word has been spoken in this house about Plates or the FSAC-whatever since that time watching *Rugrats.* Are they talking about how great it would be to live with their dad?

Fine. Let Junior Gourmet survive on Chee•tos, let him try to sleep when there's band practice at 3 a.m.

Maybe I'm being crazy; who knows what they're saying? I flush the toilet and just sit there, pulling my robe tight around me.

The boys say it at the same time: "Mom?" Morrison says, "Are you home, Mom?"

"*Um,* do *you* really listen?" I yell. "What'd I tell you about playing in my bedroom?"

"Sorry," says Morrison. "Um, sorry," says Dylan in his sissiest voice.

"What have I told you little jerks?" I come teeth-clenched out of the bathroom, but they're already gone.

•　　•　　•

Next night, Plates was at my door, grinning over his cardigan.

I led him to the kitchen, let him drink my coffee. I thought, What if I poison the cream?

Yes, I'd been stupid to go on eBay, but this had nothing to do with that. You couldn't tell me that what was happening to us wasn't just fate. Fate with its fat hands had me like a dog on a leash.

"It's simple," Plates tells me as he sips. He purses his lips, barely touching the cup, and I can picture him as an eighty-five-year-old dame or duchess. "We had occasion to talk to your children three times this past week, Mrs. McQuaid, as you know."

"Oh," I say. You'd think nothing could surprise me any-more, but this sucks all the air out of my lungs. "I didn't know." I make myself stare into Plates's grays and not look away this time.

"Yes, I think you did know," he says, soft enough to sound apologetic.

Setting my eyes on his arched, pretty eyebrows, the sweat dots under his nose, watching the point of his tongue tap wet and pink on his bottom lip, I have an unexplainable flash of the two of us dancing till we're out of breath and sweating—I have to turn away into my coffee cup. I don't realize I'm pinching my own knuckle until it starts to hurt. I don't stop it.

"Why wasn't I present at such a meeting?" I ask.

"We have—concerns. The department, I mean." He blinks, giving the gentle, head-cocked smile most people

When it's my turn to speak, I go, "Gentlemen." It's like I'm watching a movie, that's how I've planned this speech. I'm wearing my tan pants suit. "You've got to admit, sirs, it's most extremely hard to believe that one incident, one *joke—*"

"Mrs. McQuaid," Stampp cuts me off. He tilts his face toward the ceiling to calm himself. Then he fixes me with those damp eyes. "Isn't there something else you'd like to admit to us today?"

Panic gurgles in my stomach like the last slop of foam in a sink. I turn to the window almost hoping for another slow shower of envelopes; there's only burnt-edged clouds and the top of that elm tree from a different angle. "I don't think so, sir, no."

"Oh, really?" This is Plates. He's giving me quick little nods and breathing loudly from his mouth.

"Mrs. Mc*Quaid*," Stampp starts to say . . .

I don't need to hear any more. I know exactly what he's talking about. It's this: the night I found out my ex had been meeting with Plates, I went on-line for another kid-auction joke.

You may be wondering what would possess a woman to be such a moron. Doesn't every stupid mistake seem a mystery, once you look back on it?

At the time I'd been angry, wound up, drained, scared, desperate for a stress killer; I'd felt low and spiteful and hungry for a laugh at their expense. I can't tell you how badly I wanted a laugh at their expense. The last time I'd done the eBay thing it had been a lot of fun. Nobody learns her lesson show only to little kids who they're tucking in at night. "Here's a line from your son Dylan, received Tuesday last. He said, 'One thing I learned is, when your mom is mad at your dad, don't let her blow-dry your hair, 'cause it'll burn on your scalp.' "

"Why?" My eyes are closed. I imagine blood dribbling from my knuckle, just one bead forming. "Why wasn't I present at such a meeting?"

His condescension comes out as a loud huff from his nose. "Your husband—David McQuaid?—he's been present."

After that, I'm not sure I hear anything Plates says. But I start to get my brain around what's happening to me, to us.

Hours later, the kids are asleep. I go into their room; I don't turn on the light. I step to Morrison's bed. He can tell I'm there, he always knows things in his sleep, and he pulls away. Dylan, he looks so skinny, sweet-dreaming across from his brother. After a while I go back to the kitchen for more coffee. I don't feel like sleeping.

Another working afternoon, I find myself at the Human Services building, sitting in a fluorescent-lit, speckle-tiled conference room across from Mr. Plates and Mr. Stampp. There's a wide-button, black phone between us. Everything Stampp is doing—the way he lisps a little and scratches his huge shaved head as he stares—seems meaningful, cunning somehow, and scary as hell. His humid yellowy eyes look like soap bubbles shivering on pavement.

in one huge jump. Most of us climb the ladder one rung at a time. Who knows, maybe I hate myself. *Looking to unload two brats*, I'd typed stupidly, stupidly.

Anyway.

Now I'm missing most of what Stampp's saying, but I zone back in on: "We are not going to take any direct action against *you*, Mrs. McQuaid." He's smiling. I try to look calm, but by this point my anger just about suffocates me.

"But we are going to support your husband for custody," Stampp says, scratching his bald head. "If it goes to trial—which we believe and frankly hope it will not."

"Trial? Dave the *Rave*? He doesn't—"

"Yes," Mr. Stampp says. "He does."

Plates passes a folded-up notepaper to Stampp, who flattens it on the table and begins reading. " 'To whom it may concern. I admit and acknowledge that as a father I haven't always done particularly good' "—Mr. Stampp half-smirks his fat half-smirk at Mr. Plates before going on—" 'but, regarding that, I have decided with all my heart that I want to be the father that their mother as you can see, cannot. I love these children and care for them . . .' Should I skip to the part, Mrs. McQuaid, where your ex-husband expresses his doubts that you are a good person 'on account of disposition'?"

Plates speaks up, his face gone red as a blister. "You'd be smart to listen to what I'm about to tell you. Negligence is no more unusual in my day-to-day than are blaring car horns on Meadows Street." I'd never heard the guy use a loud voice, and now it's like he's got a megaphone. "Did you slap Morrison's hand 'until it was red' not long ago? Keep quiet, Mrs. McQuaid, I'm going to tell you a story." Plates is rubbing his own fat hand as he snorts. "Nineteen months back, a businesswoman told a large audience at a Republican fund-raiser that she was going to give herself a well-deserved break. How? By placing her kids in the closet for a few weeks. A funny joke, I am sure. I'll wager everyone laughed. Two months later, it was I who found those kids, still in that godforsaken closet. This woman virtually warned two hundred people she was going to do it, and we received not a single concerned phone call." The whole time Plates lectures, I'm focused on his teeth; I could swear they're more level and full than before.

"You may see yourself as a woman posting a joke on the internet." He leans in, elbows on the table, his eyes trying to bore into me. "*I* see a woman starting the ride down the ski slope marked 'unstable.' When your son Dylan falls down, why is it that you 'never' pick him up? 'Never' is *his* word, Mrs. McQuaid. Why are the boys too frightened to venture into your bedroom? Is it because you yell at them? There is quite a case built up here. We are helping the case be built, to be frank. There exists a pattern."

I turn to Mr. Stampp, whose eyes are like the ice at hockey rinks, that blue almost colorless.

"Dylan's a funny kid," I say. My voice is in rags. "He's always goofing off. That's why we call him The Goofer. Really, we do. He likes being The Goofer."

No one's listening.

Stampp tells me something and picks up the phone to start dialing, and when he passes me the receiver, I want to be nice to Dave the Rave, to sound like I'm not upset.

"Hello," Dave says. I catch my reflection in the window. My hair is gray.

The receiver gets damp with my sweat before the Rave and I start talking to each other.

Years and years ago we'd spent a few hours on Hilton Head. This'd been the dawn that Morrison was conceived. The Rave'd been on tour with The Lilacs. We hadn't been together in a while, and the band was set to run off again.

Dave and I saved cash by sleeping on the beach, not that it was so romantic with the bitter cold sand, and my mouth dry; still, at the best moment the sun was rising and the water was rising, The Rave slept on his side near me, his hands tucked under his face, his bangs covering up his eyes, the air smelling like seaweed and like salt and Drakkar, and with a flicker of the brain, I knew then his baby was in me, don't ask me how I knew it.

It's not like I'd thought of ponies and nannies, a big stone house. But we'd have to make a family now, I'd told myself.

Dave and I worked a deal on our own. No courts; easy peasy. I said fine, big shot, try it for a month—Dave'd see if he could deal with the costs of kids and such, costs that are more than financial, as I told him. He swore he'd get up early enough to drive them to school, so they wouldn't have to change districts.

The boys couldn't hold back from crying, of course, when The Rave rolled up this sunny morning—not even Morrison. I didn't say a word, just opened the fucking door, handed my ex a bucket, a mop, a towel.

"What the hell's this?" Dave's baby blues got all squinty and his mouth had trouble. His shirt showed lightning bolts around the word *Alcoholica*.

I cracked open the door a little wider and let Dylan walk out. "You'll see," I said. My voice broke, but I managed to pat Dylan on the head without losing it too badly.

As he followed his brother into The Rave's Civic, Morrison wheeled back as if to say good-bye. He was carrying the George Foreman grill I'd got him for Christmas; then he turned again, away from me and toward the car. He said, "Move over, Dickchew" to his brother, and climbed in.

And so.

Sitting at my small kitchen table in the middle of this quiet, undemanding Saturday, I have mac-and-cheese for one. Right away my place feels so big. I smoke inside. I haven't smoked inside for years. Can't say what I'm going to do the rest of the afternoon or tonight—that's an unfamiliar feeling, and I guess sort of scary. A terrible crying's stuck in my throat, wedged in there and waiting, I'm pretty sure of it. I blow my cigarette ashes around the ashtray. Two crickets are arguing at the window. Against my better judgment I've made it to middle age; I can smoke inside and it feels awfully dead here except for the crickets, who make it even more dead somehow. The crying will come even if I can't feel it just yet, and I'm betting it'll be pretty bad. Any minute now.

The Black Crowes are not my favorite band, not by a country mile. But once, when stitting on the 6 train in Manhattan, I came across a middle-aged woman who was dressed in a Black Crowes T-shirt and who told her companion, "For me, rock and roll is it. It's rock or nothing at all." Maybe I've just been blind to the obvious, but the woman's attitude seemed revelatory to me: there are thousands, perhaps millions, of sixty-year-olds in America who still listen exclusively to music made for adolescents. I wasn't really curious about why she'd chosen the Black Crowes—who make "rebellious" music that's really just a form of nostalgia for lost sounds from lost rebellions—but I began to think about the effect of rock and roll itself on the generations who have grown up knowing no other music.

Rock music and its offshoots—and I use the term broadly enough to include such youth music as hip-hop—are wonderful at moving the young; at helping bourgeois youth develop a skeptical disposition, a safe hint of the bohemian irreverence of the spirit, an aversion to complacency, and a democratic belief that the unschooled, even sometimes the untalented, can create vital art—but isn't the belief that rock and roll is the be-all and end-all of American music something to be outgrown? I guess maybe we live in a society in which nothing immature is ever outgrown.

THE SYSTEM

judy budnitz

There's a ribbon in the willow
And a tire swing rope

"Way Down in the Hole"
Tom Waits

The simplest way to put it would be to say that your father is in prison for a crime he didn't commit. But there's more to the story.

First let me tell you about the town we grew up in. That will explain a lot, I think. Things were different back then. It was a different time, a different place. What I mean is, there was a real sense of community. People looked out for each other. People would give you the shirt off their back, that sort of thing. It's not like here, where you don't know your own neighbors, where they'll steal your laundry out of the machine if you're not watching it, and then *wear your clothes right in front of you without batting an eye.* Here, if you hear strange things through the walls at night, you pretend you didn't.

Where I grew up, it was the sort of town where people stayed put. People were born there, lived out their lives there, and died without venturing more than fifty miles from the place. Small-minded, you might think. But they weren't. I mean, *we* weren't. We were broad of mind, big of heart.

It was a place of flat horizons, empty plains. The land was shaped by the weather—cracked dust bowls could change to gulchy swamp beds overnight. And the skies—you were always looking up, you couldn't help it. Wide, inescapable skies, they were the only entertainment around. They gave us spectacular dusty sunsets, blushing and subtle sunrises. You could watch the births of storms, clouds colliding, darkening, starting to swirl. Growing bigger, rolling closer, rumbling to themselves, electric strands reaching down to touch the ground like insect legs. Old men on front porches used to place bets on when the storms would strike, and how hard. They said you could measure the fury based on the color of the clouds, and their shape. The more bulbous and warty and cauliflowerish the clouds, they said, the worse the storm. "When it looks like your wife's face glaring down, you're in for a doozy," they'd tell each other.

The earth all around had been drained and leached by years of careless farming. I can't remember ever seeing crops; I think all the farmers and ranchers gave up and sold their lands long before I was born. You might see patches of hardy grass or bushes or leathery weeds, but that was it. Windstorms swept through the town, eroding away everything that wasn't fastened down. Dust, brush, clumps of earth. Swing sets. Cows. When I was a girl, I used to worry that I'd wake up after a storm to find the ground gone. I imagined the only things left would be the buildings, balancing on tall, wobbly columns of earth, with giant wind-carved mile-deep canyons gaping between. I imagined how we'd get along, rope bridges slung between the houses, walking a tightrope to school.

I was one of a whole mess of girls. My father was a barber, and how unlucky for him that he had only daughters, who wore their hair long and untrimmed. My father was the sort of man who liked to do things for other people, he'd bend over backward to help you out. And I think it broke his heart that we didn't let him expend his only talent on us. He used to sleepwalk. We'd wake from snip-haunted dreams to see him swaying in the doorway in his white nightshirt, a pair of shears flexing in his hand, murmuring, *Just a trim, girls, just a trim. Please, for me.* I think the main reason he looked forward to us getting married was so that he could indulge our husbands with a lifetime of free haircuts.

Our town, like many, was dominated by one industry, upon which the town's entire economy depended. When I was a girl, I didn't understand how our local business was any different from others. Neighboring towns held fairs, parades, elected a Beet Queen or a Dairy Milk Queen or a Nuclear Power Princess. I remember being disappointed that we didn't do the same.

Our town was home to the largest prison in the state. You could see it from any point in town, and most people drove past its gates at least twice a day. It was made up of several un-adorned, boxy buildings of yellowish brick, the same brick as our school building. If it weren't for the watchtowers and three rings of fences, you might think it was a hospital or an office complex. The prison clock could be heard all over town, you'd hear it at the end of your math class and know that over at the prison the inmates had finished a shift in the workshop. My father was the prison barber, and my mother worked in the prison kitchens. Most of the men in our town were employed by the prison, and most of the women, too.

You couldn't ignore it or forget about it. It was a daily fact of life. Prisoners made up over three-quarters of the population of our town.

Yes, it was uncomfortable to think that other people's wrongdoing put food on our table. But that's how it was. What could you do? You didn't necessarily like it, but you didn't want to go hungry either. You got used to it after a while. And though we didn't hold parades, the people in my town clearly took pride in their work. They felt they were providing a necessary service.

It was the sort of town where everyone knew each other by both name and profession, from Warden Bane to Mrs. Birdie, the prison librarian, from Miss Maudie Manguson, who x-rayed the visitors' packages and cakes, to old Mr. Crouch, who looked after the electric chair.

People were proud of the fact that it was the biggest prison in the state. People like distinctions, they like to be the best, the biggest, the superlative of something.

I know you hear a lot nowadays about prison workers abusing their authority, making life miserable for their charges. But our town wasn't like that. People were idealistic, they believed in the system, and its power to educate and re-habilitate. My father always strove to preserve the individuality of the inmates. I remember going with him on Take Your Child to Work days. He tried to please each prisoner with the cut of his choice—curls, feathers, wings, layers, stubble, shiny bald—you name it. He burned his fingers with bleaches, made gifts of expensive pomade, did his best to comply when men brought in magazine pictures of what they wanted. He had hundreds of men to trim, a ceaseless stream, and he looked like an exotic lawn ornament as he worked, arms flailing, scissors a blur. He was on his feet twelve hours at a time, never resting.

And the pressure was constant. It's a fact that a man's hair grows more quickly in prison. Maybe it's because of the inactivity, all that excess energy expended through the scalp.

And my mother, too. Though she was constrained by the budget, and by the massive amounts she had to cook, she still did her best to make the prison food resemble prison food as little as possible. I would venture to say that the prisoners ate better than we girls did, because she was usually too tired to cook for us by the time she got home, after cutting the crusts off several thousand sandwiches.

My mother's special responsibility was Last Meals. She would spend weeks ordering rare ingredients, experimenting with techniques, marinating, sautéing, stewing, stuffing, spicing, so that a man's last meal should be exactly what he desired. "It's the least I can do," she'd say.

But I'm sure she had mixed feelings about it. On the one

hand, I know she looked forward to the Last Meals, because it gave her a chance to stretch herself, explore, test herself with foods exotic and difficult. She'd get so excited when the requests came in and would be horribly disappointed if they were not sufficiently sophisticated. "Cheeseburger and fries, *again?*" she'd moan. She took great pride in rising to culinary challenges. I'm sure in a way she was proud to have the distinction of being the *last*, the *final*, the *ultimate*. How many of us can claim that, really, about anything? To be the last, the best, the pinnacle of.

And yet, on the other hand, how could she really look forward to those meals? I'm sure deep down she dreaded them.

Did I mention that our prison was a men's prison? For a long time I didn't realize that there were women's prisons elsewhere. I assumed the absence of women meant women were incapable of doing anything bad. Or perhaps they were capable, but too crafty to ever get caught.

I have said we didn't have any parades or festivals. But we did have one big yearly event: the prison rodeo. These rodeos are my most vivid childhood memories. I remember the sawdust in the arena, the smell of horses, the flying hooves, the windmilling arms and snapping heads and bobbing torsos, the strange slow-motion swoop of a man floating through the air. The *noise*. I remember the tension, the excitement, I didn't want to look, but I couldn't *not* look when all around me people were gasping and moaning sympathetically. I remember men getting hurt. A lot of men always got hurt. Some of them had never been on a horse before, but insisted on trying, they wanted to do something, or prove something.

When I remember those rodeos, I think of the smell of my hands (cotton candy) pressed against my face, peering at the action between my fingers.

The rodeos were held in the big arena on the prison grounds. The families of the inmates filled one side of the arena, and the families of the employees filled the other. There were no assigned sections, but people always segregated themselves.

Both sides cheered with equal vigor. They sounded the same to me. But I was very young then, too young to notice differences of tone and tenor. At the time I thought it was nice that everyone was being entertained.

Afterward there would be a big barbecue, ice cream and games for the kids, sack races and three-legged races and that sort of thing. We'd chase each other around on the dusty brown grass that the prisoners kept cut short, snatching fireflies out of the dark. Quit it, our fathers would say, damn kids, they'd say, and go back to their beers and slow drawly jokes that died out before the punch line. Our mothers would have their shoes off and their legs stretched out. The night would come down so slow and easy you wouldn't notice until you realized you could see stars, bright and thickly clustered and low enough to touch.

The inmates' families never lingered. The prison grounds seemed to make them uncomfortable. To me they always felt like home.

But as I was saying, the rodeos only happened when I was very young. Then they stopped.

As I got older, the prison population dipped. The population had always fluctuated quite a bit, but this was different. This was a significant and steady decline. At first we wondered if for some reason a share of our usual quota was being assigned elsewhere. But no, we were told, we were still the biggest in the state and took the largest proportion. It was just that the overall numbers were declining.

"The courts are going soft," my father suggested.

But no, it seemed that fewer people were committing fewer crimes.

"It means the prison system's actually working," one of my sisters said. "Isn't that a good thing?"

"Of course," our mother said with a worried furrow between her brows.

As the population fell and fell, as more inmates reached the ends of their terms and left us and no men came to replace them, my parents grew more and more worried. We heard their voices in the kitchen late at night, discussing.

Because more and more prison employees were getting laid off. Guards, custodians, guidance counselors, art teachers, dishwashers, dentists, secretaries, were being told to hand in their ID badges and uniforms and go home.

"I could be next," my father said.

"Impossible!" my mother declared. "You're the only one. You're essential. But me—thirty people work in that kitchen. We're dispensable."

"But . . . the Last Meals . . ."

"Nobody's awaiting execution these days. When they notice up in the head office, I'll be out on the street in a second! What then? We can't support the girls on your salary!"

Before you start thinking my mother was being overly dramatic, I should mention that back then people tended to have many more children than they do now. Pecks, packs, passels, posses of children. There were quite a lot of us girls.

People continued to lose their jobs, but my parents did not. My mother somehow managed to prove her indispensability. And as for my father, it seemed that hair growth increased as the prison population decreased, as if the inmates who were left were trying to make up for their missing brethren. My father was kept busy.

But no new prisoners came in. My parents worried more and more. So did their friends and coworkers. It was all they talked about, the numbers, the numbers.

"I don't understand it."

"Can it be that people have actually learned to behave themselves?"

"I don't believe it. Not even any petty thievery? There has to be another explanation."

"This is terrible."

"It's a kerfuffle, that's what it is."

All the people who had lost their jobs, they had nothing to do but sit and wait and watch the storm clouds. They were idle and hopeless. You could hear them singing sad songs late at night around campfires. They did not know what to do with their specialized skills. Move to a new town, start a new life, you might say. Go work in a different prison, a school, a hospital, if they were so attached to institutions. But these people had only known one life. They didn't want anything different. All they wanted to do was wait and hope that the tide would turn, that things would go back to normal. They could only hope that people would go back to killing and stealing and hurting each other so the prison would fill up and things would be just like the good old days.

"Why should we move?" they said. "This is our home."

Maybe you think it strange that people would want to cling to such a life. But I don't think I've conveyed to you properly what it was like, back in the day when the prison was thriving. How lovely it was, how sweet and sad to hear the harmonica music pouring over the prison walls at twilight, to see the men like overgrown children playing their listless games of baseball on the other side of the fence. And on our side people were content, they had a reason for being, a purpose in life. Who would want to give that up? If you'd had it, wouldn't *you* cling as long as possible to any hope of getting it back?

Those were dark times, I suppose. I confess I was not as attentive as I should have been. Because by that time I was no longer a child and I was busy falling in love. When you fall in love yourself, you'll see that it is a full-time occupation. Even when you are supposedly doing other things—working, sleeping, brushing your teeth—secretly you know you are just pretending to do them while your inner truer self has not stopped thinking about the loved one for so much as a second.

He was Bobby Bane, son of the prison warden, and he was the finest-looking man I'd ever seen, then or since. I can show you pictures but they do not do him justice. He had pointy eyebrows like a movie-star villain, sunken cheeks that looked like they'd been scooped out with a melon baller, long white teeth that a beaver would envy. Long hair that my father couldn't wait to get his hands on.

I was a fair enough specimen myself in those days. If you look at all my sisters, you can see my parents mixed in an astonishing variety of combinations and permutations: here my father's nose jutting out like a rainspout, there my mother's softly receding chin, here my mother's cheekbones merging oddly with my father's jowls. I think I got the best bit of both: my father's soulful spaniel eyes, my mother's tart and prissy mouth.

We went walking, we wrote each other letters though we lived half a mile apart. I suppose it sounds old-fashioned, but at the time it was considered romantic. I can show you the letters—read them to you someday. His penmanship was not so good but the emotion shines through, you'll see.

Meanwhile, the prison population was dwindling, dwindling. The numbers slipped from the thousands to the hundreds, and then to less than a hundred. More and more employees were let go. A shantytown sprang up on the playing field behind the school, tents and trailers and sheds of tin siding and plastic sheeting. More and more families with no income and no prospects, waiting and praying for the tide to turn, waiting to present themselves when the prison started hiring again.

But maybe it wasn't going to turn. Maybe the world really had become a better place and people were living in peace and harmony, like in songs. But what do I know. I was in love, seeing the world through rose-tinted glasses, as they say.

The prisoners continued to trickle away. Their time was up; they were given new suits and bus tickets. All the way from the prison gates to the bus station they had to endure the reproachful stares of men, women, ragged children. *This is all your fault,* their eyes seemed to say. *Why couldn't you stay put?* Some of the former inmates were so overwhelmed by accusatory stares that they ran sobbing back to the prison gates begging for entry. But the guards kept the gates closed, calling through the bars, "I'm sorry, sir, I'm sorry, sir. You're free to go now," giving them helpful proddings with pointed sticks. So they trudged wearily back to the station and awaited their buses with their eyes shut tight, fingers in their ears.

Soon there was only a skeleton staff left at the prison, pacing the empty, echoing halls, idle and anxious, pestering the remaining three inmates with offerings every few minutes. "Need some laundry done?" "Need a massage?" "Need some coffee?" "Need to talk to someone?" Even these three would not be around much longer, their release dates were coming up. Something had to be done. Men like my father, including my father, began meeting in homes, in restaurants, in the town's one bar.

"What will we do," they said, "when there are none left?"

"The funding will stop, the prison will close, and then what will we do?"

"As long as there is one prisoner, the prison will have to remain open and we will keep our jobs," someone reasoned.

"But what if there are no more criminals in need of punishment? Not even one?"

"Then perhaps we should provide one," someone said softly.

"You mean, one of . . . us?" the others said, shocked.

"For the good of everyone. Wouldn't it be worth it?"

And over a series of days and discussions, the idea began to take hold. If the rest of the state could not provide, we would have to do it ourselves. One of us would have to shoulder the responsibility, provide employment and purpose to the rest of us. And the discussions turned from *how* to *who*. Surprisingly for a town where everyone prided themselves on helping each other out, there were no volunteers.

"I have to run the damn prison, otherwise I'd do it myself," Warden Bane said.

"What about your worthless son?" someone called.

The discussion moved on to other options, but the idea that Bobby Bane was the man for the job somehow fixed itself in people's minds. Don't ask me why. Something about him made people think he'd be able to play the role of a criminal. I said myself he looks like a villain, but I meant the seductive, storybook sort. Not the real kind. If he seemed blundering and worthless in those days, it was only because he was so dizzily, blitheringly in love he could barely walk in a straight line.

Or maybe people wanted to get back at Warden Bane. They were tired of his bossy ways, though he *was* the boss. They thought if he had been smarter, acted sooner, he could have averted the present situation. Also his job would be the last to go; they resented that.

And then, well, poor Bobby. Assaulted from all sides. "Think of the kids out there, Bobby, the kids!" "Do you want to see your father lose his job?" "The whole town's depending on you, son. Step up to the plate!" "Who's going to support your grandparents now? *All* the grandparents out there?" Even his fourth-grade teacher called up to say, "Think of someone else for once." And his brother, slapping his back and saying, "I know you'll do the right thing. You've got it in you, I know it." At first he resisted, but then he began to listen. I could see him start to cave.

Whenever he stepped outside—an endless ocean of imploring, accusing faces. You never saw so many people, just waiting around, watching his every move, peering in the windows of his house, whispering through the heating vents while he slept.

I saw it happening. "Don't do it," I told him. "Don't listen to them! It's ridiculous! You don't owe anybody anything!" But already he was shining all over like a man who'd found his mission. "Let's go away," I said hopelessly. "Let's elope and go to Beet City." But already he was too far gone.

"They need me," he said dreamily. "*You* need me," he

said suddenly. "Both your folks will get to keep their jobs."

"I need you out here, not in there," I said.

"Now don't be selfish," he said, taking my hand.

After that things happened quickly. He took credit for some damage to public property, a streetlight I think, and managed to compound it with some unruliness with the police and some courtroom insolence. Soon he was returned to us in the blue van that brought in the newcomers. And just in time, too—the last of the inmates was just walking reluctantly out the gates as he was brought in.

He settled right in to his cell and spent his time chatting with the grateful, reinstated guards. My father, desperate for something to do, trimmed him once and sometimes twice a day, and my mother cooked him feasts but stuck to regulations with the plastic utensils and metal trays.

The warden managed to rehire a number of old employees by citing the special needs of the one inmate. I was allowed to see him in the visitors' hall after going through the formalities of having my coat groped and my purse searched.

"You should see the amount of mail I get," he told me excitedly. "I've got fans!"

"What about my letters?" I said.

"I got those, too," he said. "They were sort of boring, though."

Now that we had no choice but to write letters, the romance had gone out of them for me. But my sisters thought it was thrilling that I was dating a man in prison. "It's so romantic," they kept saying. "But isn't it dangerous?" they asked, as if they'd forgotten that they'd known Bobby since he was in diapers. "Isn't he just *bursting* with pent-up desire?"

Everyone thought I was being very brave and noble, and when Bobby asked me to marry him, what could I say but yes when it meant his father could rehire the prison chaplain and a few more custodians to sweep out the chapel? And afterward we were allowed conjugal visits, which meant a bit more laundry to do and a few more names on the payroll.

Bobby began to really enjoy his role after that, I think. As his sentence neared its end, his father gave him extra time for bad behavior, he had the power to do that. Bobby gave himself some tattoos and started working out and meditating. He even made tally marks on his cell wall until I told him to quit it, he wasn't fooling anybody.

"You're a fake, a decoy," I told him. "You're the little wooden duck, they're hoping you'll bring in the real thing."

If that was the plan, it wasn't working. Bobby kept on rattling around alone like a flea in a birdcage, while the giant clothes dryer in the basement flung his two little sheets around and the secretaries composed long reams of notes about him to give themselves something to file. My father groomed Bobby's poor head until not a single harassed hair dared show itself above the surface.

Then the nagging voices descended on Bobby again. "If you'd read a few books, we could rehire Librarian Birdie," they said. "There are still hundreds of people outside wanting their jobs back, why aren't you doing anything for *them?*"

"What about poor Mr. Crouch? He's got a daughter in the hospital, six granddaughters to support. If you don't give him something to do, those girls will *die*, you hear me? Do you want *that* on your conscience?"

My mother, though she tried not to mention it, was itching to do another Last Meal. "There's a quail recipe, with truffle stuffing, that I'm dying to try," she'd hint. "If you could just mention it to him . . ."

"But he doesn't need a Last Meal," I said.

"Not yet," she said. "One can always hope."

Then the rumors started. People said that if one family member "checked themselves in," other family members would be guaranteed their jobs back. Warden Bane would neither confirm nor deny. But soon there were rumors that Bobby had company. People began to lift their heads and admire the weather and talk optimistically about the future. It was not uncommon to see families in heated discussion, pointing fingers at one male or another, sometimes drawing straws, sometimes playing the clapping, rhyming games that children use to decide who will be "it" in a game of keep-away. More than once I was assailed by people in the street, they'd grab my arm and say, "Do us a favor and choose one of us. Why? No reason. Just point." And then to the others: "What the lady says, goes."

That was when I left my hometown. It was all so wearying to watch. Bobby cared only about his pen pals and his muscles. And I was pregnant with you, you see. I wanted you to grow up in a different sort of environment.

The changes didn't happen all at once, of course. It was a gradual shift, a slow reversion. Over time the shantytown was dismantled, the gray miserable hordes abandoned the streets, resumed their jobs and homes, and became recognizable again. Some families had arranged a system of rotation, taking turns spending time behind bars. The prison was filling up, though there was plenty of confusion—people had trouble remembering whether they were working or serving time. It did not seem to matter, much, anymore, as long as the daily routines continued, the floors were swept, the food cooked, the lights extinguished, the paychecks issued, and the bells rung at the proper hours for all the town to hear.

And then, to their great relief, fresh inmates from the outside started showing up again, delivered to the gates in a blue van. The world was not perfect after all.

I heard there was talk about holding another prison rodeo. I would never go back to see it, but I find it oddly satisfying to think that the spectators in the stands will no longer sit apart, since the families of workers and inmates are one and the same.

author inspiration

This was the first Tom Waits song I ever heard. And after repeated listenings over many years, its peculiar magic still hasn't worn off. This song always makes me feel wistful, nostalgic, but nostalgic for places I've never been to, nostalgic for a past not my own. Maybe it's because of the wound-down-music-box haunted-fairground feel of the music, or maybe it's the lyrics, which always strike me as ominous and yet strangely comforting.

FOUR LAST SONGS

david ebershoff

High the soul will rise in flight . . .
in the magic realm of night

Herman Hesse

I. SPRING

On a cold spring day in 1912, Mrs. Trevor Harrington, née
Olive Darwin, decided to kill her first husband. She was seventeen, a bride of two weeks, with small brown eyes and a
thin, eager face. There was always something underdeveloped about Olive, her fist as tiny and white as a chick. Her
strongest muscle was upon her ankle, sinewy and tough from
years of pressing the piano pedal. Many people agreed that
Olive wasn't pretty; gifted in music and in the garden, but
not pretty.

Trevor Harrington was sixty-six, and his new bride's first
impression of him was his hair: white, wiry hair everywhere—in his ears and upon his knuckles and on the big ball

of his belly and, like a polar bear rug, spread across his back. The last thing Olive's father had done before dying was arrange the marriage. It was his gift to his daughter, who, as anyone in Washington County could tell you, would never have children, not after the accident with the bull.

Harrington and Olive lived on a small hay farm on Fly Summit Road where they tended fifty-four acres of timothy, a dozen head of cattle, a pair of asses named George and Martha, and a lame thousand-pound pig. In the shed next to the barn Harrington tinkered with the combustion engines he salvaged from the river yards down in Troy and Albany. He would come in for supper slimed with castor oil, and Olive, who had lived a quiet but musical life with her father until only a month ago, would beg him to wash his hands.

Years before, Harrington's first wife died in childbirth, taking with her Little Sue, a baby as tiny as a kitten. He spent the following thirty years more or less alone. Most days he spoke to no one, not even to Mrs. Napp, who at noon would come to the kitchen door with a honey ham warm in the basket. Mrs. Napp would sweep up after Harrington and tackle his pile of wash, her lean but strong arms wringing the crumby sheets and the stiffening long johns until her knuckles turned white. She made such efficient work of the dishes in the sink and the mud tracks on the runner that she was gone within the hour. Mrs. Napp, who lived a hearty life until giving up at eighty-three, died about the same time Olive's father found the tender lump in his groin. His need to secure his daughter's future and Harrington's need for help with the housework coincided. Later, looking back on it, Olive would think of that moment when the tails of George and Martha swung and touched at the gray, mangy tips.

Olive's dowry consisted of the upright piano with its stiff pedal, several books of sheet music, a piano stool needle-pointed with goldenrod, and half a dozen lace napkins. Her domestic skills were capable but not exemplary. Her sewing was sturdy if not elegant. She could boil a mutton joint to a fine ashen gray while keeping the meat on the bone. She was a prize-winning gardener; her corn relish had taken second place in the cannings competition two years back. But Olive's greatest talent, everyone knew, was musical. She was blessed with a keen ear and a good memory and a small but silvery alto. Her tiny fingers moved fast and mouselike upon the upright's ivory. When she sang, the tendons leapt from her throat and the hair at the nape of her neck grew damp. In the evenings she used to sing ballads to her father—"Early Buttercup" and "Fawns in the Snow" and his favorite, "The Mohawk Girl." During the day, she would dash through her housework and the tasks in the kitchen garden in order to find time at the piano. Not long before her father's death she composed her first song, a little ditty called "Springtime For-ever."

On the first day of spring in 1912, the justice of the peace married Olive and Harrington in the Easton town hall. They returned home to the farmhouse through the fields patched with old snow and early crocus. They celebrated at the kitchen table with a pigeon pie. Olive said to her new husband, "I have a gift for you." She went to the piano in the next room and began to sing "Fare thee Well." After a few stanzas, a displeased caw came from Harrington. At first she thought it was gas from the pigeon. She ignored the unpleasant noise and continued to sing. Her back was to him and she didn't see Harrington's beaky gray lips snapping in the nest of his beard. She didn't know he was rising from his chair and moving toward his new wife in a slow, angry lurch. He came to her side and Olive looked into her husband's milky eyes, and in midnote, he slammed the upright's lid upon her right hand. "It seems no one told you," he said, "that I hate music." His tongue was wet and full on his bottom lip. "Another thing. I hate pigeon pie. Honey ham every night, that's what I like."

Then he went to his shed where he spent several hours tinkering with the engines under the kerosene lamp. Through the window she could see him bent over his workbench: he was oiling a piston and fingering a ball bearing as if it were a black pearl. His expression was lost in his hair.

Olive's hand was red and swollen and throbbing. She wrapped it in a tea towel. Upstairs in the bedroom, with her good hand she maneuvered the buttons of her nightdress and brushed out the sheets. Then she climbed in, pulling the blankets tight to her chin, her injured hand resting in a bowl of ice on the nightstand.

At first Olive couldn't sleep. Every time she closed her eyes they snapped open again. In the wall behind the bed a mouse skittered along a beam. It didn't scare her, its tiny, busy feet made her feel less alone: she imagined its bright black eyes. She wanted to stay up with it. Eventually the mouse went silent and Olive fell sleep.

A belt buckle falling to the floor woke Olive. For a moment she didn't know where she was but then Harrington climbed into bed with a smelly gasp. His stale breath reached her only a fraction of a second before his greasy hand. He was covered in castor oil: it stained his shirt and was clumped in his beard and soon Olive was slick with it, too. He rolled on top of her and slipped off and rolled back on, holding himself in place. He made a joke about greased pigs. Only later, when she was cleaning herself in the bath, would Olive realize that the castor oil had probably been for the best.

The next day she went to the shed and found Harrington with his arm deep in a barrel of oil. It was amber and slow moving and glistened in his hair. He explained that he cold-pressed his own castor oil, a sideline that brought in enough extra income to feed the pig, Priscilla, who should have been slaughtered two seasons ago. Harrington's eyes became damp as he spoke of her and her mother, Millicent, who had black spots like a cow.

"What do they use it for?" asked Olive.

"The first yield makes a fine purgative for when your pipes block up. The second makes a real nice engine lubricant."

She followed Harrington to the kitchen yard where he held up a sickly root that could have been an old cucumber vine. "See this? It's my castor plant. Come September I'll have enough seeds for a few barrels." Then he chuckled viciously. "Poisonous as hell. The stupider rabbits come round and nibble at it. At night sometimes you hear 'em screaming. Like ghosts in the field."

Olive's second evening as Harrington's wife was much the same as her first. She asked if she could play the piano and he said, "Not in my house." She reminded him that it was in fact her piano but he said, "Not anymore." She asked if she could sleep on the davenport and he said, "Not as long as I'm alive." She asked what she was supposed to do with herself and Harrington exploded with conjugal rage: it was like watching a rock hit the head of a snowman—white everywhere! "I'll tell you what you're supposed to do with yourself! You're supposed to learn how to bake a goddamn honey ham. Make it sweet as honeycomb." As if he hadn't made his point, Harrington slugged Olive in the stomach. She spent the night cuddling with an ice pack. She hadn't felt so awful down there since the accident with the bull when she was twelve.

Several days later when Harrington was in town buying scratch feed, Olive returned to the piano. The honey ham browning in the oven, she knew, would take care of her husband. Through the house she could smell the sweet, oily crust; its promise brought her a smile. Olive's hand had healed by now and today she felt as well as she had since she'd married Harrington. She played "Come All Ye Songsters," a song her mother had taught her when she was little. Her mother's fingers were long and bony and they would dance on the keys. Now when Olive sang, she thought of her mother's eyes. They were as green as a cat's.

> Come all ye songsters of the sky
> Wake, and assemble in this wood;
> But no ill-boding bird be nigh,
> None but the harmless and the good.

In the oven the ham spat and hissed. The heat weeping from the stove was so greasy it smudged the window in the door. Olive continued singing—"At the Cradle" and "Music for a While" and "Sweeter than Roses." Her voice was light and her fingers fast and the music transported her to her previous life, a girl's life of music and familial love. The bed in her old room had a pillow of velvet scraps. She would suck on it in her sleep, for years until it went bald. She kept a garden at the kitchen door, filled with peonies and pink, girlish cosmos and vegetables, from the second week of May through October. She was twelve when the bull attacked her mother; they said Olive was a fool to try to save her, running up behind the bull like that. Then a few years later her father died, the lump in his groin as big as an egg; now here she was, still at the beginning of her life.

As her singing rose, climbing the notes—*Music for a while shall all your cares beguile*—the door opened and Harrington's footsteps were heavy in her ear. But Olive couldn't stop playing—her fingers found the keys as if on their own!— and she continued to sing, under the music's spell. For a long time Harrington stood at her side. She thought perhaps her singing had beguiled him, too, but then he punched her, a left hook to the cheek that threw her from the stool.

"Where's my supper?"

"Soon, dear."

The table was set with bread and lima beans. In the oven the ham candied in its fat and honey coat. Harrington took his chair and fisted his knife and fork. Olive brought forth the ham on a platter and Harrington inspected it as if it were a newborn. "Now *that* is a honey ham." Olive carved off a slab with a thick rind of honey.

He ate quickly and licked the honey crust from his plate and slurped the oil off his fingers. He chewed down a second slice and then picked off a large chunk of honey crust and took it with him to bed. From downstairs, Olive heard the belt buckle hitting the floor followed by the groans of an old man climbing into bed. It would be there, she knew, in the crumby sheets, in the still-cold night, with the mouse busy in the wall, that he would first realize something was wrong. She waited for it, perched on her piano stool. Trevor Harrington would reach for his wife and find her side of the bed cold and then he would hear the piano and her song. Harrington would stagger to the steps, everything about him heavy and slow, and he would try to call for Olive. But a man who has eaten a ham caked in castor oil will only walk so far, and before she could finish her last song, a lied on the variations of spring, there would be the doomed thump of her husband dropping to the floor, heavy as an old dog lying down.

II. SEPTEMBER

By the time Olive Harrington was thirty-five, she had acquired, neighbors commented, an artistic air. What people had once perceived as underdeveloped they now regarded as pixieish, and this was of the style in 1929, even in the North Country. Little about Olive Harrington had changed over the years. She wore widowhood well. On cold nights she tied about her throat a black cape with a grape felt lining. Her singing had flourished to the point that she gave a much anticipated annual autumn recital in Hubbard Hall. For several years the Methodist organist, Mr. Reed, served as her accompanist. He once played the picture show in Saratoga, experience that gave him a fine sense of drama and pleasing the crowd. Mr. Reed had a long, soft face and long, spidery fingers. He wore his hair in a Cuban cut, and several women, all of them married, noted his resemblance to an Italian opera singer who was in the newspaper for abandoning his wife. Mr. Reed's eyes were black and nearly all pupil, and throughout their many months of rehearsal he kept them turned in the direction of Olive. Mr. Reed would say, "I'd do anything for her," and this was true.

It was Mr. Reed who first alerted Olive to the stranger in the audience moments before her concertina. She was backstage, practicing her scales. "Who do you think he is?" she asked. Her costume was of burnt orange chiffon, suggesting a large autumn leaf. "They say he's from New York City," said Mr. Reed. "They say he's looking to buy the dairy farm outside Shushun." Both Olive and Mr. Reed knew that the farm had five hundred stalls and five thousand acres and the last man to own it had been a millionaire. A bachelor who preferred animals to people, he died without an heir; his estate, once the farm was sold, would go to a dog home in Albany.

"What would a man from New York want with a dairy farm?" It was a good question, but there was no time to answer for two hundred people from across Washington County and even a few from Vermont had gathered in Hubbard Hall for *Mrs. Harrington's Fall Fantasy*.

After the concert, well-wishers arrived backstage. Each took Olive's warm, wet hand and congratulated her. Her neighbors appreciated her musical temperament for they believed it added refinement to the village, if not the entire county. The village also boasted a female watercolorist who had won a prize in Schenectady and a sculptress whose latest work was the giant ceramic pig, grapefruit pink and with a slot down its back, that would remain at the steps of the bank until the first snow. If Olive was eccentric, she was also tolerated. Years ago, Olive buried Trevor Harrington without gossip; she put him to rest in St. Patrick's next to his first wife and Little Sue. No one speculated; certainly no one thought to blame Olive. Maybe someone at the funeral said, *Not much of a tragedy, when you get right down to it*, but that was it.

After the admirers said good-night and Mr. Reed returned to the cottage he shared with a dozen cats, Olive sat at her dressing table wiping the Pan-Cake from her throat. She was still flushed with the excitement of her musical triumph. As she blotted away the makeup, her own glow burned through. Self-regard brings beauty to any face and it was there tonight, shining within Olive. It was then, in the mirror, she saw a second pair of eyes: a stranger lingering at the door. He held the musical program rolled up like a little wand. "Mrs. Harrington?" The man dipped his dimpled chin. He was an attractive, Nordic-looking man, not much older than thirty, with cheeks like apricots and blond hair tonicked into a luster. He introduced himself as Marcus Gardner Sutton. "I'm visiting your fine community. Up looking at a small piece of property. You have a beautiful voice, Mrs. Harrington. Did I once hear you in Salzburg?"

He was staying at the Cambridge Hotel and they dined in the flocked-wallpapered ballroom where he ordered beef au jus for two. "I understand you are a widow. My deepest regrets." Sutton's hard, squarish eyes were like two slate shingles. He spoke with an unidentifiable accent: British, but not quite. Among his many passions was tea; he was a self-described snob about it and he sniffed a bit rudely at the teapot brought to their table by the waiter. Sutton explained that he had recently sold a woman's service magazine, reaping what he called "a small but satisfactory fortune," and was looking to invest. He added, nibbling into a baked apple, "It's time I made myself a home."

"Isn't Washington County a little quaint compared to New York?"

"I'll always keep the town house open, but one can take

only so much of city living, I should say." Olive Harrington understood this, having read most of Mrs. Wharton's novels.

The next day Sutton pulled up to the farm on Fly Summit Road in an open-aired speedster. He wore a white silk scarf and a leather golf cap. They drove to Vermont and found a country dining room that served stuffed grouse and, to the trustworthy customer, fermented cider. The waiter served the cider in coffee cups and looked up nervously when he thought he heard a rap at the door. The cider was sweet and strong and it brightened the fine autumn day outside the window to a near hysteria of late color, old orange and graying red. Dizzy, and maybe in love, Olive and Sutton walked to a waterfall and watched the leaves float downstream. On the drive home he took her hand, then her knee. Later, he asked her to sing for him. In her parlor she gave a private recital, culminating with a touching rendition of "At the Harvest." Together, the eyes of Olive and Marcus misted over, while the teakettle whistled on the stove.

They were married at the end of the month by the justice of the peace in the Easton town hall. Olive wore a red maple leaf in her hair. On their wedding night they retired to Olive's bed, which she had refashioned with eight eyelet pillows. After a turn of lovemaking that caused about as much fuss as a sneeze, the two fell asleep, their little pinkies linked.

Before dawn the mouse began to scratch in the wall. Olive was so used to the noise that it didn't wake her. But the quick, shrill sound of its tiny nails scuttling up the beam startled Sutton. He clutched at Olive like a frightened child. "Is there a ghost?" Olive pressed her palm atop his head and was moved by his tenderness. "Only a mouse." This failed to settle Sutton and he couldn't return to sleep. "We can't live in an infested house now, can we? It's rather unsanitary, I should say."

"There's only one," said Olive.

"Silly, Olive. There's never only one." Sutton tried to fall back to sleep but he tossed this way and that for the rest of the night. Several times he punched the pillows in exhausted frustration. This distressed Olive and the incident set a subtle tone for their marriage: much would be the fault of Olive and for this she would pay.

In the morning Sutton kissed her forehead. He was cheery and the shine had returned to his cheeks. "Calling in the exterminator is the only thing to do. Wouldn't you agree, my dear?" From his polite, inflexible, tight-jawed voice Olive could tell that her opinion—not just on how to dispatch the mouse, but on everything—interested Sutton not at all. Recently he had changed his mind about the dairy farm and by the second week of marriage he stopped mentioning the East Side town house altogether. The exterminator came and in each corner of the house he left chunks of Swiss cheese stuffed with gray, gooey poison. "I guarantee your mouse will be dead by dawn." The exterminator's nose was red with burst capillaries and he had a wizened face that made it look as if he had outlived everyone and everything. He and Harrington had been friends; sometimes he would stop by the farmhouse and offer Harrington an extermination at half price, but Harrington never took him up on the offer.

Now Olive asked the exterminator how many vermin he thought he'd killed over the years. His voice was steady and aged and humble when he said seriously, "About a million."

When the exterminator finished setting out the poison, Sutton looked up from his teapot and said, "Olive, dear, pay the gentleman."

Over the years Olive had amassed a small but pleasing sum in her savings account. The Harrington farm was paid for and she was careful to promptly settle her account at the cooperative by the first of the month. Mr. Beckley rented the timothy fields and was good about paying on time, except the year there was snow in August. Olive took minor pride in her assets, storing her passbook and her deed in a safe the size of a Bible. She shared the safe's combination with Sutton, assuming it as much her duty as making love to him; she minded both only a little.

Each afternoon Sutton drove into the village to fetch the papers from Albany, and he spent the evening poring over the financial page, sometimes thrusting it into the fire, other times shredding it with what seemed to Olive as spite. He would join her at supper smudged with newsprint and with a sickly frown. She once inquired, "Did you keep much in the market?" Marcus instantly perked up, shaking the distress from his face, and said, "Not at all, dear. In fact, I got out just in time." Once, when he was in town, the telephone rang and a man asked for Mr. Sutton. "Would you give him a message? This is Mr. Grove from the Merchant's National Bank, Department of Loans and Liens. Please have him call back at once." When Olive delivered the message, Marcus twitched and then recomposed himself. "Never heard of him."

Olive and Marcus made a habit of dining at the Cambridge Hotel on Sundays; quickly he become friendly with many people in the village and so Olive did not notice, at least at first, Marcus's departure from the table to greet a neighbor just as the bill arrived. At church, he would nudge her to drop her coins into the dish and then pass it on himself cheerfully. Although he never ventured back to New York City, he continued to order his clothing from a shop on East Sixty-third. The shirts arrived in blue cardboard and pink-and-white string, followed, a few days later, by a small, discreet envelope, like the kind children use to leave money at church. Marcus would deposit the unopened envelope upon Olive's piano.

One Friday they took the train to Montreal and stayed at a hotel overlooking a park. Olive stumbled badly with the French menus, ordering marinated tongue when she wanted rabbit pie. When they passed the window of a furrier, Marcus steered her inside. A man with a pencil mustache helped Olive out of her cape and into ankle-length coats of squirrel and white fox. The coats were heavy and nearly swallowed Olive. When she looked at herself in the three-way mirror, she saw only her small dark eyes peering rodentlike from the fur. "Do you carry chinchilla?" asked Marcus. "Do you carry raccoon?" He turned to his wife. "Which one do you want, my dear?" Olive felt a hot anger rise in her breast. "Can't decide?" said Marcus. "Then why not take two?" Olive peeled herself out of the fur and told the clerk she would pass today. As she gathered her things, Marcus slipped himself into a gentleman's raccoon and handed the man a card: "You'll be kind enough to send the bill here."

A few weeks later a mouse returned to the farmhouse. The first clue was the pellets left upon the stove, as dark and shiny as iron filings. Then came the skittering in the walls. "It's a farmhouse," Olive explained. "If you have hay fields, you have field mice." But Marcus grumped and turned over in bed and punched the pillows with such nastiness that one night Olive got up. She wrapped herself in a flannel robe and went downstairs to her piano. She played a lullaby, the somber notes and her pretty voice covering up the mouse running between ceiling and floor. Soon from upstairs came the little piggy sound of her husband's snore. Olive continued to play, her fingers finding the notes as if on their own and her register deepening to an amber hue. *He will gather us around, all around, all around. . . .*

In the morning Marcus called the exterminator. He was out buying the newspapers when the man came and scooped his poison into the corners. "Don't touch it for a week," the exterminator warned. Marcus would want his afternoon tea and Olive set the kettle on the stove. While she waited for him to return, the telephone rang. "Is Mr. Sutton in? Would you ask him to call Mr. Grove at Merchant's National? It's rather urgent." And then, "Have you given him my messages, Mrs. Sutton?"

When Sutton returned, he took his chair beneath the

lamp and hid himself behind the shield of newsprint. Olive steeped and poured the tea. He brought the hot rim to his lips. "Mmmm, a new kind, my dear?"

"Bitter rose. Do you like it?"

"Not bad, is it?"

She began to play the piano and sing a folk song about the bounty, and Marcus said from behind the newspaper, "Lovely voice, my dear. Make any man weak in the knees, it would." He laughed at his own romantic nature.

Olive continued to play. After some time she said, "The exterminator came."

"So I smell."

"He should be dead by the middle of the night."

"Now what makes you so sure that mouse of ours is a male, my dear? It's a rather unkind thing for you to say about my half of the breed."

"It's not unkind if it's true."

"Once again, you're right, Olive dear." He rose from his chair and kissed the crown of her head the way her father used to. "Keep singing. The world's falling to pieces and the only thing that'll help is your pretty voice."

He returned to the newspaper and swallowed the last of his tea and poured another cup. Not long after, he said he was feeling sleepy and would go upstairs for a lie-down. "But do keep playing, dear. No greater lullaby than one of your songs." His feet were heavy upon the steps and Olive's fingers were light upon the keys. She played until dusk and beyond and her music accompanied the noises—the skittering mouse and the retching, strangling moans—that filled the farmhouse in the autumn night.

III. UPON GOING TO SLEEP

By the spring of 1942 nearly every man of able body, including Mr. Reed, had volunteered for duty. Washington County felt like a planet in a scientific romance, populated by only the young and the old and the female. Mr. Reed signed up to serve in a naval band aboard a carrier in the Pacific. A few days before his departure he confessed to Olive his fear of death, and they agreed to marry. The justice of the peace united them in a brief service in the Easton town hall. They did not celebrate or consummate. His departing lips upon her cheek were as velvety as a grandmother's.

Olive wrote Mr. Reed every day. Sometime after the death of Sutton she started composing song cycles, usually quattros. She would send them to Mr. Reed, the music annotated with questions: *How does this sound? Is it beautiful?* Months later a reply would arrive on paper warped with humidity: "I played your lovely 'From the Mountaintop' in chapel the Sunday past and the good sailors wept."

A year went by and then two, and despite her daily letters to Mr. Reed, she felt as if she had returned to widowhood. She gave her autumn recital, less gay this year round. She formed a canning circle to send stewed vegetables to the front, and she brushed her now silver hair to a pretty, elfish sheen. In the evenings she played the piano while listening to the war updates on the radio. The war took on a permanent feeling—the nightly recount of lines crossed and atolls gained; the murderous tally of lost tanks, downed fighters, torpedoed ships; the acute awareness of suffering, as if an antenna she didn't know she possessed had been raised. She, and others, forgot that there was such a thing as peace.

Then Germany fell and Europe was liberated and before the end of summer Japan, too. Late one night, just as Olive was falling asleep, the eyelet pillows arranged around her, noise came from the kitchen. She thought it was the mouse, but it came again, this time more like a rap on the door, and then someone was calling her name.

It was Mr. Reed. She clutched her nightdress at the throat as she let him in and watched him deposit his duffel upon the davenport. The navy had improved his posture, and years on ship had cured his cheeks to a leathery brown. But his hands were still spidery and he kissed Olive in a maternal sort of way. In their letters they had written, vaguely, about living together at the farmhouse upon his return. She had said that she would welcome him, if only because she believed she would never see him again. There comes a point, Olive knew, when a solitary person can no longer share her heart, or her house. We get stuck in our ways until our ways are who we are. It's a mysteriously fast leap—the dash from flexible youth to this. A tiny tremor shook Olive as she feared that she could not make room for her husband: Had something in her shriveled beyond repair?

And now here he was, in peacoat and cap, compassionate Mr. Reed, a man who always sided with the lamb. She had taken his name—how quickly the village had grown used to saying *Morning, Mrs. Reed*—but now it almost felt as if the name had always belonged to her and he was the borrower. She could see deep in his eyes he felt the same.

"How about some music?" proposed Mr. Reed. "I'll accompany you."

"It's late," she said a bit more harshly than she intended. "We should go to bed."

Olive and Mr. Reed studied one another; what would they do? The last thing Olive wanted was to grow to hate Mr. Reed. Oh, how cruel the tired heart can turn. She said, "I'll make up the davenport for you."

This arrangement brought immediate relief to Mr. Reed's face. Soon Olive was asleep upstairs and Mr. Reed had curled into a ball on the davenport, clutching to his breast one of the eyelet pillows. Their routine was set, their marriage defined, and each was satisfied with the terms.

Tension arises from mismatched expectations, and now that Olive and Mr. Reed knew that each wanted—or, rather, did not want—the same thing, the two fell into secure companionship. They dined together but neither felt slighted if one or the other journeyed into town or down to Albany alone. There was no obligation to report to the other every thought or whim, every hunger and thirst, every bowel movement and eruption of gas. A level of civility uncommon to marriage defined their interaction; she continued to call him

Mr. Reed and he knew never to enter her bedroom, and he never wanted to. The village of Cambridge speculated about the nature of their marriage, but the speculation was kindly and well-intended, acknowledging that Olive and Mr. Reed were happy; happier than most.

They began a series of soirees of song in the parlor, and invitations to these became coveted. People from across Washington County would perch upon the davenport, sipping tea and nibbling ham sandwiches, while Mr. Reed played the piano and Olive sang. When the guests were gone and the plates stacked in the sink, Olive and Mr. Reed embraced at the foot of the stairs and said good-night. Upon going to sleep Olive would reflect on the passage of time. She kept a notepad at her bedside and she would write down the bars of music that accompanied her dreams. In the morning Mr. Reed would play them, as if blowing upon them and bringing them to life.

She kept a kitchen garden similar to the one she had grown when she was a girl. Each year its bounty multiplied so that by late summer she and Mr. Reed delivered baskets of vegetables to the war widows across Washington County. There were tomatoes and snap beans and zucchini as big as forearms; in autumn, squashes and roots in such supply that together she and Mr. Reed built a bin in the basement to store them through the winter. Rose potatoes and yellow squash and leafy turnips and pearl onions and bloody sugar beets. Mr. Reed was a gardening novice but he was curious; he would work in the garden at Olive's side, asking her what even the most common plant was. "*That?* Why that's spinach." She ordered seeds Mr. Reed had never heard of. "What's that?" "Okra." "And that?" "A gooseberry." She would arrange the vegetables by shape and color in neat piles like at a market.

Sometimes in the late summer vegetables that even Olive couldn't identify would rise from the earth: bulbs like billiard balls and strange fleshy tubers. "It must've got into the seed pack," Olive would say. "Isn't that the fun of a garden? You never know just what will pop up." Dutifully Mr. Reed would carry the harvest to the basement. In the evenings Olive would sing her song cycles, refining them while Mr. Reed accompanied her. In the autumn she wrote a cycle of four songs about the apple, the potato, the pale cabbage, as big as a head, and the winter looming before them all.

One day she boiled a thin, crispy root without knowing what it was. Mr. Reed shrugged and declared it delicious nonetheless. Another time she served what she thought was a fingerling, but she couldn't be sure. In late October, after all the vegetables were picked, they worked together clearing the beds before the first snow. They raked and hoed and turned the soil and they could see the ghost of their breath. When they finished the last of their work for the season, they returned to the warm kitchen for some tea. Mr. Reed, freeing himself from his coat, said, "Not a bad pair, are we?"

And on days when she did not feel like cooking or an errand kept her in the village, Mr. Reed happily entered the kitchen and lit the stove on his own. Such was the day—a day in late autumn when the world is drained of color and the sun is a smudge in the hard sky—when Olive came down with the season's first flu. She took to bed in the late morning, achy and feverish. Downstairs she heard Mr. Reed cooking: the cupboards, the pans, the running water, the chopping knife. Olive was feeling weary and foggy in mind. She hovered upon the threshold of sleep for several hours. The skittering mouse, happy in the warm wall, brought comfort and memories. The sounds of Mr. Reed moving about the kitchen were comforting as well; Olive thought back to that night a few years before when Mr. Reed had turned up after the war. Never could she have imagined the ease with which they now lived. Just when you think life cannot change, it has a way of rearranging itself indeed: this was Olive's thought as the flu, a nasty bout that had already sent the hardware store owner and the justice of the peace to the hospital, overtook Olive. She shivered and her cold sweat stained the pillows. Just before her mind became unclear, it occurred to her, for a brief moment, that she might die, but the thought was too far-fetched and her mind went numb. Soon, Mr. Reed had finished his cooking and he was calling from the foot of the stairs, "Olive, can I bring you anything?"

"Play some music. It'll help me sleep."

Mr. Reed's fingers were slow and somber upon the keys, and his darkened tenor climbed the staircase wearily. He played one of her songs. It was as familiar as the voice in her head.

Upon going to sleep at night
Your hand reaches me in fright.
The touch of frost promises dawn
When the unclean spirits hurry on.

Olive drifted in and out of sleep and Mr. Reed's singing guided her into its blackness. She spent the afternoon in the delirium of flu, mindlessly nibbling upon the corner of a pillow like a rabbit upon a root. Then at last she passed out and slept. Her sleep was long and uninterrupted and transported her.

Hours later Olive woke to a quiet house. The clock's delicate chime told her it was the middle of the night. Unsure of something, she called for Mr. Reed. There was no reply: all was still except the busy mouse, scurrying relentlessly.

"Mr. Reed?" The mouse stopped. "Mr. Reed? Would you bring me a cup of tea?" She felt the urge to ask him to sit upon the bed and stroke her damp hand. He had never seen her bedroom, and any other night this would have brought a girlish flutter to Olive's breast—her ability to preserve youth's privacy. Except that the silence was frightening, as only silence in the countryside is. "Mr. Reed?"

The mouse replied by running the length of house.

She rose from bed and her footfall stopped the mouse, wherever he was. Olive imagined him twitching in the dark, the tiny mite of his heart pumping blood furiously. Silly creature, she told herself. Now she felt a bit stronger, the worst of the flu had passed. She descended the stairs with a restored presence of mind. Her keen eye peered deeply into the dark.

Olive was beginning to feel like her old self—soul fortified and erect!—until she found Mr. Reed lying in a heap on the floor, one cold dead hand reaching up the steps.

IV. AT SUNSET

This time there was an inquiry, a series of interviews, and a symphony of speculation. In the end Olive Reed wasn't charged with poisoning her husband, but many people in Washington County doubted her innocence. "Picked, chopped, fried, and ate a castor root—all on his own? Is that what she wants us to believe?" The sharpest skeptics sang, "Makes you wonder about the other poor saps, doesn't it?"

But within a few years few remembered Harrington or Sutton or, by 1970, even Mr. Reed. People knew she was a widow three times, and that was enough information about a woman as old as Olive. Those who'd never met her called her Widow Olive and her last name was forgotten, like something extinct. Gossip became myth and myth became fact: during Vietnam, wives and girlfriends with men over there went a mile out of their way to avoid passing the farmhouse on Fly Summit Road. "I know it's superstitious and all," they would say. "Even so." The young women who said this wore their hair beneath blue-and-white bandannas; they shared corduroy maternity smocks and they couldn't accurately name any of Olive's husbands or the circumstances of their deaths, but, as they say, even so.

Olive minded none of this. She tended the farm chores and continued to rent the fields to Mr. Beckley's son, and she spent several hours a day composing and singing. Because few spoke to Olive, her trips into the village were excursions of efficiency. Her voice, often unused until her nightly singing, acquired a dustiness by afternoon. Her kitchen garden thrived and her cutting bed was so extravagant in color and height that those driving down Fly Summit Road couldn't help but stare at the bursting peonies in June, or the riot of the poor black-eyed Susans in August. Hers was an idyllic life: the whitewashed farmhouse, the neat red barn, the raked and staked gardens, her music at night. She was never lonely, never felt sorry for herself. She thought of Mr. Reed often, but never with regret. She planned to live to a hundred and then die in her bed, with the mouse still skittering in the wall. There was no reason to think she might not. There was no reason for Olive to fear.

One day when Olive was in her late seventies, she woke up and discovered she could not hear. She supposed what one might suppose in such a situation: earwax, an infection, a temporary loss. But the doctor, who wasn't much older than a boy, informed her otherwise. He wrote on a piece of paper: "I'm afraid there's nothing I can do."

The doctor's name was Henry Cupper; he was part of a government program that returned army doctors to the countryside. Dr. Cupper wore bushy sideburns and a leather thong around his wrist and an open collar. There was a touching secrecy to him, as if he had been damaged at some point and had an unnatural reaction to suffering, which in fact was true. He was thirty-two and had served eighteen months in the army until he acquired a mysterious parasite after swimming in the Perfume River upstream from Hue. "Almost a year in the hospital in Honolulu," he scribbled in a note to Olive. "My system was poisoned all the way through. Even today we don't know what it was. Meanwhile, half my company was blown up in a coconut grove." Dr. Cupper remained just young enough to still say, "I became a doctor to help others."

He worked in Washington County nine months before he first treated Olive. In this time, among other duties, he delivered seven babies, set three broken arms, sewed two hundred stitches, cleared a dozen sets of blocked-up pipes, and attended the deaths of two elderly women whose hearts barely beat in their chests. Olive read of their deaths in the newspaper and tsked over the shame; later, when Dr. Cupper was treating her, he wrote in one of the many notes that the women had gone peacefully. "It was time."

He fell into a routine of dropping by the farmhouse on Fly Summit Road every Monday. After examining Olive's ears and finding no change, he would politely exchange notes with her for ten or fifteen minutes before moving on. "So many patients," he wrote on Olive's notepad. "None as patient as you." His handwriting was sloppy and difficult to read at first, but as the weeks and then months passed, she grew accustomed to its precarious slant. Once she inquired if he hoped to have a family, and Dr. Cupper proved how honest a man he was by writing quickly, "I'm afraid I'm unable to."

Once he wrote, "You must have been a beautiful girl."

He rearranged his schedule so that he visited her at the end of his rounds. She would make tea as the evening descended upon the farmland and they would pass notes, sharing the stories of their pasts. Dr. Cupper was from Dresden, an hour to the north. Before shipping off to Hue he had married the most beautiful girl in the township. "She left me within a year," he wrote. "There was a baby, but he didn't live." Olive recognized the pain around his eyes. It was all he revealed about the loss, but it was more than Olive would have expected: she wondered if each generation believed in the truth a little more than the previous. Probably not, but Dr. Cupper would make you think so. Dr. Cupper would make you believe in anything.

Sometimes she would play the piano for him. She hadn't abandoned her music, but the joy had diminished. As time went by fewer melodies arose in her head. Then they stopped altogether. She didn't dare sing for anyone, especially the doctor. In truth there was no one to sing for except Dr. Cupper. How quickly Olive had become an old old lady! Deaf and nearly mute, with tufts of flat, snowy hair around her face. Recently she had trouble sleeping, bothered by a new fear she'd never wake up. She was older than Harrington had been when he ate the ham. She was quickly becoming older than anyone she had ever known. Whenever Olive saw a little girl in the village, she would have to suppress the urge to cup her warm, milky cheeks and warn her against the on-slaught of time. But the child wouldn't believe her: What child would? The only people who believe in the reality of age are the very old; doesn't everyone else believe she will be spared?

She asked this question of Dr. Cupper, and he agreed that he had yet to meet a patient who was prepared to die. "Sometimes I find myself in the position of having to help them." It was the first time he had brought up death with her: the word scribbled on his notepad caused a lurch within.

After Cupper had been coming to see her for nearly half a year, she asked in a note, "How am I holding up, Doctor?

"Strong as a bull."

"You'd tell me if there's something wrong? If you start to see a decline?"

He promised he would.

The following Monday Dr. Cupper said he'd like to give Olive a full examination. He asked her to undress. "Lie down on your bed," he wrote. "I'll be up in a few minutes."

While unhooking her dress, Olive looked to the sunset upon the western fields. It was early November and the day was ending quickly, freezing up. Soon the sky would be black, and even after all these years it startled Olive how dark the late afternoons in autumn were: as dark as midnight at five o'clock. She unhooked her dress and it fell to the floor, the cardboard belt landing softly on her foot. Olive rolled down her stockings, and soon she was wearing nothing but her slip with the scalloped hem. Lying atop the bedspread, she felt the room's chill. Outside, soon the horizon would collapse into the blue-black of dusk; night would bury the day, again and again.

She sensed Dr. Cupper knocking at the door. She turned and found him standing in the doorframe, stethoscope round the neck. He was a handsome young man, Olive noted; he who would marry again and she hoped his wife would offer sympathy when he told her of his deficiency. Who can predict what we are capable of forgiving? Certainly not Olive, and by now she had given up.

Dr. Cupper placed the cold stethoscope upon her breast and turned away; he was looking out the window to the quick dusk. From his furrowed brow Olive sensed that he, too, was noting the injustice of time. He said something and Olive didn't understand. He had her lie upon her hip and he raised her slip to her waist and placed the stethoscope just above her groin. His fingers were warm; she knew that she must appear to him as nothing more than a pile of moley bones. His finger traced the hoof scar that dented the flesh beneath her navel; so old the scar was, it was as if it had always been there. Except that Olive remembered the accident as if it had happened only yesterday: the kick that shot her across the field and left her bleeding and half-unconscious. The shriek of her father from the porch. He shot the bull between the eyes, and the black, shiny horns hung above the front door until the day he died. Olive had lost her hearing for a week, and then it returned, with a *pop!* like a cork pulled from a bottle. *You're going to be fine,* her father tried to explain while she convalesced. *But you'll never be able to have . . .* as if she didn't already know.

"Relax, Olive," Dr. Cupper wrote on the notepad at the bedside that had once been there for her songs.

"I'm going to give you something to help you sleep."

Olive nodded, thinking that would be nice. Dr. Cupper took a syringe from his bag and held it to his eye and filliped the needle. He doused a bit of cotton with alcohol and sterilized a spot on her buttock. Soon the syringe was sinking into her, and there was a cold sensation just beneath the skin; it spread out and then passed away. Dr. Cupper returned the syringe to his bag. His hand fell to her naked hip and stayed there, stroking her just a little.

Outside, the last bit of dusk was draining from the sky. In no more than a minute, the cold night would be upon them. How permanent darkness can seem! Dr. Cupper took Olive's hand and massaged her swollen knuckles and together they looked to the window that was already frosting over. The house was silent, the world was silent; she didn't know if the mouse lived in the wall anymore. There was no one to listen for it in the night. Once or twice, knowing it was a silly thing to do, Olive had called out, *Oh, mousey mousey, are you there?* Once or twice she had sung, *Oh, mousey mousey, do you care?*

"Do you hear anything?" she wrote in a last note to Dr. Cupper.

"Not a thing. The house is still."

"Not even a mouse?"

Olive felt the movement of Dr. Cupper's chuckle. She closed her eyes. He pulled her slip down across her hip and helped her lie back into the bald pillows. The quiet was the quiet of the dead, and Dr. Cupper returned his stethoscope to his bag. For a long time he stood in the dark at Olive's side and listened to the early long night. The temperature was dropping and the wind was picking up: the nightsong heralded winter's dust. Those with a good ear would hear the music of the world cracking and drying, the brittle shiver and creak; the folding, the closing, the burrowing into the deep. At season's end and in night's morn, oh, must we always regret the cold onslaught of our final sleep?

DYING ON THE VINE

elissa schappell

*I've been chasing ghosts and I don't like it. I wish
someone would show me where to draw the line.*

**"Dying on the Vine"
John Cale**

F or years Tracy chased Ray through crowded museums
and poorly lit train stations—once, while in pursuit of
her ex-boyfriend, she'd seen the Last Supper being
played out in an airport lounge. There was Jesus, lit by the
neon of a Bud Light sign with a plate of nachos at his elbow;
Judas, at his side, was tucking into some atomic chicken
wings. The Son of God had waved at her to join them, but
she kept running. She passed up witnessing the one-of-you-
will-betray speech, just because of Ray.

In the beginning when Tracy awoke from these dreams,
her chest was clenched with sadness, and she felt sore, like
Ray had physically forced his way through her skin, she felt
invaded. Since the day he'd disappeared from her life—the
phone line he'd been pirating had been disconnected, he refused to answer her letters—he continued to cheat her. He

was a blur on a bicycle grazing her elbow in the East Village, not even braking; he was at the back of CBGB's standing hunch-shouldered in the shadows, watching her until she spotted him, then he'd make a quick escape, leaving only the faintest scent of cigarettes and turpentine.

Now, seven years later, the dreams had changed, they were gifts now. She was elated when she saw Ray in dreams. In one dream she was a kid walking down a road in her neighborhood and he'd pulled up next to her in his cherry red Nova and told her to hop in. Other times he would appear outside her apartment and she'd tuck her hand inside his jacket pocket and they'd walk talking about art and music until she realized—the way one does when you spend time with the dead in dreams—that sadly, this wasn't happening in real time. He wasn't really back, and they weren't reconciled, and she'd wake up. She no longer felt angry, or sad anymore, instead she felt a tenderness that faded to nostalgia for the girl she'd been in the dream, the first self she'd ever really liked.

At twenty-two she'd believed that love was two people pretending to be the person the other one needs them to be. It wasn't hard for her, she liked cooking for Ray, black beans and rice, eggs and green peppers and onions, she liked his artsy friends hanging around drinking cheap wine and listening to old blues records by men with names like Big Daddy and Blind Lemon, she liked that she had turned into a character who was no longer supposed to sulk in silence making just a bit too much noise as she put away the dishes she'd just cleaned, but that she now had permission to yell at Ray and throw things. In fact, one night an empty gin bottle smashing against the brick wall in the apartment had the effect of turning Ray on so much he'd stalked over and dragged into the bedroom. She didn't care when Ray couldn't get it up; after all, as he'd told her once, Jackson Pollock was a bad lay, too. She liked the way he urged her, no, *insisted* that she read her "work" to him, bad, adolescent tales of dead pets and silent fathers. It felt like playacting to her, this was the way a couple of artists young and in love were supposed to behave, and so they did. She liked the way he'd kiss her and pull off her shirt the moment they shut the apartment door, the way he brought her things he'd bought or found on the street, perfect gifts she'd never known she'd wanted, no one from her past would ever have conceived of giving her, a red-beaded lamp, a faux fur stole, a first edition of *The Sun Also Rises*. She was taken aback by how much she needed them, how right they were for her. Suddenly everything that came before seemed ill-fitting, immature, and just wrong. Mostly though, what she missed was the way she felt with Ray, every day was an awakening, it was like they were the first people to ever think what they thought, and do what they did. No one was like them.

While Ray utilized his fine arts degree from the Art Institute of Cincinnati making "frozen moments" sculptures—the fork hovering over the plate of spaghetti, the beer pouring from the bottle foaming up in the glass—she worked in a fancy little art-book store, mostly re-alphabetizing; it seemed people who buy fancy art books thought it was beneath them to put the books away properly. Through the store she'd met a man who allowed her to write movie reviews for his esoteric little film magazine that considered the fact that it paid almost nothing a symbol of integrity, badge of honor. Life was good.

Now, seven years later she was at an advertising agency as the assistant to the head of human resources—a term that sounded sinister to her, as though she were handing heavy machinery to the person in charge of drilling the best parts out of a person, or harvesting human waste—which was what the job felt like sometimes.

"I don't care what you say," her mother had said when she told her about the job, "This is as it should be—finally, a real job—a job with promise. There's no limit—"

"Mother."

Tracy's mother had thought it the epitome of irresponsibility the way she and Ray had just quit their jobs—Ray insisted on calling them their "day jobs"—and run off to Mexico, the two of them not even engaged. "What do you think your life is, a movie? Life is not a movie," she'd say.

"I know, I know," Tracy said, wanting to get off the phone.

"It's not Hollywood," her mother said.

"You're right, Mother." Tracy gave her mother the bird.

It was easier to tell her mother she was right than to listen to her tell how she'd typed up all of Tracy's father's papers in college and then law school, how she'd driven car pools, and hosted PTA meetings, the banality of it all crushed Tracy. She was not her mother, would not be her mother.

"I've got a piece coming out in the *Village Voice*," she'd

said, hoping this sounded foreign and counterculture to her mother.

"How nice," she said. "What's it on?"

She wished she'd thought before she answered, "Italian cheeses."

"How is Tad?" her mother asked. This concerned Tracy; what about Tad put her mother in mind of cheese?

"I'll send it to you," she said.

It had been years since Tracy had seen Ray anywhere but in dreams. Occasionally when Tracy was downtown, she'd think she saw him out of the corner of her eye. A short and stocky, wild-haired man in an untucked white shirt, unbuttoned almost to the waist like a young Julian Schnabel, the cuffs stained with coffee from walking and drinking at the same time, and paint-spattered jeans, which he wore like a flag. It was embarrassing to admit but the first thought that always came into her head was *What am I wearing?* Was it what had basically become her uniform: sensible pumps, a knee-length dark skirt, and a blazer? She wished she didn't think the word every time she put it on as it seemed to suggest a bold soul hacking through the jungle with a machete, which couldn't be further from reality. No, she wore a jacket, a straitjacket was more like it. Would Ray even recognize her now, her black hair cut to her shoulders, her hips not as slim? Would he even look twice?

Her second thought was always *Thank God Tad isn't with me.*

Tad had been her boss at the agency when she first started working there five years ago. It was a secret. When he came into her department, she lowered her eyes and called him *Mr. Parker*, they kissed in the supply closet, it was all so cliché. He made her laugh by sneaking up behind her in the office and doing the voices of the animals he'd written commercials for, a French bulldog frying bacon and livers, a koala bear ordering a rum and Coke on an airline. He reminded her of a koala with his gray eyes and large nose. She liked this. She also liked that he was taller than Ray, and that this would have bothered him greatly.

The first time Tad had come to her apartment, he'd said, "I like the art."

She'd thought, at first, that he was making a bad joke. She'd taken down all of Ray's paintings after a year of his absence—when it was clear he was gone. It was too hard to look at them, one was an apology, one a thank one, one a sketch of her outside a gas station he'd made when they'd driven cross-country on their third date. All that remained now were the faint outlines on the wall, ghosts of the paintings: a car on fire on a dock at sunset, a man standing in the dark with a woman pointing a gun at a tin can. Tad had walked around the room, tracing with his finger the blank spaces on the wallpaper, as though the blocks of light were some kind of abstract art, and that it was genius of her to own them. He wanted to take care of her.

One day a booklet ended up on her desk explaining that the company was now going to offer to pay part of the tuition for any sort of advance degrees that might enhance their employees' performance. As a lark, she'd applied to the creative writing program at the local college, and to her surprise was accepted.

"My mother was right, schools do look at what clubs you joined," she said to Tad. "Glee club, Small Animal Lovers, golf team . . . it all paid off."

"Don't be silly," Tad said. He didn't like it when she made fun of herself.

"Maybe it's like the SATs: if you spell your name right, you get two hundred points off the bat. Maybe they have low standards, or maybe they are mistaken in thinking I am handicapped, or some obscure ethnicity—does my name sound Burmese?"

"I'm not surprised," Tad said, pushing her hair back from her face in a way that seemed both annoyingly paternal and terribly loving. "Just don't write about me," he joked.

She didn't. She wrote about Mexico and Ray, typing with tears in her eyes, then trotted into class dumb and eager to please as a dog bringing his master his slippers and the newspaper. Always it was the same thing.

"I just don't like these people," a guy in a blue suit said, as he pulled off his necktie and stuffed into his briefcase. "And why Mexico, why not Cuba? Cuba is a happening place now. Or Nigeria, then you'd have something."

Tracy wrote down *Cuba*.

The guy smelled of cigarettes. He always smoked during the break, handing out cigarettes to all his classmates like the rich kid buying friends with candy. He insisted he couldn't write unless he was smoking.

A young red-haired man in horn rims and a wispy beard nodded. He vacillated between picking at his beard and stroking it with the sort of affection usually reserved for mammals such a guinea pigs and rabbits. "Hmmm." He always began his criticism this way, like he was tuning his voice. "I myself am more drawn to the world of Sierra Leone, I am intrigued by those death squads—do you follow me? Those children armed with AK-47s. Perhaps the story would be better suited with that sort of frame."

Tracy wrote down *Gun*.

The girl across the table in a Pro-Choice Is Pro-Death button flipped her glossy blond hair over her shoulder and shook her head. "I'm sorry, but I just don't believe any woman would be this stupid," she said, "I mean, hello, it's the year 2002, right?"

She looked at the teacher for validation.

Tracy wrote down *Stupid*.

The teacher, an experimental, or perhaps it was truer to say underpublished, poet turned fiction writer sighed, as though bored, and took his feet down from the table. He was always putting his feet up on the table in an attempt, Tracy supposed, to seem laid-back and cool. "So," he said, "what am I hearing? Do we have consensus?"

The consensus was she was stupid, and she should buy a gun, join an army of militant boys, and move to Cuba. Hadn't she tried a variation on this before?

Thankfully Tad, despite his polite inquiries into her writ-ing, seemed to have no genuine interest in reading her work (unlike Ray), so he didn't know how bad it was. He seemed content to console her.

"I can't do it . . . ," she'd wail to him. "I don't know how it ends, and you have to know how it ends, and I don't. . . ." At this he'd pull her into his arms like she was a child and pat her hair and kiss her hands, until she was embarrassed at how much he cared for her.

Finally, to put everyone out of their misery, she stopped working on her novel about Ray and Mexico. She stuffed into a box and slid it into the closet, stillborn.

The fifth of October was the sort of fall day that makes New Yorkers feel superior to everyone else on the planet. Tracy had been out buying coffee and thinking about mar-rying Tad. They'd had another *discussion* that morning. They never fought. Tad rarely even raised his voice, unless he was watching the Knicks blow a ten-point lead. No, the two of them, they discussed things. He was talking mar-riage, he was older than her, he was tired of snogging in supply closets, playing footsie, and sneaking around, he wanted everyone to know the truth. That she belonged to him.

He seduced her with talk of buying a place in the country with a barn and converting it into a studio for her. This was more appealing than she wanted to admit. After all, as he told her, they had been together for two years now (a year less than she and Ray had been together) and neither of them was getting any younger.

She'd been contemplating buying herself some sunflowers. She liked their strong fibrous stalks, the thick yellow petals and back centers, there was something so sentient about the way they turned their faces to the sun, something so beneficent in the way they died, drying up, and dropping their seeds to feed the birds. They had a purpose.

When Ray passed by her, she'd been trying to decide how many to buy—one was sufficient, but it would be lonely; three was beautiful, but too many; two, two seemed too man-and-wife. Ray's back was stooped and he was walking slowly. His tousle of dark hair was cropped short and was now ashy gray. She didn't recognize Ray, so much as feel him. She turned, almost afraid, and there he was. He looked terrible. He had dark circles around his eyes, his skin was the color of chicken fat, and he had a paunch. Her heart was racing, and her mouth was dry. She stood frozen in place. She dropped the flowers back into the bucket. Her hands were shaking. She didn't dare take her eyes off him. It was like a movie.

Should she say hello? Then she thought: *You might never get another chance.* She caught up to him easily, reached out and touched his sleeve, held on to it, tugged it, the way she had a million times before. In the time it took him to turn and fix her with his eyes, she had become the girl she once was, a lifetime ago.

"Ray," she said, "is it really you?"

"Tracy," he said in a low, raspy croak. Her eyes glanced at

his hand for a wedding band, there was none, but might Ray not be the kind of man who'd choose marital anonymity? Even his hands looked drawn to the bone and yellow. She had to stop herself from blurting out, what has happened to you?

"I feel like I am in a dream," she said. "It's you, right? How are you?"

"What can I say," he said in a hoarse whisper. "Nice voice, huh? Sounds pretty scary, don't it?"

"No," she said, "not scary"—she wiped the tears from her cheeks—"but telemarketing is probably out of the question.

"You look. . . ."

"I look like shit," he said, and smiled.

She said nothing. He wasn't moving.

"I see your stuff in the paper sometimes," he said, and took a deep breath. "I don't usually read the stories, but . . ."

"Please, please you don't have to explain." She felt herself blushing.

"I mean," he said, pausing, "I have trouble focusing, my eyes. . . . It's good though . . ."

"Thanks," she said. Here he was in front of her, he looked so awful. She wanted to ask him—what had happened? Still, she was so happy, so terribly happy.

"Well," he said. "I better go. I get tired real easy these days."

"I'm sure," she said, smiling dumbly at him, she didn't know what else to do with her face. She couldn't stop smiling at him or crying.

"Are you still at . . . ?"

"No, I moved," she said, her hands shaking. "Here, let me give you the address." She fumbled in her bag for a pen. She thought she'd have to sit down, right there on the sidewalk.

"Here." He pulled a pencil out of his pocket. She saw him palm a crystal. Was he into crystals now?

She pointed to the pencil. "Ah, some things never change," she said. She wrote her address and phone number in a faint jagged script that looked the way she imagined her pulse would look if it were graphed.

She sniffled. "So . . ."

"It's my heart," he whispered, "it's enlarged and pressing on my windpipe."

"Your heart?"

He nodded. "Makes it a little hard to communicate."

His heart? Of course, she thought, it's your heart. His heart was making it hard to talk.

"Jesus," she said, "but you're going to be okay?"

"I'm dying," he said. She wondered how many times he'd said that, and to whom. "Well, I'm on the donor list," he said, "but you never know."

"Right, you never know," she said, then smiling like Pollyanna, she heard herself chirp, "It'll happen. I know it will."

He shrugged. They looked at each other and stood there awkwardly, but neither seemed to want to move; it felt to Tracy like everyone was watching them, it felt illicit, they shouldn't be talking, but they were.

"So, call me sometime," she said, "or write me."

"I will," he croaked.

There was a moment when they might have hugged, but didn't. So they waved.

The list. That phrase rang in her head. *He was on the list.* People in hospital dramas on television were always on the list, and they always got a heart/a brain/some courage right at the last moment. In her experience that didn't happen here, not in real life.

Had he ever thought about calling her? Writing her? Was he going to wait until he died to reach out to her? Everyone knows that when someone is dying, they reconcile with estranged family members, they reel in lost and forgotten loved ones. She felt slighted. The sick are supposed to make late-night phone calls to old lovers, but she hadn't heard from him.

"It'll happen," she had said, wanting it, at that moment, to be so. "I know it will."

How grisly it all sounded, the optimism punched up with fear that somebody matching your blood and body type wouldn't die soon enough to save you. Scanning the daily papers for news of gang shoot-outs, a stabbing right through the temple of some healthy young guy who'd pledged his organs to science. They would fall back into love and have one last tempestuous fling. Then she could marry Tad; or no, then she would finally be free; or no, she would forever mourn him. How poignant!

Until Tracy saw Ray, she had considered her novel dead. Then she didn't. It wasn't until she started walking home that it dawned on her—she had the end of her book. Ray is going to die. Ray is going to die, she thought, her heart pounding hard, Ray is going to die, and I will finally be able to write our story.

What happens when the love of your life dies? For certainly he was the love of her life, not Tad, he wasn't, or couldn't be, the love of her life. No, it was Ray, always had been, and always would be. She was filled with such purpose! This wouldn't be one of those sappy *boyfriend dies and the girl goes crazy, believing his soul has been reborn in her cat* stories. No, this would be different. She rushed home and turned on the computer, she would start all over. There they were in his hospital room. She'd even give him a private room. He would be lying in bed, back against the pillows, and she would be holding his hand. There would be paint under his nails, scars on his hands—there was the cut from punching out the window in her bedroom when she said she didn't believe he loved her; there was the half-moon bite from the parrot in that bar in Oaxaca—he'd stuck his finger into the cage after the bartender told him it bit. They'd be playing hearts or backgammon on the bed like they did on the beach, a ladder of sunshine reaching down through his hospital window, a ladder like up to heaven, and a breeze barely moving the curtains. *Do you remember our bedroom in Mexico?* he'd ask, lifting his head, his dry lips straining to kiss her. *"How poor we were?"*

No, that was too mawkish. And anyway, windows in hospitals don't open, someone would pick up on that.

No, maybe she could begin with his mother calling her—having found letters from her in his belongings—or perhaps an envelope addressed to her by him in black pen, written in big block-letter capitals (TO BE SENT IN THE EVENT OF MY DEATH, it would say across the top), would just arrive one afternoon and proclaim that he had died and tell her that he had always loved her, and that he was sorry. Surely he'd be prepared for his tragic early death. After all, he had always said that his genius would not be appreciated in his lifetime, that he like his idols would die young and tortured.

Or the novel could be one of those experimental ones! Ha, wouldn't her old professor like that. It could be told through letters, and drawings, and found objects. That might be good. In the story she would reflect back on this box of letters—it would be raining outside, or just stopped raining, or she'd seen his face in a cloud—and muse about how they'd come together at the end, their chance meeting on the street—it was kismet, was it not? How they'd wept and made peace, how they had confessed their love for each other, and life would come full circle. When Ray died, life would come full circle.

What about the heart? Could one even use the heart in a story like this? In a screenplay, a Julia Roberts vehicle sure, but a real novel? The heart! Come on. No. She'd have to make his illness cancer, or some rare blood disease, a particularly virulent and rampant strain of ringworm. Wouldn't that be revenge? Ray had always wanted to go out with a shotgun blast, and she would have him lie and waste slowly away, driven mad, driven mad with longing for her—no, that was too Edgar Allan Poe.

The heart. What could she attribute to her changed heart?

That evening she wrote Ray a letter, telling him how much she had loved him, would always love him, how he'd hurt her in ways she still wasn't over. It was the sort she figured a person could only write once, maybe twice in a lifetime, the sort that feels like you've broken off one of your own ribs to write it.

She expected to get her letter back or get no response at all. When she saw the envelope in her mailbox, her name written in Ray's trademark heavy capital letters, she felt her book was blessed.

"Why did it end?" he wrote. "I don't know. It was just one of those things. I fucked up, and I am sorry."

It was just one of those things. She read this line over and over again, a dull surprise at how every time it shocked her, and hurt her, like stepping on a sprain.

"I was in a bad place, in myself, my work. I freaked out, I ran away from everybody." She wouldn't ask what that meant, she should have, and who was everybody?

Still, she'd never known Ray to apologize ever. This new Ray, this sick Ray, maybe he deserved to be let off the hook. The rules were different then. They'd never promised themselves to each other, not really. Still.

"You broke my heart," she wrote, period. She loved Tad, she did, but he didn't know her, they weren't connected like she and Ray had been. She couldn't see herself growing old with Tad the way she had once imagined growing old and white-haired with Ray. She saw them in matching white fisherman sweaters, she saw them living in a small town in Mexico, sitting on a crumbling wall that overlooked the sea, posing for the photographer that had been sent by *Art Forum* for an article they were running on Ray's newest masterworks.

Now, though, her book aside, Ray was going to die. Nothing would ever be the same, nothing was the same now. Every cup of coffee was the best coffee she'd ever had, the salsa music coming from a car that was being washed below her window was the liveliest. The pink in the evening sky so gorgeous it stopped you in your tracks. It reminded her of how with Ray everything was better, he insisted on it.

She was sad, of course, that was easy. What was harder, and ugly, was the indescribable excitement she felt, not just the shiver of having him back in her life, not the exquisite sensation of a new kind of pain, but the fact that Ray would die, and she would have something.

"I like this writing letters," Ray wrote her after their first few exchanges. "Someday these will be collected, you'll see. . . ."

They began emailing. Every time she saw a new message from him, she felt the exhilaration of cheating on Tad. Although perhaps *cheating* was too strong a word—likewise, she was also sort of cheating on Ray. After all, when he'd asked, so casually, if she was seeing anybody, she'd been oblique, she didn't want to scare him off, and it didn't feel like a lie, or a sin of omission, saying she was in a relationship, but she didn't know what the future of it was. That was true.

Tracy's fingers trembled on the keys. While writing allowed her the space to think, to control and compose her thoughts, she wanted to hear his voice, even though she knew it was hard for him, that he couldn't breathe and got tired easily. He talked to people all day long in the hospital, didn't he? She was sure he wasn't writing everything down on a little pad. He had no patience for that sort of thing. She wanted to hear his voice. How could she write his character if she didn't hear his voice?

When he wrote her that he was checked into Mercy hospital because the infection in his heart had worsened, she called him.

"Hey," he rasped, and she was suddenly sorry she'd done it. Her heart beat in her mouth.

"Hey," she said. "Just calling to see how you are."

She flicked on her computer.

"Same," he said slowly. "Hey, you want to come and save me from the Sisters of Mercy?" he croaked. "The food sucks but . . ."

"Of course," she said, her heart beating fast, "just as soon as I can."

She imagined lying down in Ray's bed with him. How many other people were visiting him? How many other women had he been with? Why did that idea make her want him again? Perhaps in the novel he would die while love-making to her, or right afterward. Maybe, in the book, she'd even get pregnant.

She typed *Sisters of Mercy*.

"I can't talk," Ray said. "Can we email? Snail mail is bull-shit. Anyway, I haven't got that kind of time." He laughed, then started coughing, right on cue.

She typed *I haven't got that kind of time* as he spoke.

"Are you typing?" he said.

"No, of course not," she said.

Tracy liked the physicalness of the letters. Like they were skin, they could be chopped off, or lost through fire—and she thought about keeping them in the refrigerator the way Robert Lowell had for fear of passing out in bed with a ciga-rette and burning his house down. She wanted the evidence. Anyone could type an email. No, she wanted his hand.

He began writing her every day, sometimes twice a day, and late at night. *Come hang out—I want you to come. When I get sprung* . . . She read that line again and again: *When I get sprung I want you to come see the paintings I did since the last time I saw you*. Poor Ray, she thought, poor Ray thought he was going to live. He fought valiantly, she would write. Right up to the end!

She was curious about the work. Had Ray fulfilled his promise? Perhaps one day he would be famous? She won-dered, too, might the sale of his letters be enough for a down payment on an apartment, a country house? A country house with a barn?

I miss you, he wrote. *I don't believe there is any such thing as an accident.*

And nor did she. Never let it be said that she denied a man his dying wish.

She imagined it would be easy to visit him. He was so sweet now, so soft. She had dreams of lying in his arms in his hospital bed, and him dying, and some part of her knowing it, but not getting up. Just lying there, making herself stay until someone else came in and discovered them there.

No, the way she figured it, the worst part of all this would be the bad coffee in the styrofoam cup, and the smell of industrial cleaner. Ray would be weak, in bed, pale and sucking ice chips. Feeling perhaps lucky to be alive, lucky to have her back in his life, and he'd be kind and warm. There wouldn't be any uncomfortable silences to fill as they would have something to distract them, something to talk about — his dying, all the time they squandered. She'd go a few times, rack up the points. *The old girlfriend*, the nurses would say, and nod their heads solemnly, appreciatively. She could just see the romance snowballing in their minds, taking on speed and shape, becoming as the days progressed more and more dangerous, a thing to admire, but not a thing to endure.

She comes, and they get back together, how perfect! It might make the local papers. It was like an opera. All that was missing was that great death scene.

●   ●   ●

She went to see him. She stood at the nurses' station in her blue miniskirt and a black turtleneck sweater, white patterned tights, and high-heeled Mary Jane shoes. Ray liked it when she dressed like this. She hadn't worn these clothes in ages. The nurses barely looked up to point the way for her; she wondered if she looked upset or resigned; did they think she wasn't his girlfriend, but maybe his sister?

"Knock knock," she said as she stuck her head in the door. Why did she say that? She hated it when people said that, why not knock? It was like people who said *Xmas* instead of *Christmas*.

"Hey," he said, muting the TV—a commercial of a pork chop slow-dancing with a box of Shake 'n Bake flitted across the screen. Was that one of Tad's? "Welcome to the good ship *Lollipop*."

She kissed his cheek. Where could he go?

A large, square-headed nurse came in and plumped up his pillow with affectionate roughness. "This is my first mate, Esther," he said hoarsely.

Esther rolled her eyes like this was part of some routine.

"Hello, Esther," she said. She'd have to remember to write this all down. Esther nodded. She felt a pang; she had always loved Ray's kindness to the waitresses and store clerks. Maybe she was still in love with him. He looked small in bed. He had an IV in his arm. In his lap she saw a book about healing the body with light. She liked this idea that Ray had become vulnerable to such nonsense as holistic healing. It would be good for the book, too. Maybe he would actually be saved by the healing power of an amethyst crystal the size of a Volkswagen, and then go on to become some rock-hound shaman.

He put the book facedown on the bedside table.

"How are you? Are you okay?" she said. She was trembling, she wanted to take his hand, but was afraid. Her mouth felt dry and pasty.

"Hey, as good as I can be with tubes sticking out of me."

"Really?" she said.

"No, I'm scared as shit," he said.

She froze. He wasn't supposed to say that.

"Who are these bastards in the white coats?"

She looked around the room collecting details for later. She was shocked that she could do this—after all, here was Ray, brave Ray saying he was scared.

"Don't worry," she said.

He pursed his lips and looked down into his lap.

"Listen, I'll stay with you," she said, taking his hand; it fit into hers perfectly. She'd never realized that the grasp of a hand could be as distinctive as someone's kiss. "I won't leave your side."

"You look good," he said to her; he stroked her forearm. "Really."

Her heart turned over against its better judgment, like a dog aware that it is losing all its dignity but must have its belly scratched.

Esther stuck her head inside the room. "Visiting hours is over," she said.

"But, I just got here . . . ," Tracy said, relieved.

Ray smiled at her. "It's cool. I am tired," he said weakly. "Thanks for coming. It's good to see you."

She smiled like Florence Nightingale and kissed his temple, his skin was so cool.

"It's going to be okay," she said, taking his hand, "better than okay."

"Don't be such a stranger," he said, and then, "thank you."

She walked out into the hall, each step faster until she was nearly jogging. She passed up the elevator and took the stairs. The racketing echo of her heels striking the steps was glorious. It was like gunfire.

Outside the hospital, leaning against the wall, she caught her breath, her side ached. One day Ray would be gone and she would be glad, grateful that she got to spend this time with him. She'd have done the right thing. Even though it would take the last of her money, she hailed a cab to take her home.

The next day they exchanged email. The time on his said 6 a.m. "Did I tell you I finally made it to Paris? It was gorgeous, amazing. I can't believe we never made it there. That is a crime. There is so much we should have done. I love you."

I love you. "I love you," she could hear him saying it as she read it over and over again. *I love you?* That was the drugs talking, or maybe the crystals.

At twelve o'clock she took a break from the book and checked her email again.

"Fuck, I am bored here," he wrote, and she wondered if he regretted writing *I love you* to her, if he was covering his ass now, "but at least I can read. Would you bring me some books, whatever is turning you on these days—"

Turning you on?

Did he love her, really love her? She felt a pang in her chest, how could she do this to him? It was a gift, she told herself. I am keeping Ray alive on the page. She wondered what he would think about what she was writing. Here he was on one screen, virtually back-to-back with his own story. Not intentionally, she didn't write him back until the next day. Instead she worked feverishly on her story, she felt like there was a train bearing down on her, gaining on her hour by hour. As she wrote, she could hear the crash of the sea outside their cottage window, smell the lime on Ray's fingers and sea salt, she could taste the fish soup she'd made with mussels they'd cut off the rocks, and feel the needle prick of fish bones in her mouth. She wrote for hours and hours, finally standing up stiff and bowlegged, the inside of her legs aching.

"Hey," Ray wrote her the next day, "I'm afraid my last letter got lost in the ether. Can't even pee this morning. It is clear now that even if I get a heart, if I live, it will never be the same. I will always be an old man."

She wrote back guiltily, "Don't say that. I'm going to come visit soon. I promise. My love always." She wrote, "T."

How many more times would they exchange emails? She had to be better about corresponding, if only for the material. They had so little time.

At night she watched TV shows where smart, good-looking people made foolish choices, then at the last minute saved themselves. She didn't think about Ray, except when she was thinking about him.

She canceled a date with Tad to write. He sounded hurt. "I miss you," he said, "but I understand." Two hours later he showed up at her door with take-out Thai food. "You've got to eat," he said, and climbed into her bed with a raft of papers from work.

"Just ignore me," he called from the bedroom. "I'll just be in here waiting for you."

It didn't occur to her that she hadn't heard from Ray for two days, until she was lying in bed beside Tad trying to sync her breath to his deep and regular inhalations and exhalations so she could fall asleep. She sat upright. "My God," she thought, "Ray is dead."

Tad slept beside her, smiling in his sleep.

She lay there for hours in the dark, too tired to get up, and too afraid to sleep. She tried to tune her mind into some cosmic wavelength—was Ray gone? Had he died? Had he been thinking of her? Was he maybe thinking of her right now in that dark and narrow hospital bed? There should be some way to know this.

The next morning she found a postcard in her mailbox with the image of a dolphin jumping through a ring of fire. Written in dark ink, it said, *I got a heart.*

What a trick. Walking back up the steps to her apartment, she read it over and over again. *I got a heart. I got a heart. I got a heart.* She went and sat at her computer, not turning it on. What did this mean? She was relieved, she supposed. "Thank God," she said out loud, as though she thought someone, say God, might be listening.

"I didn't want Ray to die," she said. Or, I don't think I did, she thought. She just wanted to be able to write her book, was that so bad? Was that so wrong? Anyway, what did this really meant exactly? She was ashamed of her ambivalence.

"Congratulations!" she emailed him. "I knew it all along!"

"Its excellent timing, the surgery is in two days," he wrote back later that day, "and they have to keep me all summer, which is awesome as I don't have air-conditioning in my place."

In the perfect world, the sick make peace and die swiftly. The healthy remain to weep and pat themselves on the back for staring down death—there is blessed catharsis. There are no awkward *We said our farewells and you told me you were always in love with me, but you haven't yet died* moments—no tapering off of phone calls because people have already said their good-byes—no disappointment in the voice of the caller when the sick pick up, like the pregnant woman everyone is waiting for to deliver—You haven't had the baby yet?

Aren't you dead yet?

She told herself, just because Ray got a heart *didn't mean* he was going to *live*, of course. She meant, she *wanted* him to live, novel or not. She just didn't know what she wanted from him now. They could still be friends, right? The only thing that was certain was that she had to finish the novel now— right now before anything else changed.

"When can you come?" Ray wrote her. "Like now. It's been too long, a hundred hours, forty-five minutes, and twelve seconds to be exact."

"How about Tuesday?"

"Tuesday's no good," he wrote. "Come tomorrow," he said.

"I'll try," she said, a little annoyed at how he'd assumed the center of her world, forgetting or not caring that he wasn't the only man in her life. Then she thought of her book. She needed him to make this book with her. So, she thought, who could refuse the possibly-dying man?

"Tomorrow then," she said.

"Cool," he said, then before he hung up, casual as could be, he said, "love you."

From *I love you*, to *love you*. How long before he'd be signing his letters *Luv ya*? How long before he was sending her Mylar balloons and teddy bears in TV shirts that read Stay Cute, or a dozen chocolate roses on long satin stems? She sat down at her desk and stared at the screen. She was close, almost done, but the ending was impossible; she wrote and erased, wrote and erased. Whose story was it? Was it her story, or his story? She paced and chewed at her cuticles.

That night, Ray called while she was in the kitchen making a peanut butter sandwich and drinking ginger ale; she heard the phone ring, and just knowing it was him, she let it ring and ring, standing at a safe distance, willing it to stop. "Hey, where be you?" he said, his voice hoarse on the machine. "Why aren't you home?"

She thought about picking it up. She'd have grabbed it if Tad was there and not away at a ten-day conference in Florida. Tad might appreciate her kindness toward her old boyfriend, but surely he'd draw the line at late-night phone calls.

"Just thought you'd want to know I'm going under the knife tomorrow," he said, pausing to let this sink in, or maybe trying to guilt her, if she was listening, into picking up.

"Okay," Ray said, "later."

There was no denying it, Ray was beginning to sound stronger, more like his old self. She wondered if he hated himself for needing her.

The next morning a postcard with a cup of coffee filled with stars stood alone in her mail slot. She almost didn't pick it up. "Walk with me, talk with me," he wrote.

He was writing, he was calling. He was everywhere. She locked up her apartment and left, walking up and down the Village, staring into windows. How many years had passed since she stopped seeing gifts that made her think of Ray? Things she thought he'd love? She didn't want to call Ray. She'd didn't want to write Ray. She wondered, what did those nurses think if they thought anything at all?

•   •   •

She went to the hospital three days after his surgery; she was taken aback by how groggy he was, how hooded his eyes were. She hoped he wasn't aware of how much time had passed.

"I'm here," she said to him. "Can you see me?" She looked around the room, anywhere but *at* him. He held her hand, and she understood how a fox would chew off its own leg to escape a trap.

Two days later he called her; his voice sounded thick. "They're kicking at me next week," he said, breathing heavily. "Goddamn insurance company . . . ," his voice trailed off. Could the story not have a thread that was some indictment of corrupt insurance practices? Wouldn't that make it of social value?

"Next week?" she said frowning. "So soon?"

It was all happening so fast now.

She didn't pick him up at the hospital. She told herself that Tad wouldn't have liked that; he was out of town and it would be like sneaking around in his absence. It was one thing to see Ray when Tad was in town, but this seemed to be taking advantage of his absence. It was cheap. Tad wouldn't understand that a man like Ray had few close friends, and those that he had were as unpredictable and irresponsible as Ray himself had once been.

Tracy didn't pick up Ray and she didn't take him home, but when she got to this point in the book—the end—she would. She'd talk about how long it took him to make it up the stairs, how he'd rested leaning on her shoulder, how a Jamaican home-care worker named Betty came by several times a day to take blood and give him meds and weeks later would accompany him on slow walks around the block. She'd joke that he shouldn't get any ideas about her becoming his girlfriend, because she was already taken, and her husband was a minister.

"I want to see you," he wrote her, "but I'm not ready to come to you." She didn't know if he meant the traveling or her. Did he not want to revisit the landscape of their past? A red woven blanket from Oaxaca thrown over the back of the old leather sofa they'd found on the street, a piece of amber carved into a swan that they'd discovered in a thrift shop in Montana, the odd assortment of coffee cups they'd collected on their drives cross-country, an ivory hand mirror inlaid with gilt that he'd once painted her holding.

She'd waited almost three weeks to visit. For a week she'd nursed along what she'd told Tad and Ray was a cold (she couldn't go see Ray and risk infecting him) but was surely depression. She sat around in pajamas, her hair dirty, working sporadically on the book, picking out words and rejecting them. She thought about taking up smoking. She was ashamed; sure she'd visited Ray in the hospital, twice even, but still. Wasn't it possible she could say that she'd been there right when he came out of surgery? He wouldn't remember. And anyway, wouldn't he want to believe it?

"Hey," he said when he opened the door.

His voice sounded tired, but it was his voice now. The

hoarseness was gone. His hair was growing out, the curl was back. He'd lost some of the paunch, his chest seemed wider, less sunken in. He even had some color in his cheeks. He wasn't dying. Still, he wasn't himself. There was no tape on his fingertips like there'd always been, from working on motors or using X-Actos, no paint stained his clothing. His shirt, buttoned up, looked ironed. On the walls hung a few old paintings she'd seen before. There was a picture of her in the dress of a Moorish woman, which now seemed quite silly, and she noticed, her heart nearly stopping, something she'd never seen before, a painting of a church identical to one in their little town.

"This," she said, drawing closer so she could see the brushstrokes.

"That is my favorite painting ever," he said.

She smiled at him. "I know this church."

"I did it when I was a kid," he said, "from a picture."

She stopped and stared into the painting; she could see now it was crude, and unrealistic, the light was all wrong, it was sloppy, she hoped he didn't know what she'd been thinking.

"It's a piece of shit," he said, "but I love it."

"So," she said, turning toward him, "are you going to have a great scar?"

"It's pretty great."

"Can I see it?" She wanted to see it. She needed to see it.

"Well," he said after a long moment. He fingered the hem of his shirt, like this was too personal a question.

"Later, maybe," he said.

"You don't have to or anything," she said.

"I can't drink coffee anymore—imagine—but I have some juice, some water . . ."

They drank iced green tea and ate cheese puffs, the kind that leave your finger pads bright orange, and he told her where he'd traveled in the past years, Russia, Italy, and Costa Rica. He'd gone back to Mexico, not to their town. His Spanish was really great now, he told her.

"But it was the best with you," he said, his voice getting soft. "That was the best time of my life."

"I know," she said. "So," she said, this was it.

"So," he said, smiling at her. He sat back in his chair, his hands laced behind his head. It would be so easy to shoot an arrow right there into his heart.

"I should go," she said, brushing the orange powder on her pants. "Look at this stuff," she said. "What is this orange stuff anyway? Agent Orange . . . ?"

"Ah shit, do you have to?" he asked. "Already?"

"I'm on deadline." She couldn't believe it was over just like that. That was it. It was over. She felt slightly sick.

"Sure, but you've got to come again." He looked a little confused, and flustered.

"Of course," she said. She couldn't get her breath.

"Look, it's not like I'm doing anything. They come and take my blood, and I hang out. I sleep a lot, eat lots of steak. Cash my disability check."

"Wow," she said. "That's the life."

"I miss you," he said, and she believed him. He did. She felt sick.

"I'll come back," she said, "don't worry. You'll get sick of me."

"Sick of you? Not possible."

How had this happened? It was because he was sick, she told herself. That's all.

"Is this driving you crazy?"

He shrugged. "What can I do? I can't work." He didn't seem bothered by this. "I am taking hundreds of dollars' worth of pills every day just to keep my body from rejecting the heart."

Rejecting the heart.

"Do you know whose heart is it?" She couldn't help herself, and who knew about the etiquette of transplants?

The whole way over on the subway she had wondered what he had done with his heart. Had he asked for it back? How could he not? How could he let it go?

"I don't want to think about it," Ray answered.

"Right," she said, but she didn't understand.

"All I know is, it was from an eighteen-year-old kid, from the Midwest."

"A boy," she said, thinking how untested and undamaged that heart would be. How she wished she'd known Ray when he had that heart.

In the silence that followed, though neither of them said it, she knew they were both imagining that the kid had died in a car accident, or a motorcycle crash, some way Ray might have once died, or should have died—a moment stolen. So rarely in life do people get the death they deserve when they deserve it. Didn't he deserve that?

"That makes sense," she said.

"It does," he said.

"Better than like a giant beaver . . ."

He gave her a funny half-smile.

"At one point, you know like the time of the dinosaurs, beavers were twelve feet tall." He stared at her. "It's nothing," she said. "I'm sorry."

"So you've got to come back soon," he said, leaving his hand on her shoulder. She knew he was about to kiss her, so she turned her head and kissed his cheek, letting her lips linger there for a long moment. She couldn't take the kiss.

"I'll be back," she said, but as she opened the door to the outside, the sun coming in, she knew that she'd never come back here. He would call her, and he would write her, and she would return calls late, she would forget emails he had sent. She'd wouldn't kill this thing between them, but she'd slowly let it die. She'd disappear, just the way he had. She would finish the book about her and Ray, and in the death scene, for Ray would die in her book, she would cry, she would cry and mourn, but then, like that, it would be over. Maybe she wouldn't understand it any better, but it would be over.

This song was written the year I had my nervous breakdown. While I didn't hear it until years later, when I saw the date of composition, I felt like it was my story. I listened to it compulsively for a very long time.

RIO

zev borow

It means so much to me
Like a birthday or a pretty view

"Rio"
Duran Duran

Diego Guiterrez stares into the mirror and can't help but wonder if another Central American strongman would have gotten a better suite. Even worse is the quick thought that one of his contemporaries, deposed or otherwise, could be decamped in New York at this very moment at another, decidedly better hotel altogether, staring into a larger mirror, with a more decorous frame, set off by more flattering lighting, a man even more mercifully alone with nothing except his own reflection. Where, he wonders, does Chávez stay? Chinaco, he knows, is usually at the Grand Hyatt. Who else? Perez, Salzar? No, no, no. He'd know if it were even a possibility. It might not make the papers—though Lord knows he reads enough newspapers these days not to miss it if it did—but still . . . It isn't as if he no longer *knew* things. And was there even a comparison between the Waldorf and the Grand Hyatt? What about The Peninsula? Had someone recently mentioned a new Four Seasons? Perhaps.

Guiterrez has a nickname. El Pollito. The little chicken. His mother gave it to him, and even though he has always hated it, it has, as they say, stuck. It is midafternoon and El Pollito is wearing a crisp, pale blue Armani dress shirt fresh out of the box, along with silver cuff links, a gift from Vicente Fox. The room is cold. The entire building practically thrums with air chilled so powerfully as to be menacing. How American, Guiterrez thinks. Of course, the truth is he loves it, that after all these years it still seduces him. When he first came to New York in the early 1970s, then just a junior member of his predecessor's security detail, it wasn't the skyscrapers or the Cadillacs that left him overwhelmed, it was the air-conditioning. That first trip had been during summer. New York was hot and thick, like home, but with even less breeze. They'd driven from the airport directly to the hotel—which one?—and as the baggage was unloaded the doors to the lobby were propped open. Out rushed a wave of air unlike any he could ever have imagined—air so ferociously piercing, so soulless, as dry and chilled as death itself. He was seized entirely. It was all he could do to keep his composure. This was cold that devoured the heat, not like the sickly, dripping coughs that spit out of rusted vents at home. This air was less a feat of engineering than brute will. Marco Polo upon first seeing the gilded court of the Chinese khan could not have been more awed. Guiterrez had turned to the soldier next to him and whispered, "¡*Dios mio!* How much could this possibly cost?"

The soldier, older, smiled and replied, "Resistance is futile, eh?"

But why resist at all? One thing Guiterrez could attest to was there was nothing better for fucking. Even this trip he'd woken up every morning with a hard-on. It also tended to make him hungry, a sensation he enjoyed almost as much. This made him recall a meal he'd had years ago with an American from the embassy. The man, surely CIA, from Texas or somewhere else in the American South, had actually cooked for him. A chicken dish, something deep-fried. He reveled in the origin of the recipe and the exact manner of its preparation and had called it "comfort food." Guiterrez hears the phrase again in his mind as he continues to stare into the mirror. Even after eleven days his skin is still tanned. He looks healthy. "The air-conditioning at the Waldorf-Astoria," he is surprised to hear himself say aloud, "is like comfort food."

Then, from the next room: "President Guiterrez?"

It is the voice of an American woman, from the State Department. Her name is Lora Schuler. "Can we get you something?"

"I am fine," Guiterrez answers softly.

He continues to stare at his reflection. His hair is thick, wavy, and mostly black. He is fifty-seven years old, and while there is some gray, it suits him. He'd always believed he would look distinguished as an older man, and the fact that now he indeed does offers a daily dose of brief, but deep, satisfaction. It is, he thinks, an example of the kind of small comfort that can help a man soldier on—to know that some things, thank God, can be counted upon. But could the same be said of the Waldorf? The lobby still shimmers, yes, but there seem to be more tourists, certainly more Asians, rich, of course, but . . . He couldn't help but detect a slow creeping to the place; a vague film or faint echo, a lingering. It unsettles him. And now he can't even come and go as he wishes. He'd been asked, no, *told*, "to stay removed from things."

Removed?

"Removed."

For how long?

"A little while. Just until the situation settles."

The situation was settled. They all knew it. He was not going home. Not that things could not have been worse. On the contrary, he was lucky to have been here when it happened. Now they would have to arrange things for him. He would get an apartment, a car and driver, nothing extravagant. He had no grand illusions, mind you. He was . . . What was it? A small fish, sure, but not so small as to toss back, not right away at least. Better to let him flop in the boat for a turn. There were favors owed, and more importantly, things he knew. Others knew more, maybe, but if nothing else, the years had allowed him an understanding of how the Americans worked when it came to these things. Smooth transitions were important, they were all too happy to attach value and ease; and he'd cooperate, and they appreciated cooperation. As for home? He would monitor things, of course, always, but the truth was his time had passed. He knew this. Perhaps, if all went well, he'd be able to go back for a visit. Stranger things have happened. But he would be fine here, happy even. There, was money, yes, not as much as some no doubt thought, as some would no doubt say, not nearly, but enough.

In the next room, Guiterrez's daughter, Arantxa, an exotic-looking young woman, the only child born to Guiterrez's first wife, a Costa Rican beauty, stands next to her father's most senior aide, Carlos Vinto. Once a member of Guiterrez's own security detail, for the past eight years he has functioned as a chief of staff. Vinto and Arantxa are staring out a window that looks over Park Avenue. Sitting near them, reading one of the dozen newspapers scattered about, is Ms. Schuler. Her pin-straight brown hair is tucked behind her ears; she is wearing a long navy skirt, a white top, and a small cross around her neck. When El Pollito walks into the room, they all turn around; only Ms. Schuler smiles. Arantxa says she likes the color of her father's shirt. Carlos asks if he is hungry for lunch. Guiterrez doesn't say anything. He considers picking up a paper, then thinks better of it and walks back to the mirror.

A few minutes later, Ms. Schuler's mobile phone rings. Minutes after that there is a knock on the suite's door. It is someone she is expecting, a colleague. She goes to the door and greets a husky blond man wearing a navy blazer and a white shirt. Arantxa and Carlos stay fixed at the window. Ms. Schuler and the man in the blazer walk into the dining area to speak more privately. After only a few moments, the man walks back to the door of the suite. Another man in a blazer is posted outside the suite's door, for security purposes. Ms. Schuler apparently wants a word with him, too; both men walk back into the suite to speak with her.

Guiterrez can see all of this because the mirror he has taken to staring at is located off the master bedroom. An open sliding door allows him to see into the suite's sitting and dining rooms. As he watches, Guiterrez notes the precision with which everyone in the room seems to move and, even, stand still. It reminds him of silent films. He also notices that when the security man walked into the suite, the door did not close entirely behind him. So, without giving it much thought, Guiterrez quickly and quietly walks out of the suite, rides an elevator down to the hotel's lobby, buys a pack of cigarettes, and walks outside and onto Park Avenue. It is just before 3 p.m. on a Friday.

The sky is clear and blue. It is mid-September and almost hot. Guiterrez smiles as the sun first hits his face and the warm air surrounds him. Another benefit of American air-conditioning, he thinks: like misfortune, enough of it can make you value even the heat of the day. He begins walking north on Park Avenue, vaguely aware that is the direction of Central Park. After a few blocks, he sees two girls dressed in school uniforms. He asks them for directions, which they relay with what is unquestionably the least possible effort and attention, an act, Guiterrez notes, of true, merciless efficiency. *They* should run a country, he thinks. Then he notices a café across the street and decides he'd like a coffee.

He takes a table in a corner, a semiconscious act of discretion. At this point, it should be noted that while Guiterrez is aware he is flouting the U.S. State Department's stated position regarding his leaving the hotel, and that back at his suite at the Waldorf there is probably a small flurry of reactive activity occurring, he does not in any way think he has committed any grand offense, and the idea that he might be in any kind of . . . danger couldn't be more removed from his mind. In fact, his simple act of . . . well, to call it defiance would be too much. Assertion? Independence? Recklessness? However it should be described, it has left him feeling lifted, and very much alive, a feeling, as it would happen, shared by a young woman he is about to meet.

Her name is Ellie Bowen. She is nineteen years old, and has lived all of her life in the very large apartment owned by her parents in the prestigious prewar building next to the café, which is where she is sitting, drinking a 7UP, when Guiterrez walks in. As it is a Friday afternoon, she has not been to sleep for nearly forty eight hours. Generally speaking, when Ellie goes out for the evening, it lasts a while. She likes being out, is good at it, and often finds that a mere six or twelve or even twenty-four hours of the doing so isn't enough to sate her. More often than not, she finishes these stretches—she likes to call them sessions—by spending an hour or so, usually alone, at the café. Not that you'd guess it from looking at her. Her long, brown hair seems like something from a magazine ad, all but posed, and backlit to flattering effect by the afternoon sun sliding in through the café's open windows. Her eyes, also brown, are clear and open wide, and her skin is smooth and deeply tanned. She is wearing a simple, white dress. She could be anyone young and pretty.

Often people think she is Latin, or Italian, sometimes Middle Eastern, none of which is true. She smiles often, and with skill, but her most charming quality, the thing that inevitably distinguishes her in a group and has been the catalyst for the high frequency of what can rightly be called singular experiences during her relatively young life, is a true faith in the power of lying. For as long as she can remember it is only when wedged deep into a dark crevice of a dense, living fiction that she feels . . . calm. For Ellie, lies are blankets, and windows, portable accessories that offer both security and possibility. Ellie and her lies share a kind of understanding; they need one another, yes, of course, but more than that, they *like* each other. The ramifications of this are, naturally, extensive, but have thus far at least been largely contained, and even capitalized upon. Not yet diagnosed, but under treatment, Ellie is an agile, fragrant textbook pathology. A true bird of paradise.

She had been sitting in the café for nearly twenty minutes before Guiterrez walked in. Now she waits until he orders, before going to his table. "I've seen you on TV," she begins.

Guiterrez looks up at her. No, she is mistaken, he says in Spanish.

"You were on a talk show."

No, she is thinking of someone else (again in Spanish).

"You were talking about rivers."

He stares at her.

"No, no, no, not rivers. That was someone else. You were talking about something bigger, something about how the world is, most of the time, a terrible and sad place where there are millions and millions of poor children dying due to neglect, because no one will act on their behalf. You said that it is understandable that most of us don't spend our lives trying to feed poor children on continents thousands of miles away, or even poor children in the cities we live in. You made it clear you understood the reality of the situation, that it's simply not feasible for most people to do that. But, *but*, you said, if we—and by *we* I think you meant, you know, not just all of us who happened to be watching you on TV at that moment—if we acted only a little, changed our behavior only in some small, manageable way, then we could do a lot to help these poor children, then we could literally save thousands, maybe millions of them."

She sits down at his table.

"I understood what you were talking about. I remembered it."

Now he speaks in English: "I'm sorry, miss, but you do have me mistaken for someone else. I have never been on television."

"Really?"

"Really."

"Never?"

"I'm afraid not."

"That's too bad."

He doesn't say anything.

"I said that's too bad," Ellie says.

"Is it?"

"Well," she says. "Yes, I think so. Being on TV is actually quite remarkable."

"I suppose I'll have to take your word for it."

"No, you don't have to, that was just my experience."

Guiterrez takes a sip of his coffee, then looks up at her. This girl is lying, he thinks. What is this about?

"I think you are lying," he says.

She smiles. "Oh, c'mon, it *isn't* something to be on television? Think about it. I'm not sure how television even works, are you? I mean how it actually works, the science of it. Waves, particles, gamma rays—who knows? But how amazing is it really that you can just flick a switch and see something happening live, right then, around the world. Just thinking of it makes me feel, I don't know, proud."

Guiterrez smiles. "Pride only gets people into trouble."

A waitress approaches. Ellie orders a 7UP. "My name is Greta," she says. "What's yours?" she asks. He doesn't respond. "Is it—"

"My name is Diego," he says.

"Great name."

He laughs, then gently closes his eyes and looks up into the sun. It is getting cooler. He rubs his eyes with his fingers.

"Is everything okay?" Ellie asks.

He looks at her. She is a attractive, sexy somehow, but short.

"Yes" — he sips his coffee — "thank you."

"Can I tell you a secret?"

"What do you mean?"

"I mean, I have a secret, something I haven't told anyone, something maybe I shouldn't tell anyone. But I want to tell someone, I think it's important that I do."

"Are you in the habit of telling strangers secrets?"

"Sometimes they're the only people you can trust."

"Are you in the habit of having conversations with most of the strangers you meet in cafés?"

"Only this one."

"Secrets are often best *kept* secret."

"Because people are afraid of them."

"People are afraid of everything."

She smiles. "Yes."

"You remind me of my daughter," Guiterrez says, even though it isn't true. "She is about your age."

Ellie looks at him. "Here's the secret I'm going to tell you," she begins, but then waits, unconsciously pausing for effect. She is about to start speaking again but suddenly realizes she wants to let the moment build, just for half a second or so more, but then that half second passes and she lets another go by, then another, and another. Now she and Guiterrez are staring at each other in silence. She does this sometimes, lets pauses grow into silence, silences into small awkward moments, small awkward moments into semi-excruciating ones. She finds it delicious, not so much that it tends to unnerve people, though she likes that it does that, too. She likes the suspense. When will she start speaking again? Now? How about now? Will the other person say something first? She once told someone that for her it feels like the moment right before a movie starts, but better, sharper, scarier.

Guiterrez likes Ellie. He can't help but think to himself, She doesn't know who I am.

"The other day I was walking though the park," she says. "The weather was like this, gorgeous. It was the weekend and the park was crowded, with lovers, children, parents. I was walking around just looking, just watching. I think it became too much for me. I'd been watching a small boy play, he was five or six years old and running around a patch of grass near a playground. I couldn't tell who his parents were, or where they were. There were lots of parents around watching their kids, drinking bottled water, packing things away into various packs and pockets. I was sitting on a bench nearby and this little boy ran over to me. He was very cute and said hello. I asked if he was having fun. He said he was. Then I asked him where his parents were, and he pointed back toward the playground, toward where most of the adults were standing. Then I asked him if he was a fast runner. Oh, yes, he said . . ."

Ellie stops. The waitress puts down her 7Up. Ellie smiles at her and takes a sip before continuing. "I asked him if he could run far. He said he could. I told him I didn't believe him. He said he could run as far and as fast as I could imagine. We went back and forth about it for a while, me saying, 'I don't believe you,' and him saying, 'I can, too.' Then I told him to prove it to me and pointed in the direction opposite the playground, toward a hill way in the distance. I told him to run as far and fast as he could in that direction, and that I would watch, and if he did it, I would believe him. And he said okay and took off."

She stops.

"And?" Guiterrez says.

"And then I just got up and walked away."

"And you think something happened to the boy?"

"I don't know. But my secret is not that this thing happened, it's that I do things like this all the time, and even more than that, it's that it doesn't bother me. I don't think about it afterward. Like with the little boy, I just kept sitting there, then got up and walked away. I didn't even watch to see how far he ran. And right now, telling you, I don't feel guilty about the little boy, or wonder if he ever found his parents again, or if something awful happened to him. It's just something that happened, something I made happen. I do things like this and just walk away."

"Maybe you should see a priest."

"I don't know any priests."

"Maybe you should see a psychiatrist?"

"Another thing is that I steal things, not so much from stores, but from other people, people I know, and people I don't. In general, the truth is that I can just be . . . I guess *cruel* is the best word, usually for no real reason. Sometimes I think it's that I don't have some kind of gene that most other people have that keeps them from doing certain things. I've never hurt someone, like, you know, physically or anything, never hit someone or anything like that. Truthfully, I don't think I'm a cruel person. It's just that maybe I think about people in a different way. I mean, I don't walk away from people. I don't not want to let them in or whatever. I want to let them in. I want people close to me. You know, I hate even going to sleep."

"You are quite a young girl," Guiterrez says.

"Maybe. I don't know." Another sip. "It's like . . . Everything, it all means so much to me. Like a birthday, or . . ." She stops.

"Or a pretty view," says Guiterrez.

"Yes, exactly," she says.

He laughs.

"I'll tell you a secret of mine," he says.

"You think I'm a stupid girl."

"Listen."

She does.

"I have hurt people, physically. I have killed people, shot them, strangled them, drowned them, tortured them. I don't know how many, more than ten, less than twenty, with my own hands. But I have been the cause of many more deaths, hundreds more, people whom I ordered killed, and people whose deaths I could have stopped, but didn't."

He looks at her, tries to read her face, but can't. "I don't believe I'm a cruel person either."

"I know who you are," Ellie says to him.

"You are a stupid girl," Guiterrez says to her.

They stare at one another. She stands up.

"Do you think *I* am lying?" Guiterrez asks.

She smiles at him, and it—the smile—ends up being the most honest thing to have come out of her in a while, perhaps ten days. "I don't know," she says. "But I enjoyed our conversation."

Now he smiles, too. "So did I."

Before leaving, Ellie stops at the café's bar and asks the bartender to bring a bottle of Cristal Champagne to the older man sitting in the corner, her boyfriend, for his birthday, that she has forgotten his present in her car, but will be right back with it. When she is outside, she immediately takes out her cell phone and calls a friend with news of how she just slept with Diego Guiterrez, the famous Formula One race car driver. Soon after, Guiterrez walks back to the Waldorf, hungry for dinner.

author inspiration

Upon first hearing about the idea for the *Lit Riffs* collection of stories, my first instinct, other than dismay at the chosen title, was to choose a song that would in some way be surprising and fun, even more so than a song I really loved, or at least liked, or at least knew most of the words to. This notion was further solidified in my head after I saw an initial list of songs other writers were choosing (not sure if that list has any resemblance to what finally made it in the book). Lots of folks were picking what I thought of as smarty-pants, hyperliterate stuff. I kinda just shook my head. I mean, what's the point of trying to write a short story based on a Dylan song? (I always thought Dylan songs were short stories, only better.) Anyway, for me, "Rio" came up right away. For one, I fucking love the song, it usually makes people smile, even if they're shaking their head in the process. I sort of think you can divide the world into people who appreciate Duran Duran, and people who don't, and I'd rather vacation with the people who do. To me, Duran Duran in general, and "Rio" in particular, shimmer with the absolute brain-freeze purity of pop-rock's transcendent ridiculousness, whatever that means. And I like the drums and guitar. And, good Lord, the lyrics, to "Rio" especially, are an L.A. sunset, a hot breath of everything and nothing all at once. I love shit like that.

KING HEROIN

nelson george

I'm a world of power and all know it's true
Use me once and you'll know it, too

"King Heroin"
James Brown

What you are about to read are excerpts from the memoirs of a man who calls himself Edgecombe Lenox aka Edge aka King Heroin. As comical as the name might strike some of you, Edge is not a jokester. He is a man who takes himself very seriously and you should as well, because in the seventies he was the biggest, smartest, most successful heroin dealer in Harlem, New York, which made him one of the biggest drug kingpins in the country. In the thoroughfares of the city he was called Mr. Untouchable because the authorities, try as they might, failed repeatedly to convict him.

When I was on the street, there was a kind of style, a kind of cool, even grace, you won't find anymore. It was in the way we spoke. The way our threads lay, the way we hung and laughed and made things happen. All that style has been replaced by a lack of brotherhood that disgusts me. It's like the world has no center anymore.

I know I sound nostalgic and old. Maybe even silly. But I know what we tried to do. We tried to impose order on the street without having to hurt people—though we always kept our options open. It's the difference between a .45 and an Uzi. We never sprayed a street indiscriminately; we aimed precisely, we took out who needed to go and let civilians live in peace. After all, they were our customers. If you weren't in the game, you couldn't be hurt by the game. Play at your own risk. You could have lived on 145th and St. Nick your own life and not been hurt by my people.

Well, no. That's actually a lie.

No need to lie. Not now. We really went out of our way not to shoot civilians. We just destroyed the world around them, block by block, like a damn virus. I mean Harlem was crumbling when I came of age. All the families that could were running out to Long Island or Queens or Jersey. All the cops and the TA workers and the mailmen. Shit, half my lieutenants had houses in Englewood or St. Albans living that comfortable-ass Negro American dream.

Harlem was left with nothing but poor people, sad people, and weak-willed suckers and people like me—pimps, thugs, jackleg preachers, crooked cops, and peddlers of narcotics. These two groups of people, prey and predator, victim and victimizer, working men and people in the life, were what Uptown was all about after the marching and protesting had died down. Those whom civil rights had helped were gone. For those who got left behind, there was me and my crew with cellophane bags of white powder to take your mind where your body couldn't afford to.

When a junkie shoots up, his blood slides into the needle and is visible as the dope heads into his system. The needle and the vein become one milky, red-tinted substance, a new thing that bonds them together. That's how my business worked. We commingled with the streets. We took over corners. We bogarted buildings. We owned police precincts. We injected ourselves into everything that linked Harlem to the rest of Manhattan.

We ran Harlem because we could. There was no master plan. At least not at first. Not overtly. Not like we blueprinted it one night at Jagazzy's. I think there was some racial pride involved. The Irish and the Jews and the Italians had all been sucking brown people's money out of Uptown since before Duke Ellington opened his jar of pomade. So we were just asserting our ethnic rights.

But I'd be lying a bit again. All that makes me sound like some damn nationalist on a soapbox in front of Micheaux's on 1-2-5. Like behind all my dealing was some submerged political agenda. Power to the people! Free Huey! We shall overcome with a brick of China White cut with baking soda in the hand that wasn't giving the black power salute.

Fuck that. We were criminals.

Now I can say that. I don't have to act righteous anymore

or justify myself like I used to. I ruled Harlem because it was there to be taken. I didn't do it for black people or "the movement." At the time I would not have admitted that. I would have quoted Malcolm or the Honorable Elijah Muhammad. I would have painted my organization in the bronze hues of salvation and empowerment. I would have given donations to Operation Push and even them Tom-ass niggas at the NAACP. And, like half the people from my generation, I would have been full of shit.

Back then, everything we did could be explained by the struggle. You see, I preached discipline and force, and we enforced with cruel brutality. Even selling dope was a way, perhaps, to punish our weak-minded. If they were sad enough to buy my shit, should they survive? Jerry Butler sang, "Only the strong survive," and that, beloved, meant me and mine.

You know, we never made anyone buy our product. We set up shop but never bought ads. No billboards. No newspaper ads in the *Amsterdam News*. No jingles on 'LIB. We just made it available and the customers—the silly, stupid, and needy—lined up twenty-four hours a day, seven days a week, 365 days a year, and sometimes twice on payday.

IN THE YARD

Every day I saw my tortured children. Man-children with eyes that surveyed the yard as if it were a street corner to capture. Most of them had bulked-up shoulders hunched like rottweilers as they strutted like streetwalkers. I would have liked to have had a hand in raising them. I could have brought them up like all the ones I once loved and schooled. I could have given them some class and some discipline to go along with all that heart. Yeah, these new jack, hip-hop, jiggy young ones got heart for days. If I'd had niggas like these back in the day, things would have ended right. I truly believe that.

In a way I did raise them, I guess. I laid the foundation in the dope game that they've been following for twenty-odd years. They followed my path, straight from the concrete heaven of Lenox Avenue to the concrete hell the Feds built out here in Marion, Indiana. Yeah, we all ended up in the same place—might any way—but I know I could have changed the journey for all of us.

About once a month a newbie would stroll by my bench, acting like he didn't give a fuck. Some even stepped to me, trying to treat me like some crusty, old man not be respected, who had no knowledge of crack, the chronic, or that E shit they fuck with now. But I knew that they knew and they knew I knew what they didn't. Sometimes it would take time—but then we had plenty of that—before they broke down and asked to hear what only I could relate. They'd finally acknowledge that while there were many a serious motherfucker in that gray steel Midwestern hell, there was only one who'd had the president of the United States drop a dime on them. That's why they sought me out. I'd been that dangerous—I'd been that large. That's why I was the only Edgecombe Lenox.

THE BODIES OF BOYS

julianna baggott

*Me and Crazy Janey was makin' love in the dirt
singin' our birthday songs*

"Spirit in the Night"
Bruce Springsteen

I didn't love the boys then the way I love them now, their lean hips, their hairless, muscled chests, their neck-laces—a lot of Italian horns bobbing in the dips of collar-bones—their loping gaits, their swelling pricks, their soft wet lips, and teary eyes, some were already deeply sentimental. Then I loved them with deep primal biology; I loved them because of an internal bent, a moist yearning imprinted heav-ily on my genes, perhaps passed down through my mother, stunted (and fattened, too) by her need for romance. I loved them like we were a country at war, like I was a bullet-wounded nurse, and sometimes I was compelled by a sweep-ing maternal drive. I had no choice. But now, bodies, bodies, boys, they are the home of my youth. Not a row house in As-bury Park, but the bodies of boys, sprawled out, adoring, that's the place I was raised.

I've tried to convince myself that collegiate academia is more like rock and roll. I don't get up in front of my students like some old crank in a mustard-crusted cardigan arm-flapping, a chirping prattle, memorized book dust. No, I'm the kind of professor always trying to reveal our dirty little secrets in something other than fat-headed lingo. For example, the first day of class, Feminist Studies, entry level, I gave a talk on Self-Esteem Warfare. Michael Hanrahan was just another student, second row, halfway back, a boy, unusual, yes, in a class always dominated by brassy young women. I started with: Self-Esteem Warfare was a plot hatched by the mediocre minds of desperate, well-intentioned high school administrators. Until this point, they had been alternately bawling and shrugging in the face of calamity: the deterioration of society via the loose morals of high school girls wearing frosty lipstick, bicentennial tube tops, MIA dog tags, and tight jeans. The notion is this: girls have sex with boys because girls lack self-esteem and are seeking approval and love that is insufficient in their lives. In other words, we ached for our daddies. Freudian Theory had made its glorious way to the masses—I do not recall for them Mrs. Glee with the rub-rub of nylons as she patrolled the halls; the eggy Mr. Flint picking at the dismal sour creep of his boxer shorts; the breathless tenacity of them all, charging to catch us, electrified by their own urges, really, for each other, for us, our then beautiful bodies, rubbery and buoyant.

Boys have sex because it feels good. There's no stopping them. And, here we have the most logical example. Who could have stopped Michael Hanrahan, the boy who came in so very late each class that I told him I needed a written explanation? His car skidded across a thin plain of water, smashed into a telephone pole. He died driving too fast in the rain, his dick hard. And no one could have stopped him. It would have been un-American to try. (Maybe if he'd been relieved . . . maybe if there'd been a bullet-wounded nurse beforehand to tend to him.)

The administration set out to cure girls of their tragic flaw, this weakness not for pleasure or even an inevitable biological yearning, but for acceptance. It was a nationwide call to arms, but I focus on New Jersey, specifically Asbury Park. (No one this far north knows Asbury Park, the ghetto on the Jersey shore, boarded-up casino, The Adriatic with its old regulars in fishing caps, listening to lounge music under leaky skylights, the minigolf course overgrown except for patches of indoor/outdoor carpet, hotels looking like Eastern Block old-age homes, the old Tilt-A-Whirl, the abandoned fun house, auto body shops, auto parts, paint shops and detailing, signs like "New Jersey's Hottest Nite Spot," closed, the old Greek statue: the Patriarch of Eternal Graces or is it Infinite Love? All I know is the adult-movie theater thrives and the ocean is the ocean, big wide blue, the widest eye.)

I don't tell my students that I'm talking about one girl, like me. I don't even say: We will call her X. I don't render my large mother or my witless father, or Mrs. Glee and Mr. Flint, deflated by another ball-busting school year, hunched over their gardens, hosing down their cars, because it's summer. But nearly the end of summer. Because isn't it always the end of summer? Isn't there always a mist on the beach, a huddle of kids, arms stiff, hands in pockets. And girls, like X, like me, dumpling-eyed with ringing hips and punching hearts, strung out on screaming guitar and growling motors, aching. (My ass remembers the hot hood of a car.) And, the truth is, let's set it straight, I was confident enough to get it. Weren't there other girls who sat in their bedrooms, damp and listless?

I tell them that not all sexually active girls lacked self-esteem. The prior argument, even as historically recent as the fifties, was that a girl shouldn't have sex because of biological consequences of pregnancy, of which she alone had to bare the brunt. My mother and father know this argument too well. My mother told me that she knew of a girl who'd gotten rid of a baby before she showed. She could have done that, but didn't. She would stroke my hair, me, her baby, and say, "Look, here you are, the joy of my life." But it never rang quite true, her soft sack under her chin wagging, not quite.

The pill did away with this argument. And a new one had to be fabricated. Self-Esteem Warfare was dirty pool. It allowed judgment not just on a girl's abilities at self-restraint. No, it gave the girls sticks and asked them to poke at each other's soul. Are you insecure? It asked. Do you like yourself? Are you some sad, lost girl that we should all feel so very sorry for?

I've gotten drunk with the other women in my department. After a meeting, we went out for drinks, under the guise of bonding. And I gave in, drank too much, told sordid tales.

Things that I don't think of now, or try not to—driving some-one's Camaro into a chain-link fence for love. Little stories that end: You know how that goes, followed by a semicircle of silence and blank stares. And a mousy cardigan picked up the slack by telling the story, so boldly, of the first penis she ever saw. When she was a freshman at Williams, a frat boy whipped his out on a fire escape at a party. She got so flustered she cried. I don't belong here. The other women cheer her on. They leer at the boy, now a man somewhere in an easy chair. How could he? Men are savage, blah, blah, blah.

I didn't miss my daddy. I would like to admit to nothing short of perfection: our cheeks were pink, our knees like wax fruit never bruised. Our mothers chirped like birds and our fathers kept map-folded handkerchiefs in their back pockets. But Asbury Park wasn't short on grim reality. Some people develop a split personality; I developed a split landscape, shrugging off the boardwalk, worn and rotting, held together by rusty nails that could slice open feet, the roller coaster's click, click, click and its labored whining motor, its seat belts frayed and busted, the gray, sickened ocean and wheezing gulls, for the terrain of boys. The administration was right. I was lacking. Things like love were insufficient. But this is always true. It's the human condition.

Wasn't it true for Michael Hanrahan? His handwritten note appeared in my mailbox: *Dear Professor, I'm in love with you. I find it hard to come to class on time because I get nervous and pace and loose track of time. Sincerely, Michael Hanrahan.*

Loose track of time, maybe that was it, that alone. If time is a track, it is loose. His beautiful slip, *loose*, it's why I asked him the next day to come and see me after class, in my office. Humans are weak. It isn't Asbury Park's fault, is it? Even though we all know that a town can rip the bones from your back. And my back was weak, ironically. I was that girl in the brace. Stiffened in a case, I wasn't allowed to slouch unless I slipped out of it, out of the house, into the night.

And I did. I don't recall names. I've worked hard not to recall names. I don't go back. Funerals are the only exception—my mother's enormous casket, the men staggering, legs stiffening, under its weight. I don't carry yearbooks in a box when I move.

Let's call him D, that first boy. I remember our radio-lit bones, our pearly oils, how the car, sealed shut, filled with steam so like a bathroom pumped with hot shower water I could only think of my mother, her big body, sausage-taut, rocking me on the tub's edge. It's what you do with a child suffering midnight croup. I don't have children, but I know this much. Each cough clanged my ribs, my own voice was an animal bark and moan. Slowly my throat opened again, my body went slack with something near sleep, my hand a tiny pink star on her large sagging breast covered by her thin nylon nightgown. The car was hot like that. I cried out urgently. We both eventually relaxed, a cooling sweat. I rested my hand on the doll-hat nipple of his tan chest, a cure. It was the end of summer, like it is now. It began to rain, like it did when Michael was driving too fast. He wasn't going home.

No one rushes home. He was going somewhere else.

D drove me home past unwashed churches, seam-rusted silos, a man caught in his headlights, shoveling a raccoon from the roadside. I stood in front of my house after he pulled off. Our house tilted forward, an errant tooth in the row, because my fat mother sat nose pressed to the window, staring out at the street; this was somebody's idea of a joke. During the day she could look out on the kids with broom-stick handles and halved tennis balls, and in the evening the dim, red-fringed windows of the lantern-strung Chinoiserie, where couples leaned together in the dull glow. I was fifteen. (I absorbed her desire.) She'd been waiting for me, dimpled, pale arms perched in an open window. But when I arrived, her face slid inside. She wouldn't ask about the night. She was a nervous woman. (One night, she put her head down on her arm on the sill and her heart stopped, a dead muscle.) What could she have said? I was late. Shouldn't she have said something?

The basement's bare bulb shined through the window wells; and the dark house, belly-lit, seemed to hover just above earth like a spaceship. My father lingered under-ground, wide fingertips running over the greased gears of other people's clocks and toaster ovens, a side job. Through the open upstairs windows, where curtains billowed like veils, I could hear my mother from their bed, calling his name, calling. But he didn't come. And then her face ap-peared again in the window. An urgent whisper, "What the hell's amatter with you? Why aren't you coming in?"

"I'm taking my time."

I didn't want to go inside. I had a little brother and two little sisters who wrestled their clammy sheets in a shared bedroom while I stayed outside. I was somebody else now, my back brace hung to twist on a hanger in my closet, a broken cocoon, old skin. I felt like everything had changed. It seemed possible for the house to heave from earth in a whir of chewed screens and shingles, dust ruffles and dust. It didn't. My father pulled the chain on the basement bulb and turned on the front-porch light. In the slow dilation of morning it burned like a golden pear, like fruit on fire.

And so I became the girl you see in a pack of boys. High, windblown from riding in the backseat. Someone's arm slung around me, one day this one, another day that. (A mercenary, a tender nurse, a mother, angel. My father once said, "Be kind to boys. They're not as tough as they seem. Don't break their hearts." He was drunk, confused. He'd cut his finger with a paring knife. I was twelve. I promised.) They needed me more than I needed them. Doesn't it take a certain confidence to take in these boys, knowing their bound to become Atlantic City bus drivers? To offer some small condolence of the body before they go on to install parts at a Chrysler Plant somewhere? I was a soft spot, a comfort. And none of them had that. Or some did, I suppose. But I wasn't drawn to them.

Once there was a cake and we were drinking rosé and we were at that lake. This was toward the end of it, summer, yes, and the end of all of it for me. There was a fight. A bloodied face. A boy running into the lake. Arms outstretched. One staggering onshore, calling him back. (See, they loved each other, too, not just me. They howled for each other. These beatings were born from the steam of desire and pride.) One passed out in the grass. And another one was with me under a tree, bare dirt. There was a cake, but it wasn't anybody's birthday. I was riding this one boy. So pretty, and when we were done, he sang "Happy Birthday." And his voice was rough, but nice. I said, "Were you a choirboy?"

And he just smiled. "I can sing."

And I sat up, topless, skirt bunched at my waist, and saw the other boys, and I couldn't keep them all safe forever. The song had stitched my heart. The boys were dangerous. Each one was shining lit from within; their souls were torches. I had to let them go, let all of it go, and it was hard to do. And maybe even then I knew it was wrong to let it go, despite rhetoric to the contrary.

I loved it: the dirt, the cake, the skin, the cars, squealing tires, the radio pitched and reeling. But I was already seeing it through a certain head-tilted gaze. I knew it was something else. That there was a larger swirling, what? Import? Implication? I was reading it. I couldn't stay in the body even though I tried.

Michael Hanrahan, second row, he was there as I show slides of Tibetan women hauling timber like crosses on their shoulders, and then of the veiled bedouin. I could feel him twist in his chair. I could see him, leaning in, watching me, my body carnival-lit, a reflection of color when I moved across the wide screen. I proceeded to the Gimi men in their gourd masks sticking their tongues through pigs' teeth. I made the appropriate American correlations: consumer debt, spiked heels, football fanatics. Did my mother ever make such connections? When the *National Geographic* arrived each month, she put it in a wicker basket next to the toilet with its dreamy bright blue water, and she'd stack the old one in the attic, neatly, each month rising like a child, by quarter inches. Did she ever imagine her life splayed in captioned photographs: the female of the tribe taking a pot from the stove, ladling beans and chopped dogs onto plates? (Isn't that what we do in these classes?) Would they have said she seemed invisible, that we grunted into our food? Once, she slapped my father, pleading, "Talk to me." He said nothing, steam rising from the beans to his red cheek like a Raji at the base of a bus-sized tree trunk where he has lowered hive after hive and now sits stunned from bee poison, the roar of a million angry wings in his ears, and my mother, by the sink, cried like a Raji woman wringing honey from a comb.

I don't want to be like my mother, but I sit at a window of sorts in a house that tilts forward with all of my urgency; academia provides the view. And the boy, now dead, he was so real. The class filed out. Someone threw on the lights. The projector fan buzzed. He followed me to my office, sheepish. Once inside, he said, "You got my note."

"Yeah, I did."

"It's true."

"I figured it was." I'm sitting in my office chair. It's old wooden slat-back on wheels. The floors are institutional tile.

I tell him to sit down. There's a small blue couch. He edges into it slowly, presses his shoulder blades back, cocky, but looks at the floor.

He looks like all of them. Do I have to go over it? Half pimp, half Little League. I want to tell him that I know him, drunk, naked, stung. I know him beat-up, passed out. I know how he drives, distracted, screaming lyrics. I know how he plays air guitar in the shower, how he lathers his head with his knuckles and how he shakes it when he comes up for air in a lake. I know how he throws up. I know how he'd put his hands behind his head when I'm going down—my mouth, my teeth, they remember too much—and I know how he'd like me to ride him so he can take in a view. I know him in his parents' basement, on public golf courses, swimming pools. I know him on the beach, on a basketball court, up against a tennis wall. I know him in the school gym, along a row of clanging lockers. I know what his car smells like and that his dick curves because some overzealous doctor circumcised him too tight, an underestimation.

I lean over and put my hands, one on each of his knees, and let them slide down his thighs. There's a small window in my office door. It isn't locked. I tell him that he can call me at home. I write the number on a slip of paper. He looks at it, folds it, and puts it in his pocket.

Once upon a time, the high school administration developed an arsenal of filmstrips. What had once been the uplifting story of an armless woman (she could trim her sons' bangs, bake a cake, stir batter, swat a fly, all with her toes) was replaced with stories like *Cathy, Cathy!* about a promiscuous girl who needed love and a virgin football player talked into having sex with her in a van. Projectors were wheeled into stuffy, chalk-dusted classrooms. Lights off, the room took on a backseat feeling, the expectation of groping. The filmstrips did no good. Jealousy, I preferred it to sympathy. Afterward the beleaguered eyes of the ethics teacher dogged me all the way to the door. "I want to talk to you."

But she had nothing to say. She kept things vague. "Is there something wrong? Do you need help?"

I stared at her. An underbite and stitched eyebrows, concern knotting at her nose. "No," I said. "I'm as fine as you are. We're all fucked-up."

"Don't speak that way to me! I'm reaching out."

"Was there a teacher memo on that?"

"I should give you detention."

"Okay, but in your professional opinion, do you really think that would help?"

I'm proud of this now. Can you tell? I didn't have a vocabulary for any of it then. I thought I was alone. There was a movement going on, but not in Asbury Park.

Michael Hanrahan called once it was dark. His voice was hushed, like he was calling from his parents' kitchen phone. Or his roommate was around. "Should I come over?"

There have been grown-up men. A techie who appreciated that I could dance to Ozzie. An engineer who confused work and love. A Harvard grad, fallen on hard times, selling his hand-me-down golf clubs. I'd been good for a long time.

But this kid was one of my people. I'd be able to recognize him anywhere. Smart, but beaten, that dogged accent, rough hands. "I think you should."

My mother called, too, at dusk the night she died. It had only been six weeks. That's relevant. She said, "Why don't you get married? I thought you would get married young. But no, you and your boys, boys, boys. I saw you once. Your father and I were driving to your aunt Rita and uncle Marty's. They were going to play calypso music. And, out on the highway, you were there, doing a backbend out a car window with your shirt pulled up. I didn't tell your father."

"Why didn't you say anything to me?"

"Because."

"Because why?"

"It doesn't last. That's why. Do you do that now?"

The kid was knocking at the front door in fifteen minutes. He picked up a gourd off the coffee table. "Nice gourd."

I was going to tell him about a tribe, but didn't. It was a lecture. I didn't want to be rehearsed.

We sat on the floor. I lit a candle. We drank wine. It made my nose itch. I asked, "Do you believe in original sin?" I asked, "Do you know Yeats's 'Crazy Jane'?" I recited, " 'My friends are gone, but that's a truth nor grave nor bed denied, Learned in bodily lowliness and in the heart's pride.' "

A true feminist, a single woman, should keep condoms in the house. I should have had them in a candy dish on the coffee table, like at the campus health center. But I didn't. Once my mother and father were doing it in some parking lot somewhere, two stupid kids, and they didn't either. It's why I exist. And Michael Hanrahan didn't have anything either. "That's okay," he said. "I'll go out and get some." He was being grown-up, mustering all of his adult manners for me. He buttoned his shirt, his chest disappearing.

I looked out the window. "It's started raining. Do you want an umbrella?" My umbrella was a Monet print, bought at a museum gift shop on a day they'd forecasted sun.

He shook his head, and I thought of him pawing out across a certain lake at night. I can't make it okay, only understandable. That's the most I can hope for. When I think of him now, I imagine the radio cranked, the scrim of water, an intersection nestled in a forest of telephone poles, Michael, his dick tensed against his jeans. I could have saved him, right? And while he was gone—he never came back; all night as I waited, no one called me; he didn't, after all, even have my ridiculous umbrella in his car—I thought of what I might tell him. I'd tell him, of course, "Don't love me." I'd confess, "My mother died not long ago." And "I was once someone else." I would stretch against him and marvel, "My house, my old street, my entire raucous hometown, how could you walk around carrying it with you and not know, and not have the tiniest idea?"

Walker Percy once wrote Springsteen a letter appreciating his Catholic imagery. This literary gushing is nothing new. My letter, if I were bold enough, would center on Bruce's women. Maybe I'd confess how his line "You ain't a beauty but, hey, you're all right and that's all right with me" was a relief at sixteen, when I was a scrawny girl living just south of Jersey. I'd tell him that his women are strong and flawed, ordinary and real—Sandy, Wendy, Mary. He wants to save them, but it's clear that he needs them if he's to save himself. Even in the middle of a song about drunken rowdiness like "Spirit in the Night," he slips in the line "I'm hurt," and it's Crazy Janey who offers to heal him, and the song takes on a new weight, a dirty ache. When I was asked to contribute, there was no hesitation. I'd been following Crazy Janey in my mind for years, and she rose up, heroic, nostalgic, still desperate as ever.

LESTER BANGS has been regarded as the most influential and irreverent critic of rock and roll. Although an untimely death in 1982 cut short a writing career at a premature thirty-four years of age, his hyperintelligent and impudent pieces for such publications as *Creem, Rolling Stone,* the *Village Voice,* and London's *NME (New Musical Express)* conveyed his aggressively candid and honest style with prose that echoed Jack Kerouac and Hunter S. Thompson. His subjects in his many travel essays and general music criticism ranged from Lou Reed, Miles Davis, Bob Dylan, and the Rolling Stones to more obscure musicians like Brian Eno and Captain Beefheart. The piece featured in this collection, "From 'Maggie May,' 1981," was one of many pieces that became lost in his vast catalog of work and has been resurrected for this collection as a celebration of his sometimes experimental work, which helped to inspire the other pieces in the book.

JONATHAN LETHEM is the author of six novels, including *The Fortress of Solitude* and *Motherless Brooklyn,* which won the National Book Critic's Circle Award. He's also the editor of *The Vintage Book of Amnesia* and *The Da Capo Year's Best Music Writing 2002.* He lives in Brooklyn and Maine.

AMANDA DAVIS is the author of the novel *Wonder When You'll Miss Me* and *Circling the Drain,* a collection of short stories. Davis was raised in Durham, North Carolina, and lived in New York City and Oakland, California, where she taught in the MFA program at Mills College. Her fiction, nonfiction, and reviews have been published in *Esquire, Bookforum, Black Book, McSweeney's, Poets and Writers, Story, Seventeen,* and *Best New American Voices 2001.* She was killed in a plane crash in March 2003 at the age of thirty-two.

JT LEROY is the author of the international best-sellers *Sarah* (being made into a film by Steven Shainberg) and *The Heart Is Deceitful Above All Things* (being made into a film by Asia Argento). LeRoy's third book will be out from Viking in 2004, and his work appears in the short story collection *The Best American Nonrequired Reading 2003,* edited by Dave Eggars. He is the associate producer of Gus Van Sant's *Elephant,* which premiered in competition at the 2003 Cannes Film Festival, where it won the prestigious Palme d'Or and Best Director prizes.

LeRoy's writing has appeared in such publications as *McSweeney's, Black Book, Film Comment, Spin, GQ, Paper, Interview, The Face,* and *Filmmaker.* He will soon be published in *The Sunday Times* of London and writes a monthly column for the magazine *7 X 7*. LeRoy is also slated to write a book about Gus Van Sant's *My Own Private Idaho* for the influential BFI Film Classic series. He is working with Last Gasp publishing and artist Cherry Hood on a graphic novel version of *Harold's End.*

LeRoy is part of the rock band Thistle, currently recording their debut release. He is working with No Hands Productions, the creators of the hit series *Blue's Clues,* on an original children's feature film.

TOM PERROTTA'S most recent novel is *Little Children.* His other books are *Joe College, The Wishbones, Bad Haircut,* and *Election* (the basis of the acclaimed 1999 film starring Matthew Broderick and Reese Witherspoon). Perrotta's nonfiction has appeared in *Rolling Stone* and *GQ.* He lives in Massachusetts.

TANKER DANE is an accomplished guitarist and street poet. He has been serenading in the New York City subways for several years and still finds it strange why the tips were fewer and far between during the heyday of the dot-com era. This is his first published work.

LISA TUCKER is the author of two music-inspired novels: *The Song Reader* and *Shout Down the Moon.* She grew up in small towns outside Kansas City and St. Louis, Missouri, and has toured the Midwest with a jazz band and worked as a waitress, writing teacher, office cleaner, and math professor. She has a graduate degree in English from the University of Pennsylvania, and a graduate degree in math from Villanova

University. Her fiction has appeared in *Seventeen* and *Pages* magazine. Her book reviews and essays have appeared in a variety of publications, including *The Philadelphia Inquirer*. She currently lives with her husband and son in New Mexico, where she is at work on another novel.

Visit the author's website: www.lisatucker.com

AIMEE BENDER is the author of two books: *The Girl in the Flammable Skirt* and *An Invisible Sign of My Own*. Her fiction has been published in *Harper's*, *The Paris Review*, *Granta*, *GQ*, *Fence*, *McSweeney's*, and other journals, as well as heard on NPR's *This American Life*.

ANTHONY DECURTIS is executive editor of *Tracks* magazine and a longtime contributing editor at *Rolling Stone*. He is the author of *Rocking My Life Away: Writing About Music and Other Matters* and editor of *Present Tense: Rock & Roll and Culture*, both published by Duke University Press. His essay accompanying the Eric Clapton box set *Crossroads* won a Grammy in the Best Album Notes category. He holds a PhD in American literature, and he teaches in the creative writing program at the University of Pennsylvania.

HANNAH TINTI grew up in Salem, Massachusetts. Her work has appeared in *Story*, *Alaska Quarterly Review*, *Epoch*, *Sonora Review*, *Story Quarterly*, and *Best American Mystery Stories 2003*. Her short story collection, *Animal Crackers*, will be published by Dial Press in March 2004. She is currently the editor of *One Story* magazine.

NEAL POLLACK is the author of three books: the rock novel *Never Mind the Pollacks, Beneath the Axis of Evil,* and the cult classic *The Neal Pollack Anthology of American Literature.* He is a columnist for *Vanity Fair* and writes regularly for many other fine publications. Visit his website, www.nealpollack.com, for daily satirical commentary on important matters of the day. He lives in Austin, Texas, with his family.

TOURÉ is the author of *The Portable Promised Land,* a collection of short stories published by Little, Brown. He's also a contributing editor at *Rolling Stone* and the host of MTV2's *Spoke N' Heard.* He studied at Columbia University's graduate school of creative writing and lives in Fort Greene, Brooklyn. A novel called *Soul City* will arrive in September 2004. Visit his website at www.toure.com.

VICTOR LAVALLE is the author of a short story collection, *Slapboxing with Jesus* (Vintage), and a novel, *The Ecstatic* (Crown/Vintage), which was chosen as a finalist for the 2003 PEN/Faulkner Award.

HEIDI JULAVITS is the author of two novels, *The Mineral Palace* and *The Effect of Living Backwards.* Her fiction and nonfiction have appeared in *Time, Esquire, McSweeney's, Zoetrope, Harper's Bazaar,* among other places. She is a founding editor of *The Believer.*

ARTHUR BRADFORD's first book, *Dogwalker,* was published by Knopf in 2001. His first feature film, a documentary

called *How's Your News?,* was broadcast on HBO/Cinemax in 2002 and is now out on video.

JENNIFER BELLE is the best-selling author of two novels, *Going Down* and *High Maintenance,* and a book for children, *Animal Stackers.* Her stories and essays have appeared in *Black Book, Ms., The New York Times Magazine, The Independent Magazine, Harper's Bazaar,* and *Mudfish.* She lives in New York City, where she leads a writing workshop in her home and is at work on her third novel.

ERNESTO QUIÑONEZ was raised in Spanish Harlem. He is the author of the novels *Bodega Dreams* (Vintage, 2000) and *Chango's Fire (HarperCollins Rayo Imprint, 2004).* He lives in New York City.

DARIN STRAUSS is the award-winning author of the international best-seller *Chang and Eng,* and of the New York Times Notable Book *The Real McCoy,* which was named one of the 25 Books to Remember of 2002 by the New York Public Library. He is also a screenwriter and has adapted *Chang and Eng* for Disney films. He teaches at New York University, and his work has been translated into thirteen languages.

JUDY BUDNITZ is the author of the books *Flying Leap, If I Told You Once,* and a forthcoming story collection. Her stories have appeared in *Harper's, The Paris Review, McSweeney's, Fence, Story, Prize Stories 2000: The O. Henry Awards, Best American Nonrequired Reading 2003, Lost Tribes,* and others.

DAVID EBERSHOFF is the author of the novels *Pasadena* and *The Danish Girl* and the story collection *The Rose City.* He Lives in New York City and is finishing a new novel, *The Lost Family.* He can be reached at www.ebershoff.com.

ELISSA SCHAPPELL is the author of *Use Me,* which was a runner-up for the PEN/Hemingway award, a New York Times Notable Book, a Los Angeles Times Best Book of the Year, and a Border's Discover New Writers selection. She is currently a contributing editor at *Vanity Fair* and a founding editor and now editor-at-large of *Tin House* magazine. Her work has appeared in, among other places, *The Paris Review, Spin, Spy, Nerve.* She lives in Brooklyn.

ZEV BOROW has written for *Spin, The New Yorker, The New York Times Magazine, GQ, Details, Wired, Vibe, ESPN the Magazine,* and *McSweeney's.* He also writes scripts for television and is the cofounder of G-NET Media, which produces video-game-related TV projects.

NELSON GEORGE is the author of numerous fiction and nonfiction works, including *Hip Hop America* and *Post-Soul Nation,* a history of the '80s in black popular culture. His next novel is *The Accidental Hunter.* He also executive produced the HBO film *Everyday People.* He can be reached at www.nelsongeorge.com.

JULIANNA BAGGOTT has published dozens of short stories and poems in such publications as *The Southern Review, Chelsea Poetry,* and *Best American Poetry 2000.* A recipient of fellowships from the Delaware Division of Arts, the Virginia Center for the Creative Arts, the Ragdale Foundation, and Bread Loaf Writers Conference, she won the 1998 Eyster Prize for short fiction. She is the author of two novels, *Girl Talk* (Pocket Books, 2000) and *The Miss America Family* (Pocket Books, 2001) and a collection of poems, *This Country of Mothers*. She lives in Newark, Delaware, with her husband, poet David G. W. Scott, and three children.

As many as 1 in 3 Americans
have HIV and don't know it.

TAKE CONTROL.
KNOW YOUR STATUS.
GET TESTED.

To learn more about HIV testing,
or get a free guide to HIV and
other sexually transmitted diseases.

www.knowhivaids.org
1-866-344-KNOW